AN UNTENABLE ARRANGEMENT

"Aren't you forgetting something, Julian? This is my home, and you will live up to the terms of our agreement—to be an exemplary host and husband. Don't forget, I still hold that promissory note."

He started toward her. She gasped as he grabbed her by both shoulders; his mouth sought hers in a fierce, punishing kiss that ignited a raging inferno in her blood and left her helpless with desire. When he released her at last and stepped back, his eyes were black with passion and his breath was coming in short, ragged gusts.

Stumbling back against the dressing table, Chandra said in a shaking voice, "You promised—you agreed this would be a platonic marriage . . ."

He had control of himself now. "Don't worry. This won't happen again."

DISCOVER THE MAGIC OF REGENCY ROMANCES

ROMANTIC MASQUERADE   (3221, $3.95)
by Lois Stewart

Sabrina Latimer had come to London incognito on a fortune hunt. Disguised as a Hungarian countess, the young widow had to secure the ten thousand pounds her brother needed to pay a gambling debt. His debtor was the notorious ladies' man, Lord Jareth Tremayne. Her scheme would work if she did not fall prey to the charms of the devilish aristocrat. For Jareth was an expert at gambling and always played to win everything—and *everyone*—he could.

RETURN TO CHEYNE SPA   (3247, $2.95)
by Daisy Vivian

Very poor but ever-virtuous Elinor Hardy had to become a dealer in a London gambling house to be able to pay her rent. Her future looked dismal until Lady Augusta invited her to be her guest at the exclusive resort, Cheyne Spa. The one condition: Elinor must woo the unsuitable rogue who was in pursuit of the Duchess's pampered niece.

The unsuitable young man was enraptured with Elinor, but *she* had been struck by the devilishly handsome Tyger Dobyn. Elinor knew that Tyger was hardly the respectable, marrying kind, but unfortunately her heart did not agree!

A CRUEL DECEPTION   (3246, $3.95)
by Cathryn Huntington Chadwick

Lady Margaret Willoughby had resisted marriage for years, knowing that no man could replace her departed childhood love. But the time had come to produce an heir to the vast Willoughby holdings. First she would get her business affairs in order with the help of the new steward, the disturbingly attractive and infuriatingly capable Mr. Frank Watson; *then* she would begin the search for a man she could tolerate. If only she could find a mate with a *fraction* of the scandalously handsome Mr. Watson's appeal. . . .

Available wherever paperbacks are sold, or order direct from the Publisher. Send cover price plus 50¢ per copy for mailing and handling to Zebra Books, Dept. 3638, 475 Park Avenue South, New York, N.Y. 10016. Residents of New York and Tennessee must include sales tax. DO NOT SEND CASH. For a free Zebra/ Pinnacle catalog please write to the above address.

An
Unscrupulous Bride
Lois Stewart

ZEBRA BOOKS
KENSINGTON PUBLISHING CORP.

For my sons—
James, Michael and David

ZEBRA BOOKS

are published by

Kensington Publishing Corp.
475 Park Avenue South
New York, NY 10016

First printing: January, 1992

Printed in the United States of America

Prologue

Hindustan, 1798

It was so hot. Not even the faintest breeze stirred the trees crowding in on the rutted track. As Diana Meredith fanned herself in a desperate effort to create a cooling current of air, her arm brushed against the carved woodwork of the palanquin. She recoiled. The wood was burning to the touch.

It was so hot that even the birds were silent, and no rustling sounds came from the underbrush to indicate the activity of jungle animals, apparently keeping to their lairs until evening came. However, in the eerie silence, Diana could hear clearly the labored breathing of her four bearers as they strained to carry the heavy weight of her litter in the humid heat, and the faint tinkle of the silver bells that adorned the Begum's elaborate palanquin. In the distance, the rhythmic clop of sandals striking the baked earth was also audible, marking the presence of her father's Sepoy company, to the front and rear of the little procession of palanquins and heavily laden bullocks.

The sound of marching feet was reassuring to Diana. These were unsettled times in northern India, after the incessant native wars of the previous half century. The cautious traveler did not move a foot beyond town or settlement without armed protection against bandit raids or marauding jungle animals. When the Begum—the

5

widow of the recently deceased Nizam of Bhulamphur, a small principality in the foothills of the Himalayas—decided to visit Calcutta, she'd asked for a military escort. Happy to extend a courtesy to the widow of the former ruler, the commander of the English garrison at Bhulamphur had ordered Diana's father, Major Geoffrey Meredith, to accompany the Begum on the six-hundred-mile journey to Calcutta.

Diana mopped at the beads of perspiration that had formed on her forehead beneath her straw bonnet, and tried to settle her skinny ten-year-old body more comfortably on the flattened pillows of the palanquin. Even though the curtains of the litter were drawn completely back, the interior of the palanquin was like an oven. If only the monsoon season would come, and break the oppressive heat of the past three months, Diana thought longingly. She sighed, shaking her head. It was only the end of May, and the rains were still several weeks away.

In one part of her mind she knew it wasn't any hotter here in the jungle than it was in the cantonment at Bhulamphur. Somehow, though, the heat always seemed more bearable on the veranda of her father's bungalow, facing the wide *maidan*, or parade ground. There a servant brandishing a six-foot-long peacock feather fan could augment the faintest hint of a breeze. Her mind wandered back to the previous evening . . .

Unable to fall asleep because she was so excited about the journey to Calcutta in the morning, Diana slipped out of bed to enjoy the comparative coolness of the veranda. Huddled against the wall, her knees drawn up to her chest, she sat there, watching the stars and listening to the night sounds, until well after midnight. At last, as she was beginning to feel drowsy, she heard voices at the front of the house. Papa must have returned from dinner at the regimental mess. His *dubash* and his Sepoy personal servant had met him at the door and would soon be guiding his stumbling steps to his bed.

She rose quickly and went into her own bedchamber.

Papa's room, like all the family bedrooms, opened onto the veranda. It would never do for him to find her out here at this hour. When he was in his cups, Papa's temper was very uncertain, and he always drank too much in the mess. Not that he was unique in that respect. Most officers of the East India Company Army were heavy drinkers. As Miss Banks, her governess, had once said dryly, there was very little for the officers to do except to drink wine and shoot wild animals.

After a few minutes, Diana heard the murmur of voices from the direction of the dining room, and realized that her father, contrary to his usual custom, hadn't gone straight to bed. Could he have a visitor at this hour?

Curious, as she usually was about everything and everybody, Diana quietly opened her door and walked softly down the corridor to the dining room door, which was slightly ajar. As she peered into the room, she gasped in surprise. She didn't know the name of her father's visitor, a burly man in a richly decorated *chapkhan* and elaborate turban. However, she recognized him as one of the officials she'd seen in court processions of the late Nizam of Bhulamphur. What possible business could this official have with an officer of the East India Company in the middle of the night?

Apparently Papa was puzzled, too. His voice slurred by too much claret, he was saying impatiently, "Has there been a change in the arrangements? My orders are to meet Her Royal Highness's entourage at the main gate of Bhulamphur at dawn tomorrow. Does she wish to postpone her departure?"

Diana had caught her breath apprehensively at her father's remarks. Was she to be cheated out of her eagerly awaited visit to Calcutta? When the major had received orders to escort the Begum to Calcutta, he'd decided to bring his family with him. Now, if the Begum had changed her mind about going, Papa's orders would be cancelled.

"No, no, Her Highness has no wish to postpone her

departure," the court official had replied in rapid Hindi, which Diana understood and spoke almost as fluently as her native English. "There will, however, be a small change of procedure. You see this box?"

Diana edged a little closer to the door. She craned her neck to look into a corner of the room, where four servants, wearing the livery of the Begum's household, were standing beside a large trunk, banded with iron and fastened with stout leather straps.

The court official continued, "For reasons which I won't go into, Her Highness does not wish to leave the palace with this box among her baggage. She prefers that you include it in the baggage train carrying your own household possessions. You will return the box to Her Highness when you reach your destination." He paused. "One more thing: mount a heavier guard than usual on your personal possessions. No one—I repeat—*no one* is to have access to this box. Is that understood?"

"Yes, certainly. I'm happy to oblige Her Highness," Major Meredith said. It was clear to Diana that Papa was far from understanding his new instructions. She was so absorbed in this intriguing nocturnal conversation that she failed to notice a quiet footfall behind her.

Strong fingers dug into her shoulders, and a voice hissed in her ear, "For shame, my girl! Ladies don't eavesdrop. You come with me."

Resignedly, Diana allowed her redoubtable governess to lead her down the corridor. At the door of Diana's bedchamber, Miss Banks peered down at her charge from her bony height of almost six feet, saying severely, "Not only have you behaved most improperly, Diana—listening to your father's private conversation, and in your nightshift, too!—but you'll not be fit to start a long, fatiguing journey without a good night's rest. Lily's been asleep for hours. Your sister, too."

"I'm sorry, Miss Banks," said Diana meekly.

The governess sniffed. Her bark was decidedly worse than her bite. She gave Diana a little push. "We'll speak no more about it. Into bed with you, now."

Yawning, Diana climbed into her bed and adjusted the netting around it. She was feeling a little tired by this time, but she still wasn't sleepy. Her mind was too busy for sleep. Why on earth would the Begum want Papa to carry her box in his personal baggage train? And why had she sent her emissary to make the arrangements so mysteriously at so late an hour?

Diana's thoughts shifted as she became aware of Lily's deep regular breathing in the bed next to hers. Her six-year-old niece apparently hadn't had any difficulty falling asleep. But then, it wouldn't have occurred to Lily to wonder about their reception in Calcutta. After all, she'd been a baby when the family arrived in Bhulamphur, and she was still too young to realize that something was very wrong with her mother's social position.

Diana lifted her head from the pillow. She could hear the faint sound of her older's sister's footsteps on the polished wooden floor of the room on the far side of her own. Phoebe was often restless at night. Sometimes she cried. Diana had never quite understood why her sister was so unhappy, or why the wives of the officers of the regiment never came to drink tea, or never invited Phoebe to their bungalows. It was something to do with Phoebe's daughter Lily, that much Diana knew. Lily's father had not been . . . well, acceptable.

Diana yawned. Now her eyelids were beginning to grow heavy. Perhaps one day Miss Banks would explain to her about Phoebe and Lily . . .

Diana jerked her head upright, confused about her whereabouts for a moment, until the swaying motion of the palanquin told her where she was. Her lack of rest the night before had finally caught with her, she reflected with a grin. She'd fallen sound asleep riding in the palanquin, despite the intense midday heat. But something had awakened her. What was it? Suddenly she heard a burst of

9

frantic shouting, followed by the crackling of musket fire. At that same moment, her bearers dropped the heavy palanquin to the ground with a crash.

Recovering from her initial daze, Diana scrambled out of the litter, her eyes widening at the scene around her. The bearers had also abandoned the palanquins in which Miss Banks and Phoebe and Lily had been riding. The Begum's servants were still holding her elegant gilded palanquin off the ground, but they were not moving. Like the other bearers, huddled by the side of the track, they were gazing fearfully toward the front of the column, where they could glimpse their Sepoy escorts locked in fierce fighting against a horde of screaming assailants. From the rear of the column, a straggling band of Sepoys, in their high blue turbans and red jackets, was attempting to squeeze past the halted palanquins and the train of bullocks to come to the aid of their comrades in the van.

Diana sprinted toward Miss Banks, who had crawled out of her palanquin and stood holding her arms protectively around Phoebe and Lily. Phoebe was unstrung, crying out hysterically. Lily had buried her head in Miss Banks's skirts.

"Phoebe, try to get hold of yourself," Miss Banks ordered. "This will be over soon. Your papa's men will soon chase away these bandits."

Diana wasn't so sure. She'd caught the faintest hint of a quaver in the governess's tone. She managed to keep her own voice steady as she said, "I heard the bearers muttering something about the Pindaris, Miss Banks. Are they the ones who're attacking us? And who are they?"

Miss Banks had recovered her usual composure. "I believe the Pindaris are irregular horsemen who are loosely attached to one or another of the Mahratta chieftains. When they aren't on campaign with the Mahrattas, they go off on plundering expeditions on their own." She stiffened as an exultant roar went up from the center of combat. In moments a disorganized group of Sepoys came streaming from the head of the column in full retreat. In close pursuit was a mob of fierce-looking bearded horsemen in towering turbans and loose flowing garments, brandishing enormous, curved swords. Before the horrified eyes of Miss Banks and her charges, the horsemen cut down several of the Sepoys in their tracks.

While the main body of the Pindaris continued their grim pursuit of the fleeing Sepoys, a number of the brigands dismounted to deal with the occupants of the palanquins and their bearers. In a few bloodthirsty seconds, they inflicted a dreadful carnage. While several of them made a merciless assault on the cowering bearers and the Begum's personal attendants, another dragged the Begum herself out of her palanquin and killed her with a single sweeping blow from his scimitar. Maddened with fear, Phoebe broke loose from Miss Banks and tried to escape into the underbrush, followed by a Pindari with an upraised sword.

Acting purely on instinct, ignoring Miss Banks's frantic call, Diana raced after the brigand. She fell to her knees when she stumbled over the corpse of one of the Sepoys. Before she could rise, she saw Phoebe's lifeless body sink to the ground in a bloody heap. The Pindari spotted Diana and started for her. Without a second's hesitation, she picked up the fallen Sepoy's bayonet and jumped to her feet to plunge the blade into the Pindari's chest. Then she whirled, speeding back to stand in front of Miss Banks and Lily with the bayonet pointed menacingly at two Pindari warriors who were bearing down on her.

They had almost reached her—she realized later, when the fury of battle had died away, that it would have been child's play to knock the weapon from her hand—when a stentorian voice roared in Hindi, "Stop! Leave the child alone!"

The Pindaris halted in mid-stride. The speaker dismounted from his magnificent horse and walked slowly over to Diana. He was an awesome old man, tall and corpulent, with glittering, intense black eyes and a flowing white beard. He wore a helmet and upper body

11

armor studded with sharp spikes. He paused in front of Diana, who stared back at him defiantly, keeping her bayonet leveled. After a long, thoughtful look, he chuckled, reaching out to tilt up her chin with a bony finger. "Good girl," he said. "You have the courage of a lion. For this I will spare you. You remind me of my daughter. She died fighting off her father's enemies."

Chapter One

The port of Woolwich, near London, 1809

Frederica Banks stood at a window in the parlor of the White Swan Inn in Woolwich, looking out over High Street. The view was certainly not very prepossessing. What a shame that they'd purchased passage on an East India Company ship so heavily loaded that it had docked at Woolwich rather than at Blackwall, the usual port of arrival. Woolwich was a dull and uninspiring place. The narrow, irregular High Street was lined with mean brick dwellings, shabby shops, and graceless public buildings. There was nothing of charm or beauty about it.

Frederica hugged her shawl closer to her shoulders as the wind blew an icy blast through the panes. After living in India for thirty-five years, she'd forgotten how cold it could be in England in January.

Thirty-five years. Could it be that long? Yes, she'd been almost twenty-five when she went out to Bengal to join her brother Walter. She was sixty now. Poor Walter. It had been years since she'd thought very much about him. He hadn't been much of a success, for all his high hopes and ambitions when he received a commission in the East India Company army. Five years after his arrival in India, he'd been cashiered from his regiment for extorting a bribe from a native official. Not that he was unique in his offense. He'd simply been too greedy, had asked for too

13

much. Then he'd become a mercenary officer in the service of the Mahrattas, the warlike Hindus who controlled most of western and central India. Within a year he was dead, killed in a senseless skirmish, and she was left alone in this strange, forbidding country, a penniless spinster without family. It had been the greatest stroke of luck of her life when Major Geoffrey Meredith had hired her to be the governess of his two motherless daughters.

Frederica turned her attention to the window again, her eyes sharpening as she spotted Chandra and Lily making their way up the street. When their ship had docked this morning after the long voyage, Chandra had rejoiced at the opportunity to stretch her legs on dry land. Poor Lily. Her slight shoulders hunched against the wintry blasts, she looked miserably uncomfortable. Chandra, now, that was a different story. Nothing ever daunted Chandra.

Frederica snapped her fingers impatiently. She *must* stop thinking and speaking of Diana as Chandra. Why was it so difficult? But she knew why, of course. Eleven years ago, the girl who'd been christened Diana Elizabeth Meredith had, in effect, become another person. She was Chandra, first the captive, then the child-wife of Mohammed Asaf Khan, the most powerful Pindari leader in northern India.

Frederica shivered. The details of that blood-soaked day of terror in the steaming jungles of Hindustan were indelibly imprinted on her memory. Major Meredith was killed almost immediately in the Pindari attack on his column of Sepoys. A few men in his company managed to escape the massacre by fleeing into the brush. Among the civilians in the party, there were only three survivors: herself, the child Diana, and Phoebe Meredith's daughter, Lily.

Even now, Frederica felt a stab of raw fear when she recalled the climactic moment when that scrawny, redheaded child had confronted Asaf Khan with the dead Sepoy's bayonet. Diana's courage had impelled the Pindari chief to spare her life, and those of her governess and niece. He'd taken them off to captivity in his

14

stronghold in the foothills of the Himalayas.

Asaf Khan was already old and weary and battle-worn. He had no family. All his wives were dead, and his children, too. His beloved only daughter had died, fighting off a rape by members of a rival Pindari band. Gradually, over the years, Diana Meredith had taken the place of his daughter in Asaf Khan's affection. He'd given her a new name. The fact that she was named after the pagan goddess of the moon offended his Moslem sensibilities. "I'll give you a proper Indian name," he'd snorted. "You'll be Chandra. That's the Sanskrit word for moon."

Diana-Chandra was ten years old when she began her captivity in Asaf Khan's camp. Several years later, Asaf decided to marry her. It was a purely platonic gesture. In Asaf Khan the fires of sexuality had burned low. He was impotent, he'd explained privately to Frederica, when the governess mustered the courage to protest the marriage. What he wanted from Chandra was companionship. He delighted in the quick play of her mind, in her sturdy independence and complete lack of fear. By marrying her, he'd also given her a position that his lawless followers might respect if he became ill or died.

As it happened, when he knew his time was short, Asaf Khan had been able to send Chandra and her former governess and her niece away to the safety of the English settlements in Bombay. Though he'd informed her that he was providing for her financially, the size of the fortune Chandra found waiting for her in Bombay had stunned her. Fifty-five *lakhs* of rupees. A half a million English pounds.

Frederica turned away from the window as Chandra and Lily entered the parlor. "Did you enjoy your walk?" the governess asked the girls.

"It was very restorative, Freddie. You should have come with us," Chandra replied with a grin. She and Lily had long ceased to call their governess "Miss Banks," or even "Frederica." The three of them had drawn so close during their years of alien captivity that all formality had gone by the board. Miss Banks was just "Freddie," the senior member of their tiny family of three.

Lily hurried over to the fireplace to spread her hands before the flames. "It's too cold a day for walking. My fingers are numb. I think they're frozen," she complained.

"Oh, nonsense, Lily," Chandra said bracingly. "It's not much colder here than it is in Hindustan at this time of year."

"Yes, it is. Much colder. And the next time you want to go for a stroll, you can go by yourself. *I'll* not stir from the fire!"

As she listened to the girls wrangling, Frederica reflected that Lily had changed very little since her childhood, except that she was taller. The slight graceful figure was the same, and the pretty, dark-skinned face with its soft brown eyes.

Chandra. Oh, yes, Chandra had changed. The plain-looking child had become a beautiful woman. She wasn't scrawny any more. Her tall slender figure curved in exactly the right places, and she held herself like a queen. The untidy red hair had deepened in color to a rich dark auburn. The once faintly freckled skin had a creamy fairness that set off the large, long-lashed green eyes.

Ramesh Lal, their Indian servant, came into the parlor, making the traditional three salaams, bending his body and head very low as he touched his forehead with his fingers. He was in native dress. His turban consisted of a long strip of blue cloth wound around a tall conical red cap, with the ends of the cloth falling over his shoulder. His *kurta*, a loose, shirtlike garment of white cotton, hung almost to his ankles over baggy trousers. His dark face was almost hidden by a full beard and a sweeping pair of mustachios.

The exotic appearance of the tall and powerful Ramesh had occasioned little comment on the six-month voyage from Bombay. Most of the passengers were longtime residents of India, familiar with native dress. Here in Woolwich, however, since their ship had docked early this morning, Frederica had been amused to observe that Ramesh was the object of acute curiosity on the part of the

16

local population. Wide-eyed children dogged his footsteps, and the inn servants treated him with a wary respect.

"The cook has informed me your dinner is ready, lady. Do you wish me to serve it?" Ramesh addressed his words to Chandra, as was his invariable custom. There was no question about where his allegiance lay, Frederica reflected. Ramesh had been a trusted servant in Asaf Khan's household. It was he who had smuggled Chandra and her governess and Lily out of the Pindari camp to the safety of Bombay, when Asaf realized that death was approaching. Ramesh owed his excellent English to the lessons Frederica had given him in the camp over the years, but he usually disregarded her completely. Frederica didn't resent his single-minded devotion to Chandra. The former governess found it rather amusing.

"Yes, serve the dinner immediately, Ramesh. I'm starved," said Chandra.

As Ramesh silently and deftly served the meal that the inn's kitchen staff had wheeled into the parlor on a serving cart, Frederica noticed that Lily was merely pecking at the really excellent roast beef, saddle of lamb, and steak and kidney pie. It had been many years since Frederica had tasted English cookery, and she herself was thoroughly enjoying it.

"You're not hungry, Lily, after your brisk walk in the cold air?" she asked.

Lily put down her fork. "I—I don't like this food. I wish we could have a Burdwan stew, or a dumpoked fowl stuffed with almonds and raisins, or a curry."

Chandra looked up from her plate. "You can hardly expect to be served Indian dishes in an English inn. You'll soon grow accustomed to the food here. You may even find you like it."

Lily's pretty face twisted in a mutinous scowl. "I'm sure I'll never like English food. I don't like anything about England. It's cold and dull and dirty. I wish we'd never come here!"

"Lily." Chandra's voice cut through the air like a knife. "Get hold of yourself. You're acting like a child. We'll be living in England for six months, perhaps as long as a year. Why can't you at least make an effort to enjoy your stay here?"

Her eyes filling with tears, Lily jumped up from the table and ran out of the parlor, slamming the door behind her. After a moment, her lips clamped grimly together, Chandra followed her niece out of the room.

Lily had locked the door of her bedchamber. "Lily, please let me in. I'd like to talk to you." Chandra repeated her low-voiced request several times. Lily didn't answer. Chandra shrugged. She certainly wasn't going to allow her disagreement with Lily to become a spectacle for the inn servants. Slowly she walked down the stairs and into the parlor.

"Lily's tired. She's decided to go to bed," she informed Frederica.

The ex-governess nodded, without saying anything. Though she'd been away from England for so many years, her strict upbringing as a clergyman's daughter wouldn't allow her to discuss personal problems in front of the servants. Ramesh's face remained expressionless. With a flicker of amusement, Chandra reflected that it was quite useless to attempt to conceal family squabbles from Ramesh. He was always acutely aware of whatever affected her, just as he'd been aware of all the nuances of her existence in Asaf Khan's harem. Nevertheless, she sat down and resumed her interrupted meal, choosing safe conversational subjects like the abominable English weather, until Ramesh began clearing the table. "Leave the claret," she told him when he'd loaded the serving cart. "The mem-sahib and I will each have another glass."

Ramesh removed his hand from the claret bottle and wheeled the cart to the door, where he paused to bow respectfully three times.

After he had left the room, Chandra laughed, saying, "Poor Ramesh. I daresay he'll keep trying to his dying day to deliver me from the demon of drink."

"Yes, it always surprises me that Ramesh observes the religious laws against alcohol so strictly. Asaf Khan certainly didn't."

"No. He considered himself a good Moslem, but he was also a free soul. He liked his wine." Chandra became thoughtful. "He was inclined to interpret other aspects of Islamic law rather loosely, too. My inheritance, for instance. Under the law of the Koran, since Asaf had no surviving children, I was entitled to one-fourth of his estate as his widow. The rest of his estate should have gone to any surviving relatives. Instead, he left his entire fortune to me. He said any surviving relatives he might have were too distant to have any right to his hard-earned money."

Frederica gasped. "Hard-earned! That's hardly how I would describe robbery and plundering and murder!"

"Yes, and Lord knows what else," Chandra said, as a flood of dark memories invaded her mind. She shut her lips firmly. Not even to her old governess would she reveal the fears that had assailed her during the closing weeks of Asaf Khan's life. He'd never intruded on her physically during the seven years of their marriage. He was impotent, yes; he'd made no bones about telling her that in the very beginning, apparently to make it clear he regarded her only as a daughter. During those last weeks, however, as his vitality slipped away, he must have felt the need to reassure himself that he was still in some way a man. He'd begun to come to her bedchamber at night, sitting on her divan, gently touching her face, running his fingers through the thick masses of her hair, murmuring his regret that he hadn't met her when he was a young man in his prime. Nothing had actually happened, though with each passing night she'd grown more apprehensive. And then suddenly, knowing he had days or mere hours to live, Asaf had ordered Ramesh to execute the plan he'd drawn up months before, to remove Chandra from the camp before his death.

The governess broke into her ex-pupil's train of thought. "Chandra—I mean Diana . . ."

A conviction that had been lurking in the back of Chandra's mind for some time suddenly surfaced. "Freddie, you can stop trying to remember to call me Diana. It's a lost cause."

"But . . . I thought you wanted to make a clean break with your life in Asaf's camp. You said the name Chandra would keep reminding you of the things you wanted to forget."

"I know. But somehow I can't make myself believe I was ever Diana. I think of her as totally different person. Not me at all. I *feel* like Chandra."

"Well, if you're sure . . ." Frederica sighed with relief. "I must say, I'll be easier in my mind. I simply could not remember to call you Diana!" The governess cleared her throat. "Chandra, don't you think you were a little severe with Lily? In fact . . ." Frederica drew a deep breath, "In fact, sometimes I think you act a little too authoritative to everyone!"

"Authoritative?" Chandra blinked in surprise.

"Yes," said Frederica a little uncomfortably. "Sometimes you're positively royal, like a ruler, or the wife of a ruler—"

"Or the wife of a Pindari brigand?" Chandra asked dryly. Her eyes met Frederica's, and they both began to laugh.

"About Lily, though," Frederica continued. "Doubtless she shouldn't have allowed herself to be upset by the cold English weather, or English food. The fact is, though, you really can't blame her for being a little nervous about this visit to England. She's spent her entire life in India. She doesn't know a soul here, she doesn't know how to act, or what to expect . . ."

Frederica's voice trailed away. Then she added, hesitatingly, "Lily may be worrying about her reception here in England, because of her mixed blood. When she was a small child, it never occurred to her that she was different, and of course, in the Pindari camp it didn't matter what her ancestry was. It's never mattered, either, to you and me. On board ship, however—probably you didn't notice—

some of the passengers snubbed Lily, or avoided her company altogether. She must have wondered why. Perhaps she guessed why."

"Yes," said Chandra. "I noticed." She'd known for a long time the answer to the question that had plagued her in her childhood: why was her sister Phoebe a social pariah?

Poor Phoebe. She'd been so pretty, so gentle, so eager to please. Lily closely resembed her. But Phoebe's complexion had been dazzlingly fair, her hair a light brown, her eyes blue. If only she'd loved more wisely. It wasn't just that she'd borne a child out of wedlock. That would have been disgrace enough. It wasn't even that her lover had been a half-caste. Actually, if Phoebe had fallen in love with and married the light-skinned by-blow of a prominent and wealthy Englishman by his quasi-official mistress, the union—at least in India—might have been tolerated. But Phoebe hadn't married such a man. She'd had an illicit affair with the offspring of a common British soldier and a native servant girl. For that, English society in Calcutta, and later at the army cantonment in Bhulamphur, had cast her out. The entire Meredith family, and Frederica Banks, had shared in her social ostracism.

"As a matter of fact, I'm having second thoughts about this visit to England," said Frederica suddenly. "Everything was so confused when Asaf Khan died. Ramesh rushed us out of the camp and down to Bombay. And then, before Lily and I quite knew what was happening, you'd booked passage on a ship to England."

Chandra raised her eyebrows. "Another example of my dictatorial ways?"

"Now, Chandra, don't you fly up into the boughs. I wasn't criticizing you. *Somebody* had to take charge at that time. It wasn't feasible to go back to Calcutta. We'd been virtual outcasts there years ago because of Phoebe's— because of Phoebe's indiscretions. Calcutta society would certainly have viewed you with suspicion if, after supposedly dying in that massacre, you turned up as the wife of a notorious bandit chief. No, it was better to start our lives anew somewhere else. But I've been thinking: mightn't it have been wiser to go to one of the French or Portuguese settlements in southern India? There's no color bar there—"

Interrupting Frederica, Chandra said, "And Lily, if she had a generous dowry, would have no difficulty making a good marriage there. Yes, I've thought of that."

"Well, then . . ."

Chandra drew a deep breath. "I think it's time to tell you the real reason I decided to come to England. It wasn't to satisfy some kind of sentimental yearning to see the land of my parents' birth, or to live among English people after all those years in Asaf's camp." She rose abruptly. "Wait. I'm going up to my bedchamber. I have something to show you."

When Chandra returned to the parlor a few minutes later, she carried in her hands a carved wooden box. She placed the box on the dining table. Her fingers trembled as she raised the lid.

"Oh-h-h," Frederica breathed softly as she gazed, spellbound, at the jewelry arranged on the velvet lining of the case. Emeralds and diamonds glittered from a marvelously intricate necklace and matching earrings, bracelet, and tiara. The gems in the parure were all large and flawless. The exquisite emerald that formed the pendant of the necklace was the size of a hen's egg, or a pigeon's. Frederica raised her eyes to Chandra. "Where did you get these beautiful things? From Asaf Khan?"

A shudder ran through Chandra's body. She could remember every detail of that night, seven years ago, when Asaf clasped the necklace around her neck and placed the tiara on her head and told her the terrible story that would change her life forever. Clearing her throat, she said, "Asaf gave me the jewelry on the day we were married. He told me they once belonged to the emperor Jahangir—and after that, to the Nizam of Bhulamphur."

"There's something horrible about these jewels, isn't there?" said Frederica slowly. "Something so horrible you could never bring yourself to talk about it. That's why you never showed them to me." She sat down, her fingers clamped tightly on the arms of her chair. "Tell me."

Choosing a chair opposite Frederica, Chandra sat in brooding silence for a long interval. Finally she said, "Asaf Khan was paid to ambush our column on the day of the massacre, when Phoebe died, and the Begum, and Papa. Didn't you ever wonder at the sheer butchery of the attack? Heaven knows, Asaf was a cruel and bloodthirsty man, but he was also very efficient. Normally he raided for plunder, not for the pleasure of killing. When he attacked us that day, however, his instructions were to kill the Begum and her household servants and all the European members of the party."

Her face turning pale, Frederica forced out her words between stiff lips. "If it wasn't for you, Chandra, and your incredible bravery, Lily and I would be dead, too. Who paid Asaf Khan to massacre your father's party. And why?"

Now that she'd broken the bonds of silence that had preserved her grisly secret for so long, Chandra found it easier to go on with her story. Ignoring Frederica's question about the identity of the man who'd ordered her father's death, she began, "As I'm sure you remember, Freddie, Papa had orders to escort the Nizam's widow, the Begum, on a visit to Calcutta. What he didn't know was the Begum's real reason for her visit: to deliver a fortune in jewels and gold to the man in the East India Company whom she'd bribed to oust her stepson from the throne of Bhulamphur and put her own infant son in his place. The night before the journey was to begin, she sent one of her court functionaries to Papa with a heavy box containing the treasure, which he was to carry with him among his own household effects."

"That was the man who called on your father late that night. I caught you eavesdropping on the conversation and sent you to bed," exclaimed Frederica with a surprised look.

"Yes. Poor Papa. He didn't know what the box contained, and he didn't understand why the Begum

23

didn't take her belongings with her in her own baggage train. But of course, she was afraid her stepson might suspect she was leaving the palace with valuables."

Caught up completely now in the story, Frederica said, "Someone obviously found out that the treasure would be accompanying the Begum and informed Asaf Khan about it. Who was it?"

"No one found out about the treasure. No one who didn't previously know about it, that is. The same East India Company official who'd accepted the Begum's bribe, also paid Asaf Khan to ambush Papa and his Sepoys. Well, paid isn't the right word. The official offered to share the Begum's treasure with Asaf if he would commit the actual theft and the murders. You see, the company official had no power to overthrow the Begum's stepson. He allowed her to believe he could do so, because he desperately wanted her jewelry and her gold. So he betrayed her to Asaf, and to ensure that there would be no witnesses to connect him to the treachery and the murders, he ordered Asaf to kill the Begum and all the Europeans in the party."

Chandra motioned to the carved wooden box and its glittering contents. "Those emeralds were renowned all over northern India. They were the most valuable items in the collection the Begum was taking to Calcutta, to pay off the corrupt East India Company official. Asaf was fascinated by the emeralds's history. He decided to keep them as part of his share of the Begum's treasure. I think it bolstered his ego to know that he owned gems that had once belonged to a Mughal emperor."

Her eyes wide with horror, Frederica asked, "Why did Asaf tell you about this? He was fond of you. I suppose he wanted you to return his affection. So why did he tell you something that could only make you view him with revulsion?"

"Because he believed in revenge. He'd tracked down the murderers of his only daughter. I believe they died a very unpleasant death. He thought my honor demanded I do the same."

"Logically he should have expected you to revenge yourself on *him*," snapped Frederica. *"He* was directly responsible for the deaths of Major Meredith and Phoebe."

Chandra shrugged. "Actually, Asaf didn't really feel any guilt. For one thing, he considered himself merely the instrument of the East India Company official. For another, he felt that he'd repaid his debt to me, if there was one, by sparing my life, and yours, and Lily's."

"Humph," Frederica sniffed. "Terrible man. It may sound unchristian to say so, but I'm very happy he's dead! Well, my dear, I'm glad you've shared this dreadful story with me. You've borne the burden of this secret all alone for too many years. I hope it's eased you to talk of it. Now, though, I think you ought to put it out of your mind and get on with your life."

"I can't do that, Freddie."

"Chandra . . ." A frown furrowed Frederica's brow. "You're planning something rash. I can feel it in my bones. A few minutes ago you spoke about your real reason for coming to England—"

"I came here for revenge," said Chandra calmly. "Asaf Khan was right. Honor demands that Papa and Phoebe and yes, the Begum, too, and all those innocent servants, be avenged. I intend to find Papa's real murderer—the man who hired Asaf to ambush the Begum—and make him pay for his crimes."

Frederica looked dumbfounded. "You mean you're going to report him to the authorities? But couldn't you have started proceedings in India? And do you have sufficient proof to bring this man to justice? After all, you have only Asaf Khan's testimony against him, and Asaf is dead."

"Well . . . Actually, I don't know the man's name."

"What? Asaf refused to tell you?"

"Asaf never met him in person. The man was so anxious to keep his identity secret, that he communicated with Asaf solely through letters carried by an intermediary, a seedy half-caste clerk employed by one of the European shopkeepers in Calcutta. Asaf pressed the clerk for

25

information, of course, but the clerk knew his employer only as someone connected to the East India Company. The first letter was signed with an intricately drawn symbol. Subsequent letters bore the same symbol, apparently to assure Asaf that he was still dealing with his original contact."

"I don't understand," said Frederica blankly. "You say you came to England to punish your father's murderer. You don't know the man's name, or anything else about him, except a vague suggestion that he is, or was, connected to the East India Company. You're not even sure he ever left India to go to England. How, then, do you expect to expose him?"

Biting her lip, Chandra thought with a sinking sensation that Frederica had inexorably fastened on the weak point in her scheme. It was a flaw that had already occurred to her, after Asaf's death and her escape from the Pindari encampment had left her free to make concrete plans to avenge her father's murder. She'd always managed to banish such qualms to the back of her mind. As she was going to do now, she told herself firmly. Somehow she'd find a way to bring down the mysterious man who'd ordered the massacre of her family.

"I do have some clues to the killer's identity," she told Frederica with more confidence than she actually felt. "The man must have been either a highly placed official in the Calcutta offices of the East India Company, or somebody close to such a man. In such a rarified political matter, the Begum would have wanted to deal with a person in power, or close to power. It's safe to assume, too, that the man returned to England soon after the massacre to enjoy his ill-gotten gains. Asaf told me the man's share of the robbery was worth at least a hundred thousand pounds. Why would a wealthy Englishman remain in Calcutta, with its hellish climate, if he didn't have to? So now I've narrowed the field. I'm looking for a man from a prominent family—otherwise he wouldn't have achieved a high position in the company—who returned from India within the past ten years with a large fortune.

26

Someone who's undoubtedly a member of the upper crust of London society. All I have to do is find him."

"Oh, Chandra . . . It's all so vague, a few flimsy facts. No, not even facts. Impressions. How can you possibly hope to find one unknown man in a vast city like London?"

Chandra flashed a crooked smile. "You don't like the source of that vast fortune Asaf Khan left me, but it's going to help me find Papa's murderer. I plan to buy a great house in the most fashionable part of London, and establish myself as a famous and wealthy hostess whose invitations will be sought after by everyone who matters in London society. Then I'll trick the murderer into betraying himself."

"How?" asked Frederica, sounding both fascinated and skeptical.

"By giving the grandest party that London's ever seen." Chandra picked up the Begum's necklace and gently swung it back and forth in front of her. The gems blazed with a scintillating fire as they caught the light from the lamps on the mantel. "I'll wear the emeralds at that party," Chandra continued. "That will give the killer a nasty shock. The last he heard of the emeralds, they were in the possession of Asaf Khan. He'll wonder how I obtained the gems, and what connection I have with Asaf. And then I'll lure him into the open by hinting I have proof of his identity."

Chandra returned the necklace to the case and pried up the velvet lining to remove a folded slip of paper, which she handed to Frederica. "This is one of the notes that Asaf received from the killer, notifying him about the exact date of the Begum's journey to Calcutta. Possibly the handwriting is disguised, but there's no mistaking the signature." Chandra pointed to the curious symbol at the end of the note, a series of intricately interlocking circles. "That symbol is unique. It will trap Papa's murderer."

It was clear from the growing dismay in the governess's long bony face, that Chandra's arguments were beginning to convince her. "You're making yourself into a stalking

27

horse," Frederica faltered. "You may be in great danger, if you succeed in finding this man. You realize, don't you, that he might try to silence you by killing you?"

Her eyes flashing, Chandra exclaimed, "I'm willing to take the risk. I won't allow that man to escape the punishment he deserves. It's not only that he's a murderer, a cruel, merciless killer for gain. Don't forget the years that you and I and Lily spent in captivity. Years when we were at the mercy of a volatile and dangerous-tempered man who might at any moment fly out of control. Years when we had to grit our teeth to keep from screaming under the strain of trying to please him. Years when we'd go to bed at night never knowing whether we'd survive till morning. Papa's murderer owes us something for those lost years, too." Chandra's voice broke. She looked away.

Frederica stared at her, appalled. "I didn't realize you felt that way, Chandra. I thought Asaf showed you only his gentler side. You were always so calm, so cheerful. You never gave the slightest indication that you lived each day in fear of your life, just as the rest of us did."

Oh, the devil. I succeeded in keeping my feelings to myself all these years, in order to spare Freddie and Lily my fears. What possessed me to speak of them now? Chandra managed a smile for Frederica, saying, "Lord, Freddie, you sound positively Gothic. If I'd lived each day in fear of my life, I vow it would have stunted my growth. And look how tall I am now. Almost as tall as you are!" A knock sounded on the parlor door. She looked up, saying, "Come."

The landlord entered, bowing. "I've jist 'ad word from the livery stable, Miss Banks," he said to Chandra. "Yer travelin' carriage won't be ready ter take ye ter London until the day after termorrer. Somefing aboot repairin' the swingletree."

"Miss Banks?" Frederica inquired after the landlord had left the parlor. She gave Chandra a hard look. "The last I heard, you were still Miss Meredith."

"I can't risk arousing the suspicion of Papa's killer by appearing in London under my real name, can I? I'm

28

adopting you as my aunt, Freddie. Lily and I are your nieces, your brother's daughters. Didn't you once tell me that you and your brother Walter were the only surviving members of your family? So if anyone should become curious about us, there's no one he could go to for information."

Frederica said urgently, "Chandra, please don't go on with this scheme. It's much too dangerous. Let's leave England before it's too late."

Chandra's mouth hardened. "I'm not leaving this country until I see Papa's murderer dangling from a gibbet!"

Chapter Two

Lieutenant the Honorable Tristan Loring paused at the door of the game room at White's, peering into the crowd of players. The gamblers certainly appeared to be out in force. Tristan nodded to one of the attendants. "Evenin', Jack. Do you know if my cousin Julian Ware is playing here tonight? I was supposed to meet him at the club for supper."

"Oh, and indeed, sir, Mr. Ware is 'ere right enough," replied the attendant, rolling his eyes. "There 'e is, at the table in the far corner. 'E's been 'ere, playin' whist, since eleven o' the clock last night wifout a break. I've jist brung 'im another bottle o' claret."

"Dipping pretty deep, is he?" asked Tristan, raising his eyebrow.

"Oh, no, sir. Leastwise, no more'n 'e kin handle. Mr. Ware, 'e's got a werry good head for the drink. The other gentlemen at the table, now . . ." The attendant shrugged.

Tristan laughed. "Oh, I'd lay my blunt on Julian to drink all his fellow players under the table. You say he's been playing whist for"—he pulled out his watch—"he's been playing for nigh on to nineteen hours. Is he winning?"

"Cain't swear ter it, sir, but I *will* say there's a mighty tall heap o' rhino on his corner o' the table. I'd guess 'e was winnin' big. 'Course, 'e'll prob'ly 'ave ter leave soon. One o' the gentlemen was sayin' that Mr. Ware will be deliverin' a speech i' the 'Ouse o' Commons ternight."

"Is he now, by Jove? He didn't mention it. Well, I'm glad he's winning," Tristan went on cheerfully. "He can pay for our dinner. *My* pockets are to let." He strolled across the room to the table in the far corner.

Julian Ware glanced up from his cards to smile at his young cousin as Tristan walked up to stand behind his chair. Several other men were standing around the table, their eyes intent on the play. Julian's face was slightly flushed, Tristan noted, but the hand pouring a glass of wine was perfectly steady.

As Tristan watched, Julian played the last card of the hand and gathered up a seventh trick. His voice, too, was steady. "Another rubber," he remarked to his partner, "thanks to your good cards."

"*And* another treble. I make it eight points with the rub. Eight more points at one hundred pounds the point," replied his partner, rubbing his hands together gleefully.

"Damned if you don't have the devil's own luck, Ware," grumbled one of the opponents, staring at the piles of coins and bank notes at Julian's elbow. "I must have been out of my mind to agree to play for a hundred pounds a point, the way your luck's been running. Much more of this, and I'll have to sell my hunters."

"And I'll be off to visit the cents-per-cent tomorrow, unless our luck starts to turn," said the man's partner with a grimace. "Shall we cut for deal? Time's a wasting."

"One moment, gentlemen. I'd like to sit in," said the man standing next to Tristan. The speaker was a tall, dark men whose rather florid good looks were overemphasized by his elaborately arranged coiffure and his tight, dandified clothes.

Julian gave the man a straight, unfriendly stare. "None of your friends here tonight, Forrest?"

The man flushed. "Whether I have friends here or not is beside the point. I believe I'm within my rights in asking for a seat. The rules state that if, after a rubber, another player wishes to join the table, the original players will cut, the player with the highest card going out."

"There'll be no need for a cut, Captain Forrest. I don't care to play anymore. You may have my seat," said Julian curtly. He rose. Motioning to his winnings, he said to his partner, "You can settle with me later." He bowed to the other players at the table. "Thank you, gentlemen. It's been a pleasure. Shall we be off, Tristan?"

As he walked with Julian toward the door of the card room, Tristan murmured, "Speaking of cuts, that was a cut direct, if I ever saw one. You made it very clear you didn't like Basil Forrest."

"I've reason to believe Captain Forrest is a Captain Sharp. I can't prove he cheats, or I'd have had him blackballed from every club in London. But I won't play cards with him."

A few minutes later, sitting opposite Julian at a table in the dining room, Tristan looked closely at his cousin. Julian displayed no evidence of his mammoth gambling session and his hours of drinking, except that he needed a shave. His eyes were clear, his skin fresh and unlined. He was a handsome, vital man, tall and powerfully built, with a cavalryman's grace. He had intensely blue eyes beneath a mop of black curls, a bold nose, and a sensual mouth above a deeply cleft chin. Tristan had hero-worshipped him from childhood.

"How much did you win today, Julian?" Tristan inquired after the waiter had served the first course and poured the wine. "Or rather, how much did you win last night *and* today?"

"Don't know exactly. I had no luck at all during the first hours of play, but then, toward morning, I made a recovery." Julian grinned suddenly. "It's amazing how fast your losses evaporate when you start winning at a hundred pounds a point! Baird and I must have won fifteen rubbers at an average of six points each."

"Nine thousand pounds. Forty-five hundred each," said Tristan after a quick calculation. He sighed. "I always seem to be at point-non-plus. I wish I had some of your skill at cards. I know you support yourself—and support yourself very well—on your gambling winnings. You certainly don't have any other substantial source of income. You receive only a small allowance from the family settlements, and, of course, you had your major's pay, before you sold out of the dragoons."

Pausing in the act of raising his wineglass to his lips, Julian frowned, saying, "If you're in low water, don't think of playing cards to raise the wind, Tris. You're no gambler. You've no head for cards at all. Actually, I'm no gambler, either. I never go near a hazard table or a faro bank. Whist isn't a gambling game. It's a game of skill. I happen to be a very good whist player." He set down his glass. "If you need money, I'll be happy to grease you in the fist. I'm full of juice at the moment."

"No, thank you. It's very good of you, but I haven't a notion when I could repay you," Tristan replied stiffly. Now that he was almost twenty-one, he occasionally found himself resenting his big cousin's unconscious assumption that his eight yers of seniority entitled him to give Tristan advice.

"No offense meant," said Julian mildly.

Tristan flushed. "Sorry. I didn't meant to react like an overly sensitive schoolboy. It's just—oh, confound it, I'm tired of living hand-to-mouth on a lieutenant's pay, with nothing to look forward to except a slim chance to snare a wealthy heiress, as Mama is always urging me to do. I tell you, Julian, it's sheer hell being a younger son!"

"Really?" Julian shook his head. "You amaze me." His eyes met Tristan's, and the two men burst into laughter. Julian was a younger son of the Earl of Daylesford. His Aunt Georgiana, his father's only sister, was Tristan's mother. Georgiana had been the second wife of the late Baron Eversleigh. She had never become reconciled to the fact that her stepson had succeeded to the title rather than her adored only son, Tristan.

Cocking an eyebrow, Julian said sympathetically, "I thought you looked a trifle blue-deviled. Aunt Georgiana's been matchmaking again, I gather."

"Oh, Lord." Tristan sighed. "Yes, she's found me a new heiress. Friend of hers met the young lady at a Christmas party in Yorkshire. The gal will be making her come-out in London this spring. You know, Julian, it's all well and good to marry a girl with a fortune. Dash it, I certainly couldn't support a wife on a lieutenant's pay. But is it asking too much to want a little mutual affection between me and the woman I marry? Frankly, I think you've got the right idea: forget about marriage. Find a charming ladybird, who, if she doesn't love you, will make you think that she does!"

Reaching for the claret bottle, Julian retorted, "Pray don't hold me as an example! *My* ladybird left me for greener pastures." He poured himself another glass of wine. "Madelon was your typical Frenchwoman. She never put sentiment before pure gain. Lord Mayfield offered her more than I could afford, and off she went."

"You don't seem crushed."

Julian tossed down his wine. "I'm looking for greener pastures, too," he grinned.

His fit of ill humor fading under the influence of Julian's ebullience and an excellent claret, Tristan applied himself to his turbot and a plump capon. After a moment he observed, "I hear you're speaking in the House tonight." He put down his fork. "Julian, it's none of my affair and all that, but I've often wondered why you resigned your commission last year and entered Parliament. If there was anyone who enjoyed the military life, it was you. I always thought you'd have a regiment one day."

His cousin remained silent for so long that Tristan feared he'd been guilty of prying. At last Julian said, "You know how Ashley prides himself on our family lineage."

"Yes, of course." Tristan couldn't hide his mystification at this reference to Julian's older brother, the present Earl of Daylesford. "Mama feels the same way. Always going on about how the first Baron Daylesford came over with the Conqueror, and how the barony was raised to an earldom on the field of Agincourt. There's something about Crusaders, too. To hear Mama talk, a duke is nothing to a Ware of Daylesford!"

A faint smile curved Julian's lips. "Yes, Ashley and

34

Aunt Georgiana have always been in complete agreement about the greatness of the Ware family. Ashley, you see, doesn't want our line to die out. He and I are the last of the family in the direct male descent, as you probably know. There's also a very distant collateral branch in Northumberland. Ashley asked me to sell out of the regiment, so I wouldn't run the risk of dying in battle before I fathered a son."

"Well, but . . . My God, isn't Ashley being a trifle fustian? He'll have a son of his own some day. Oh, I know he and Irene have been married for some years, but they're young, there's plenty of time—"

Julian shook his head. "There isn't any time at all. Irene is ill. She had a bout of joint fever when she was a girl. Now her heart is affected."

"Good God, I didn't know. How long . . . ?"

"Oh, she probably won't die suddenly," Julian reassured Tristan. "With proper care, she could go on for some years. Ashley hopes so. You know how he adores her. But she'll never recover her health, and the doctors have warned against the danger of pregnancy. Mind, Tris, you're not to mention this to your mother, or to anyone else."

"No. No, of course not." Shaken, embarrassed, Tristan searched his mind for another topic of conversation. "Julian, do you *like* being in Parliament? I went to a session at the House once. Must say it wasn't what I expected. Some of the members were stretched out on the benches asleep, others leaned against the pillars telling jokes, while some poor fellow was trying to give a speech about the family affairs of the Prince of Wales. Might have been interesting, too—how *did* the Prince succeed in becoming a bigamist?—but I couldn't really hear the speaker over the hoots and catcalls of the members. I swear to you, some of them were baying like hounds!"

Julian laughed. "You must have been listening to Mr. Whitbread. He's not a very inspiring speaker. Sometimes we do accomplish something important, though." His tone changed. "I thought politics was a little boring myself, when I first took my seat. I only stood for Parliament because Ashley asked me to do so. Well, what else was there for me to do? I couldn't go into trade! Now, though, I feel I can do something really worthwhile by sitting in Parliament."

At Tristan's bewildered look, Julian went on quickly, "Look, Tris. At this moment, Napoleon controls all of Europe. England has no allies except a mad king in Sweden and an unreliable dynasty in Naples. Napoleon's Continental Blockade is starving our industries by preventing our goods from entering Europe. If we don't strike a military blow against Napoleon somewhere in Europe, we may be shut out of the continent for years to come."

"Yes?" said Tristan cautiously, but without complete understanding.

"So now we have a War Secretary, Lord Castlereagh, who believes as I do. He wants to use British troops to smash Napoleon's forces in Spain and Portugal. I agree with him. I intend to support him. And you know, Tris, I've been thinking: someday, I might even be a member of the government. Secretary for War, or even Prime Minister!"

Julian paused, looking mildly surprised by his own remarks. He broke into a chuckle. "My eye and Betty Martin, I do go on, don't I? Don't be alarmed, Tris. His Majesty is never going to send for me to kiss hands. The kingdom is safe from me."

Despite his cousin's lightly assumed air of self-derision, however, Tristan realized that Julian was far more serious about his new profession than anyone in the family had previously suspected. Julian the Nonpareil, the Corinthian of Corinthians, as Prime Minister! The thought boggled the mind.

A servant brought Julian a note. The amused expression faded from his face as he read.

"Something wrong, Julian?"

"No, I daresay there isn't," said Julian. But Tristan heard the note of worry in his voice. "The note's from

Ashley. He just wants me to drop by after the session in the House tonight. But—it's his handwriting. When he's troubled about something, he tends to drive his pen right through the paper."

Tristan knew that the two brothers had always been exceptionally close. He said apprehensively, "Perhaps Irene is ill."

A worried frown creased Julian's forehead. "Lord, I hope that's not it. She's been quite stable now for months."

"Well . . . Keep me informed."

"I will. Thanks, Tris."

The speech went pretty well, Julian thought with relief as he rode away from the House of Commons in a hackney cab later that evening. Not that it had been an important speech, he hastily reminded himself. Merely a few words of praise for the work of the recent Court of Inquiry, which had approved the terms of the Convention of Cintra ending the fighting in Portugal last summer. However, several members *had* congratulated him. Lord Castlereagh, never noted for his warmth of manner, had nodded almost cordially.

The glow of his modest achievement had faded by the time the cab made the turning out of Piccadilly into Old Bond Street. As he neared Berkeley Square, his uneasiness about Ashley's note began to resurface. It wasn't just the handwriting, that hurried, slashing style that since Ashley's childhood had always indicated stress. Why did Ashley want to see him at this late hour? If it was about family business—or, more important, Irene's health— surely Ashley could have mentioned the subject in his note.

Well, he'd discover the reason for the summons soon enough. The cab had stopped in front of a house on the west side of Berkeley Square, not far from the gardens of Lansdowne House. Julian stepped out of the cab, instructing the driver to wait for him, and walked up the

37

steps of Daylesford House. A footman answered his knock immediately and ushered him along the corridor to the library.

As Julian entered the room, the Earl of Daylesford was sitting slumped in a chair behind his desk, a nearly depleted decanter of wine at his elbow. He rose and walked over to Julian, his left leg dragging more than usual. A hunting accident in his late teens had left him with a permanently painful left hip and a decided limp, which always became more pronounced when he was tired or out of sorts. Slapping Julian on the shoulder, Ashley said in a voice slurred by alcohol, "I knew I could count on you, little brother. Sit down. Let me give you a glass of this port. It's quite decent. Oh." He stared owlishly at the empty decanter. "I'll ring for another bottle."

A little later, settled into a chair opposite the desk, glass of port in hand, Julian watched his brother as he paced nervously back and forth across the room, pausing every few seconds to gulp from his glass. Ashley's face looked drawn and tired. He seemed to have lost weight recently. *He's changed so much,* thought Julian.

When they were younger—and before Julian had grown to his present height of six feet two—the brothers had sometimes been taken for twins. Not anymore. Ashley's brooding resentment over his crippled leg, added to the devastation he felt at his wife's illness, had left their toll. His blue eyes had dulled, his skin had taken on the faint flush of the habitual drinker, and he'd lost the *élan*, the sparkle, that had once made him irresistible to everyone, old and young, male and female.

There'd been three Ware brothers in the beginning. Following the death of Edward, the oldest brother, Ashley had become the heir to the earldom at the age of twenty-one and succeeded to the title several years later. But before that, the two younger brothers had enjoyed an idyllic childhood, untroubled by the weight of any future family responsibilities, living an active outdoor life at the Daylesford estate in the Chiltern Hills of Buckinghamshire. They'd been so close, Julian thought wistfully.

They were still close, but now there were times when he felt older than Ashley, protective and concerned, rather as if their roles had been reversed.

"What is it, Ashley?" Julian said quietly. "Is it Irene? Is she ill?"

"What?" Ashley ceased his distracted pacing and threw himself into a chair. "No. Irene's well. As well as she ever is."

"Then what's amiss? Why did you send for me?"

Ashley stared at his brother out of hunted eyes. "I'm done up, Julian. Fast aground. I dropped fifty thousand to Jack Matcham's faro bank last night. Or rather, early this morning. I can't pay it. The banks won't loan any more on my mortgages. Not a moneylender in town will give me another shilling."

"God, Ashley!" Julian exploded. "I've warned you, time and again, that you'd end up under the hatches. You're just like Papa. No head for cards at all. He'd have landed in the River Tick if he'd lived long enough."

Like his son, Ashley, the twelfth Earl of Daylesford had been an enthusiastic but inexpert gambler. Only his wife's immense fortune had kept the earl solvent until his premature death at the age of forty-six. Ashley, too, had married money. Irene was a great heiress. But for some time, Julian had suspected Irene's money was long gone, squandered at the tables.

Ashley winced. "Oh, everyone knows what a nonpareil you are, little brother. *You* never make mistakes. You're the gambling champion of the ton," he gibed.

"I don't play if I can't pay, that's true," replied Julian quietly.

Ashley's face crumpled. "I'm sorry. If I'd taken your advice, I wouldn't be in this fix. It's just . . . you see, I fall into a fit of the megrims when I think about losing Irene, and then I have to drink, or play cards, do *something*, before I end up queer in my attic. Julian, please help me. I've nowhere else to turn. If I can't raise the fifty thousand, I'll have to put the estate on the market. Well, you'd have to break the entail first, of course. We can't let that happen.

39

The Ware family has been living at Wolverton Abbey since the eleventh century!"

For a moment, sheer exasperation overcame the sympathy that Julian felt for his brother. "Ashley, you must know I don't have fifty thousand pounds, or anything approaching that sum."

"You could borrow it."

"From whom? You need collateral for a loan, and I don't own anything except the clothes on my back and my horses."

"You have expectations."

Flashing Ashley an incredulous stare, Julian retorted, "You mean because I'm your heir presumptive? There's not a banker or a moneylender in London who'd advance me a loan on an estate that's already sinking from the weight of the mortgages you and Papa loaded onto it."

Ashley reddened, but kept his temper. "I was thinking of Great-uncle Josiah's property in Barbados. It must be worth fifty thousand, or close to it, and you're his heir."

"Uncle Josiah enjoys changing his will," said Julian shortly. "Last year his nephew, Jack Bradford, was his chosen heir."

"And this year you're the lucky man." Ashley's voice deepened into desperation. "Please, Julian. Help me, and I swear I'll never touch another card as long as I live."

How many times have I heard that promise? Julian drew a deep breath. He had no great faith in Ashley's good intentions, but he was genuinely fond of his brother, and he had a deep family loyalty. "Very well. I'll try to raise the money. I'll see a cents-per-cent in the morning, before I go to Woolwich. Tomorrow evening I'm invited to a dinner at the Royal Artillery Barracks."

Julian climbed into his curricle slowly and carefully, trying to avoid any sudden move that might jar a monumental headache back into life. He had a hard head for liquor, and he usually knew his limits. However, in the scant year he'd been away from the military, he'd forgotten

40

how freely the wine flowed in the company mess. In any case, he couldn't very well allow the artillery to outdrink the dragoons!

Well, any discomfort he was feeling this morning had been well worth it, he reflected, as he drove away from the long facade of the Royal Artillery Barracks, and entered the road crossing Woolwich Common. He'd discovered how much he'd missed the easy give-and-take of his regimental days, the rough military humor, the knowledgeable talk of battles and strategy. Last night in the mess, for instance, the officers had talked about the ominous rumors coming from Spain about General Moore's retreat, with a detachment and an understanding that none of his political friends would have displayed.

Though the sun was shining brightly, it was a bitterly cold morning. The spume of his horses' breath rose like puffs of smoke in the chilly air, and he could feel the cold penetrating his ankle-length, many-caped greatcoat. He called to his tiger, perched behind him, "You going to be warm enough, Amos?"

"Yes, sir. Leastwise, I reckon as I won't be freezin' ter death, guv," came the shivering reply.

"I'll get you home as soon as possible," Julian said, touching his whip lightly to his pair. "You're not dressed for this weather."

"Now, guv, don't you spring them elegant bits o' blood jist ter save me from catchin' my death o' cold," exclaimed the tiger in alarm.

Grinning, Julian continued to drive his team at a spanking pace, past the Royal Military Academy on the left and on toward the junction with the Dover-Canterbury road. As he neared a wooded, rather isolated area at the foot of Shooter's Hill, he rounded a sudden curve and slowed, his eye riveted on a traveling coach halted at the side of the road, which appeared to be under attack by a crowd of roughly dressed men.

Apparently the assault was barely underway. As Julian watched, he saw a youth riding the "cock horse"—the extra horse hitched to the front of the team to assist the

41

carriage up the steep hill—being knocked off his mount. An elderly coachman was feebly attempting to resist an attempt to topple him from his perch. The door of the carriage was ajar, and a tall woman and a dark-complexioned man wearing flowing robes and a turban had leapt out on the road in front of the coach, gleaming knives in their hands, defending themselves against the attack.

Pulling sharply on his reins, Julian halted his team and jumped to the ground, tossing the reins to the tiger. He rushed into the fray, grabbing one large ruffian who was brandishing a heavy stick and sending him crashing to the roadway with a leveler to the jaw. Out of the corner of his eye he glimpsed another thug bearing down on him and whirled to catch the man's arm, twisting it behind his back and forcing him to drop the ugly knife in his hand. Then Julian drove his fist hard into the pit of his opponent's stomach. The man doubled up with a grunt of pain and dropped to the ground.

Wheeling to take on yet another of the ruffians, Julian observed with considerable surprise that only four of the thugs remained. Two motionless bodies were sprawled on the roadway near the carriage. Then there were the two men he himself had milled down, who were beginning to show signs of life. Even as he watched them, they lumbered to their feet and darted away. He made no effort to stop them. He walked over to the woman. "Are you all right?" he inquired, his eyes widening at the sight of the bloodstains on the wicked-looking poniard in her hand.

She was a stunning creature, despite the rather outlandish appearance she presented in a voluminous cape of Russian sables and a hat loaded with ostrich plumes. Tall and graceful, she had a pair of magnificent long-lashed green eyes set in an exquisite, fine-boned face. She gave him a level glance, seemingly unperturbed by her brush with danger.

"I'm quite all right, thank you," she said, in a voice faintly tinged with an unrecognizable accent. "It was kind of you to come to our rescue, even though I fancy those thugs would have become discouraged soon enough when they saw what had happened to their friends." She motioned to the two unmoving bodies, who, Julian suspected, were quite dead.

She turned away from him to face the bony-faced middle-aged woman who had just scrambled out of the carriage, followed by a slight young girl with a pretty, heart-shaped face and large brown eyes. Pale with shock, the older woman gasped, "Are you hurt, Chandra?"

"No, of course not, Freddie. The damage was all on the other side, as you can see. There's nothing for you and Lily to worry about any longer," said Chandra calmly. She frowned suddenly as she studied the carriage, which definitely appeared to be listing to the side. "Ramesh, have a look at the right rear wheel," she ordered the exotically dressed man who had stood shoulder to shoulder with her during the attack.

After a few moments, the man Ramesh returned from his inspection, spreading his hands in a helpless gesture and speaking a few words in an incomprehensible tongue. The green-eyed woman stared at him with an angry impatience. "A broken wheel, what does that mean, Ramesh? How is it broken? Can it be fixed?"

"If you'll allow me, ma'am . . ." Julian moved around the carriage to look at the rear wheel. He came back to report, "You have a damaged collinge hub, ma'am. You need the services of a wheelwright. If you'd care to accept a ride in my curricle, I'd be delighted to take you—or your coachman, if you'd prefer—to the nearest posting stop, where you could arrange to have the wheel repaired."

"Thank you, I prefer to come with you, so I can make the arrangements myself," replied the woman named Chandra, with an air of instant decision. "This is a hired vehicle, so I think it would be best simply to hire another, if one is available." She turned to her two companions. "I shan't be gone long, and meanwhile you'll be quite safe here with Ramesh and the coachman to guard you."

The women, especially the young girl, Lily, still appeared apprehensive, and Julian couldn't blame them for their fears after the horrifying attack they'd experienced. He flashed them a reassuring smile. He thought it unlikely that the thugs would return after the drubbing they'd taken. Taking Chandra's arm, he helped her into his curricle.

"The wind isn't too cold for you?" he asked, as they drove off.

"No, not at all," she answered briefly, and Julian felt foolish. *Nobody* swathed in those furs could possibly feel cold, even in a blizzard. She wasn't a very communicative person, he concluded a little later, after he'd failed to draw more than the briefest of responses to his polite overtures. He'd never before met a young woman who seemed so perfectly self-possessed. Or who evinced so complete a lack of interest in himself, he thought wryly. It was really quite wounding! Especially since, on his part, he'd felt instantly, powerfully, drawn to her. One glance from those wonderful green eyes, and he'd felt a stab of desire in his loins.

A short drive brought them to the Bull Hotel at the top of Shooter's Hill, the last posting stop before London. Pausing before entering the inn, Chandra gazed at the distant steeples and smoke-wreathed buildings of the great city, eight miles away on the horizon, and at the sweeping vistas of the Thames valley below. Her face became momentarily alive with a vibrant interest.

"You're perhaps returning to London after a stay on the Continent, ma'am?" Julian ventured.

"No. I've never been to London." There it was again, the civil, noncommittal reply.

The proprietor of the Bull Hotel regretted that he had no large traveling carriages for hire. However, he'd be happy to send a message to a livery stable in the nearby town of Eltham, inquiring about the availability of a coach, if the lady cared to wait.

"Please do so," said Chandra.

"Meantime, can I offer you some refreshment, ma'am?" Julian inquired. "Some tea, perhaps, after your cold drive in an open carriage? An early nuncheon?"

44

"Thank you. I'd like a cup of tea. But please don't feel you must stay with me, sir. We're complete strangers, after all. And I assure you that I'm very capable of taking care of myself."

Julian was beginning to feel quite challenged by this cool young woman. He bowed. "It's my pleasure, ma'am. I wouldn't dream of leaving you stranded here, until you've found proper transportation." He beckoned to a waiter and requested a private parlor.

While he was helping Chandra out of her sable cape, Julian fixed his eyes incredulously on the ropes of pearls and lengths of filigreed gold chain that hung around her neck. Chandra was wearing enough jewelry for any three necks, and the hackneyed expression, "worth a king's ransom," came readily to his mind. She whipped off her hat with what sounded like a sigh of relief and a barely audible mutter of, "What silly things, hats. I can't think why they wear 'em."

Now Julian could see his new acquaintance without the enveloping cover of that splendid fur cloak, and the sight was a definite shock. Chandra was wearing a gown of heavy purple satin, hideiously incorrect as to material or color for day wear, with elaborate ruffles and yards of lace. Her hair, which, since she'd removed her bonnet, he could now see was a glorious dark auburn, was pulled to the crown of her head and hung down her back in a thick braided rope almost to her waist.

"Er—may I introduce myself, ma'am? My name is Julian Ware."

She bowed her head. "I'm Chandra—Chandra Banks." Was there the faintest hint of hesitation in her reply?

After a discreet knock, a waiter entered the parlor with a tray containing a teapot and cups and a plate of pastries. Julian pulled out a chair for Chandra and sat down opposite her. "Will you pour, Miss—it *is* Miss?—Miss Banks?" A little later, as he stirred sugar into his tea, he remarked, "I fear you were the victim of a very unusual circumstance, ma'am. Long ago the vicinity of Shooter's Hill was a haven for highwaymen. However, for many years the area has been safe for travelers."

"Oh, I don't think the ruffians who attacked my carriage were local men. I believe they followed me from Woolwich," said Chandra. "I distinctly recall encountering one of them in the hall of the White Swan Inn last night, as I was going up to my bedchamber. I was wearing my rubies. He stared at them so hard I thought his eyes would pop out. Doubtless he and his friends were after the contents of my jewelry box."

Chandra's tone was so matter-of-fact that Julian almost choked on the pastry he was eating. How much jewelry did she own? And where had it come from? Trying not to sound too inquisitive—although, for some reason, he was intensely curious about this odd, attractive woman—he said, "You were staying in Woolwich, Miss Banks? You were visiting the Arsenal and the Dockyards, perhaps?"

"No. My aunt and my sister and I merely spent two nights in Woolwich after our ship docked, while I made arrangements for our journey to London."

"So you've come from foreign parts. From your servant's costume, I'd guess you've been traveling in India. Am I right?"

"Not precisely." Chandra gave him a look of cool indifference. "I was born in India."

Mentally mopping his brow, Julian plowed on. Chandra Banks was exasperatingly non-forthcoming! "Your father served with the East India Company, I presume. Or in the army."

Now he'd caught her attention. A spark of—well, he couldn't place the emotion—a spark of *something* animated her face. She replied, "My—my father served briefly in the East India Company army, yes. Then he took service with one of the Mahratta chiefs. He's dead now."

Understanding dawned on Julian. All the pieces of the puzzle came together. He thought he knew exactly who this young woman was. Her father, perhaps cashiered from the company army, had become a mercenary attached to the marauding Mahratta chieftains. He'd died in some meaningless clash. And he must have left his family destitute. If he'd provided for his children, if he'd belonged to a respectable family, surely his relatives would have brought his orphaned daughters home to England. Chandra's jewelry? It was highly improbable that an insignificant soldier of fortune could have accumulated a fortune in gems as his share of the loot from some plundering raid.

No, Julian decided, more likely than not, the jewels had come to Chandra by other channels. Judging by her lack of taste, her unsuitable, overly ostentatious clothing, her forthright, unladylike manner—even, it occurred to Julian, her willingness to accompany a strange man in his curricle—Chandra was no lady of quality. At some point she'd been the companion of some nabob who'd rewarded her with a fortune in jewelry. Had she come to England to look for fresh conquests?

Julian felt both disappointed and encouraged by his assessment of Chandra's situation. He was becoming more attracted to her with each passing minute, he admitted to himself, and he hated the thought that she'd been the fancy piece of some disreputable Eastern adventurer. And she'd certainly given him no indication at all that she felt any liking for him. He decided he'd taken the wrong tack with her. Perhaps, like his ex-mistress, Madelon, Chandra responded only to a businesslike approach. Although a little finesse probably wouldn't hurt.

Relaxing, Julian made small talk, trying to draw Chandra out, exerting all his charm. They'd finished the plate of pastries, and were drinking their third cup of tea, when the landlord of the Bull came to the parlor to announce with satisfaction that his confidence in the livery stable at Eltham had not been misplaced. Miss Banks's traveling coach was waiting at the door of the inn.

Chandra put on her beplumed bonnet. As Julian held out her sable cape, he asked casually, "Where will you be staying in London?"

"I don't know. As I told you, I've never been to London."

"May I suggest the Clarendon Hotel, or the Pulteney?"

Julian settled the cape around her shoulders and took out his card case. Holding out one of his calling cards, he said, "And will you send me word where I can reach you?"

The green eyes grew chilly. Chandra ignored the calling card. "Why should I do that?"

"Because I'd like to see you again."

The eyes became even chillier. "I'm not accustomed to making friends with complete strangers, Mr. Ware."

Julian smiled. "Oh, come now, we're not strangers any more. We've fought together against bandits. We've broken bread together. Well, pastries, anyway!" He put out his hand, gently lifting up one of the ropes of pearls she was wearing. "You seem to like jewelry. I patronize one of the finest jewelers in London, Rundell and Bridge. I'd like to gift you with one of their creations. What would you fancy?"

"Nothing you could give me," Chandra snapped, as her hand darted out to deliver a stinging blow to his face. "I'm not for sale, Mr. Ware."

Nursing his smarting cheek, Julian watched Chandra march out of the parlor. *Wrong tactics. Even poorer strategy*, thought the ex-major of dragoons. Somehow he'd badly misjudged Miss Chandra Banks.

Chapter Three

Well, that obnoxious coxcomb Mr. Ware had been useful in one respect, Chandra mused, as she stood at the window of her hotel bedchamber, looking down at the busy traffic in New Bond Street. She'd taken his advice about booking rooms at the Clarendon hotel when she arrived in London yesterday, and she was well satisfied with her choice.

At the thought of Julian Ware she could feel her cheeks burning. Insufferable, conceited man. He'd taken her for a loose woman, someone who would fall into his arms like a ripe pomegranate, simply because he offered to buy her an expensive piece of jewelry. Her cheeks burned even hotter. What right did he have to judge her like that? She shrugged her shoulders impatiently. Why was she wasting time thinking about him? It was unlikely in the extreme that she'd ever lay eyes on him again.

The Clarendon was a far cry from the miserable inn near the docks where she and Freddie and Lily had stayed in Bombay, waiting for their ship. There the amenities in each room had consisted of an earthen water jug, a meager strip of toweling, and a lumpy mattress. The Clarendon had porcelain half-tubs, in which you could almost submerge yourself, cocks that supplied water at the turn of a handle, a profusion of wide towels, fine glassware, and large standing mirrors. The proprietor was a Frenchman—a waiter had informed her that their host had once

49

cooked for royalty—whose dinner last night had been superb, according to Freddie. The ex-governess's memories of eating non-Indian food seemed to be rapidly reviving. Even Lily was recovering her usual sunny spirits, as she contemplated visiting the myriad of shops that lined both sides of New Bond Street.

Shopping, however, would have to wait. Today Chandra had more important things to do. She walked over to the wardrobe. Perhaps she didn't need her sable wrap today. At breakfast their waiter had said a warming spell was setting in. She plucked out of the wardrobe the long, close-fitting coatlike garment that the modiste in Bombay had called a "pelisse." It was what all the fashionable folk in England were wearing, she'd assured Chandra.

After she'd put on the pelisse and buttoned it, Chandra stood in front of the cheval glass and examined her reflection with a rather doubtful stare. She didn't much care for the brilliant orange color of the garment, which she thought made her complexion look sallow. However, the pelisse was certainly rich-looking enough, with its profusion of heavy gold braid decorating the front and sleeves. The modiste, a vivacious half-caste lady, had claimed that the color and style of the pelisse were "All the cracks in London, madam," whatever that meant, and Chandra had taken the lady's word for it.

After all, what did she, Chandra, know about English fashion? She'd worn nothing but native dress—the soft, luxurious, sinuously draped Indian silks and brocades and satins—for many years. When she arrived in Bombay after Asaf Khan's death, she'd needed a complete Western wardrobe immediately. Freddie was of no help in choosing such a wardrobe. Thirty-five years ago, when the governess had last lived in England, the styles had been very different. So, on the recommendation of the inn-keeper, Chandra had turned to Mademoiselle Roselle, who, he said, sewed for the finest ladies in Bombay. And indeed, in very short order, Mademoiselle had produced trunk loads of clothes for her three new customers. To the unaccustomed eyes of Chandra and Frederica Banks and

Lily, the gowns and pelisses and bonnets had looked quite splendid.

"Come," Chandra called, in answer to a knock on the bedchamber door.

Frederica hurried into the room. "I was afraid you'd already gone. Chandra, I don't think you ought to make a personal visit to this banker. Oh, I admit it's been many years since I lived in England, but in my day, ladies of quality didn't take care of money matters personally. Well, of course, they didn't stay in public lodgings without a male member of the family being present, either, but . . . Look, why don't you write to the banker, asking him to call on you at the hotel?"

"Since I *have* no male members of my family left, Freddie, I must take care of all my affairs personally, financial or otherwise," said Chandra coolly. "I really don't see why it should raise any eyebrows if I visit my banker. After all, I'm not going there alone. I'll be well escorted."

"Oh, yes, Ramesh . . ." Frederica fidgeted with the fringes of her shawl. "I've been meaning to talk to you about him. I think you should put him into livery, or at least a plain dark suit of some kind. And he should shave off his mustachios and whiskers."

"Why?" asked Chandra in surprise.

"Haven't you noticed how people stare at him? You're calling unwelcome attention to yourself by employing a servant who looks so—so outlandish."

"Ramesh would despise wearing Western clothing. He thinks it's ugly. And he'd certainly refuse to shave off his whiskers. You know very well that facial hair is a religious obligation for Muslims. So is shaving one's head. People would *really* stare if Ramesh took off his turban and walked around with his bald pate showing! As for calling attention to myself, don't forget why I came to London. Eventually I want everyone to know me. Ramesh's 'outlandish' appearance can only be helpful."

Although she looked unconvinced by Chandra's arguments, Frederica made no further objection. Chandra put on her bonnet, a velvet confection topped by enormous plumes dyed to patch her pelisse. Checking the time, she opened the case of the large gold watch, ablaze with diamonds, that was pinned to her bodice. The watch had been one of Asaf Khan's last gifts. Even the hands were adorned with minutely tiny diamonds. "Time to go," she told Frederica. "I'll be back soon. Tell Lily we'll go shopping this afternoon."

As she walked down the stairs, Chandra reflected that Freddie was becoming more English by the hour. The patterns of thinking and acting that had governed her behavior during her years in India, and especially during her stay in the Pindari encampment, were dissolving now, and she was beginning to act far more like the prim, vicarage-reared spinster who'd left England to join her brother so many years before. Take her objection to Chandra's visit to the banker, for instance. It was too priggish for words.

In the front hall of the Clarendon, Chandra found Ramesh waiting for her. With a graceful, sweeping salaam—which caused every head in the foyer to turn, guests and servants alike—Ramesh said in Hindi, "Lady, the carriage awaits."

The "carriage" was a hackney cab. Eyeing the ramshackle vehicle, so obviously a castoff from a previous, more prosperous owner, Chandra made a mental note to buy her own town carriage as soon as she could find the time to do so. She glanced down the street. Yes, she'd like something like the elegant closed carriage, with its crested door panel and richly fringed hammercloth, which had just turned the corner into New Bond Street. She drew a sharp breath. Immediately in front of the town carriage was a two-wheeled open vehicle drawn by a magnificent team. The driver's handsome face beneath the dashing top hat was unpleasantly familiar.

Julian Ware recognized Chandra at that exact moment, and reined in his team so abruptly that he caught the coachman of the town carriage behind him utterly by surprise. In a desperate effort to avoid crashing into the curricle, the coachman tried to edge past the smaller vehicle, but the street was too narrow. The town carriage, too, came to a halt with a loud grinding noise, as its front left wheel locked into the right wheel of the curricle.

The two vehicles having collided virtually in front of the Clarendon Hotel, Chandra's hackney cab was hemmed in. She remained standing on the trottoir, watching the aftermath of the accident with a feeling of malicious amusement.

As Julian Ware hurriedly stepped down from the driver's seat, the door of the town carriage opened and an elderly gentleman leapt out. Or, rather, he fell out, having refused to wait for his footman to pull down the steps. His face distorted with rage, he picked himself up and hobbled over to Julian Ware. "A pretty how-d'ye-do, young fellow my lad," he bellowed. "I daresay you fancy yourself a bang-up driver. Four-in-Hand Club and all that rot. What *I* say, cow-handed drivers like you shouldn't take the ribbons."

Julian Ware's face had turned a dull red. "I'm very sorry, sir. As it happens, I do belong to the Four-in-Hand Club, and I assure you I'm usually a competent driver. You see, I recognized an acquaintance . . ." He darted a frustrated look at Chandra, who lifted her chin and stared past him as if he were invisible.

The old gentleman's eyes followed Julian's gaze. "I might have known," he sneered. "You young cawkers, you always have your eye out for the petticoats."

Turning even redder, Julian said coldly, "If you'll allow me, sir, I'll try to disengage our vehicles so we can have a look at the damage." He climbed back into the curricle and slowly, very carefully, inched his team forward. In a few moments, with one last protesting grinding sound, the curricle pulled free. Julian drove it up the street a few feet to a vacant spot in front of a shop. Leaving the curricle in the charge of his tiger, he walked back to the irate old gentleman, handing him a card. "I fancy no real harm's been done to either vehicle, sir. Pray accept my apologies for any inconvenience I've caused you. Send me a bill for any repairs." He bowed and started across the street toward Chandra.

Hastily she reached for the door handle of the cab. By the time Julian Ware reached the hackney, Chandra and Ramesh were seated snugly inside. Julian rapped on the glass. Ignoring him, Chandra kept her eyes fixed straight ahead. A moment later, when the indignant old gentleman's coachman drove the town carriage away, Chandra's driver eased his vehicle into traffic through the opening left by the town carriage's departure. Chandra wished there was a rear window in the hackney. She would have enjoyed looking back to see Julian's expression. If he imagined he could resume his rakish pursuit of her, he was badly mistaken.

To eyes and ears accustomed to the jungle solitudes of Hindustan, the noise and bustle and sheer size of London were bewildering, even frightening. The rush of traffic, with its multitude of vehicles of every description. The horde of humanity thronging the busy streets. The magnificent public buildings and churches. The bridges over the mighty river. The drive seemed to go on interminably, but at last, having passed an imposing structure that Chandra later learned was the Mansion House, the residence of the Lord Mayor of London, the cab stopped in front of a substantial-looking building. In a moment the driver opened the door. "Number 12, Lombard Street, ma'am. Harley's Bank."

Followed by Ramesh, Chandra entered the building. In a small anteroom, a clerk sat behind a desk, busily inscribing figures into a ledger. He looked up as Chandra came in. A stunned expression crossed his face.

"I should like to see Mr. Harley, please," said Chandra crisply. Afterwards, she would look back on this moment and laugh until she cried. To the unfortunate clerk, the sudden appearance in his staid, male-oriented establishment of a tall young woman in a blindingly colored orange pelisse and a bonnet with soaring orange plumes, accompanied by a powerful, dark-visaged individual in flowing robes and a huge turban, must have been

54

unnerving. At the moment, however, Chandra felt only impatience. "Mr. Harley, please," she repeated.

"Er—which one, ma'am?"

Chandra stared the man down. "Is there more than one?"

"Er—yes, ma'am. Mr. Harley senior *and* junior."

Shrugging, Chandra snapped, "I'll see whichever Harley is available." She fixed a steely eye on the clerk. "Immediately."

The man who rose from behind his desk to greet Chandra a few moments later was a plain-featured, rather nondescript-looking man of middle height, with keen gray eyes and a pleasant smile. If he felt any surprise at seeing a lady in his office, he showed no sign of it.

"Good morning, ma'am. I'm Simon Harley. I'm my father's partner. How may I help you?"

"How do you do, Mr. Harley. My name is Chandra Banks. I've come to open an account with your bank."

"Ah. Splendid. Will you sit down—is it Miss?—Miss Banks? And you, too, sir," he added to Ramesh, sounding somewhat uncertain, as if he doubted whether the tall dark man spoke English. With one of graceful salaams, Ramesh took the chair indicated. Mr. Harley returned to his chair behind his desk.

Chandra reached into her reticule for a folded document. Handing it to Mr. Harley, she said, "That is a bill of exchange drawn on the banking firm of Solari and Son in Bombay, India. I believe the firm is well known to you, as you are to them. I should like to deposit these funds in your bank until further notice."

"Certainly." As he examined the bill of exchange, Mr. Harley's agreeable smile faded into an expression of astonishment. "This is a very large sum, Miss Banks. The largest sum I've ever handled, frankly, in a single transaction." He studied Chandra appraisingly. "You said 'until further notice.' May I ask what you meant by that?"

"Only that my stay in England won't be permanent."

"I see. You're merely visiting friends or family here.

After your visit, if I might ask, do you plan to return to India?"

"I've made no definite plans, Mr. Harley. And I have neither friends nor family in England. That's why I must call on you for assistance during my stay in London."

Mr. Harley inclined his head gravely. "I'm quite at your disposal, ma'am."

"Thank you. Well, first of all, I must tell you that I propose to establish myself in London society. The ton, I believe it's called. So I will require a house with a good address, suitable for lavish entertaining. Since I know nothing about fashionable or desirable residential quarters in London, I'll depend on you to find me a suitable house and direct me to a place where I can find the servants to staff it. My *dubash*—my steward—will, of course, be in charge of the household." Chandra motioned to the impassive Ramesh. Continuing, she said, "You will also recommend reliable tradesmen. For instance, I will need at least one town carriage and the necessary horses." She paused, eyeing the banker with a questioning lift of her eyebrows.

"Naturally, I'll be delighted to render you any assistance in my power," replied Mr. Harley promptly. "However . . ." He hesitated briefly. "You'll forgive me, ma'am, if I seem to intrude, but I should consider myself derelict in my duty to a client if I didn't ask you this: how do you propose to establish yourself in London society if, as you say, you have no acquaintances here?"

"I see no difficulty," said Chandra coolly. "Once it becomes known that I'm a single woman of unlimited wealth, I presume folk will flock to make my acquaintance. You see, my aunt, who will be living with me, and who spent her youth in England, has told me all about the 'Nabobs,' the East India Company men who returned from India with a fortune and then proceeded to make their mark in English society. I'll be, in effect, a female Nabob!"

A faintly dubious expression crossed the banker's face and immediately faded. He made no further objection.

"Finding just the right house may take some time," he warned Chandra. "If you'll give me your direction—"

"The Clarendon Hotel, on New Bond Street."

"Thank you. I'll keep you informed of my progress in locating a suitable house. Do you have any special requirements as to size, gardens, anything of that sort?"

Chandra rose, saying, "Just make sure the house is expensive, and looks it! Goodbye, Mr. Harley. I rely on you."

The banker insisted on escorting Chandra outside to her hackney cab, where Ramesh with his towering height and bright blue turban attracted the usual number of curious stares from passing pedestrians. As Chandra rode back to the Clarendon, she reflected with satisfaction that she'd made a good choice in selecting Simon Harley as her London banker. He seemed intelligent and discreet, properly deferential but not toadying. She liked him very much. What a shame, really, that bankers didn't move in the highest social circles. Mr. Harley might have been very useful in introducing her to the right people.

Arriving back at the hotel, Chandra was walking across the hallway to the staircase, when a tall figure emerged from an anteroom and blocked her path. "Miss Banks, I'd like to talk to you."

Chandra froze in her tracks. She tried to look past him, ignoring his presence. Despite herself, she found her eyes drawn to the handsome face with the long-lashed, intensely blue eyes and that sensual cleft in his chin. She noticed his clothes, too. Even with her scanty acquaintance with Western dress, she recognized that Julian Ware's blue coat, fitting like a second skin, and the pantaloons that hugged his long legs without a crease, represented tailoring of the highest order. "I have nothing to say to you, Mr. Ware."

Stepping closer, he said in a low voice, "Can't we go into one of the parlors where we can speak privately? I realize now that I grossly offended you when we last met, and I'd like to apologize—"

"I don't want your apology. Let me pass."

He put his hand on her arm. "Please, Chandra," he murmured. "Won't you let me explain? I want so much to know you better."

Julian's touch and his nearness sent a surge of electrical awareness through Chandra's body. Suddenly she wanted to touch her finger to that wicked cleft in his chin. She muttered between her teeth, "Release my arm, sir. And don't call me Chandra."

Julian's fingers tightened. "Give me a minute, one short minute," he pleaded. "I know I can—" He broke off as two powerful hands closed on his shoulders and effortlessly lifted him away from Chandra. "Let me go, you damned fool," he exclaimed angrily, attempting, without the least success, to tear himself out of Ramesh's iron hold. In a few moments, however, becoming aware that he was the object of fascinated attention on the part of several hotel servants and a brace of Chandra's fellow guests, he ceased struggling. Turning a bright red, he told Chandra, "Call off your bodyguard. I've been very dense, but I do finally understand that you don't wish to talk to me. I won't trouble you again."

Hesitating only for a split second, Chandra nodded to Ramesh, who removed his hands from Julian's shoulders and stepped aside to stand behind her, quietly watchful.

Bowing, Julian said, tight-lipped, "Good day, Miss Banks," and strode swiftly toward the door of the hotel without looking back.

As she walked up the stairs to her rooms, Chandra wondered why she didn't feel more exhilarated by the set-down she'd given Julian Ware. Had he given up a shade too easily? And if he had, why should she care?

"Chandra, can I wear your carbuncles tonight?"

Chandra waved Lily toward the large ebony and gold jewel case that stood open on her dressing table. "Take what you want." She herself was trying out the effect of a necklace of honey red fire opals interspersed with large gold beads. She decided the opals were rather overpowered by her gown of heavy, elaborately flounced maroon velvet, adorned at neckline and hem with rows of large yellow silk roses. Diamonds would display better. She selected a necklace consisting of several rows of enormous diamonds, added a rope or two of pearls, and adjusted a pair of diamond earrings fashioned vaguely in the shape of chandeliers and very nearly the same size. She adjusted a towering toque of matching velvet and stood up, her toilet complete.

Tonight marked the beginning of Chandra's campaign to enter the ranks of London society. She and Lily and Freddie were about to attend a performance of a play at the Theatre Royal, Drury Lane. It was true, as Freddie had pointed out, that the Season wouldn't start until the spring, and the town might be a little thin of company. On the other hand, Parliament was in session, and there would probably be a goodly audience of notables at the play. In any case, one had to start somewhere!

The past two weeks had been very busy ones. Simon Harley, the young banker, had been almost too indefatigable in his search for suitable real estate. He'd dragged Chandra all over the fashionable parts of the city to look at houses. South Audley Street, Park Lane, Arlington Street. Berkeley Square, Hanover Square, Cavendish Square. In the end, Chandra had bypassed a house in St. James's Square, which, Mr. Harley informed her, had been the most fashionable address in London some years ago, when no less than six dukes and seven earls had made their homes there. Instead, she'd chosen a large mansion in the newer and more prestigious Grosvenor Square.

Actually, Chandra hadn't much liked any of the houses. They all seemed overfurnished and uncomfortable. In Asaf Khan's encampment in the foothills of the Himalayas, she'd grown accustomed to bare rooms furnished only with cushions and divans and glowing Persian carpets, to low roofs shadowing cool verandas overlooking a peaceful inner courtyard with luxuriant plants and playing fountains.

It would be some time before she could move into the

Grosvenor Square house. The previous owner, an elderly peer, had lived a hermitlike existance there for many years, and Mr. Harley had told Chandra that the furniture was hopelessly old-fashioned. She would undoubtedly wish to replace it. So Chandra had spent a number of days making the rounds of the furniture emporiums and had ordered numerous pieces. She'd also visited several labor exchanges in search of servants to staff the house, and had bought a town carriage. And she'd sent Ramesh to a place called Tattersall's to purchase horses. According to Mr. Harley, ladies of quality did not frequent the premises of Tattersall's, and Chandra had bowed to his warning.

All in all, Mr. Harley had been most helpful during these past weeks. Once more Chandra found herself wishing that his social status were higher. She could certainly use a friend in the ton.

Dressed for the evening, Frederica came into Chandra's bedchamber, her forehead furrowed with misgiving. "Really, Chandra, I don't see how I can wear this—this thing!" She motioned to her gown of black taffeta. "These feathers around my neck, they make me look as though I'm about to take flight!" She gazed at the two younger women, shaking her head. "Do you know, sometimes I wonder about the taste of that modiste in Bombay," she said slowly. "That gown Lily's wearing, for example . . ."

"What's wrong with it?" Lily asked with a hurt expression. She glanced down at her dress of bright pink satin and the necklace of enormous deep red garnets, set *en cabuchon* instead of faceted.

"Well . . . I'm not sure pink is your color. And those carbuncles. Aren't they rather large?"

Lily's big brown eyes filled with tears. Since their arrival in London, she'd felt a little left out. Chandra had been too busy to spend much time with her, and Lily by now had had her fill of shopping in Oxford Street and New Bond Street. She'd been looking forward with great excitement to their visit to the theater.

Frederica said hastily, "Don't pay any attention to me, child. What do I know of high fashion? You look lovely.

You always do." Lily's piquant little face brightened. Compressing her lips, Frederica didn't allow herself to make any comment about Chandra's toque, which was festooned with the same bright yellow roses that trimmed the gown, and dripped with trailing ostrich feathers. "It's time to go, if we're not to be late for the play," she announced.

The new carriage waited for them in front of the hotel. After handing his ladies up the steps, Ramesh took his place at the rear of the carriage, protected against the cold night air by his *anga*, a splendid brocaded coat with full sleeves.

As the carriage swung east along Oxford Street, Frederica reminisced about another visit to Drury Lane many years before. "Papa brought me to London as a special treat for my twenty-first birthday. Mr. Garrick was in his last years as manager. Oh, what a great actor that man was! I felt so privileged to see him play *Hamlet* and *Macbeth*. Well, of course, *that* Drury Lane has been torn down. I understand this new theater is enormous. The second largest in all Europe, one of the waiters at the hotel was telling me."

It *was* enormous, thought Chandra a little later, after the carriage had deposited them at the Catherine Street entrance to the theater, and the attendant had ushered them to their box. She looked around rather blankly at the huge stage, the soaring ceilings, and the five great tiers of boxes on either side of the stage. And staring at her from a box directly opposite was a pair of eyes set in a familiar face. Eyes that close up would appear an intense blue.

Georgiana, Lady Eversleigh, gazed at her nephew with something less than enthusiasm when he walked into her box. She was a slim, elegant woman, still remarkably handsome in her mid-forties. "Good evening, Julian. Tristan told me you might be joining us. Allow me to introduce you to my friend, Miss Amberley."

Julian bowed to the thin, rather mousy girl who sat

61

beside his aunt. Miss Amberley seemed painfully shy. Her voice, when she returned his greeting, was almost inaudible, and she responded to his polite remarks with bare monosyllables. She actually seemed a bit afraid of him. Julian grinned inwardly. He wouldn't have put it past his aunt to warn Miss Amberley about his rakish propensities, in order to prevent him from poaching on her son's territory. Julian turned away in relief to sit down beside Tristan at the front of the box.

"By Jove, Julian, I thought you weren't coming," muttered Tristan. "Cut it pretty fine, you did. Performance will start any minute."

"I promised I'd support you, old fellow," said Julian below his breath, trying to keep a straight face. Miss Amberley was Lady Eversleigh's lastest candidate in her campaign to find Tristan a rich wife. Georgiana had invited the girl to London on a preliminary visit before the start of the Season. Yesterday Julian had received a frantic note from Tris, imploring him to accompany his mother's party to the theater.

"I can hear that laugh in your voice," muttered Tris. "It isn't funny, confound it. I need your help. Mama keeps leaving me alone with that girl. *She* never says a word, and *I* can't think of anything to say, either."

"You could make her an offer," Julian murmured.

Tristan tossed his cousin a murderous look. However, Julian's attention was elsewhere. He was staring fixedly at a party of four that had just entered the box directly opposite them across the auditorium.

"Good God, what a smashingly beautiful girl," Tristan breathed, momentarily forgetful of his mother's presence. He flashed a guilty look behind him. Fortunately, Lady Eversleigh was engrossed in relating a long anecdote to Miss Amberley. "I've never seen anyone as lovely," Tristan half-whispered.

"Nor have I, even if she's wearing that atrocious hat smothered in ghastly roses and feathers," grunted Julian.

"What feathers?"

"What feathers? Are you blind, man? Those ostrich

feathers slithering down her neck like a waterfall."

"Well, she's wearing a sort of little cap of flowers, but—Julian! I don't meant that tall woman in the dark red gown. I'm talking about the girl in pink."

"Oh. Her." Julian glanced at the slender dark young girl whom he'd last seen with Chandra on the Woolwich road. "She's pretty enough, I daresay. Chandra, though—"

"Chandra?" Tristan's voic quickened with interest. "You know the lady?"

"We've met. Don't get your hopes up. I can't introduce you. Chandra's not—that is to say, she—er—she doesn't care for the acquaintance."

Tristan's eyes were brimming with laughter. "Spurned your advances, did she? I can't remember when that last happened." He gazed at the tall, turbaned figure in the rear of the opposite box. "By Jove, that's an unusual-looking fellow standing behind the lady. Some kind of servant, I take it."

"That's no servant," said Julian morosely. "That's a bodyguard. A fiendishly effective one."

Tristan chortled. "As you've found to your sorrow, no doubt! Julian, who is she? She looks—well, you know. Not quite the thing."

"She looks like an expensive tart."

"Oh. And is she?"

"I'm not sure. No, I don't think so."

From behind them came Lady Eversleigh's voice, saying reprovingly, "Really, Tristan, we have a guest. Are you and Julian going to spend the whole evening talking to each other?"

Across the way in the opposite box, Frederica tugged at Chandra's sleeve. "Isn't that—?"

"Yes," said Chandra shortly. "That's the man who helped us beat off those thieves on the Woolwich road."

"I wonder if he'll come over to speak to us. I never really thanked him properly for coming to our rescue."

63

"I doubt it," replied Chandra, even more shortly. She hadn't told Freddie about Julian Ware's insulting offer, or his subsequent attempts to contact her.

"That was such a frightening time, I didn't notice how handsome he was," Lily observed. "He's dressed very plainly, though, don't you think?"

"He is, isn't he?" Frederica agreed. "In my day, men were more elegant, in their velvets and brocades and gold lace. Still, he's a very handsome man."

He's magnificent, confound him, even in that severe black coat and breeches, thought Chandra, feeling an illogical resentment. If Julian Ware had been plain-looking, like the young man sitting with him, it might have been easier to put him completely out of her mind. After their encounter in the hallway of the Clarendon Hotel several weeks ago, Julian had made no further attempt to see her. However, Chandra hadn't been able to stop thinking about him. If only he hadn't been so insulting . . . Chandra dismissed the thought. She couldn't possibly consider associating with a man who treated her like a common doxy. With relief, she noticed the curtain beginning to rise on the vast stage. Now she could concentrate on the play.

According to the playbill, *The Foundling of the Forest* was a brand-new production. It was a wildly melodramatic story about the misfortunes of Florian, a foundling who is in love with Geraldine, the daughter of a nobleman. A dastardly villain, the Baron Longueville, is plotting to kill Florian. The play wasn't remotely Shakespearean in tone, as Frederica halfheartedly remarked during the opening scenes, but to Chandra and Lily, who had never seen a stage performance, it was pure magic.

During the first interval, while she was still bedazzled by the excitement of the play, Chandra came down to earth rather suddenly. Becoming aware of a slight scuffle at the rear of the box, she turned to see Ramesh in the act of pushing a gentleman out the door. *So, Julian Ware hadn't given up so easily. Well, she'd soon put him straight.* She called to Ramesh in Hindi: "Let the gentleman come in."

But the gentleman who entered the box wasn't Julian Ware. He was a tall, slender man, in his early thirties, good-looking despite his elaborately arranged black curls and overly tight clothes. He bowed gracefully. "Your obedient servant, ma'am. My name is Basil Forrest. Captain Forrest, of His Majesty's 10th Hussars. Pray excuse the intrusion. However, short of introducing myself, I saw no way of making your acquaintance, and I do think we have something in common."

Frederica hissed, "Send him away, Chandra. You can't allow strange gentlemen to accost you like this in public."

But Chandra was intrigued by the little mystery. She said to the man, "Tell me, sir, what we have in common."

"Why, it's your servant. I noticed immediately that he's dressed like a Pathan." Captain Forrest smiled confidently. "Correct me if I'm wrong, but I assume you've recently arrived from northern India, and that you may be a stranger in town. Now, as it happens, I served for a number of years in Bengal. If I can be of any service in— er—helping you, as a fellow expatriate, to settle yourself in London—"

He broke off as a tall figure bounded into the box past Ramesh and elbowed him away from Chandra. "Look, here, Ware, what's the meaning of this?" spluttered Forrest.

Ignoring the captain, Julian drew Chandra aside, speaking in a voice so low that it was inaudible to the other occupants of the box. "Chandra, you may not want my company, but in heaven's name don't make the mistake of associating with this man. He's a Greek, for one thing, and I've heard rumors he's a gazetted fortune hunter."

Even if Chandra had known that the term "Greek" referred to one who cheated at cards, it would have made no difference to her. She was too angry. Drawing herself up to her full height, she said icily, "I thought you quite intelligent when we first met, Mr. Ware. Now I see I was mistaken. You're very obtuse. Let me say it again, I trust for the last time: I don't want your friendship, and I most definitely don't need your help in choosing my friends. I'd like you to go."

The blue eyes sparked, and a muscle twitched in Julian Ware's cheek. Then, his face expressionless, he bowed, saying, "At your service, Miss Banks," and walked quickly out of the box.

Gazing after Julian's retreating figure, Basil Forrest said with satisfaction, "Good riddance, that. Ware's too high in the instep. A set-down will do him good." He smiled at Chandra. "Now, ma'am, may I bring you some refreshment? Tea? Lemonade? Something for the other ladies, too, of course."

Catching Chandra's eye, Frederica gave her a warning shake of the head. Chandra's own common sense told her it was improper to admit Captain Forrest into her acquaintance without a formal introduction. For all she knew, he might be angling after the same casual favors that Julian Ware wanted from her.

Chandra thought quickly. If she dismissed the captain, Mr. Ware might assume he'd succeeded in interfering in her affairs. Not for anything would she give him that satisfaction. Then, too, hadn't the captain said that he'd served in Bengal? Her heart quickened. Could Basil Forrest be in some way connected to the mysterious figure who'd ordered Papa's massacre? Or could he perhaps lead her to others in London who might help her locate her quarry?

"Thank you, Captain Forrest," she said graciously. "We'd be pleased to have some lemonade. And perhaps you'd care to join us to see the rest of the play?"

Chapter Four

Frederica Banks paused on the threshold of the drawing room of the house in Grosvenor Square. Chandra was standing in the middle of the large, completely unfurnished room, deep in conversation with a soberly dressed gentleman. Frederica cleared her throat.

Chandra glanced up from the sheaf of papers in her hands. "What is it, Freddie?"

"My dear, Captain Forrest is here to see you."

Chandra muttered a low-voiced phrase in Hindi. Then she said, "I'll be with you in a moment, Freddie," and turned to her visitor. "Well, Mr. Bannister, I think we've settled everything. I won't keep you any longer. When can you start putting up the wallpaper?"

"Tomorrow, if that suits you? And the carpets, I believe I can promise you, will be here next week." Mr. Bannister bowed. "Good day, ma'am. It's a great pleasure doing business with a lady who knows her mind as well as you do."

After the tradesman had left, Frederica said accusingly, "Shame on you, Chandra, for saying what you did when I told you Captain Forrest was here. Many's the time I've heard Asaf Khan using that expression, but I certainly never thought I'd live to see the day when *you'd* talk so vulgarly! If that poor Mr. Bannister had had even the remotest idea of what you were saying—"

Chandra flashed the governess an unrepentant grin.

67

"Fortunately, Mr. Bannister doesn't understand a word of Hindi. And it made me feel much better! Tell me, pray, why Basil Forrest is calling when I told him particularly that I was going to be very busy these next few days, moving into this house."

Frederica shrugged. "He wants to introduce you to one of his acquaintances."

Opening her mouth, Chandra closed it again at Frederica's sudden glare. "Oh, the devil," she said weakly, substituting the phrase for a much more robust quote from Asaf Khan.

"That's better," said Frederica with a nod of approval. "What's that?" she asked, motioning to the papers in Chandra's hands.

"Designs for the new wallpaper in the drawing room. Here, what do you think?"

Frederica stared blankly at the sample of wallpaper. "It looks like the old Egyptian writing in one of Papa's scholarly books."

"Exactly. Hieroglyphics. Picture writing. It comes with a frieze of ibises around the ceiling."

"But—"

"It's the lastest fashion, Freddie. I'm decorating the house in the Egyptian style. Look over there in the corner. That settee is the first new piece of furniture to arrive."

Frederica walked over to the settee and inspected it carefully. "It's a crocodile," she said, sounding dazed.

"It's shaped like a crocodile, yes. Well, you know, crocodiles live along the Nile. Mr. Bannister says pieces like this are all the rage. You should see the dining room chairs I've ordered. Jackals on the backrests, no less. And Mr. Bannister has his eye on a lotus-leaf chandelier."

"Jackals? Why those nasty things? They used to make our nights hideous with their incessant yowling in Bhulamphur."

"Surely you remember, Freddie: the jackal was the symbol of the Egyptian god, Anubis."

"That's all very well and good, but in one's dining room—"

"We must be fashionable if it kills us," said Chandra firmly. She put down her papers on the settee. "It's no use putting it off," she sighed. "I'll go see Basil Forrest. Perhaps I can discourage him quickly."

"Don't be too sure of that. I don't think the captain discourages that easily."

Freddie was probably right, Chandra reflected, as she walked down the corridor from the drawing room to the morning room. Perhaps she'd made a mistake that evening a week ago, when she'd asked Basil Forrest to share her box at the Drury Lane theater. Basil had accepted the invitation enthusiastically, and she'd enjoyed seeing Julian Ware's reaction. He'd glowered at her all through the next act of the play, and then he'd left his box, not to return for the rest of the evening. Unfortunately, her triumph over Mr. Ware had had a price tag. Since that night, she'd been obliged to see a great deal more of Basil Forrest than she cared to. The captain had taken to calling at the Clarendon Hotel every morning, to invite her to ride in the park, or to offer his services as escort on sightseeing excursions or shopping expeditions.

She walked into the morning room, which was still furnished with the old-fashioned belongings of the previous owner, as were three of the bedchambers and the kitchens. Otherwise, Chandra had moved into a very nearly empty house. She'd previously disposed of most of the original owner's articles of furniture, planning to replace them with the new pieces she'd ordered. Or rather, Ramesh had disposed of the furniture, realizing a tidy sum from the transaction, unless Chandra was mistaken. In India, a *dubash*, or steward, took no salary. Instead, he provided for his retirement by assessing a commission on every tradesman supplying provisions for his master's household. Chandra saw no reason to believe that Ramesh had changed his way of doing business now that he was living in London.

As Chandra entered the room, Basil Forrest and his companion rose from their chairs and bowed politely. "My dear Miss Banks," said the captain, "I trust our visit isn't inconvenient?"

"Not at all," Chandra replied, lying smoothly. "I hope you'll forgive me for receiving you so informally, however. This is the only room on the first floor that contains any chairs! We're virtually camping out these days, as you can see. I decided to move into the house while it was still unfurnished, so I could supervise the renovations. I think it's important to keep an eye on workmen, don't you?"

"Er, quite. Will you allow me, Miss Banks, to present my friend, Mr. Alfred Taney?"

Chandra bowed to the rather weedy, undersized youth, whose complexion still showed signs of adolescent eruptions. "How do you do, Mr. Taney. Won't you sit down?"

"Alfred's father served with the East India Company," said Basil. "Fact is, Mr. and Mrs. Taney took me under their wing when I first arrived in Bengal."

"Indeed." Chandra gave Alfred an encouraging smile. "When did you and your family return from India, Mr. Taney?"

"Two—no, three years ago. M'father's a member of the board of directors of the company now," said Alfred with an air of importance. "Perhaps you'd like a tour of East India House? Very impressive building, I'm told. Oh, and your sister, too, of course."

"Alfred saw Miss Lily when we were driving in the park the other day," Basil explained.

Light dawned. Alfred Taney wanted to meet Lily. "I fear we'll be too busy for the next few days to visit East India House, Mr. Taney. Later, perhaps?"

Basil gave Alfred a meaningful glance, and the young man, looking flustered, rose to his feet, saying, "Er, you'll excuse me, Miss Banks? I—er—I have another engagement."

After Alfred had gone, Basil remarked, "I don't mind sharing your acquaintance with Alfred, Miss Banks, but I wasn't going to allow him to monopolize your company, either!" He sat down beside Chandra on the settee, gazing

70

into her eyes with an expression that he probably meant to be soulful, but which reminded her of nothing so much as a doleful spaniel. "We've known each other for only a few days, but . . . Dare I ask for the privilege of using your Christian name?"

Suppressing a strong urge to laugh, Chandra said gravely. "Yes, you may call me Chandra. And I'll call you Basil, shall I?"

A look of bliss settled over the captain's face. Reaching for her hand, he said, "Chandra, I know it's too soon, but I must tell you, I'm falling in love with you."

Chandra snatched her hand away. She averted her head, saying, in a tone that she hoped conveyed a maidenly confusion, "Please, Basil. It *is* much too soon."

Basil was overcome with remorse. "My emotions were too strong for me, Miss B—Chandra. It won't happen again, I promise."

"I'm sure it won't. And now, if you don't mind—I'm so busy today . . ."

Chandra smothered a smile as she watched Basil leave the room, his very back revealing his reluctance to go. Then a thoughtful expression settled on her face. Was there any profit in continuing her friendship with the hussar captain? Her suspicion that he was, or was *connected* to, the mysterious man who'd ordered her father's murder was no longer very strong. Quite frankly, she doubted that Basil Forrest was either intelligent enough or conniving enough to be such a thoroughgoing villain. He was probably just what he appeared to be, an unremarkable young man who'd transferred from India to more desirable duty with a regiment based in England. From bits of information he'd dropped, she knew he came from a modest background—minor country gentry—and he was penniless except for his military pay. Obviously, to maintain any kind of social position, he needed a wife with money. Oh, Chandra didn't doubt that he was genuinely attracted to her, but she was also sure that her fortune was an even bigger attraction.

As for Basil's contacts with former servants or soldiers of

the East India Company, well, yes, he'd introduced her to a number of young officers with Indian army connections. They, like him, were so impecunious that it was unlikely they'd ever profited from a share in the Begum's treasure. Today, of course, Basil had brought Alfred Taney to the house. Alfred's father, now, was a likelier suspect: he'd returned from India to become a member of the prestigious company board of directors. But Taney, senior, had returned to England only a few years ago, so in that respect he didn't fit the mental profile Chandra had drawn up to describe the man who ordered the massacres.

Chandra sighed. Basil Forrest might be a feeble reed, but he was the only person she'd met thus far who might be able to obtain for her information about former Anglo-Indians now resident in London. She'd best cling to his acquaintance for the time being.

Ramesh appeared in the doorway of the morning room, bowing his usual low salaam. "Good. Your visitors have gone, lady. I'll serve your luncheon now." He walked into the room and proceeded to arrange chairs around a small table. "It will, of course, be easier to serve you according to your rank when we have a proper dining room," he said with an air of reproach.

"The house will be in order soon, Ramesh."

"As you say, lady. I believe you will enjoy your meal today. I have taught the cook to prepare a curry."

"Really?" Chandra said, surprised. "How did you manage that?" One of the first servants she'd hired was a rotund woman who came highly recommended by the people at the Labor Exchange. "Cooked for a viscount for many years before he died," they'd told her. "None of those fancy French sauces or the like. Just proper English cooking."

"I simply gave the woman her orders and she followed them," said Ramesh austerely. "She kept muttering something about heathen practices, but I soon put a stop to *that*. Heathen practices. What a phrase to hear on the lips of an infidel!"

Later, while they were eating luncheon, neither Frederica

nor Lily seemed to consider the incident of Ramesh and the curry as amusing as Chandra thought it was.

"I do hope," worried Frederica, "that Ramesh will be able to manage the servants when we have a full staff. This isn't India. He can't treat English servants like an Oriental slave driver."

Lily saw no humor at all in the situation. "Ramesh must have done the right thing," she said enthusiastically. "This curry is quite good. Certainly it's the best food I've eaten since we came to England!" She paused, looking faintly guilty. After her angry outburst on the day they docked at Woolwich, Chandra knew that Lily had tried very hard not to complain about things English.

Chandra smiled at her. "You have a new admirer," she teased. "A young man, a friend of Basil Forrest, who saw you driving in Hyde Park. His name is Alfred Taney, and his father is a director of the East India Company. He wants to give us—of course, he really means you—a tour of company headquarters."

Turning faintly pink, Lily murmured, "That might be interesting." Shortly afterwards, she excused herself to go up to her bedchamber to practice on her sitar. Chandra had never had the patience to master the intricate rhythms of the long-necked, lute-shaped native instrument, but Lily had become quite proficient.

"Do you think it's wise to allow Lily to go out driving with a stranger?" Frederica asked when Lily had gone.

"Alfred Taney isn't a stranger. Basil introduced him."

"Oh, Captain Forrest." Frederica's tone was dismissive. "He's a stranger himself—or should be," she added pointedly.

Chandra ignored the jab. "Alfred might be a valuable acquaintance. His father is apparently an important man. He might be useful in helping me to make the contacts I need to establish myself in society."

"I don't think so, Chandra," said Frederica, shaking her head. "I don't think Basil Forrest or any of his friends will help you to realize your ambitions."

Two weeks later, Chandra had to admit that Frederica

was right. She sat one afternoon in her newly refurbished drawing room in her newly refurbished house in Grosvenor Square, and as she looked around the vast room, empty of people save for herself, she faced the fact that she needed more than a grand mansion and enormous wealth to launch her career in the inner circle of London society known as the ton.

Making a sudden decision, Chandra walked across the room to the bell rope. In moments, a footman answered her ring. The house now had a full complement of servants, and the footman, like the other male servants, was wearing a plain dark blue livery. Too plain, Chandra had thought, opting for a little gold braid, but Frederica had insisted on a chaste severity. The footman's carefully powdered hair looked strange to Chandra, too. She sometimes wondered if it itched.

"Send word to the stables that I want the carriage in half an hour," she ordered the footman.

"Yes, ma'am. Shall I notify Mr. Ramesh, too?"

"No," said Chandra hastily. "I won't take him away from his duties." Ramesh's intuition was always acute, and she didn't want anyone to know about her errand today.

An hour later, at the Harley bank in Lombard Street, the clerk ushered her immediately into Simon Harley's office, without checking to see if his employer was engaged. The clerk's alacrity was a tribute to the size of the bill of exchange she'd deposited in the bank, Chandra thought with a glimmer of amusement.

Simon Harley looked up from his papers with an expression of mingled surprise and pleasure. "Miss Banks, I'm delighted to see you, naturally, but you needn't have come here," he said, as he jumped up to pull out a chair for her. "I would have been happy to come to you. Why didn't you send for me?"

"Because I didn't want anyone to overhear our conversation."

Simon sat down behind his desk. "Surely you aren't afraid that your family or your servants will eavesdrop on your private conversations?"

"No. But what I wish to discuss with you is *very* private."

Simon sat back in his chair, his eyes intent and wary. "I'm quite at your disposal, Miss Banks. You're not dissatisfied with the house, now that you've moved into it?"

"No, no. The house is beautiful. It's—" Chandra paused. "Simon, that is to say, Mr. Harley—"

"I'd be honored if you'd use my Christian name," said Simon swiftly. A faint color crept into his cheeks. "I'd be even more honored if you'd give me your friendship."

"Oh, you've had that for some time," she replied cheerfully. "And my name, by the way, is Chandra."

Simon and Chandra exchanged pleased, rather astonished smiles at the sudden change in their relationship. Then, his expression quickly becoming grave, Simon said, "Something's troubling you, Chandra. How can I help you?"

"Well . . . Do you remember my telling you I expected fashionable folk to flock to my acquaintance, once I'd bought a grand London house and the word had spread I was a female Nabob? I was wrong. I haven't met a single prominent member of the ton." Chandra cocked her head at Simon. "You don't seem surprised."

He gave her a cautious look, without speaking.

"Well, at least you're not saying, 'I told you so,'" Chandra sighed. "I still wish to be a famous London hostess, Simon. I'll just have to go about it differently, that's all."

"Yes?" Simon sounded still more cautious.

"Yes. What I need is an aristocratic husband. Someone of impeccable lineage, with the *entrée* to the most exclusive circles in London. I want you to find him for me."

Simon stared at Chandra in stupefaction. He opened his mouth, but no words emerged. Finally he spluttered, "Me? You're asking *me* to find you a husband?"

"Who else? You see, I don't want a *real* husband. Or a

permanent one." Chandra colored. "I merely want a figurehead, a man who can give me a great social position for a few months, a year, and whom I can then discard."

Recovering his composure somewhat, Simon snapped, "Are you trying to bubble me, Chandra? You must know such a scheme is impossible. For one thing, no man would marry you on those terms."

"No? Not even if it came to a choice between going to debtors' prison and becoming my platonic, temporary husband?"

Simon's jaw dropped. "In heaven's name, what are you suggesting?"

"Something very simple. You're a banker and a man of business. I'm sure you often hear rumors of financial difficulties involving prominent people. Look around you, make some inquiries, find me an impoverished aristocrat who's deeply in debt. Then buy up those debts and throw the aristocrat into debtors' prison. We'll let him stew in his anxieties for a bit, and then we'll offer him his release from prison on those terms I mentioned."

"No!" Simon clenched his fists. A muscle twitched in his cheek. "I won't be a party to this. It's infamous. You—you should be ashamed of yourself, Chandra, selling yourself for an empty social position!"

Rising, Chandra transfixed Simon with an icy stare. "I was asking for your help, not a moral judgment. Very well, if you won't cooperate, I'll conduct my own search. Good day, Simon." As she turned to go, she added, "You needn't worry that I'll transfer my account to another bank. You've been most efficient in performing your professional duties. It was my own mistake, after all, thinking I could combine business with friendship."

"Chandra, please—don't go. I had no right to say what I did." Simon swallowed hard. "I'm your friend, not just your banker. I'd do anything in my power to help you, only . . . For God's sake, *think*. I said this scheme was impossible, and it is. You can't marry someone and then walk away from him, scot-free, when your use for him is over. The moment you marry, both your person and your fortune will pass out of your control. Your money will belong to your husband for his lifetime, and after that to *his* heirs, not to yours. Under English law he's not required to return a penny of it, if you decide to divorce him. And, I might add, you can obtain a divorce only by an act of Parliament!"

"Good God," Chandra said blankly. She sat down, her mind churning furiously. Presently she asked, "Couldn't you fix it?"

"Fix what?"

"There must be some way to keep my money in my own hands if I marry. Wait. Supposing I give, or deed, my fortune to my aunt. As soon as I've gotten rid of my husband, Freddie could give me back my money."

Despite his shock at this unorthodox financial proposal, Simon's professional interest was aroused. "I daresay we could set up a premarital trust," he said slowly. "Some families are beginning to do that in order to safeguard a daughter's portion from a grasping husband. Do you have absolute confidence in your aunt?" he asked suddenly.

"Yes. I'd sooner doubt that the sun will rise tomorrow than question Freddie's loyalty."

"Very well. Under those circumstances, if you made over your fortune to Miss Banks in a paper transaction, I could agree to set up a trust. Your—your husband would be unable to touch a shilling of your funds."

"I knew you could fix it." Chandra gave Simon a long, steady look. "I take it you've decided to search for that impecunious aristocrat?"

"Against my better judgment, yes." Simon threw up his hands. His voice sounded desolate. "Chandra, can't I dissuade you from this madness? *Why* is a great social position so important to you? You have everything else. Beauty, riches, the opportunity to travel. You could have love—" He broke off, averting his eyes at the betraying words.

"I'm sorry," Chandra said gently. "I can't explain, except to tell you that it's a matter more important to me

77

than life or death."

Simon had his mask in place again. "I'll inform you when I find a suitable candidate. It may take some time."

It didn't take as long as Chandra had anticipated. Several days later, as she was dealing with a domestic crisis, a message from Simon arrived.

Having returned from a drive with Basil Forrest, Chandra had stepped into the foyer, past an attentive footman, and collided with Lily, who'd come rushing down the hallway from the direction of the music room.

"Good heavens, Lily, what—?"

But Lily was beyond speech. Her face flaming, she tore past Chandra and up the stairway. Racing after her, Chandra found Lily sprawled across her bed, sobbing uncontrollably.

Settling herself on the bed next to Lily, Chandra stroked her niece's back gently, murmuring, "Darling Lily—Nalini—what's wrong?" Without thinking, Chandra used the Indian name that Asaf Khan had bestowed on Lily in the camp, and which the girl had fiercely rejected as soon as she was free. "Nalini" was the Indian name for the sacred lotus, a form of water lily.

As Chandra continued to speak softly and soothingly, Lily cried herself out. She sat up, mopping her tear-swollen face with the handkerchief Chandra handed her. "Don't call me Nalini," she said crossly. "I'm English, not Indian."

"I won't. Lily, why were you crying like that?"

"Alfred Taney," Lily spat out in a tone of loathing. "I was playing my sitar for him in the music room, and he tried to kiss me. He—he grabbed me. He wouldn't let me go. Look, my gown is torn. Chandra, he has spots on his face!"

Chandra's lips compressed in a straight line. She'd allowed the young man to visit because of his father's position as a director in the East India Company, even though she knew he was besotted about Lily. It was one more proof, if she needed it, that Frederica had been right in her prediction that Basil Forrest and his friends wouldn't bring her the social recognition she craved. She doubted very much that Alfred Taney would have dared to take liberties with a girl in the highest circles of London society. If Simon Harley wasn't successful, and soon, in his search for a suitable aristocrat . . .

"Alfred won't bother you again," Chandra promised. "Wash your face and change your clothes, Lily. We'll go shopping this afternoon."

Outside the door of Lily's bedchamber, to her no great surprise, Chandra found Ramesh waiting for her. He was always acutely aware of what was happening in the household. "Taney sahib has gone, lady," he informed her, with a faint quiver of his mustachois. "He did not wait for me to summon his carriage. He seemed in a great hurry. And here is a message for you." He produced a note on a salver.

She read Simon's brief note quickly. "I'm going out again immediately, Ramesh. Please order the stables to put the horses to."

"You will want me to accompany you, lady?"

"Oh, yes." Chandra shrugged her shoulders resignedly. Although Ramesh had gradually and reluctantly abandoned his notion that Chandra should be suitably veiled in public, he still became rather restive when she insisted on going out without a male escort. She avoided wounding his sensibilities as much as possible. However, she reminded herself to leave him in the anteroom of the bank with Simon's clerk, where he couldn't overhear her conversation.

Simon's face, when he rose to greet her in his office a little later, was quite composed. His smile, however, was a little strained as he remarked, indicating the papers on his desk, "I'm tempted to believe that the entire aristocracy of England is on its way to the River Tick."

"You've found a number of possibles, then," said Chandra, as she sat down and looked at Simon expectantly.

"I have. So many that my main problem was winnowing them down to the most promising, so to speak."

"You had to eliminate all the married men, for one thing," said Chandra with a rather forced attempt at humor.

He didn't appear amused. Picking up a sheet of paper, he began, "Here, for example, is a viscount who has mortagages of one hundred thousand pounds on his ancestral estates. And here's a baronet from an old family who borrowed sixty thousand from his banker to repay a debt of honor." Simon glanced up from his papers. "Actually, I fancy that excessive gambling is responsible for most of these financial problems. Well, to get on with it, I also have a duke's son, drowning in debt, whose father has refused to rescue him. I gather the duke's son went to the well once too often." He paused. After a moment, he said, "I could go on, but I think it unnecessary. There's one man, among those I've investigated, who it seems to me is a better choice for our—your—purposes than the others."

"Who is he, Simon?" Chandra's mouth felt a little dry.

"The man is the younger brother of an earl. The family is very ancient and distinguished. At the moment, this man is heir presumptive to the title. He's reportedly young, handsome, and a leader of the ton. For what it's worth, he's also a member of Parliament. I—er—recommend him because it would be a very simple matter to obtain control of his debts. He borrowed fifty thousand pounds from a moneylender without security. Consequently he was obliged to give the lender a promissory note made out to bearer *and* on demand. I've already sounded out the moneylender. For a substantial fee, he's entirely willing to let me have that promissory note, because he's developed strong misgivings about the loan."

"I should think so. What possessed him to make a loan of that size to a man without security?"

Simon said dryly, "The client is the heir to his aged uncle's estate. However, the uncle has an unfortunate habit of changing his will frequently."

Now that she was at the sticking point, Chandra felt a

80

curious reluctance to go on with the scheme she'd put in motion. Her entire future might depend on the decision she was about to make. She had to force the words out. "What's his name, Simon?"

"Julian Ware. He's the younger brother of the Earl of Daylesford. Very old family, I'm told. Came over with the Conqueror, or some such." Simon cleared his throat. "Do—do you want me to proceed in this matter?"

Chandra didn't answer immediately. She couldn't. She felt dizzy from a rush of conflicting emotions. Oh, she'd love to see Julian Ware's face when he discovered she had him at her mercy. It would pay her back a hundredfold for that insulting encounter on the Woolwich road. But could she risk it? Originally she'd planned a platonic marriage, a marriage of convenience, one in which neither partner would have any feelings for the other. Whatever else it turned out to be, a marriage with Julian Ware wouldn't lack emotion.

She heard herself saying, "Yes. Proceed, Simon."

Chapter Five

Tristan Loring and his cousin, the Earl of Daylesford, paused on the threshold of a room on the "state side" of Newgate Prison. Inside the room, Julian Ware sat at a wooden table, playing cards with three other men. He looked up, waving his hand. "Just finishing a rubber," he called out. A few minutes later, as his card-playing companions were leaving the room, one of them said, "It's good thing we don't have any rhino to lose, Ware. You'd have cleaned us out in that session."

"Believe me, nobody hates to waste an opportunity for gain more than I do," said Julian cheerfully. "However, there's no help for it here, gentlemen. We wouldn't be in debtors' prison if we were in funds, would we?" The good humor faded from his face after the men left. He looked tired and discouraged.

"By Jove, Julian, this infernal place looks worse every time I come here," Tristan exclaimed as he and the earl entered the room.

It was a fairly large room, about fifteen feet square, but there its good points ended. The windows were dirty, and the wooden floor was uncarpeted. The furniture consisted of three rough bedsteads, stacked on top of each other in a corner, with a fourth bedstead, spread with blankets, in another corner, and the wooden table and four chairs.

Julian shrugged. "Look on the bright side, Tris. Think how much worse it would be if I hadn't paid my twenty-eight shillings a week for four beds, thereby entitling me to a private room. Or supposing I were lodged in the male debtors' section of the prison. I might be living in a room with thirty or more companions. Here, at least, I can play a game of cards in peace."

"Julian, for God's sake, you could be staying in a private room in the keeper's house. You don't have to live in squalor like this," his brother expostulated.

"The keeper charges thirty guineas a week for his accommodations. I can't afford it. And don't say you'll find the money, Ashley. I may be here for a good long while. It could get very expensive. Unless you've found someone who'll loan me fifty thousand pounds?"

Ashley shook his head, saying despondently, "I've been everywhere. I can't raise a shilling."

Tristan burst out, "Julian, how in heaven's name could this have happened?"

"I owe fifty thousand pounds, remember? There are people imprisoned here who owe as little as fourpence. And not one of them will be released until he's paid his debt, even it it means he rots in prison for the rest of his life."

"Yes, but . . . You've never owed anyone a shilling until now. Oh, I daresay you've put off paying your tailor, or your bootmaker. Everyone does that. But you're a good risk. Vansittart, the moneylender, had security for your loan. Well, security of a sort. You're the heir to your great-uncle's property in Barbados."

"Not enough, apparently. Doubtless he started wondering about Great-uncle Josiah's inconvenient habit of changing his beneficiary."

"There's more to it than that, I fancy," said Ashley suddenly. "I finally choked some of the truth out of the moneylender, Vansittart. He admitted he'd signed over your promissory note to a partner at Harley's Bank. I went there today. The partner, a Simon Harley, wouldn't tell me anything."

"Keep after him, will you, Ashley? Try to find out why Harley's bank wants that promissory note." Julian began

83

restlessly pacing the floor. "It's only been a week . . . And I know some of these poor devils have been in Newgate for years . . . But this is a critical time in Parliament. I ought to be there. Take this investigation of the Duke of York, and the allegations that his mistress, Mary Anne Clark, had been selling commissions and exchanges and promotions for years, and that the Duke knew about it. Lack of confidence in our commander-in-chief could endanger our whole campaign in Portugal."

Tristan snickered. "Yes, it's hard to think of the duke as a commanding leader when his letters to 'Darling' are being read aloud to six hundred members of Parliament!"

Ignoring Tris's jibe, Julian went on in a worried tone, "Mrs. Clarke has even insinuated that Sir Arthur Wellesley was involved in selling commissions. Sir Arthur has been unofficially selected to be our next commander in Portugal. This investigation could ruin the career of the only competent general we have left, after Sir John Moore's death at Corunna."

Julian abruptly ceased his pacing. "Sorry. Didn't mean to enact a Cheltenham tragedy."

"I'll go to Jasper," said Tristan suddenly, speaking of his halfbrother, the present Baron Eversleigh. "He's got plenty of juice. Must have. M'father squeezed every penny, and left it all to Jasper."

Julian's tense face relaxed in a grin. "I wish you luck. Jasper squeezes pennies fully as hard as your father ever did. Aunt Georgiana will have something to say about it, too. You know she considers me a bad influence on you, Tris."

"But, Julian, you can't stay here in Newgate with no prospect of release," protested Tristan.

"I wouldn't be the first." Julian struck his right fist into the palm of his left hand. "Damnation, if I just knew *why* someone at Harley's bank bought up my note and threw me into debtors's prison . . . " He broke off, staring at the tall woman who had appeared in the doorway. Behind her stood another, taller, figure in a bright blue turban and long, flowing garments.

84

*   *   *

Chandra paused to gaze at the two great forbidding masses of unwindowed wall, united in the center by the many-windowed keeper's house with entrance lodges on either side. She shivered, feeling a kind of malignant emanation from the prison. It was as if the emotions of desperation and agony suffered by the countless wretches, guilty or innocent, who had been incarcerated on this site over the centuries, still remained trapped in those cold stones.

A large crowd of people was clustered around the entrance lodges, waiting to be admitted to the prison. Simon Harley had told Chandra that friends and relatives could visit the prisoners in unlimited numbers, from early morning until nine o'clock at night. Simon had also told her that prison regulations required that visitors be searched for weapons or other articles that might be used by prisoners to escape. As she approached the lodge, closely followed by Ramesh, she could see male turnkeys running rough hands over the persons of the men visitors. Hard-looking, frowzy women were searching the female visitors.

When his turn came, Ramesh stood in front of the turnkey with his great arms folded across his chest, skewering the man with a steely glance. Gulping, the turnkey muttered, "Er—any knives or other dang'rous weapons, guv?"

Ramesh shook his head.

"All right, then, guv. In ye goes."

Ramesh moved protectively behind Chandra. Eyeing his vast bulk apprehensively, the woman searcher brushed a perfunctory hand down the front of Chandra's pelisse and motioned her on, to the resentment of the other female visitors who weren't so favored.

At the inner entrance, one of the gatesmen—prisoners appointed to escort visitors to the various wards—accepted a coin from Chandra, saying, "The state side, ma'am? Yes, indeed," and led the way into the prison.

Simon Harley had begged Chandra not to go to Newgate. "It's not fitting for a lady," he'd said. She hadn't been inside the place for more than a few minutes before she realized what Simon had meant. The prison was dark and dirty, with a pervasive smell of unwashed humanity. Prisoners swarmed around her, jostling her as she walked; apparently they were unconfined, at least in the daytime. Many of them were in rags; most were thin and malnourished-looking. On the felons' wards, most of the inmates were wearing heavy iron manacles that clanked as they walked. There was a strong odor of alcohol, which was natural enough, since a high proportion of the prisoners and their visitors were drunk. Several times a male prisoner lifted a hand to Chandra, only to be lifted bodily out of the way by Ramesh's stout arms.

Chandra was relieved when the gatesman finally led them into a cleaner, less crowded part of the prison, where the prisoners were apparently accommodated in rooms containing four beds each. Laughter and the clink of glasses came from several of the rooms as she passed by. The gatesman stopped in front of one of the rooms. The door was open. "Mr. Ware, ma'am," said the gatesman.

Chandra met Julian's amazed eyes. "May I talk to you, Mr. Ware?"

"Er . . . certainly. Won't you come in, Miss Banks? Oh, and allow me to present to you my brother, Lord Daylesford, and my cousin, Mr. Loring."

Their polite expressions barely concealing a lively curiosity, the two gentlemen bowed respectfully. Chandra recognized one of them as the young man who'd accompanied Julian to the performance at Drury Lane. The young man who'd stared so hard at Lily.

"Julian, Tris and I must be going," said Lord Daylesford hastily, in response to a meaningful glance from his brother. He bowed to Chandra again. "Your servant, ma'am."

"Meeting a feller at White's," mumbled Mr. Loring, as he edged himself out of the room.

Julian stood with his hand on the door, looking

questioningly from Chandra to Ramesh, who had not entered the room.

"Ramesh will wait for me in the corridor," said Chandra calmly.

Julian shut the door and turned back to her with outstretched hands, his eyes alight with laughing anticipation. "My dear Chandra, I knew you couldn't stay angry with me forever! You're the most welcome visitor I've had since I came to this cursed place. How in the name of all that's holy did you find me here?"

"I put you here, Mr. Ware."

Julian froze in mid-stride. "What?" he said, sounding dazed, as if he couldn't possibly have heard what he'd thought he'd heard.

"I have your promissory note for fifty thousand pounds. When do you propose to pay me?"

Now Chandra's words had penetrated. Julian's lips were compressed in a thin line. The brilliant blue eyes were almost black with anger. "Since you're responsible for my being in Newgate, Miss Banks, you must be aware that I can't pay you. So there's something else you want from me. What is it? Or are you simply taking a petty revenge for a fancied insult during our encounter on the Woolwich road?"

Chandra blurted, "Fancied insult! You treated me like a—a—"

"Like a whore?" said Julian brutally. "That's what you looked like, you know, in those flamboyant clothes, loaded down with all that paste jewelry." His eyes raked her bright green velvet pelisse with its rows of gold Hussar braiding encrusting the sleeves and the bodice, and at the matching velvet bonnet with the impossibly high plumes that nearly reached the ceiling. "You haven't changed your style of dressing, I observe."

Choking with fury, Chandra exclaimed, "What I wear is my own affair. And my jewelry isn't paste." She paused, well aware that she'd allowed Julian to take the offense. She forced herself into calm. "Neither my clothing nor my jewelry is at issue here."

Julian walked over to the wooden table, where he sat down and poured himself a glass of wine. Leaning back in his chair, his right hand on the table with his fingers around the glass, he said coolly, "Perhaps you'll enlighten me, Miss Banks. What *is* at issue?"

I won't let him make me lose my temper again. Trying for an equal coolness, she said, "Put as simply as possible, you have a choice between remaining in debtors' prison for the foreseeable future, and becoming a married man. My husband, in fact."

Julian's face registered pure shock. His fingers tightened so convulsively on the wineglass that half its contents spilled on the table. "You want to marry me?" he spluttered. "Why, for God's sake? Unless you've been disguising your feelings perfectly, you despise the ground I walk on!"

"I wish to establish myself as a prominent hostess. To do that, I require a distinguished social position. I've had my banker, Mr. Harley, check into eligible candidates, and you seem to fill my qualifications, Mr. Ware. You come from a good family, I understand you're received in the best circles, you're reasonably personable . . ." Having delivered this last barb with considerable satisfaction, Chandra went on, "My personal feelings—or yours, for that matter—are beside the point. I neither want nor expect you to—to fulfill any marital duties."

Recovering his composure somewhat, Julian growled, "What you mean is, you don't want to sleep with me. The feeling's entirely mutual. and before you go any further, my poppet, my answer is no. I don't want to be your husband, marital duties or no marital duties."

Chandra bit her lip. *He has a knack for throwing me off balance. If I married him, could I control him?* "Perhaps, before you make your decision, you should listen to what I have in mind."

Julian drained what wine was left in his glass and poured himself another drink. "Fire away, Miss Banks. This might be amusing."

"Very well. I propose a platonic marriage of convenience for one year. During that time, you will act as my host in the house I've just purchased in Grosvenor Square, introduce me to your family, friends, and associates, and, in public, act like a devoted husband. At the end of a year, I will return your promissory note, marked paid. You may then divorce me whenever you choose. My banker informs me that a divorce involves an act of Parliament. That should be very easy for you, in your position as a member of the House of Commons.''

"It would also leave you in a delicate social position. There are very few divorced ladies in the highest ranks of London society.''

"I'll risk it,'' Chandra snapped. "After a year, I'll be so securely established that I won't need you *or* the marriage. Well, Mr. Ware? Will you accept my proposition?''

Julian glared at her. "I'm damned if I will! I'm not for sale, Miss Chandra Banks. I'd rather rot in Newgate for the rest of my life, than be leg-shackled to a brazen harpy like yourself!''

Shrugging, Chandra said, "It's your choice.'' She walked to the door, pausing with her hand on the handle as she turned to face him. "I'll give you three days. If I haven't heard from you in that time—oh, by the way, I'm living at Number 11, Grosvenor Square—I'll instruct my bankers to look into other possibilities. I daresay there won't be any difficulty. I'm told London is swarming with indigent aristocrats, including dukes' sons and baronets in their own right. Don't get your hopes up,'' she added. "Whether I choose someone else or not, you'll stay here in Newgate until you pay me that fifty thousand pounds!'' She wrinkled her brow in a thoughtful frown. "As a matter of fact, I may have made a mistake in choosing you in the first place. I'd only be an 'honorable,' wouldn't I? The Honorable Mrs. Julian Ware. It has a rather plebeian ring.''

"Deuce take you, Julian, you haven't been listening,'' Tristan complained.

"What?" Julian shook himself out of his dark thoughts. It was the afternoon of the fourth day since Chandra had issued her ultimatum. "I'm sorry, Tris. What were you saying?"

"Only that I went down to Eversleigh Manor to see Jasper. Would you believe it, that brother of mine is such a cheese-parer he's not going to open the London house for the Season this year. Says he can't afford it. You'd think the tipstaffs were after him." Tristan sighed. "I should have known it was a useless trip. I asked him to cover your promissory note. He said you'd made your bed, now you could lie in it. I'm sorry, Julian. I did think there was a chance of prying the rhino out of my brother."

"Don't worry about it, Tris." Julian sounded absent-minded again. He pulled out his watch to check the time.

"Expecting someone? Julian! Is it that smasher, Miss Banks?"

"Er—yes. She'll be here shortly."

"You sly dog! I thought you were looking like the Top of the Trees today," said Tristan, casting an admiring eye at his cousin's irreproachable coat and pantaloons, at his cravat, a masterpiece of the art, and at the curling perfection of his black locks. "You won't need me, certainly. I'll take myself off," Tris added, reaching for his hat. At the door he paused. "Didn't you once tell me the lady didn't wish for your acquaintance?"

"Evidently she changed her mind. It's a feminine prerogative," Julian said dryly.

"Well, then . . ." Tristan hesitated. "You remember that pretty little friend of Miss Banks? The gal in the pink gown at the theater? *Now* can you introduce me to her?"

Before Julian could reply, a knock sounded at the door. Tristan opened it, bowing to Chandra. "Afternoon, Miss Banks. A pleasure to see you again." He waved to his cousin. "Until later, Julian. Don't forget—er, you know—to think *pink!*" He sidled past Ramesh's large frame on guard in the corridor and disappeared.

Closing the door, Chandra observed, "You cut your time limit rather fine, Mr. Ware. By late last evening, I'd quite given you up."

"Condemned prisoners naturally struggle to stay out of the hangman's noose as long as possible. Surely you can understand that."

Chandra glared at him.

"On due reflection," Julian continued, "I decided that living with you was preferable, if only marginally, to staying in this hellhole." He cocked his head. "Disappointed to get my message, Miss Banks? Perhaps you already had a replacement in mind for me?"

"No one specific. I may have been leaning toward the duke's son. After all, one wishes to obtain the best value possible for one's money! Do I take it, then, that you've decided to accept my offer?"

"I have. With one proviso."

"You surprise me, Mr. Ware. You're hardly in any position to impose conditions."

Julian restrained a strong impulse to grab Chandra by that lovely thick braid of auburn hair and shake her until her head rattled on the slender stem of her neck. "It's a very minor condition," he assured her. "I'm prepared to be an exemplary husband in public. I'll be a dutiful host, I'll squire you wherever you wish to go. I'll not by the lift of an eyebrow reveal my real opinion of you. But in private I wish nothing to do with you."

The green eyes flashed dangerously. "That suits me perfectly. In fact—" Chandra opened her unfashionably large reticule and took out a bejeweled poniard, "in fact, I should remind you that I carry this with me at all times and in all places, *including* my bedchamber!"

"My dear Miss Banks, have you forgotten we've already mutually agreed that we have no desire to sleep with each other? Let me assure you that under no circumstances will you have need of that weapon to protect your person from me. I've no intention of ever going near your bedchamber."

Observing the sudden tightening of Chandra's lips, Julian felt a perverse satisfaction at having provoked a reaction from her. This woman might have him at her mercy, but he wasn't going to make it easy for her. He wasn't going to play the role of her tame lapdog.

Quickly recovering, Chandra said coolly, "I agree that it's important to clear up any possible sources of misunderstanding. For example, I should tell you that you'll profit from this marriage only to the extent of recovering your promissory note. You'll have no access to my fortune. I'm making over my assets to my aunt, Frederica Banks, who in turn will set up a trust, the income of which will be solely at my disposal."

Julian had to choke back a rush of cold fury. "I don't want your money," he said contemptuously. "I just want to be rid of you, once and for all, when this sham of a marriage is over."

"Amen to that, Mr. Ware. However, before we can speak of ending the marriage, we must begin it. I'd like to have the ceremony performed as soon as possible. We can begin discussing the arrangements immediately after you're released from prison."

"Which will be?"

"My banker is completing the formalities now. You should be free to leave by the end of the day. Come see me tomorrow in Grosvenor Square."

The imperiousness in Chandra's voice and manner grated on Julian's already lacerated sensibilities. "Has it ever occurred to you that you might catch more flies with honey than with vinegar? Do you always order, never ask?"

For a moment Chandra looked nonplussed. "Oh, you mean my request to call in Grosvenor Square. But that was just business. Ours is a business, not a personal, relationship."

"Business? I'd say, rather, that it smacks of trade!"

Despite her intention not to lose her temper again, Chandra felt a quick surge of anger at the note of utter disdain in Julian's voice. "Perhaps trade *is* the right word," she snapped. "My—my father made his money in the indigo trade. Make of it what you like. But I still want to see you at my house tomorrow." She turned to go.

"One moment, Miss Banks. As a cavalry officer, I was

accustomed to obeying the commands of my superior officers. I'm a civilian now, and you're not my commanding officer, and I don't take orders from you. If you don't accept that, then perhaps you'd better leave me in Newgate."

After a moment's hesitation, Chandra shrugged. "Oh, very well, if it will make you feel better . . . *Please* come to see me in Grosvenor Square tomorrow, Mr. Ware."

Julian bowed. "Certainly, Miss Banks. Oh, one more thing," he added, as Chandra again turned to go. "You have the advantage of me. You apparently know all about my background. Please tell me something about the family into which I'm to have the honor of marrying. It's information I'll need to know in any event, if I'm to send a notice to the *Times* and the *Chronicle*."

He listened in silence while Chandra described her "grandfather," the Reverend Theophilus Banks, a vicar in the Midlands, who was now dead. She talked of her "father," the vicar's only son—and Frederica Banks's brother—the mercenary soldier who had died in the Mahratta wars, leaving a daughter by each of his two marriages.

"And a fortune to each, I presume," commented Julian.

"No. He left his money to me."

"Odd." Julian lifted an eyebrow. "So," he went on, "you have no immediate family except your younger sister and your aunt, Miss Frederica Banks. You'd almost think you existed only in a vacuum." He shook his head. "It will certainly mean a rather small number of guests on your side of the aisle for the wedding, will it not?"

"Exactly, Mr. Ware. I'm depending on you to supply the family connections and the guest lists I lack. Until tomorrow, then."

"Well, sir, it's *about* time," said Julian's valet, in heartfelt gratitude later that afternoon in Julian's cell in Newgate. Bates arranged his master's belongings with loving care in one of several large portmanteaux. He glanced scathingly around the room. "This is no place for a gentleman, *or* a gentleman's gentleman. Mind, I've done the best I could, Newgate or no Newgate."

"You've done admirably, Bates," Julian interrupted. He'd found it impossible to prevent the valet from coming daily to Newgate during the period of his incarceration, even though it was ludicrously apparent that fashion had no place in the prison. Bates had his own sense of the proprieties.

The Earl of Daylesford paused abruptly on the threshold of the room. "What's this?"

"My lord, we're leaving this dreadful place," said Bates, with a beaming smile, as he began strapping shut the portmanteaux.

"Run along, Bates," said Julian. "I'll be with you directly. I'm going to White's tonight. I need to replenish my coffers."

"How did this happen?" asked Ashley, when the valet had withdrawn with the bags. "Who loaned you the money to redeem your promissory note?"

"Does it matter?" Julian muttered. He was instantly annoyed with himself for evading Ashley's question. He knew he was being childish. Not even to himself did he want to dwell on the fact that the price of his freedom was entrapment in a hated marriage.

"Well, I'd certainly like to know who succeeded in obtaining your release, when your own brother couldn't raise the wind to get you out of here," said Ashley savagely.

Julian looked at his brother's strained, guilt-ridden face, and felt a rush of sympathy. Poor Ashely. He blamed himself for Julian's predicament. He'd blame himself even more if he knew the truth about this marriage.

"If you don't mind, Ashley, I'd rather not say where I got the money. It's—er—it's a rather delicate matter."

"That's up to you, certainly," said Ashley stiffly.

"I do have some other news you ought to know. I'm getting married. To that tall handsome girl who visited me the other day while you were here. Miss Chandra Banks."

Ashley stared. "I gathered from Tristan that you just met the woman."

"Actually, I've known her for some time."

"How long?"

"Well . . . five or six weeks, at least."

Ashley looked his disapproval. "Who is this Miss Banks? Who are her family? Where do they live?"

"Her grandfather was a clergyman. Apparently he held a modest living in the Midlands. Her father went to India as a soldier, then became a military adventurer who accumulated a fortune before he died. Chandra was born in India. She's never lived in England. She has no living family except an aunt, who lives with her, and a younger sister, Lily, who I believe is of mixed blood."

"You believe? You don't *know?*"

"Lily looks to be of mixed blood. It's not something you can very well ask about, you know," said Julian defensively.

Ashley threw up his hands. "It won't do, Julian. You can't be considering such a mésalliance. This Miss Banks seems to be a nobody from a barely respectable family. Her sister's position may be most irregular. If the sister *is* a half-caste, how could we possible present her to society as a member of our family? Think about what you owe to the Ware name. You know you're the only hope to continue our family line—"

Julian interrupted him. "Ashley, I *must* marry Chandra Banks." There was nothing for it now. To curb his objections, Ashley had to know the truth. Briefly Julian told his brother how Chandra had obtained her hold on him through the promissory note.

"No, Julian, I won't let you do this," Ashley exclaimed in horror. "It's all my fault. If I hadn't lost that money playing faro, you'd never have pledged that promissory note. I'll sell the estate. It will take some time to break the entail and find a buyer, but then we can repay this Banks woman the entire amount."

"It's too late for that. You'll have to accept this marriage, Ashley. It will only last a year, and then I'll be free of Chandra. In the meantime, I've made a bargain with her, and I intend to keep it. I promised her I'd be an exemplary husband to her in public. That means she must be received into the family, and my friends must extend a welcoming hand to her."

Ashley's lips thinned to an ugly line. "I see we have no choice," he said bitterly. "Very well, I'll not be the cause of scandal. I'll receive her. But don't expect me to be more than civil to that dreadful woman."

Chapter Six

The following morning, when Chandra brought her into the morning room to hear the news of the betrothal—and the events that had led up to it—Frederica was frankly horrified. "You're selling yourself into a loveless marriage for the sake of revenge!" she exclaimed, with an involuntary glance at the book that lay face downward on the table next to her chair. *The Count of Monteverde,* or, *The Bride of Evil,* it was called. Since the governess's return to England, she'd been reveling in the lurid Gothic romances she'd been forbidden to read in her sheltered girlhood.

"You've been reading too many of those novels, Freddie. You have it the wrong way around," said Chandra dryly. "It's Mr. Ware who's selling himself, not me. And you needn't be concerned about a loveless marriage. This isn't going to be any kind of a marriage at all, except on paper. It's a business arrangement. I've hired Mr. Ware's services, so to speak. He'll be my host and my escort and otherwise do as I say, for as long as I need him, and then we'll part company."

Frederica said sharply, "Don't forget, I've met the gentleman, the first time under unusual circumstances. He was trying to save our lives! I don't think he's the kind of man you can order around like one of your *kitmatgars* or peons in Asaf Khan's camp. Especially after you've had him thrown into debtors' prison. Chandra, how could you

97

do such a thing? It was no better than blackmail, and well you know it. What must Mr. Ware have thought of you?"

"What he thinks of me has very little to do with anything. I can manage Julian Ware."

"'Pride goeth before destruction,' as Papa used to say," retorted Frederica. "He also said, 'Wisdom is better than rubies.' Chandra, unless you're very careful, you'll come to grief with that man."

Conscious of the rush of color to her cheeks, Chandra tossed her head, saying, "Don't be ridiculous, Freddie. Julian Ware is just a man, no more, no less. I told you I could manage him."

"There's something more, isn't there?" Frederica said suddenly, peering closely at Chandra. "You're not indifferent to this man Ware, are you?"

Remembering a long list of Julian's taunts and jibes, Chandra said resentfully, "No, I'm not. He's conceited and insufferable and I can't abide him! But he can be of use to me, and that's all that matters."

"Oh, Chandra, I don't like this. I'm not a fanciful person, but I feel in my bones something dreadful will happen if you persist in this marriage. Break it off. Better yet, give up this scheme of revenging your father's murder."

"Freddie, stop it. Nothing on earth could make me give up my search for Papa's killer." Chandra broke off as Lily burst into the morning room. Lily was looking very pretty in a gown in a becoming shade of deep red. The angry color in her cheeks matched the gown.

"Why, what is it, child?" asked Frederica.

"It's that Alfred Taney. Chandra, you told me he'd never bother me again. And yet, as I was coming down the stairs a few minutes ago, who should the footman be ushering into the foyer but Alfred. So I called Ramesh, who threw him out!"

"Oh, dear. I told him he might call," said Chandra in a hollow voice. "He wrote me such a penitent letter, I decided we should give him another chance. He comes from such an excellent family, you know. Well, there are only twenty-four directors in all the East India Company, and Alfred's father is one of them! And since we know so few people in London, I was really looking foward to meeting such a distinguished man. Alfred promised faithfully he'd be a perfect gentleman in future."

Lily looked dissatisfied, and Frederica shot Chandra a hard glance. Chandra could easily read Freddie's mind. The governess knew quite well why Chandra had chosen to overlook Alfred's boorish behavior in regard to Lily. It wasn't that she cared a fig for the Taneys' social position, which was upper-middle class at best. Chandra was after much bigger game. She wanted to continue to pick Alfred's brains, and those of his parents, about the family's contacts in the East India Company.

"You may find you have neither the time nor the opportunity to cultivate the Taneys, now that you'll be moving in such different circles," Frederica remarked with an air of limpid innocence.

Touché, Chandra acknowledged silently. She cleared her throat. "Lily, I have something to tell you."

"Married?" Lily gasped, when Chandra had revealed her plans to marry Julian Ware. "To that man who tried to rescue us from the bandits? What a romantic story, Chandra. Poor Mr. Ware was in *prison?* Oh, for debt. Not for any terrible crime. And you visited him there? It's easy to see how friendship could develop into—into love very quickly under the circumstances!" She paused, a frown appearing between the delicate wings of her eyebrows. "Does this mean we'll be staying in England?"

"Oh." Chandra wished suddenly she could take Lily completely into her confidence, to avoid telling lies and half-truths at every turn. But she and Freddie had decided the grisly facts of Chandra's vendetta would be too heavy a burden for Lily's childish shoulders. "Darling Lily, am I being selfish? My betrothal happened so fast I quite forgot my marriage would involve you, too. Do you still dislike England so much?"

"N-no. I wish we knew more people, though. Younger people. *Not* like Alfred Taney with those dreadful spots!"

Chandra reflected with a wry amusement that Lily seemed to dislike Alfred as much for his spots as for his graceless personality.

A footman came into the morning room with a tray. "Are you at home, ma'am?"

"If that's Alfred again, no, we are *not* at home," muttered Lily.

Chandra looked up from the card she had taken from the tray. "Ask Mr. Loring to wait in the drawing room," she told the footman. When he left, she rose, shaking out her skirts. "Come along. You're about to meet the first of my new relatives. A Mr. Tristan Loring. He's Mr. Ware's cousin." She chuckled. "I met him in prison, too. He was visiting Mr. Ware."

"Is he nice?" asked Lily, as she and Frederica and Chandra started walking down the hallway toward the drawing room.

"Oh, yes. Quite nice. He's young, too. Younger than Mr. Ware." Chandra gave Lily an encouraging smile.

In a puzzled voice, Lily asked, "Are you going to keep calling Mr. Ware 'Mister' after you're married?"

"You must remember this has been a whirlwind courtship, Lily," said Frederica hastily, "Chandra and Mr. Ware are still in the process of getting to know each other. As for calling Mr. Ware 'Mister,' my dear mother always referred to my father as 'Mr. Banks' both in public and within the family. I was quite old, actually, before I realized his Christian name was Theophilus."

Chandra shot Frederica a look of gratitude. *All the same, though, Lily has a point. Perhaps among older, more conservative people, and in clerical circles, husbands and wives call each other "Mr." and "Mrs.," but I can't risk the slightest doubts about the genuiness of my marriage. Julian and Chandra it will have to be, if it kills us.*

Tristan Loring rose as the ladies entered the drawing room. He wasn't, thought Chandra, someone you would notice instantly on the street. He was a slender young man of medium height, unremarkable in his looks save for a lively pair of gray eyes and a quick smile of pure charm that transformed his plain features.

"Miss Banks, what a pleasure to see you again. Thank you for receiving me," said Tristan with a deep bow. He looked expectantly from Lily to Frederica.

"My aunt, also Miss Banks, My sister, Lily. May I present to you Mr. Tristan Loring?"

When they were seated and Chandra had rung for refreshments, Tristan said, "I couldn't wait to tell you how happy I was to hear the great news. I rushed over here immediately when Julian told me about your betrothal. I hope I'm the first to welcome you into the family."

"You are, yes," replied a startled Chandra. "Er—I wasn't aware that anyone knew about the betrothal yet. Mr.—Julian talked of sending a notice to the newspapers."

"Oh, I didn't learn about your betrothal from the newspapers. I met Julian at White's last night. Or, rather, early this morning. By Jove, I was never so surprised to see anybody in my life. I thought he was still in debtors' prison. But no, there he was, big as life, sitting at his usual table, decimating his opponents, also as usual, at whist. One of the club attendants said he'd already been there for ten hours. That wouldn't be a record for him, of course. Not long ago he was in a marathon session that lasted nineteen hours. Won thousands."

"Mr. Ware gambles a great deal, does he?" inquired Frederica. Chandra could hear the faintest hint of reproof in her voice. Freddie's papa, the vicar, had been much opposed to card playing.

"Lord, no. Well, Julian doesn't call it gambling," said Tristan blithely. "He says whist is a game of skill." He cleared his throat. "Look, Miss Banks, I came to ask you and Miss Lily and you, too, ma'am—" he bobbed his head to Frederica, "if you'd care to go for a drive. The weather's turned quite mild since last week."

"Unfortunately, I'm very busy today. Possibly, however, my aunt and Lily . . ."

Her dark eyes shining, Lily murmured, "I'd like very much to go driving with you, Mr. Loring."

"Oh, please . . ." Tristan turned a bright red. "I say, won't you call me Tris? Mr. Loring sounds so formal. After all, we'll soon be relatives!" He flashed Frederica a coaxing smile. "I don't have any aunts on either side of the family. May I adopt you, Miss Banks?"

After a moment of blank surprise, Frederica laughed, saying, "I don't have a single nephew, either. I'd be delighted to be your Aunt Freddie. And yes, Lily and I accept with pleasure your invitation to go driving."

Chandra watched them leave, feeling both pleased and relieved at Tristan's friendly gesture. She hoped Tris's visit was an omen that her entrance into the Ware family would continue to go smoothly. Now, as soon as Julian arrived, they could proceed to make the wedding plans. Yesterday, at Newgate, he'd promised to visit her today.

Several hours passed, and Lily and Freddie returned from their drive, having extended a luncheon invitation to Tristan, which he accepted with alacrity. He stayed on to have a game of backgammon with Lily, and left reluctantly because he'd promised to escort his mother to Somerset House to view the latest exhibition. "Mama really doesn't care for art," he explained with an engaging frankness, "but she likes to appear knowledgeable about which paintings are all the crack."

The house in Grosvenor Square seemed to lose some of its vitality when Tristan removed his cheerful presence. And still Julian didn't come. Doubtless he was still playing whist amid scenes of debauchery at White's, which Chandra assumed to be some kind of gentleman's club, instead of keeping his engagement with her. By mid-afternoon she'd grown decidedly snappish.

At three-thirty a footman escorted Simon Harley into the newly renovated Egyptian drawing room. He gazed about the room with a slightly bemused air. The finishing touches included several tables supported by figures of Egyptian gods, a large crystal obelisk with inscribed Egyptian figures, and a sofa in the form of a Nile boat. "Er . . . what an unusual room," Simon murmured. When Chandra didn't reply, he looked at her more closely, inquiring, "Is something wrong?"

"N-no." She'd already burdened Simon with enough of her problems, Chandra decided. "Pre-wedding jitters, maybe," she said ruefully.

A shadow crossed Simon's face. "I understand Mr. Ware obtained his release from prison yesterday. You're—you're still determined to go through with this marriage?"

"Yes, Simon, more than ever."

Simon shurgged. "Then you'll be interested in looking at these." He took from his case a sheaf of legal-looking documents. "These are the trust agreements. In this document, you sign over your assets to your aunt. In the second document, she puts your fortune into a trust in your name, which becomes effective on your marriage. For the duration of the marriage you—not your husband— have the sole use of the income from the trust. If for some reason during the course of your marriage, you require a large sum over and above the amount of your income from the trust, you may apply to your trustee to grant it to you from capital. I presume Miss Banks would comply with your request."

"Oh, yes. Freddie would give me any sum I required. Don't worry about it, Simon."

"Let's hope you're correct," said Simon. His tone was dubious. "To proceed with the description of your trust. If your husband dies, or if you are divorced, your principal reverts to you. In effect, by the purely legal maneuver of creating a trust, we retain the control of your money in your hands. The sticking point, in my view and that of the solicitor who helped me draw up these agreements, is, of course, the moment after you sign the first document and before Miss Banks signs the second. In that moment you *could* become an instant pauper, if Miss Banks decides to retain your assets."

Chandra smiled into Simon's concerned eyes. "You're an expert on banking matters. *I'm* an expert on Frederica Banks. She'd rather be trampled by a herd of maddened elephants than cheat me out of a shilling." She turned thoughtful. "Simon, I thank you for all you've done.

103

Could I ask you to do one thing more?"

"Anything at all."

"Well . . . You have so many contacts in the business community. Could you be on the watch for information about men who served in India about ten years ago, either with the East India Company or its army, and who returned to England with substantial fortunes?"

"I could, yes," said Simon slowly. "Why do you want to know this?"

"I can't explain. I can only say that I must have this information for use in a very—in a desperate situation."

Simon studied her for several moments. "Chandra, I know I have no right to pry . . . You didn't come to England for vanity's sake, did you? I don't think you really care a fig for social success. You want position—notoriety, even—merely as a means to an end. And now I'm beginning to think it may involve some kind of danger. Won't you let me help?"

Impulsively Chandra took a step toward him and clasped his hands. "You're such a good friend, Simon. You can help me most by obtaining that information for me."

A voice behind them said, "Will you receive Mr. Ware, ma'am?"

Hastily Chandra broke away from Simon and turned to face the door.

"Miss Banks is expecting me," drawled Julian, as he brushed past the footman into the drawing room. With his great height and lounging grace, and the candlepower of those intensely blue eyes, he immediately dominated the room, she thought resentfully. He raised an inquiring eyebrow at Simon.

Chandra introduced them. "Mr. Ware, Mr. Harley."

The men bowed to each other. "Harley," repeated Julian. "Would you be the banker who's responsible for my recent stay in Newgate Prison?"

Simon colored faintly. "I've been acting as Miss Banks's banker, certainly."

"You're to be commended, sir, for your devotion to Miss

Banks's interests," said Julian suavely.

Looking goaded, Simon muttered, "Thank you." To Chandra he said, "I must be going. Please sign those documents at your leisure and return them to me. Good day, Miss Banks, Mr. Ware."

After Simon left, Julian took out his snuffbox and inhaled a delicate pinch of snuff. Dusting off his fingers with his handkerchief, he said, "I see you believe in combining your business relationships with your personal relationships. Interesting."

He looked handsome but dissolute, decidedly the worse for wear. There were lines of weariness in his face, and a puffiness around those bright blue eyes. He needed a shave. His cravat was wilting. A strong odor of wine wafted from his person. In short, he was still a little bit on the go, and it was obvious he'd come straight to Grosvenor Square from the gambling and drinking session at his club where Tristan Loring had observed him in the early hours of the morning.

"You're late," blurted Chandra. She was positive Julian had delayed his arrival purposefully, to make it clear to her how much he resented being trapped into this marriage.

The half-smile on his lips faded. "Late?" The single word cut like a knife.

"I told you I wanted to see you today to begin making arrangements for the wedding."

"So you did. And here I am. Your most humble, obedient servant." He swept her a low bow.

The open derision in his eyes caused Chandra's temper to explode. "Yes, here you are, half seas over, after you've gambled the night and most of the day away. You're in no condition to discuss *anything!*"

Stiffening, he asked, "You've been keeping tabs on my activities? A little premature, is it not? We're not married yet."

"No, I haven't been spying on you," she retorted. "Your cousin Tristan Loring was considerate enough to call this morning with his felicitations. He told us how much you'd been enjoying yourself at White's." Swallowing her

105

anger, Chandra went on, "Well, now that you *are* here, shall we discuss the wedding? When shall it be?"

He shrugged. "Whenever you like. After all, the sooner we begin, the sooner my year of captivity will be up!"

Chandra's mind reverted longingly to several of the more grisly torments that Asaf Khan had inflicted on his enemies. She gritted her teeth, saying, "In three weeks time, then, after the publication of the banns."

"Banns? Isn't that a bit excessive? I suggest we have a quiet ceremony by special license. There's no need to call attention to our situation."

Chandra glared at him. "You mistake the matter entirely. I *want* public attention. That's why I'm marrying you. The *only* reason I'm marrying you."

His lip curling, Julian remarked, "Perhaps you'd like me to arrange a service at St. George's, Hanover Square."

Chandra lifted her chin defiantly. "Is that the most fashionable church in the city for weddings?"

"It is. Westminster Abbey is, I fear, a cut above our touch."

Ignoring his sarcasm, Chandra said, "Good. St. George's it will be, in three weeks' time. Do you know a bishop who might perform the ceremony?"

"Ah, yes. That would add the crowning stroke of vulgar ostentation that you seem to crave." He gazed around the drawing room, as if he were taking in its details for the first time. "Good God. What in the fiend's name possessed you to have a canopy of palm trees painted on the ceiling of this room?"

"I went to the most expensive upholsterer and furniture maker in London for advice in decorating this house," Chandra flared. "I'll have you know Egyptian style is all the crack in home furnishings these days."

"Not in the circles I move in," Julian said coolly. "I prefer to live like a gentleman, myself. That doesn't include sitting on furniture with feet shaped like lions' paws, or an Egyptian boat." He took another long look at the boat-shaped settee, and shuddered. "Carlton House to a charley's shelter, it's only a hardy soul who could avoid seasickness after sitting on that thing!"

Chandra swallowed against the hard lump of hurt that had formed in her throat. "In future, pray keep your criticism of my clothing and my house to yourself, Mr. Ware. Your opinions are nothing to me."

"Perhaps not, but you'd be wise to pay attention to them. My tastes are shared by my friends in the ton, the very people you apparently wish to attract. Your hair, for example. Why do you wear it down your back, like some Indian peasant girl?"

Julian made a sudden move toward her, picking up the heavy braid of hair that hung from the crown of her head. His nostrils widened and he inhaled a sharp breath. Chandra knew he'd caught the sweet, heavy scent of her jasmine perfume. Her own heart began to pound. Holding the braid in one hand, he drew it slowly through the fingers of the other as if he were caressing the thick silky rope. "You have such beautiful hair," he muttered. "It feels alive, as if it wanted to escape its bonds and curl around my fingers . . ."

His face flamed, and he dropped the braid as if it were a burning coal. He said in a suffocated voice, "Your hair is lovely—you're lovely—but you'll never become the prominent hostess you want to be, if you don't change the way you look, the way you live. You couldn't achieve your goals if you were to marry a man a hundred times more important than I am in the social scheme of things. If the Prince of Wales were free to be your husband, he couldn't bring you into fashion!"

If there's the smallest grain of truth in what he's saying . . . I can't allow hurt feelings to damage my chances of finding Papa's murderers. Suppressing an urge to stamp her foot and screech like a fishwife, Chandra said calmly, "Since you appear to know so much about female fashions, Mr. Ware, why don't you come shopping with me and help me to choose something more becoming?"

A flabbergasted look crossed Julian's face. The reaction gave Chandra a good deal of pleasure. "You want me to go shopping with you for clothes?" he gasped.

107

"I do. This marriage is a business proposition. I daresay I shouldn't neglect any opportunity to make it successful." She glanced at the elaborate diamond watch pinned to her gown, a taffeta confection in a bright red shade. "I believe the shops are still open. Shall we go?"

"Now?"

"Why not? Time is money, according to my banker, Mr. Harley."

"Mr. Harley appears to be a fount of wisdom," snapped Julian. He took a deep breath. "If you really want me to accompany you to a dress shop, I'm quite at your disposal."

"Thank you. Did you drive yourself here? Or shall I order my carriage?"

"I came in my curricle. It's very cold today. Perhaps you'd be more comfortable in a closed carriage."

"Oh, no, that's all right. I have my sable cape. I'll be quite warm enough." Chandra paused as she noticed a flicker of a smile curving the corners of Julian's lips. "There's something wrong with my cape, too? I'll have you know those are the finest Russian sables obtainable. Asaf—" Chandra paused again, biting her lip. She'd nearly given herself away. "The—the friend who gave them to me said they were worth a nizam's ransom."

"Your—your friend was doubtless correct. Their value, however, doesn't make them any more appropriate in a London wardrobe. When you wear those sables, you look like a walking fur tent."

Chandra drew a quick, sharp breath. *I'll pay him back for this some day.* Aloud she said stiffly, "In that case I won't wear the cape. I'll ring for my carriage."

A little later, sitting beside Julian in her town carriage as it moved out of Grosvenor Square, Chandra had to rid herself of an illogical conviction that the interior of the vehicle had somehow shrunk. It was Julian's size, of course—his long legs and the breadth of his powerful shoulders—that created the illusion of crowding. Since their first meeting, they had never been in such intimate proximity in so enclosed a space.

His thigh brushed against her when the carriage made a sudden turn. His touch sent a shiver of excitement coursing through her body. She was conscious of an electriclike current flowing between them, drawing them together. Warm, enticing thoughts of how it would feel to lie clasped in his arms, with his strong, slender fingers caressing the sensitive skin of her throat, crept into her mind.

Abruptly she shifted her position, jamming herself into her corner of the carriage. *I'm an idiot. I'm imagining things. If he knew what I was thinking . . .* "Are there any shops you especially recommend?" She was surprised to hear how calm her voice sounded.

He peered out the window. "Where are we? Brook Street? Not far from here, near the junction with New Bond Street, there's a modiste who's much patronized. My Aunt Georgiana buys many of her clothes there, I believe, and, according to the *on dit,* she dresses in the first style of elegance."

A rather timid-looking girl came forward to serve them when they entered the shop. Her eyes widened at the sight of the tall woman in the orange-colored pelisse and hat. "I'm afraid Madame herself isn't here at the moment," she apologized. "May I help you?"

Julian cleared his throat. "Miss Banks requires a new wardrobe. What can you show us?"

"Well, sir, most of our creations are made to order, of course. Madame would be most happy to design something original for you, Miss Banks. A ball gown? A walking dress? Perhaps I could show you some materials. A sarcenet, or a *Soie de Londres,* or even a Zephyr cotton."

Julian said impatiently, "Do you have nothing made up?"

"Well . . . There *is* one gown that was returned when Lady Newfield suffered an unexpected bereavement. Wait just a moment." The clerk soon returned with a gown of *crêpe lisse* in a pale yellow, with tiny puff sleeves and an edging of delicate green and gold leaves at the neckline and hem. "Will you try it on, Miss Banks? I think it could easily be altered to fit you. Lady Newfield is also a tall lady."

"It's very plain," said Chandra with misgiving. "Such a pale color, too."

"It's perfect," said Julian suddenly. "Simple. Elegant. That pale yellow complements your coloring. Try it on."

In the dressing room, as the clerk helped her out of her pelisse and gown, Chandra reflected how much she missed her *ayah*, or ladies's maid. Kamala, the Eurasian girl who'd served her for so many years in Asaf Khan's encampment, had been reluctant to leave her family and her country for an unfamiliar and intimidating future in England.

"Do you like the gown, Miss Banks?" said the clerk anxiously a few moment later. "It might have been made for you, truly. As I told you, it needs only the slightest alteration."

"M-m-n . . ." Chandra stared at her reflection in the cheval glass. The yellow gown *was* very plain, but its simple lines served to set off the soft curves of her slender figure that had been concealed by the ruffles and furbelows of the clothes she'd had made in Bombay.

"Ah, madame, *c'est ravissant!*"

Chandra turned to face the blonde, rather buxom woman who stood in the doorway of the dressing room. The newcomer was no longer a girl, and she wore a liberal amount of powder and paint, but she was still strikingly attractive.

"I am Madelon LaRivière. I own the shop," the woman remarked in a strong French accent. Advancing into the room, she took another critical look at Chandra. "No, I was not mistaken. The gown is quite perfect for you, madame." She glanced at Chandra's discarded red taffeta dress and the orange pelisse that the clerk had draped carefully over a chair. She raised her eyebrows. "The yellow gown is quite different from the red taffeta, *n'est-ce-pas?* But then, variety is the spice of life, *vous comprenez*. I'll leave you, madame, to make up your mind

110

about the gown. Later, perhaps, we could talk of creating another dress for you?"

After Madame LaRivière had left the room, Chandra turned back to the cheval glass for another lingering view of herself in the pale yellow gown. She decided Julian was right. The delicate yellow of the material seemed to enhance the creamy pallor of her skin. Yes, she'd take it. But first . . . She walked out of the dressing room in the direction of the show room, feeling a little flutter of excitement at the thought of showing herself to Julian in the gown he'd selected. At the door of the showroom she stopped, frozen in place by the sound of Madame LaRivière's spiteful, laughing voice.

"*Mon cher* Julian, so that's the lady who replaced me! I'm feeling quite chagrined. That beanpole of a girl, with that dreadful hank of hair hanging down her back, and those dreadful clothes. Has she no taste at all? Red taffeta with that complexion! That orange pelisse, fairly dripping with braid! Julian, *mon amour*, if you *must* have this woman in your keeping, please don't appear with her in public. Think of *my* reputation, if not your own!"

Chandra stumbled back to the dressing room on trembling legs that threatened to give way under her. She felt a sharp stabbing pain in her heart, and it was difficult to draw a breath. "Help me out of this infernal dress," she ordered the clerk.

"But, Miss Banks, I thought you liked—"

"You thought wrong."

Nervously and in silence, the clerk undid the tiny buttons on the back of the yellow gown. Chandra tore it off so roughly that she heard a seam rip. She pulled on the red taffeta dress, thrust her arms into the sleeves of her pelisse, and jammed her bonnet on her head. Then, snatching up her reticule, she stalked out of the dressing room and into the show room.

Breaking off what Chandra vaguely perceived was an argument with Julian, Madelon LaRivière gasped, "Madame—you are not buying the so beautiful gown?"

"I wouldn't buy an elephant from you if you came

111

recommended by the head elephant keeper of the Nizam of Hyderabad," snapped Chandra, making for the door.

"Chandra, is something wrong?" Julian exclaimed.

Stonily ignoring him, she sailed past him out of the shop, heading for her waiting carriage. Her well-trained footman saw her coming and had the door of the carriage open and the steps down before she reached the vehicle. As she was about to climb into the carriage, Julian caught up with her, laying his hand on her arm.

"Look here, Chandra," he began angrily, "I can see you've got some sort of bacon-brained notion in your cockloft, but is that any reason not to talk to me?"

Wrenching her arm from his grasp, she exploded into fury. "Bacon-brained? Is that how you describe taking me to a modiste shop owned by your discarded mistress, so that the pair of you could ridicule me behind my back?"

Julian took an involuntary step backward, staring at Chandra in shock. "Wait, I didn't know—"

"You didn't realize I'd overheard you? It would have been far better for you if I hadn't, Mr. Ware. You can start packing your belongings for another stay in Newgate. We're not getting married in three weeks, or ever!"

Chapter Seven

The announcement in the *Morning Chronicle* and the *Times* of the coming marriage of Miss Chandra Banks, daughter of the late Captain Walter Banks, of the Bombay Presidency, India, to the Honorable Julian Ware, second son of the late Earl and Countess of Daylesford, caused intense interest and speculation among the faithful readers of those newspapers.

In her house in Berkeley Square, the Countess of Daylesford pushed herself upright from the mounds of pillows at her back, gasping, "Ashley! Look at this!" She thrust the *Times* at her husband, who was sitting beside her bed, sharing a pot of morning chocolate with her.

He scanned the brief announcement. "Here's another," he said, handing her the *Morning Chronicle*. "They seem to be worded identically."

Settling back against her pillows, Irene gazed thoughtfully at the earl. "You already knew about Julian's betrothal. Why didn't you tell me?"

Ashley moved his shoulders restlessly. "Oh, the devil, Irene, I didn't want to to worry you about something that might not happen—that I hoped would never happen."

Irene smiled. "Darling Ashley," she said softly, "you go to such absurd lengths to protect me. I'm really not as fragile as you think."

Ashley looked at his wife with a brooding tenderness. This morning she seemed almost well. A frilly lace cap

113

adorned with blue ribbons, which covered most of her blond hair, drew attention from the pallor of her finely drawn features, and the voluminous folds of her equally frilly bedrobe concealed her extreme thinness.

"What's wrong with this marriage?" she asked presently. "Of course, the betrothal *is* happening like a bolt from the blue, and I never heard of this Miss Banks, but—"

"She's an immensely wealthy heiress from India. Her father apparently was a freebooter who made a fortune in the Mahratta wars."

"Oh. The family isn't respectable?"

"Barely so," said Ashley shortly. "The grandfather was an obscure country vicar."

"Well, I daresay Julian should be grateful his bride has money, considering his predicament of the past few weeks." Irene sat bolt upright again. "Ashley! You're not telling me everything. Is there a connection between Miss Banks's fortune and Julian's release from debtors' prison?"

Unable to suppress his resentment, Ashley said bitterly, "That damnable woman put Julian into Newgate in the first place. She bought up his promissory note and then blackmailed him into marrying her!" At Irene's appalled expression, Ashley exclaimed, "Oh, my God, I wasn't supposed to say anything, not even to you. I promised Julian I'd receive this woman into the family, so there wouldn't be any scandal."

"Then that's what we must do, my love, regardless of our feelings," said Irene quietly. "We'll pay a call on her today."

At about the same time, a short distance away from Berkeley Square, in a house in South Audley Street near the Stanhope Gate, Georgiana, Lady Eversleigh, turned away from her dressing table as her abigail admitted her son into her bedchamber. "Tristan, I hoped I'd catch you before you reported for duty," she exclaimed, presenting her scented cheek for his dutiful kiss. She winced, as she always did, at the sight of the single epaulet on the right shoulder of his red dragoon guards jacket. "Darling, it's simply not right. You should have at least a majority," she said plaintively, a comment she repeated every time she saw him in uniform.

"Well, Mama, perhaps the Horse Guards will send me to the Peninsula, and there, if I'm very fortunate, all my superior officers will be killed and I'll receive a battlefield promotion. I'll go instantly from lieutenant to general, even if it means I must do so over a mass of dead bodies!"

"Naughty boy," she said fondly. Becoming business-like, she picked up a folded copy of the *Times* from her dressing table. "Now, then, what's this about Julian getting married? This Miss Banks, who is she? She sounds like a real nobody."

"All I know, Mama, is that Julian only met her recently, when she came to England from India, she's a smashingly lovely girl, and she's rich as Croesus. Her younger sister is also very lovely," Tristan added, with an offhand air that didn't deceive his mother.

"Miss Banks has a sister?" Lady Eversleigh's eyes grew pensive. "Do you know, dear boy, I think it would be a real act of kindness on my part to call on Julian's betrothed. To welcome her to our family, as it were."

At Mrs. Artemus Taney's breakfast table in Golden Square, which was not quite as fashionable a residential location as it had been in its heyday, but was still an eminently respectable address, the lady of the house peremptorily demanded her son's attention. "Alfred, do put down that fork. I wish to speak with you. I vow, I sometimes think you have a giant worm in your stomach. You eat and eat, and yet you stay thin as a stick."

"Yes, Mama," said Alfred obediently, continuing to chew a large mouthful of bacon. His spotty complexion hadn't improved.

"Now, then, Alfred, you've been prattling of late about a Miss Banks, who arrived recently from India. I wonder if she could be the same Miss Chandra Banks who's about to marry the Honorable Julian Ware." Mrs. Taney pointed to the announcement in the *Morning Chronicle*.

Alfred reached for another piece of toast. "Shouldn't doubt it, y'know. Chandra's an unusual name. Her sister Lily told me it means moon. So Miss Banks is getting married. Odd. M'friend Basil Forrest says she's been in London for a few weeks only. Must have been one of those whirlwind courtships, I daresay. Why do you ask, Mama?"

Mrs. Taney cleared her throat, looking faintly embarrassed. "Well, you recall you asked me to invite Miss Banks to tea."

"Yes, and you said you'd never heard of a family named Banks, and probably the lady was a social climber you didn't care to know."

"Oh, I don't think I said precisely that. You misunderstood me. If Miss Banks is about to marry the brother of the Earl of Daylesford, she's no mere social climber. The Wares! One of the oldest, most distinguished families in the kingdom! Alfred, since you're acquainted with Miss Banks, you must make me known to her."

In Grosvenor Square that morning, Chandra came down to breakfast later than usual. She'd had a restless night. Her eyelids felt gritty, as if grains of sand had crept under them. Frederica, draining her third cup of tea, checked a movement to rise from the table when Chandra entered the dining room.

"I was just coming up to you, Chandra. Did you know about this?"

Chandra took the *Times* from Frederica and skimmed the announcement of her betrothal. "No, I didn't know," she said grimly. "If I *had* known it was to be published, be sure I'd have prevented it. Julian must have sent this item to the newspaper before he came here yesterday," she muttered, half to herself. Her eyes flashed. "He couldn't have had the gall to do it afterwards!"

"Chandra, I don't understand," Frederica faltered.

116

"You told me yesterday that Mr. Ware was going to announce your betrothal in the newspapers, and you seemed quite pleased."

"Well, I'm not pleased, I'm furious! I've changed my mind about marrying Julian Ware, Freddie. As soon as I've had a cup of tea, I'll go straight to the offices of the *Times* and order them to print a retraction."

"You'll do no such thing. Lord, I suspected you and Mr. Ware had quarreled when you returned to the house alone yesterday afternoon, your cheeks as red as fire, and Mr. Ware's curricle still waiting out in the square. And then, when you didn't come down to dinner . . . Chandra, *did* you and Mr. Ware quarrel?"

"Yes, we did. I never want to see him again. I should have listened to you. It was a harebrained scheme, asking Simon Harley to find me a husband! I must have been queer in my attic!"

"Sit down, my dear, and listen to me," declared Frederica, sounding as formidable as she had in the old days, when, as their governess, she'd kept the Meredith girls firmly under her thumb. "Now, tell me: have you given up on this notion of marrying a prominent aristocrat so you can establish yourself as a famous hostess and discover who ordered the murder of Major Meredith?"

"No, of course not. I haven't taken the right way of going about it, that's all. I'm sure some eligible suitor will come along. One of Basil Forrest's friends, for example—"

"Captain Forrest will never introduce you to anyone save riffs and raffs, and well you know it. And in the unlikely event he should produce a presentable man, it wouldn't profit you at all. No gentleman of good repute would offer for a female who'd been branded as fast for crying off from her engagement as mere day after it was announced in the newspapers!"

"You're trying to roast me, Freddie," said Chandra uncertainly.

"I was never more serious in my life. You'll not have a shred of reputation left if you jilt Julian Ware." Frederica

117

rose. She walked around the table to Chandra's chair and patted her shoulder. "Think about it. Don't do anything rash."

After Frederica left, Chandra swallowed a cup of tea and ate a mouthful of toast that tasted like sawdust. She remained seated at the table for a long time, occupied by her black thoughts, aimlessly pushing a bit of bacon around her plate, while servants peered into the dining room and crept away again, unnoticed by their mistress.

Could Freddie be right, Chandra wondered? If she threw Julian over, would she lose her reputation, and with it, her chance to avenge her father's death? But how could she consider marrying a man—even platonically, even temporarily—who had taken pleasure in exposing her to the humiliating gibes of his ex-mistress? Chandra felt a renewed burst of searing rage at the thought of the conversation she'd overheard between Julian and Madame LaRivière. How much they'd probably both enjoyed it! How could she trust such a man to uphold the terms of their bargain? To—how had Julian put it?—to act toward her in public as a devoted husband? On the other hand, if Freddie was correct, she ran the risk of branding herself a heartless flirt if she jilted Julian.

Ramesh came into the dining room. "The food doesn't please you, lady?" he asked in Hindi. His face was aloof, expressionless, but Chandra knew by the quivering of those splendid mustachios that Ramesh was aware of his mistress's troubled mental state and was intensely curious.

"I'm not very hungry this morning, Ramesh."

"Ah. So. Does the mem-sahib wish to receive a visit from the Captain Basil Forrest?" The mustachios were quivering even more wildly. Chandra had realized for some time that Ramesh did not appreciate Basil Forrest. Perhaps it was Basil's clothes. More than once, Chandra had caught Ramesh's disapproving eye fixed on Captain Forrest's wasp-waisted coats, so tightly fitting that he seemed in danger of splitting a seam with the slightest movement.

Chandra sighed. A visit from Basil might take her mind off her dilemma. "I'll see Captain Forrest."

Basil, too, had seen the announcement in the *Morning Chronicle*. When Chandra came into the drawing room, he hurled himself toward her, clasping her hands in both of his. "Chandra, my own, my love! It must be a mistake. You *can't* marry Julian Ware. You must know he's a toplofty high stickler, loose in the shaft. A gazetted fortune hunter, too. Well, as to that, he must be at point-non-plus. Why else did they clap him into debtors' prison? No, Chandra, you mustn't marry this man. He can't love you as I do. You can't possibly love him."

Chandra pulled her hands away from Basil. She wanted to shriek, "Of course, I'm not going to marry Julian Ware!" But Freddie's solemn warnings held her back. She mustn't be too precipitate, if there was even the slightest chance that marriage to Julian would help her discover her father's murderer. She temporized. "La, Basil, I thought you were a man of the world. You know as well as I do that people in polite society usually don't have the luxury of marrying for love."

Basil's face fell. "Oh, I know that, all too well," he said bitterly. "I must have been dicked in the nob to think I had any chance with you. I have no prospects, no nothing . . ." He bent his head.

Chandra felt a flicker of sympathy for him. She didn't doubt that her money would be as welcome to Basil as it was to Julian, but she was also prepared to believe that the hussar captain had genuinely strong feelings for her.

After a short silence, Basil said fiercely, "Very well, I accept that you can't marry me, Chandra. But I can be your *cicisbeo*. You won't deny me that privilege?"

"*Cicisbeo*? What's that?"

"Well, actually, I heard about it from a feller whose father made the Grand Tour, before the wars with Boney made it impossible to travel on the Continent. It seems that in Italy it's very unfashionable for a married lady of high rank to be seen in public with her husband. So these ladies are always escorted by their—er—their official lovers, their *cicisbeos*. Naturally, I wouldn't expect you to—well, you know," Basil floundered. "Not unless you really wanted to, that is."

Chandra covered her mouth with her handkerchief, simulating a cough while she fought back an urge to laugh hysterically. What an idiot Basil was. He needed a keeper. "Oh, I don't think that would be feasible, Basil. We have very different standards in England. You wouldn't wish me to appear a brass-faced lightskirt, I'm sure."

"No, no," muttered Basil, turning a bright red.

"But I hope we'll continue to be friends."

"You can count on my friendship to my dying day," Basil said fervently, and kept saying it, until finally she was able to persuade him to leave.

Chandra had very little opportunity for contemplation for the remainder of the morning. Basil Forrest was only the first of many callers.

Georgiana, Lady Eversleigh, arrived. Tristan's mother was handsome, exquisitely dressed, and determined to please. She gazed around the drawing room, saying graciously, "I see you've redecorated in the latest mode. The Egyptian style is all the rage, I hear." Turning her attention to Chandra, she said, "My dear Miss Banks, I could scarcely believe my eyes this morning when I read that announcement. I was so happy to learn my nephew is to be married. He and his brother, as I'm sure you know, are the last of our family line. I was beginning to think Julian was a hardened case. In fact, it was just recently that Tristan told me he thought his cousin would never allow himself to be 'leg-shackled.'"

Smiling and attentive, Georgiana was also extremely inquisitive. Chandra had wearied of fending off questions about the Banks' family tree by the time Lily poked her head into the drawing room to tell Chandra that she and Freddie were going shopping. Introduced to Georgiana, Lily chatted briefly before going on her way.

With Lily's departure, the iron beneath Georgiana's gentle, butterfly charm emerged. "Miss Lily is surely not your full sister," she said bluntly.

"No, she and I are half sisters. Lily is the daughter of

120

my father's second wife."

"I see. The lady was of foreign extraction? French, perhaps, or Spanish? Or—mixed blood?" If words had been objects, Chandra thought, Lady Eversleigh would have picked up the loathsome phrase, "mixed blood," between fastidious fingers and tossed it into the rubbish heap.

Chandra said coldly, "Lily's mother belonged to an Indian family."

A mask descended on Georgiana's face. In a few moments she rose to go, offering Chandra a stiffly formal welcome into the family. The footman who showed her out brought back a tray containing several visiting cards.

"Show Mrs. Taney and her son in," Chandra told the footman resignedly.

Alfred Taney's mother was a sharp-nosed, hard-eyed woman whom Chandra disliked on sight. A gushing effusiveness failed to conceal an essential vulgarity. "My dear Miss Banks, you must forgive my tardiness in calling on you. Here my Alfred has been telling me so much about you, and I've longed to meet you. But then one thing after the other prevented me. Isn't that so, Alfred?"

"Yes, Mama."

"So, of course, when I saw the announcement this morning, I said to Alfred immediately, 'We must go call on Miss Banks to offer our felicitations.'"

"So kind," murmured Chandra. She had no doubt at all that it was the magic of Julian Ware's name that had brought Mrs. Taney to Grosvenor Square.

"A month hence, Mr. Taney and I will be giving a dinner for the directors of the Court of the East India Company. We would be delighted to see you and Mr. Ware among our guests."

Chandra's ears perked up. How many directors were there in the Court? Twenty-four? What a tremendous opportunity to extend her contacts with the East India Company! "Why, Mrs. Taney, I'd be very pleased to accept your invitation," she said, beaming. "I was born in India, you know. It will be wonderful to talk with people who've shared my experiences."

Once more the footman came in with his tray. Chandra's eyes widened at the names on the cards. "Ask them in."

Mrs. Taney fairly quivered with ecstasy when the Earl and Countess of Daylesford entered the drawing room. However, Ashley's aloof bow and forbidding stare reduced both Mrs. Taney and Alfred to a helpless silence, and they left shortly afterward.

"Ashley darling, that wasn't very kind of you," murmured Irene, her tender little smile taking the edge from her criticism.

"I don't know any Taneys," said Ashley shortly. "I don't care to know any Taneys." He gave Chandra a level look. "I came to offer my best wishes, Miss Banks, and to welcome you to the Ware family. I hope you'll make my brother very happy. And now . . ." He consulted his watch. "Now I have an urgent appointment elsewhere. I'll leave Irene to make your further acquaintance. Don't bother to ring. I'll show myself out."

Chandra watched his limping progress toward the door. When he'd gone, she said abruptly to Irene, "He knows, doesn't he?"

Irene colored. The faint glow in her cheeks gave a momentary illusion of health to the fine-boned beauty of her thin face. She was of medium height, but her extreme fragility made her seem much smaller. "Miss Banks, really, I don't know what you mean . . ." She paused, coloring again at Chandra's disbelieving look.

"I think you do, Lady Daylesford. Your husband has learned that I blackmailed his brother into marrying me, and he hates the very thought of the marriage." Chandra's face hardened. "It's very likely, you know, that the earl's sensibilities will cease to be lacerated. I'm considering breaking off my engagement to Mr. Ware. I—I've come to the conclusion that we really won't suit."

Irene gasped. "How can this be?" She stared at Chandra's grim expression. "Have you and Julian quarreled?"

"No. Yes. It doesn't matter." Despite herself, Chandra couldn't keep the anger and resentment out of her voice.

Up to this point, Irene had been polite but detached, obviously determined to do her duty by a future sister-in-law, whom she must have been as reluctant as her husband to receive into the family. Now a note of sympathy crept into her tone. "My dear, can I help? I'm beginning to understand that this marriage must have been very important to you, judging by the lengths to which you—" Irene broke off, biting her lip. "Forgive me. This is no time for recriminations. The marriage is also important to Ashley and me. We certainly don't want to see Julian back in debtors' prison." She paused, giving Chandra a questioning look. "Am I correct, is that what will happen to him if you break off your engagement?"

"There's the matter of his promissory note for fifty thousand pounds," said Chandra stonily. "Would you expect me to swallow that? I'm not a philanthropist."

"Oh, dear. Miss Banks, would you care to talk? Sometimes, after a misunderstanding, it helps to clear the air."

"There's been no misunderstanding," flared Chandra. "I understand Mr. Ware perfectly." Feeling incredulous, she heard her voice pouring out the angry accusations, and couldn't seem to stop herself. "He thinks I dress and act like a whore. He says a gentleman couldn't live with my Egyptian furniture. And he has a right to his opinions, I daresay. But he had no right at all to drag me to his mistress's dress shop so that he and she could make fun of me behind my back!"

Irene looked appalled. "My dear Miss Banks, you must be mistaken. For one thing, Julian has no mistress, to the best of my knowledge. Some time ago I believe he had a Frenchwoman in his keeping, but she was no modiste. In any case," she added firmly, "Julian would never do such an ungenerous thing. He doesn't have a mean bone in his body. I'm disappointed to hear that he criticized your dress and your furnishings to your face. That's not like him, either. He—he must have been under a good deal of stress."

Oh, yes, I goaded him, Chandra thought suddenly. *We goaded each other.* "Lady Daylesford," she began abruptly, "are my clothes really so wrong?"

Irene examined Chandra's gown of puce-colored velvet, liberally festooned with strings of dangling beads. She cleared her throat. "Miss Banks, if that gown is a typical example from your wardrobe . . ."

"It is."

"Then I'm sorry. Your clothes must be quite dreadful." Irene's face flamed with embarrassment, and she put her hand to her mouth as if to prevent the escape of any further criticism.

"It's all right, Lady Daylesford. I asked for your opinion."

Irene said quickly, "Believe me, I didn't mean to hurt your feelings." After a pause, she added, "I must tell you I'm selfish enough to hope you'll decide to remain engaged to Julian. He and my husband are very close, and Ashley would be plunged into torment again if Julian went back to Newgate. If you do decide not to break your engagement, I'd be most happy to go shopping with you for a new wardrobe, and to advise you about the wedding, or any other matter that might be troubling you." She rose, saying, "I must go. I've taken quite enough of your time. Will you think about what I've said, Miss Banks?" She added, "I really mean this: whatever happens, I'd like to be your friend."

Irene sounded sincere, thought Chandra after Lady Daylesford had left. *I wonder what it would be like to have a woman friend of my own age?*

Chandra paced restlessly up and down the drawing room. She had to make a decision about Julian. She'd already dillydallied for too long. Today, at least by omission, she'd allowed Lady Eversleigh, Alfred Taney and his mother, and Basil Forrest to believe that she still intended to become Mrs. Julian Ware.

Irene was not to be her last caller this morning. Julian

strode into the drawing room just ahead of a footman who was saying plaintively, "But sir, I'm supposed ter announce ye—"

"It's all right," Chandra told the footman. "You may go."

"I didn't send in my card because I thought you might not see me," said Julian. He looked more presentable this morning than he had yesterday after his all-night gambling session. His coat and pantaloons were impeccable, his cravat was tied with a masterly knot, his thick dark curls were brushed in a fashionable Brutus, and he was freshly shaved.

"Oh, I'd have received you, Mr. Ware. I have things to say to you."

Julian nodded. "And I to you." He lifted his hand as she opened her mouth to speak. "May I go first? After that, I'll be quite at your disposal." He gave her a level, unsmiling look. His usual air of casual self-confidence was considerably toned down. "I want to apologize to you for criticizing your taste in clothing and furniture. You were perfectly justified in becoming angry. However, you were incorrect in assuming that, when I took you to that dress shop, I was aware that Madelon LaRivière was the proprietress. I was not. Madelon and I parted company some time ago. I didn't know she'd bought the shop from its former owner. And whatever you may have heard, or thought you heard, I did not join Madelon in 'making fun of you behind your back.' Actually, I told her I couldn't with propriety discuss my fiancée with her. When she persisted, I informed her she could go to the devil."

"Your tongue is well hung, Mr. Ware. I daresay you thought your little apology couldn't fail to turn me up sweet."

"What?" Julian turned a dull red. "You think I came here to attempt to persuade you to change your mind about breaking off our betrothal? On the contrary, I'm quite relieved that you've cancelled our arrangement. At least in Newgate I won't have to deal with you *or* your tantrums! No, I came to see you because I was ashamed of the way I'd acted, and I wanted to put the record straight about Madelon LaRivière. Now that I've done so, I'll bid you good day." He wheeled, heading for the door.

There was a roaring noise in Chandra's ears. Oh, she was handling this badly. He'd put her completely off balance. Was he telling the truth when he said he didn't know his ex-mistress owned the dress shop? Yes, probably. Julian Ware had too much arrogant pride to allow himself to lie in such a matter. She heard herself saying, "Wait, Mr. Ware."

He half-turned, his body poised and tense as a drawn bowstring. "Yes?"

"I don't want to cancel our bargain," she blurted. "For one thing, it would take time to find another—another candidate, and I wish to proceed with my plans as soon as possible. For another, my aunt tells me that I risk being considered fast if I cry off from this engagement. Is that true?"

"Probably," said Julian, shrugging. "The ton might speculate that you had a bigger catch in mind. Otherwise, why would you throw over a splendid specimen like me?"

Chandra gritted her teeth against the provocation. Would the next year be one long sparring match? Did she really have any choice, with the announcement of her marriage graven in stone in the columns of the *Times* and the *Morning Chronicle*? Drawing a deep breath, she asked, "Mr. Ware, are you still willing to accept the proposal I made to you?"

Julian's lips tightened. After a moment, he said, "Yes. I won't deny I resent being forced into this marriage. If you'd broached your offer *before* you had me clapped into debtor's prison—"

"Would you have said yes?"

Julian's lips curved into an unwilling smile. "No. I don't threaten easily. I daresay I wouldn't have given in to you until I was faced with the brutal reality of prison. Now that I've enjoyed the delights of Newgate, well, let's just say I'm not made of the stuff of martyrs. I've no wish to return to prison."

"Then shall we consider ourselves engaged again?"

"If you wish." He paused. "If that's all . . . ?"

"Not quite. While this marriage lasts, Mr. Ware, I want the world to believe it's genuine. Could we have a little less of the atmosphere of an armed truce when we're together?"

"You needn't worry about that," he said, a little stiffly. "I told you once, remember, that I'd act the devoted husband in public."

"I think we could, both of us, use a little more common civility in private, also," said Chandra dryly.

The blue eyes kindled with a sudden amusement. "Agreed."

"And I'm sure we'd convey a more convincing facade if we used our Christian names."

"Very well—Chandra. It's a pretty name. Much, much prettier than Banks!"

Chapter Eight

Chandra clutched Simon Harley's arm with an iron grip. His fingers closed comfortingly over her hand in its elbow-length kid glove.

"Chandra, your hand is as cold as ice," he murmured. "And you're trembling. Are you sure you want go through with this ceremony? You can still change your mind."

"It's a little late for that. The wedding march will start at any moment."

As she stood in the vestibule of St. George's Church, Hanover Square, waiting for the organist to begin, Chandra's mind swarmed with a series of kaleidoscopic impressions of the past three weeks . . .

Her hair, for instance. Instinctively she reached for the heavy braid that had hung down her back since her earliest days in Asaf Khan's encampment. The braid was gone. Irene had persuaded her to send for a hairdressing genius named Monsieur Anatole, who had promptly snipped off eighteen inches of her hair and arranged the rest of it in graceful coils on the crown of her head. For several mornings thereafter, Chandra had felt she was seeing a stranger in the mirror when her newly hired abigail was dressing her hair for the day.

There were memories of Irene. She seemed so gentle and self-effacing, and yet she had an effortless knack for accomplishing what she wanted to do. She'd taken Chandra to her own dressmaker, and with a few quiet suggestions, had transformed her new sister-in-law's wardrobe. Gradually Chandra's own eyes had grown accustomed to the simple lines and muted colors of her new clothes.

Irene had taken Freddie and Lily in hand, also, to the governess's heartfelt gratitude. Gazing at her reflection in the cheval glass one day in her plain high-necked gown of dove gray *Barége*, with mancherons at the shoulders and wrists, Frederica had sighed with pleasure. "I feel so much more the thing in clothes like this. Bless Lady Daylesford! Do you know, Chandra—" Frederica lowered her voice and she blushed hotly, "do you know, I believe that dressmaker in Bombay was sewing for workers in a brothel!"

Callers. During the past few weeks, callers had virtually worn out the door knocker of the house in Grosvenor Square. Most of the names meant nothing to Chandra, but Frederica, having been an avid reader of the personal notices in the newspapers during her girlhood, was deeply impressed. "Chandra! The Duke and Duchess of Bedford! Lady Jersey! Countess Lieven! Mr. Hughes and Sir Lumley Skeffington! Everyone who *is* anyone in London society!" More practical than impressed, Chandra had tucked away in her memory all the noble names. They would add to her consequence in her campaign to become a social lioness. Some of them almost certainly would be sources of information about her father's murderer.

Then there was Julian. She stirred uneasily. She was finding it easier to use his Christian name, and she was beginning to know him better. However, she still felt a constraint in his presence, even though he'd been on his best behavior since they'd agreed to renew their battered betrothal. Charming, attentive, he'd acted the part of the perfect fiancé. And yet, gazing into those deeply blue eyes, Chandra could always detect a flicker of ribald mockery, which sent her into a helpless rage. Control his outward behavior she might, but she couldn't control his inmost thoughts.

During the period of her engagement, Tristan's lighthearted friendship had been a great comfort, even in such a small matter as dancing lessons. Chandra and Lily had never learned to dance. Declaring himself an absolute dabster on the dance floor, Tristan had volunteered to teach them the latest steps, assisted by Frederica. Though the minuets and gavottes of her girlhood were now outmoded, Freddie could still remember the lively movements of the country dance.

During this time, Simon had been an even greater comfort. Dear Simon. He'd tried to refuse the honor of escorting her down the aisle on her wedding day, protesting, "Chandra, I assure you, it wouldn't be at all the thing!"

Even Frederica had been aghast at her choice of the man who was to give her away. "Chandra! Mr. Harley won't fit in. He's *trade!*"

"He's my friend, Freddie. My only male friend. Who else is there to give me away?"

The organ swelled triumphantly. Simon's fingers tightened on her hand. "Chandra, it's time."

Lily, who had been standing quietly in front of them, flashed Chandra a nervous smile and began the long walk down the tunnel-vaulted nave with its flanking galleries supported on Corinthian columns. On legs that felt numb, and holding firmly to Simon's arm, Chandra followed Lily down the aisle. Every pew in the church seemed occupied. And then she was standing in front of the sanctuary beside Julian, who looked impossibly handsome and also quite pale.

The brief ceremony passed in a blur. She had only a vague memory of walking to the vestry on Julian's arm. As she signed the register with the name Chandra Banks, she had to restrain an inane impulse to giggle. She'd married Julian under a false name. Was the marriage legal? And did it matter?

In the carriage she rode in silence with Julian to Daylesford House in Berkeley Square, where Irene and

130

Ashley were hosting a wedding party in their honor. She felt unreal, disembodied, as if it were somebody else, not Diana Elizabeth Meredith, who sat beside this aloof, handsome stranger. The March afternoon, merging into twilight, was cold and blustery, and she shivered beneath the folds of her Lyons shawl.

Unexpectedly, Julian reached over to take her hand. "You're deathly cold. Are you ill?"

"No." She disengaged her hand. "Merely finding it a trifle difficult to realize we've actually done it. I'm the Honorable Mrs. Julian Ware!"

"So you are. I'm finding it hard to believe, myself. Leg-shackled at last!"

Chandra was beginning to feel more normal. She flashed him an impudent smile. "Indeed. My heart bleeds for all the females in London and throughout the kingdom, who must be wearing the willow for you. What a shame you can't tell them you'll be free in a year's time."

"I think they'll survive the disappointment," Julian said dryly. His voice changed. He said, grudgingly, reluctantly, "You look lovely today."

Her heart caught. She'd known, without any false modesty, that she looked beautiful in her wedding gown of pale green silk, adorned with tiny yellow roses and garlands of delicate lace, with a wreath of pastel flowers encircling the glossy coils of her hair. She hadn't expected Julian to notice or comment. Why should he? This was a business arrangement.

"Thank you," she managed to say. "Irene chose the gown."

"But *you* wore it . . ." The air suddenly seemed to quiver with a tremulous expectancy. Julian's blue eyes locked into hers, and he put out his hand in an odd groping movement.

The carriage stopped. A footman appeared at the door. "Daylesford House."

For almost an hour, Chandra stood with Julian and Ashley and Irene at the entrance to the ballroom, while they greeted the swarm of guests streaming up the grand

131

staircase of Daylesford House.

"My dear, I've heard nothing but compliments on the wedding," said Irene happily. "Everyone says you're the most beautiful bride of the year. Isn't that so, Ashley?"

"You look charmingly, Miss Banks—Chandra." There was no warmth in Ashley's voice. Since the betrothal had been announced, he'd been civil, if only barely so. Chandra doubted that he'd ever be reconciled to his brother's mésalliance. Ashley's face softened as he glanced at Irene. "You aren't overtiring yourself? Wouldn't you like to rest? Julian and Chandra and I can receive our guests."

"No, dearest, I feel very well." Irene's cheeks were faintly pink. She didn't look ill. "In fact, I'm enjoying myself immensely. It's been too long since we entertained, Ashley."

Chandra was very conscious of Julian's tall figure standing beside her. When she accidentally brushed against his arm she could feel the hard, controlled muscle beneath the perfectly tailored broadcloth coat. She found herself wondering if every woman he met felt the pull of the powerful male physicality that seemed to surround his person like an aura. As the thought crossed her mind, she looked up at him and met the gaze of those intense blue eyes. Hastily she glanced away. Julian was very perceptive. Sometimes she thought he could read her mind.

At one point during their stay in the receiving line, Julian said beneath his breath, "Unless I'm mistaken, you've bagged every important name in the ton, Chandra. This affair is developing into what my Aunt Georgiana would call a delightful squeeze. Everyone in London knows who you are now. That's what you wanted, isn't it? You must be very happy." There wasn't a trace of ridicule or of resentment in his voice. He merely sounded amused.

She grinned at him. "I couldn't have done it without you, Julian. Or, rather without the power of the Ware name. So I must thank you for my success."

After a startled moment, he chuckled, the smile lingering on his lips as he turned to greet Lord and Lady Sefton.

The line of guests coming up the stairs was thinning out now. Irene said gaily, "I think we won't wait for the latecomers. The orchestra is striking up. Julian, you and Chandra must open the ball."

As they walked to take their places in the first set, Chandra involuntarily tightened her fingers on Julian's arm. Instantly he clasped his hand over hers. Every nerve in her body seemed extraordinarily sensitive. She went through the steps of the reel in a kind of a spell. The faces of the other dancers were a blur. She was aware only of the touch of Julian's hands and the gravely intent look in his eyes when they met during the dance.

As they came off the floor, the spell was broken. Basil Forrest, resplendent in his hussar's uniform, came up to them with a beaming smile. He said to Julian, "Afraid I was a bit late for the receiving line, old fellow, but I wanted to extend my best wishes for your happiness." He shook his head. "Mind, I can't deny I'd have cut you out with Chandra if I could, but the best man won, eh?"

Julian's eyes were pools of blue ice. "I wasn't aware I'd ever competed with you, Forrest," he said in a low tone that cut like a sawblade. "Be assured I would never do so voluntarily. I limit bouts of friendly competition to my friends."

The hussar's face flamed crimson. He bowed jerkily to Chandra and moved on.

"That was cruel," Chandra muttered.

"I don't choose to associate with court cards like Forrest," Julian muttered back. "Why was he invited here—if in truth he *was* invited?"

Chandra said in an angry half-whisper, "He was invited because he's a friend of mine. And when he comes to call on us in Grosvenor Square, I expect you to be civil to him."

"Then you'll expect in vain," Julian said savagely. "I choose my friends, even if I can't choose my wife!"

133

Chandra felt as if she'd been plunged into a tub of icy water. Her tenuous belief that maybe, just maybe, she and Julian could coexist for the next year, if not as friends, then as friendly enemies, began to crumble away. She turned her face away from him, not speaking. As soon as they reached the edge of the dance floor, she was besieged by a horde of would-be partners, and danced every dance for the remainder of the evening. She paid little attention either to her performance or to her partners. However, thanks to Tristan's tutelage, she did know the steps, and she must have executed them adequately. At least, nobody seemed critical.

Between dances, she chatted aimlessly. Or, more accurately, she listened to snatches of conversations.

Frederica said in an awed voice, "You said you'd find a way to become a part of London society, and you have. Chandra, the Prime Minister was in the church!"

Lily said dreamily, before Tristan dragged her off for another dance, "This is the grandest evening of my entire life."

Simon Harley inveigled her into sitting out a dance behind a large potted palm. "Is something wrong? I thought Mr. Ware was looking like a thundercloud a bit ago."

"No. Nothing's wrong."

"Well . . . remember, if ever you need me, just send me a message."

Lady Eversleigh remarked, as she watched her son partner Lily in a country dance, "My dear Chandra—I may call you that?—I think we really must give the young people a tiny hint. Two dances, or at most three, with the same person are quite enough!"

Mrs. Artemus Taney simply gushed. "Such a lovely wedding, Mrs. Ware, and we—Alfred and I and Mr. Taney—are so grateful to you for allowing us to share in your happiness."

While the abigail brushed out the heavy coils of her

hair, Chandra leaned back in her chair at the dressing table, feeling her tight nerves beginning to relax at last. Since her confrontation with Julian at the ball, she'd felt on edge, as if a catastrophe were imminent. Why was he behaving so unreasonably? Granted, he didn't like Basil. Obviously they'd quarreled in the past. But wasn't Julian's reaction to Basil's presence at the ball out of all proportion?

She hadn't spoken a word to him after their quarrel. In fact, she'd caught no more than fleeting glimpses of him during the evening. After the ball, driving back to Grosvenor Square in the berline, he'd sat hunched silently in a corner of the carriage, while Frederica and Lily had chattered excitedly about the evening.

Well, now it was over, this long and demanding day. Whatever the consequences, whatever her regrets, she was Mrs. Julian Ware, and she could start using her new position to accomplish the task that had brought her to England.

"Do ye wish me ter braid yer hair fer the night, ma'am?"

Chandra twisted her head to stare in surprise at the abigail. "Of course, braid my hair. Why ever not, Betsy?"

The girl blushed. "Why, I thought as 'ow it were yer wedding night an' all . . ."

Chandra felt the hot color flooding her own cheeks. Before she could reply, the bedchamber door opened. Julian stalked into the room. He carried a glass of wine in one hand. He was fully dressed except for his coat and waistcoat. "Mrs. Ware won't need you any more tonight," he told the abigail curtly. When she scuttled away, he closed the door behind her with a decisive bang.

Chandra rose slowly from her chair, drawing her white silk bedrobe closer around her. Suddenly she felt icily cold. "What do you want?" she asked. The effort she made to maintain her self-control caused her voice to sound harsh.

"I want to talk, of course." He drained the glass of wine. Chandra suspected from the glitter in his eyes that a number of glasses had preceded it. "You forced me into this marriage so you could use your position as my wife—

135

so you could use my *friends,* my family—to give you entry into the highest levels of London society. Why, then, are you associating with scum like Basil Forrest, and fawning parasites like the Taneys?"

"You're talking about my friends," Chandra snapped. "Take Basil. He may not be an out-and-outer like you, but he's perfectly inoffensive—"

"Inoffensive? The man cheats at cards! Not too long ago, he caused the death of one of my good friends, Jack Armbruster. Forrest used barred dice to win a fortune from Jack, who then went home and killed himself."

Chandra gasped. "But—if that's true, why is Basil still received in society?"

"Because I can't prove it, that's why."

"You could be mistaken. Or, even supposing Basil did cheat, you can't know he intended your friend's death. He's no monster."

"I'm not mistaken about Forrest. Whether he intended Jack Armbruster's death is beside the point. I'm not mistaken about the Taneys, either. They're a pack of social climbers. Mrs. Taney cornered me tonight, you know. She informed me that you and I were to be the guests of honor next week at a dinner she's giving for the directors of the East India Company. You neglected to tell me about that. Mrs. Taney further informed me that her husband was buying an estate in the Chiltern Hills near my brother Ashley's seat, and she intimated she would feel much more comfortable in her new home, if her husband were at least a baronet!"

"I'm sorry you didn't find her interesting—"

Julian threw up his hands. "My God, woman, don't you know that Artemus Taney has been angling for a peerage ever since he came back from India? And now that you've befriended her, his wife expects me to get that peerage for her husband. Chandra, it was never a part of our bargain that I had to associate with Cits and Captain Sharps, much less to welcome them to my house!"

The clammy vice around Chandra's heart became a little tighter. She could understand why Julian didn't want to associate with Basil Forrest and the Taneys. She herself felt no obligation to Basil—had he really caused a man to commit suicide?—and she wouldn't care if she never saw the Taneys again, but she couldn't drop them. She needed them to supply her with information and contacts in the web she was spinning to entrap Papa's killer. Nor could she give Julian any reasonable explanation for continuing to see these people. She would simply have to destroy the tenuous beginnings of understanding and friendship that had sprung up between them during the past few days and weeks.

"Aren't you forgetting something, Julian? This isn't your house, it's mine. I'll invite anyone I choose to be a guest here, and you'll live up to the terms of our agreement, which is to be an exemplary host and husband. Don't forget, I still hold that promissory note."

Julian's face paled, and then turned a dull red. The wineglass slipped from his hand and crashed to the floor. He started toward her.

Chandra whirled and wrenched open the top drawer of the dressing table. Turning back to him, the jeweled poniard in her hand blazing in the light of the candles, she exclaimed breathlessly, "Stay away from me. You saw me use this on those bandits on the Woolwich road. I won't hesitate to use it again."

With a fluid, lightning-swift movement, Julian forced her arm behind her back and twisted it until, with a muffled cry of pain, she dropped the poniard to the floor. "You hurt me," she mumbled, rubbing her throbbing wrist.

She gasped as he grabbed her by both shoulders with sinewy fingers that bit into her flesh, while his mouth sought hers in a fierce, punishing kiss that ignited a raging inferno in her blood and left her helpless with an unfamiliar consuming desire. He released her at last and stepped back, his eyes black with passion, his breath coming in short ragged gusts.

Stumbling back against the dressing table, Chandra said in a shaking voice, "You promised—you agreed this

137

would be a platonic marriage . . ."

He had control of himself now. "Don't worry. This won't happen again. I don't want you, Chandra. I just wanted to show you that I could take you if I wanted to, and what recourse would you have? Tell the world I've taken you to bed against your will, and you expose the sham of this marriage. Society would shun you." He laughed. "It's checkmate, my dear. In a sense your promissory note is useless. Oh, you could toss me back into debtors' prison, but the scandal would destroy your chances to become a great society figure."

"But you'd still be locked up in prison," Chandra said between stiff lips.

"Yes. Unfortunately." He flashed her a mocking smile. "So we're tied to each other for one full year from this date. You to a man who despises you. I to a woman who's tricked me and used me and whom I'll never willingly see again once my year as a prisoner is up. What juicy memoirs we could write if we had a mind to!"

Chandra's chest was so tight she felt it might explode. "I hate you," she said.

"The feeling, my dear wife, is mutual."

Chapter Nine

After several days of clouds and drizzle, the sun was shining brightly in Hyde Park on this May morning. A slight breeze ruffled the waters of the Serpentine, as Chandra and Basil Forrest put their mounts to a slow canter along the banks of the stream in the direction of the Stanhope Gate. Chandra nodded and smiled to several early morning riders. After a month of marriage to Julian Ware, she had a wide circle of acquaintances. In fact, thought Chandra a trifle smugly, it was safe to assume that she was well on her way to "knowing everybody who *was* anybody."

Glancing behind him at Ramesh, stately on a powerful horse, Basil muttered, "Must you always bring that fellow with you, Chandra?"

"I must have a groom with me, Basil," Chandra replied, shocked. "It wouldn't be at all the thing for me to ride with you alone."

"Well, but you must have hordes of grooms in your stables. Why *him?* He doesn't like me. His eyes keep boring into the back of my head, as if he expected me to attack you, or some such thing!"

Repressing a giggle, Chandra said, "Ramesh is an old family servitor. This country is still strange to him, and he feels very protective toward me." It was true, of course, that Ramesh, for some unfathomable reason, had a fixed dislike for Basil, but it was Chandra's own idea to have her servant accompany her on her rides in Hyde Park. In her quest to become one of the best-known women in London, Ramesh's presence in her company was a definite plus. His exotic appearance caused heads to turn wherever he went.

"You haven't come out with me very often of late, Chandra. Our last ride was a sennight ago."

"I'm sorry. I've been so busy. The Season has started, you know. I vow, I received more invitations than I can possibly accept. Two and three to an evening, sometimes. Wednesday I went to my first assembly at Almack's. Basil, I can't understand why folk are so impressed with the place. Three rooms, none of them so very grand. Music and dancing. Punch and lemonade and sandwiches. And the patronesses! All of them with faces like lemons, except maybe Lady Jersey. She laughs a lot."

"Chandra!" gasped Basil. "Don't let anyone hear you saying things like that. I know people who would lie and steal to obtain a voucher for Almack's. *I* would! Do you realize that, of some three hundred officers of the Foot Guards, only five or six have been admitted to Almack's?"

"Really? I had no idea I was in such exclusive company. I must try to appreciate my advantages more."

They had left the Serpentine by now, and had made the turn for the Stanhope Gate. "When will I see you again?" asked Basil. "I don't move in your circles, as well you know. Will you come riding with me tomorrow?"

"No, not tomorrow. But soon, I promise."

"I bumped into an old friend last evening at Astley's. Served with him in India. He's been living in the country since he retired. Would you like to meet him? You're always so interested in talking to the old India hands."

"Why, yes, I'd like very much to meet him. Bring your friend to tea on—let me think—on Thursday next." The occasion would be a waste of time, Chandra was sure of it. None of Basil's friends had been useful to her, so far, in divulging any fact that might point to her father's murderer. However, she couldn't afford to overlook any source of information. That was why she was still cultivating Basil. But oh, what a paperskull he was!

Back in Grosvenor Square, after she'd changed from her riding clothes (a smart, simple ensemble in dark green velvet selected by Irene), Chandra headed for the dining room and her usual hearty breakfast. Frederica trailed into the room some moments later, and Lily later still. Neither of them was a particularly early riser.

"Well, then, Chandra, tell us about your evening at Carlton House," Frederica exclaimed, after she'd provided herself with a plate of grilled kidneys."

"Yes, don't leave anything out," said Lily eagerly. "Who would ever have thought, back in Asaf Khan's encampment—" She stopped short. Without explaining their reasons, Frederica and Chandra had impressed on the rather puzzled Lily that she was never to talk about their years of captivity in northern India, but occasionally she forgot in the privacy of the family group. "Who would ever have thought," she finished lamely, "that one day, Chandra, you'd be invited to a palace!"

"Well, Carlton House isn't really a palace, you understand. I'd call it a very grand house. There's a lovely Chinese drawing room, all in yellow silk, and a dining room walled with silver, and a huge Gothic conservatory hundreds of feet long—"

Frederica broke in impatiently. "Oh, I daresay the house is splendid, but tell us about the Prince of Wales." Her voice softened. "I saw him once, when I went to divine services at the Chapel Royal. He was young then, not yet twenty, and he was so charming, so handsome, like a young god." Frederica sighed reminiscently. "They called him Florizel in those days."

"Well . . . I shouldn't call him godlike now, Freddie. He's very fat. I think he wears stays. I could hear them creaking." At the look of disillusionment on Frederica's face, Chandra added hastily, "But he's certainly charming. He was most gracious to Julian."

"And why ever not?" Frederica demanded. "Julian's a rising politician. Tristan was telling me and Lily last night, that Julian is speaking in the House tonight. You never mentioned it, Chandra."

"Tristan was here last night?"

"Yes, he came to play backgammon," said Lily happily. "He says I'm getting to be such an expert that soon he won't be able to beat me! Oh, by the way, I hope you haven't forgotten that Lady Eversleigh is giving a party this evening for Tris's twenty-first birthday."

"No, no, I'm looking forward to it."

It was really amazing, Chandra thought, as she walked to her sitting room after breakfast, how easily and naturally Freddie and Lily had adapted to their new life in London. Frederica had apparently fully accepted Chandra's marriage. It was as if Freddie had put out of her mind the circumstances of the marriage and Chandra's reasons for entering into it. Not once since the wedding had Freddie tried to dissuade Chandra from her vendetta, or even mentioned it. And Lily was happy, blossoming under Tristan's attentions and those of the other young men who swarmed about her. If she noticed that few of the young ladies among her new acquaintances—or their ambitious mamas—had offered her the intimacy of close friendships, she never commented. Chandra fervently hoped that their stay in London would end before Lily became aware of the color bar that held the possibility of such unhappiness for her.

Chandra sat down before her desk in the sitting room, eyeing the stack of invitations with dismay. Surely the pile was twice as high as yesterday's. She leafed through the invitations. Balls and dinner parties, routs and soirees, at addresses only now becoming familiar to her. Melbourne House. Holland House. Ashburnham House. There was even an invitation from royalty. The Duchess of York requested the pleasure of her company and Julian's at Oatlands for an evening entertainment.

Feeling slightly bemused, Chandra sat back in her chair.

Who, so short a time ago in Bombay, could have imagined her present life? Or who, she thought suddenly, could have imagined how much she'd be enjoying it? She liked being admired. She liked wearing beautiful clothes, especially now—with Irene's guidance and her own fast-developing taste—that she knew how perfectly suited the clothes were to her. She liked the excitement and the gaiety and the stimulation of the London social scene. When the purpose for which she'd come to England was accomplished, she'd miss her life here. Some aspects of it, at least.

Well, no matter. She must attack this pile of invitations and decide which ones would best advance her campaign to become the most prominent hostess in London. "Come in," she called absently at the knock on the door.

Ramesh entered with his usual sweeping salaam. She noted with apprehension that the splendid mustachios were bristling. Speaking in Hindi, he said, "Lady, is it your will that I continue to serve you?"

"Certainly. Surely you know how much I value your devotion."

Ramesh smoothed a complacent finger over his mustachios. "I thank you, lady, for the confidence you repose in me. So, it is understood that I am in charge of your household? No one is to countermand my orders?"

"Yes, of course." But Chandra had a sinking feeling, as if catastrophe, invisible as yet, was slinking up on her around the nearest corner. "Is something wrong, Ramesh?"

Before he could answer, another knock sounded at the door, and Julian swept into the room without waiting for a response. He carried some papers in one hand. Fixing a hard eye on Ramesh, he said, "Here already, are you? I might have guessed." He motioned toward the door. "I wish to speak to your mistress. Alone."

Ramesh stiffened. His hand groped for the knife he no longer carried at his belt, and then fell to his side. He turned to Chandra, his face like carved stone save for the betraying mustachios. "Is it your desire that I leave your presence, lady?"

143

"Yes. Please. I'll talk to you presently," said Chandra hastily.

Ignoring Julian as if he were invisible, Ramesh swept Chandra a slow, magnificent bow and strode out of the room, with the air of a *mahout* in full control of his elephant.

Rising, Chandra said coldly to Julian, "What have you done to offend Ramesh?"

Julian stared at Chandra, his eyes kindling into blue flames. "What have I—? Have you gone queer in your attic? I, offend Ramesh? Good God, Chandra, the fellow's a servant. As the head of his household, I collect I can say or do as I like to him!"

He looked almost handsomer when he was angry, Chandra thought regretfully. If only he weren't so attractive, it would be far easier to ignore him and his poisonous barbs, which she'd been trying her very best to do since their wedding night. After the wounding things they'd said to each other that night, they'd been living under an armed truce, avoiding each other as much as possible.

To give him credit, Julian had been scrupulous in fulfilling his social obligations. Nearly every night, dutiful and attentive, he'd escorted her to balls and dinners and the theater. No one could fault him in public. In private, the wall of antagonism between them was almost palpable, resulting in a constant tense sparring that rubbed her nerves raw. He made no attempt at all to hide his feelings when he was alone with her. He despised her, he resented her, he couldn't wait to be free of his shackles. Chandra often wondered if they'd survive a year together without attempting to do each other bodily harm.

Chandra went straight to the attack. "Ramesh has served me and my—my family for a very long time. When he's distressed, I'm distressed. He's upset this morning. Are you responsible?"

Julian glared at her. "No, I am not. And if I were, it wouldn't signify. The fellow, as I've said, is a servant. As it

144

happens, however, Ramesh is disturbed because he's been besieged by a clamoring horde of tradesmen, all of them bent on having a piece of his hide." He waved the sheaf of papers in his hand. "These are accounts from, as far as I can gather, very nearly every reputable merchant in Mayfair. When a deputation of tradesmen came to the house this morning and failed to get any satisfaction out of Ramesh, they demanded to see me. They have this pathetic notion, you see, that I have some authority in this household."

"I don't understand," said Chandra slowly. "What's this about tradesmen? Hasn't Ramesh paid our bills? I can't believe he'd be so remiss. In India, he managed a much larger establishment than this."

"You'll forgive me if I don't perfectly understand the situation. However, I gather that Ramesh refused to pay any tradesmen's charges that do not include a generous commission for himself. The merchants naturally regard this as thievery. Or perhaps blackmail would be a better word."

"Oh, dear. A half anna on each rupee," murmured Chandra.

"What?"

"A *dubash*—steward, butler, whatever you call the position here—normally doesn't receive a salary in India," Chandra explained. "He takes a commission on each transaction."

"How big a commission?"

"Well, I've heard it's half an anna on each rupee. An anna is—let me think—about one-sixteenth of a rupee. And a rupee is—oh, about two shillings."

His eyes narrowing, Julian shuffled through the stack of bills in his hand. He made a swift mental calculation. Looking up, he said dryly, "Mathematics was never my strong suit. At a venture, however, I'd say that Ramesh has been trying to collect considerably more than half an anna to the rupee on these accounts." He flicked through the bills again. "Most of which appear to be in arrears."

"Oh, dear," Chandra repeated in a hollow tone. "Poor Ramesh, he's confused by this strange country. He's merely providing for his future, as he's always done, but now he doesn't know what his future will be, or even where he'll be next year, or the year after—"

"You surprise me. Won't he be in this house, assisting you to become the most famous society hostess in London?" inquired Julian, raising his eyebrow.

I must watch my tongue. I nearly gave myself away. "I merely meant that I might very well buy a larger house someday, adding to Ramesh's responsibilities," she said hastily. "Are the tradesmen still here?"

"No. I sent them away with a promise their complaints would be attended to."

"I see." Chandra wrinkled her brow. After a moment she asked, rather reluctantly, "Do you have any suggestions for me about how I should handle this situation?"

"Yes. Hire a proper butler to manage your household. And do it soon." Julian deposited the stack of bills on her desk. "Here you are. These papers are your responsibility. And I must remind you that this is the last time I intend to be a buffer between that barbarian servant of yours and half the respectable merchants of London. I have my own affairs to take care of."

Chandra felt a quick stab of anger at the curt indifference in his voice. It was one more indication, if she needed it, that he regarded their lives as completely separate. "I won't dismiss Ramesh," she said sharply. "He's my rock. I can always depend on him."

Shrugging, he replied, "Doubtless you'll do as you see fit. Just don't involve me, please. Although . . ." A thoughtful look crossed his face. "Common sense, and, I must admit, a consideration for my own comfort, impels me to suggest a solution to your problem."

"Which is?"

"Why don't you persuade Ramesh to abandon his commissions and accept a salary equivalent to *two* annas on the rupee on all household expenditures? Judging by the size of these accounts, I daresay he'd be the highest paid domestic servant in all of England." As Chandra gazed at him with surprise slowly merging into approval, he bowed and turned to go. At the door he paused, saying, "I'm speaking in the House tonight. I trust we have no late evening engagements?"

"No. Tristan's birthday dinner will be earlier, of course." At the knock on the door she responded, "Yes?"

A footman reported, "Mrs. Taney has arrived, ma'am."

"Lord, I'd forgotten I'd asked her to lunch." Chandra glanced down at her gown of sprigged muslin. It would do. "Tell Mrs. Taney I'll be down shortly."

After the footman left, Julian said, "Thank you, Chandra."

"Oh? For what, pray?"

"For not expecting me to help you entertain Mrs. Taney."

"Not at all. I'm saving you for bigger game. Royalty, for example. The Duchess of York has asked us to be her guests."

She knew from the slight flicker of a muscle in his cheek that she'd hit home, and felt slightly better about this, their latest encounter.

As she walked down the stairs, she wasn't anticipating much pleasure from her luncheon with Mrs. Taney and the other wives of the directors of the East India Company whom she'd met at the Taneys' dinner party some weeks before. She was using the ladies, of course, but she didn't feel the slightest pang of remorse. Equally they were using her, she knew, trying by virtue of her position as a member of the Ware family to enter the magic world of the *haut ton*. During the luncheon she hoped that a comment here, an inadvertent recollection there, might trigger a clue to the identity of her father's killer. She sighed. She had no great expectations of the luncheon. After all these weeks, she was no closer to solving her mystery than she'd been on her arrival in England. It was true that she'd heard of several men, ex-East India Company, or ex-Indian army, who might loosely fit her specifications, but she had no real reason to suspect any of them. Her search must go on.

The luncheon wasn't a success. No interesting tidbits of information surfaced. And Mrs. Taney, whom she was beginning to dislike intensely, tried to monopolize Chandra. It was soon clear that the director's wife was after a favor. "My dear Mrs. Ware," she began plaintively, "I look at you, so happy at the beginning of your married life, and I do hope you'll be spared the disappointments that some of us have suffered."

"Is something wrong, Mrs. Taney?"

"Not wrong, precisely. It's just when one has children, one wants the best for them. My Alfred, for example. My heart bleeds for his unhappiness. Poor boy, he yearns to become a member of White's." Mrs. Taney brightened. "Mr. Ware belongs to White's, does he not?"

"I believe he does." Chandra added with an air of discovery, "I have it! Why doesn't Alfred ask Julian to nominate him to the club?"

Mrs. Taney's face fell. Obviously she'd hoped that Chandra would volunteer to ask Julian to nominate her son. Chandra put her napkin to her mouth to hide a grin. She'd had a sudden vision of Julian's outraged expression if she were to request him to make Alfred Taney a member of White's.

There was one bad moment at the luncheon. One of the ladies commented, "I understand you spent some years in Bombay, Mrs. Ware. In what part of the city did you live?"

Chandra's blood ran cold. She knew practically nothing of Bombay, except for the commercial area around the waterfront where she'd stayed while awaiting ship for England. Fortunately the speaker, a garrulous lady fond of the sound of her own voice, answered her question herself. "Surely you lived in Malabar Hill. It's quite the most desireable area," she said wisely. "But not near the Towers of Silence, I trust?"

"Oh, no," replied Chandra, with the firmness of ignorance.

"I thought not. One shouldn't criticize any religion, heathen or no, but really! To leave one's dead exposed high on a tower for the vultures!"

"Er . . . no. No vultures," said a startled Chandra. *Tread carefully, my girl. This makes twice in one day that you've come near to betraying yourself.*

Lady Eversleigh's house, though situated in a fashionable neighborhood, wasn't large enough for lavish entertaining. The family group assembled for Tristan's birthday celebration filled her drawing room and dining room comfortably.

"You must think this is a paltry affair," she told Chandra, as they sat together in the drawing room, enjoying a glass of wine before dinner. "I should have liked to invite many more people—Tristan has so many friends!—but as you see, I have no room in which to put them. One would think, since my stepson never stays in his townhouse, that he'd be happy to allow me and Tristan the use of it, but . . ." She sighed, an air of gentle melancholy enveloping her like a veil. In her short acquaintance with Georgiana, Chandra had learned that Tristan's mother was seldom without a grievance. She'd never reconciled herself to the reality that her adored Tristan was a younger son with dim prospects.

Lady Eversleigh's expression brightened as she glanced across her tiny drawing room at a small dark girl who was talking to Irene. "Miss Amberley is charming, don't you think? I was so happy she could be with us tonight." Her voice became low and confidential. "My dear Chandra, I must ask you not to speak of it just yet, but I have every hope that Tristan and Miss Amberley will soon make a match of it."

Chandra rather doubted it. From Irene she'd learned that Georgiana had been dangling eligible heiresses in front of Tristan since his eighteenth birthday. Tris had always managed to wriggle out of the net. Tonight

149

Tristan was being elusive again. He greeted Miss Amberley cordially enough when she arrived, but then he retreated to a seat on a sofa between Frederica and Lily, where he sat regaling them with the tale of the amusing accident that had occurred that afternoon on parade. Lily was looking unusually lovely in a gown of deep apricot silk.

Chandra glanced down at her own dress of pale blue-green sarcenet and wondered why it had taken her so long to perceive that she and Lily had arrived in England wearing clothes whose colors were wrong for each of them and perfectly suited to the other. Lily's dark beauty was complemented by the bold, vibrant hues that clashed with Chandra's own more delicate coloring and rich auburn hair.

A little later, talking to Irene, Chandra noted that her sister-in-law was looking more fragile than usual. "You aren't ill, Irene?"

"Oh, no. A little tired, perhaps. Dear Ashley, he always worries about me so much. He wanted me to stay at home tonight, but I couldn't miss Tristan's twenty-first, could I?" She flashed a loving smile at her husband, who was standing at the fireplace, deep in discussion with Julian.

Chandra gazed at the brothers, marveling once again at how alike and yet how different they were. They resembled each other so closely, and they were both superbly dressed in black evening coat and breeches, but Julian, with his magnificent dark good looks and his air of abounding vitality, completely eclipsed his brother, who looked haggard and worn.

"Darling Ashley," murmured Irene. "His hip has been so painful recently. He'll never admit it, of course, but I can always tell by his limp." She studied Chandra. "We haven't had much time to chat of late. Is everything going well?" Irene colored. "I don't mean to pry, my dear. However, you did begin your married life under difficult circumstances. I'm so fond of you and Julian. I keep hoping you'll be as happy as Ashley and I have been."

150

"Oh, Julian and I are rubbing along tolerably well," Chandra assured Irene. "We can't hope to be as happy as you and Ashley. I don't think anybody can."

Irene smiled, catching Ashley's eye across the room. A smile of such radiant sweetness curved his lips that Chandra's heart caught. The open, shameless adoration between the pair made her realize more cruelly than words could have done, what a lifeless caricature she had in her own marrige.

Lady Eversleigh had obviously planned the evening to throw Tristan as much as possible into the company of Miss Amberley. Tris overset her arrangements. When, after dinner, the gentlemen joined the ladies in the drawing room—except for Julian, who had left to attend the sitting in the House—Lady Eversleigh said brightly, "How lovely, we've exactly two full tables for whist. Tristan, you'll play with Miss Amberley and Irene and me."

Tristan, who had been whispering to Lily, looked up with a grin. "Sorry, Mama. No cards for me tonight. I have a famous scheme: we'll all go to hear Julian's speech!"

Georgiana frowned. "I don't know that your mama would approve, Miss Amberley. I understand some of the speeches are not fit for female ears."

And Ashley said, "It would be too tiring for Irene, Tris. I'm taking her home."

So in the end, Tristan escorted only the ladies from Grosvenor Square to the gallery of the House of Commons. Chandra peered down at the seat of English government. It was much less impressive than she'd expected. The room was quite small, for one thing, dimly lit by a single chandelier. At one end of the room, a man in a black robe and a long wig presided on a kind of throne. "The Speaker," Tristan whispered. In front of the Speaker, three clerks sat at a green baize table on which lay a gleaming golden mace. On either side of the central aisle rose tiers of benches covered in green leather.

If the chamber itself was insignificant, Chandra found

151

the Honorable Members outrageous. Most of them weren't listening to the speeches. Some were actually napping. Many lolled on the benches, talking audibly to each other, or emitting an occasional "Hear, hear" or a catcall. Others wandered in and out, bowing jerkily on departing and arriving again to the Speaker on his dais.

"There's Julian, on the back bench," murmured Tristan. "No, not there to the left. The Government side of the aisle is to the right of the Speaker."

The current speaker, a venerable member in countrified clothes, concluded his remarks to a vast indifference on the part of the Honorable Members. Chandra saw Julian's tall figure unwind from the back bench, and in spite of herself she felt a spurt of sympathy. Would anyone listen to him?

"See those red stripes on the sides of the carpet?" whispered Tristan. "The stripes are about two swords' lengths apart. They mark as far as a member can go when he's addressing the House."

The members were as noisy and unruly as ever when Julian stepped up to the red stripe on the Government side of the aisle. In moments, however, the tumult began to die down. Julian's tall handsome presence had a natural dignity, and his voice was clear and carrying.

"Mr. Speaker," he began, "I have been much troubled of late by the scurrilous attacks made on a gallant soldier. I refer, of course, to General Sir Arthur Wellesley, who, in the course of a lightning two-week campaign that included a magnificent, daring attack across a river in full flood, has driven our French enemies out of Portugal and liberated the great city of Oporto. Now his enemies are saying that Sir Arthur 'got himself into a scrape.' One Honorable Member has even intimated that Sir Authur lied in dispatches. And why is the general being criticized? Because he did not capture the entire French army, because he did not immediately continue the drive into Spain." Julian's voice rang out in a great peal. "As a soldier myself, Mr. Speaker, I submit to you that Sir Arthur Wellesley deserves, not a barrage of carping criticism, but the heartfelt gratitude of the nation."

A ripple of applause followed Julian's final remarks. As he walked back to his seat, one of the members on the front bench rose and shook his hand. The applause grew louder.

"Oh, my word, did you see that?" Tristan was nearly beside himself with excitement. "That was Castlereagh, the Secretary for War. Everyone says he's a cold fish, never has a soft word for anybody. And he congratulated Julian in front of the whole House of Commons!"

"Oh, Tris, I collect this means great things for Julian," Lily exclaimed, her face glowing. "Perhaps one day *he* might be Secretary for War!"

"Why settle for that?" said Tristan recklessly. "He could be prime minister, or—or—"

"Don't get carried away, Tris," Chandra cut in dryly. "The king's position is secure. This is a hereditary monarchy, recall."

Chapter Ten

"The terms of this 'salary' you offer me are very generous, lady," said Ramesh uneasily. "With your permission, however, I would rather abide by the old ways."

It was the morning after Julian's speech in the House. Fortified by a more than usually substantial breakfast, Chandra had just broken the news to Ramesh that he would henceforth be running the household under new rules. He would, in fact, be a butler.

"Ramesh, I, too, prefer the old ways," said Chandra solemnly. "You don't think I like living in this cold foreign country, in a house without a veranda and gardens and playing fountains? You don't think I like wearing these strange clothes instead of the gorgeous silks and brocades in which I was used to gladden the eyes of my husband, Asaf Khan?"

"No, lady," came Ramesh's puzzled reply. "But then, why—?"

"I must tell you something important, and secret, Ramesh. I came here on a mission, actually one that Asaf Khan suggested to me, and when I've accomplished that mission I can leave England. You will supervise a proper household again."

Ramesh raised his head alertly. "The sahib will accompany us?"

"No," said Chandra shortly. "Mr. Ware and I will be

parting company." Ramesh's eyes gleamed with satisfaction. "Until I leave here, however, you can best serve me by adopting the English ways. Is it agreed?"

"It shall be as you wish, lady." The wonderful mustachios were quivering with emotion. He lowered himself in a profound salaam. Opening the door, he nearly collided with Ashley, who was standing just outside, his hand poised to knock. Ramesh bowed to the earl and went on his stately way.

Chandra rose. She didn't attempt to hide her surprise. Ashley had never sought her out before. "You wished to see me?"

"Yes." Plainly Ashley wasn't paying a friendly visit. He seemed both angry and ill at ease, as if he was unsure how to broach the subject that had brought him here. He kept pulling his gloves between his fingers. At length he said abruptly, "Julian badly wants a political career."

"So I'd gathered."

"He made an impressive speech in the House last night."

"Yes, of course. I heard him."

"But you didn't hear what Lord Castlereagh—the Secretary for War—said to him later at White's. Castlereagh offered Julian the post of undersecretary in his department."

"Indeed." Chandra shot the earl a puzzled look. "Is that an important post?"

"It's the first big step up on the political ladder. However, when Julian came to my house last night to tell me about it, he also told me he intends to refuse the offer."

Even more puzzled, Chandra asked, "But why, if he's so ambitious?"

"Because, if he accepts office, he'll have to stand for reelection to his seat, and he can't afford the twenty thousand pounds an election campaign would cost him."

"But why, in heaven's name, must he stand for reelection? He's already a member of Parliament."

"The requirement to be reelected on assuming office was one of the provisions of the constitutional compromise of 1707," Ashley replied impatiently. "But that's neither here nor there. The fact is that Julian hasn't the money to run for office, and he can't admit to Castlereagh why he won't stand,, without revealing the sham of his marriage. Everyone in London knows he married a wealthy heiress. They'll naturally wonder why Julian doesn't dip into his wife's fortune for his election expenses."

"Wait. Doesn't Julian represent your family constituency of Wolverton? Can't you, as the landowner, simply reappoint him?"

"Wolverton isn't a nomination borough," replied Ashley, even more impatiently. "All freeholders are eligible to vote. And the elections are always hotly contested. There's a faction in the borough, for example, that's very opposed to sending British troops to fight in Europe. Julian, on the other hand, is heart and soul in favor of the war in Portugal. Contested elections are always expensive."

"You mean you buy votes?"

Ashley looked at Chandra with cold dislike. "In certain cases, yes, I suppose it does amount to that. Some electors regard their votes as property; they expect to receive a dividend, either in cash, or in places or pensions for relatives, or in renewal of their leases. Some of them want something as simple as a meal and lodging for the night and transportation to the hustings on polling day. But take my word for it, very few electors are completely altruistic."

"I see. Shall I guess why you came to me, Ashley? You want me to pay for Julian's reelection campaign."

"Yes, I do," Ashley exploded. "It's little enough repayment for throwing him into debtors' prison, for forcing him into an unequal marriage. It's to your advantage, too, my dear sister-in-law. You married Julian for his position. Wouldn't you enjoy the added cachet of being the wife of the Undersecretary for War?"

Ignoring the contempt in Ashley's voice, Chandra thought about the statement for a moment. "Yes, I would," she decided. "I think Julian's political advancement would be a social asset to me. Tell him he can have the money."

"Tell him yourself," said the earl savagely. "I'd as lief not be within a league of him when he finds out I informed you about Castlereagh's offer. In any case, he's so damnably stiff-necked that you'll have to put pressure on him to accept your rhino. I'm not sure you'll succeed. Last night I asked him why he didn't apply to you for the money. He said he'd rather be hanged, drawn, and quartered than be forced to ask you for a farthing. Then he left Daylesford House." The earl eyed Chandra accusingly. "I fancy he intended to drown his disappointment at White's."

"And I, of course, am responsible for Julian's getting foxed." At the taken-aback expression on Lord Daylesford's face, Chandra chuckled. "Thank you for bringing this matter to my attention, Ashley. I'll do my best to persuade Julian to stand for reelection. As you pointed out, it's to my own advantage."

After her brother-in-law's departure, Chandra walked down the corridor to Julian's bedchamber. Possibly he hadn't come home last night, she reflected as she tapped lightly on his door. He might still be at White's, engaged in one of the marathon drinking and gambling sessions that Tristan seemed to admire so much.

She was wrong. From the other side of the door a voice growled, "Yes, what is it?"

She opened the door to find Julian sitting in front of his dressing table. He flashed her a brief, morose glance, then resumed his task of tying an intricate knot in his cravat. His valet hovered solicitously beside him, a pile of pristine starched linen cloths on his arm, ready to supply his master with a spare if the current attempt failed. As Chandra watched, Julian added the last touch to a Trône d'Amour, and the valet heaved an audible sigh of relief.

"Thank you. I won't need you anymore," Julian told him. Waiting until the door had closed on the valet, Julian rose from his chair and confronted Chandra. He looked quite dreadful. His eyes were bloodshot. His skin was pasty. A muscle twitched in his temple. Chandra guessed that wine, not cards, had been first on his agenda last evening, and that he was probably nursing a monumental headache.

Whatever the state of his health, he sounded normally provocative. "To what am I indebted for this visit, my dear wife?" he jibed. "One thing for certain, you have no conjugal purposes in mind!"

Chandra hadn't been in this room since Julian had moved into it. The bedchamber, like most of the bedrooms in the house, retained the furnishings of the house's original owner. Thriftily, Chandra had seen little reason to redecorate rooms that the public would never see. However, the room seemed subtly to have changed with Julian's occupancy. Now it had an aura of masculinity, compounded principally of shaving soap and the smell of freshly laundered linen. And something else, the indefinable sense of male bravado that Julian projected so effortlessly.

"I came to talk about your reelection campaign," she said calmly.

The muscle in his temple stood out like a rope. "What, pray, do you know about that?"

Chandra moved to a chair and sat down, settling her skirts. "Ashley told me about Lord Castlereagh's offer. I think you should accept it."

"Brothers!" Julian exclaimed in a tone of loathing. He stared at her. "Then I presume Ashley also told you I intend to refuse the post of undersecretary on the grounds of lack of funds to fight a reelection campaign."

"He did. Biting off your nose to spite your face, I call it. As you must be aware, I'm prepared to advance you any sum you may need."

His eyes glinting dangerously, Julian retorted, "You don't know me very well, do you, Chandra? Rather than ask you for a shilling, I'd prefer to—"

"I know. You'd rather be hanged, drawn, and quartered. Such an unpleasant death, I was used to think, when

158

Freddie read stories to me and Lily about the olden times. What fustian, Julian!"

Crossing his arms across his chest, he leaned back against his dressing table. "Call it what you like. I won't take a penny of your money."

"So this is what it amounts to, a gentleman's honor," said Chandra contemptuously. "I was taught that a gentleman always keeps his word. But then, you're not really a gentleman, are you? You're an *aristocrat*. You're breaking the terms of our bargain, Julian. You promised to give me a position in society, and now you're reneging."

He straightened, his eyebrows drawn together in a puzzled frown. "What in the fiend's name are you talking about, Chandra? How am I—?"

Chandra cut him off. "You needn't think to feel obligated to me, if that's what you're afraid of. I'm not offering to pay your election expenses out of the milk of human kindness. Personally, I don't care a fig if you win or lose this election, or any elections in the future. While I'm married to you, however, I want my money's worth. I want all the consequence I can get, and that includes being Mrs. the Honorable Undersecretary for War!"

The blue eyes were brilliant with anger. "You're every bit as mercenary and selfish and grasping as I thought you were, that day in Newgate. Very well, I'll stand for reelection. Thank God, you've relieved me of the necessity to feel the slightest shred of gratitude toward you!"

It's the last week of May. The Season is almost a third gone, and what have I accomplished? I still haven't the faintest clue to Papa's killer. Seated at her desk, Chandra flicked the pages of her appointments diary, crammed with engagements for virtually every day until the end of July. She wasn't savoring the balls and routs and dinners as much as she had in the beginning, and, much as she hated to admit it, she knew why. Julian had been away from London for two weeks, campaigning in Buckinghamshire. Though they were so often at each other's throats when they were together, there was an excitement, a vibrancy in the atmosphere when Julian was present, that was lacking when he was gone.

"Do you mind, Chandra? I told the footman not to announce me."

Chandra looked up at Irene with a welcoming smile. "Of course not. I'm delighted you came. I haven't seen as much of you lately as I would have liked."

"Oh, I've been staying close to home," said Irene with a laugh. "Before Ashley left with Julian for Buckinghamshire, he made me promise to rest as much as possible. You know he fusses over me. You'd think I was an invalid." She sat down, pulling rather nervously at the strings of her reticule. "Have you received any news from Julian?" she said at last.

Chandra shook her head. After a moment's hesitation, she said, "Irene, dear, what's the use of pretending? You know Julian and I have a marriage of convenience. There's no reason why he'd feel impelled to write to me. We're civil to each other, but neither of us has any interest in the other's affairs."

"Oh, Chandra, that's such a *waste* of the happiness you and Julian could share. I'd hoped by this time . . ." She broke off, smiling ruefully. "Forgive me. I daresay I can't expect all marriages to be like mine! The thing is, Ashley has been writing regularly to me. He says Julian's re-election campaign isn't going very well."

"Oh? I'd have thought since Julian's the brother of the principal landowner—"

"It's the war, I believe. The opposition is making the most of the fact that a local regiment suffered heavy losses in the battle of Corunna last January. Chandra, I think you—both of us—should go to Buckinghamshire. Julian needs our help."

Chandra stared at Irene in surprise. "He needs *our* help? In what way?"

"Mainly by just being there, to indicate our support and concern. By entertaining the electors at dinner at Wolverton Abbey. By inviting their wives to take tea with us."

MORE PASSION AND ADVENTURE AWAIT... YOUR TRIP TO A BIG ADVENTUROUS WORLD BEGINS WHEN YOU ACCEPT YOUR FIRST 4 NOVELS ABSOLUTELY *FREE* (AN $18.00 VALUE)

Accept your Free gift and start to experience more of the passion and adventure you like in a historical romance novel. Each Zebra novel is filled with proud men, spirited women and tempestuous love that you'll remember long after you turn the last page.

Zebra Historical Romances are the finest novels of their kind. They are written by authors who really know how to weave tales of romance and adventure in the historical settings you love. You'll feel like you've actually gone back in time with the thrilling stories that each Zebra novel offers.

GET YOUR FREE GIFT WITH THE START OF YOUR HOME SUBSCRIPTION

Our readers tell us that these books sell out very fast in book stores and often they miss the newest titles. So Zebra has made arrangements for you to receive the four newest novels published each month.

You'll be guaranteed that you'll never miss a title, and home delivery is so convenient. And to show you just how easy it is to get Zebra Historical Romances, we'll send you your first 4 books absolutely FREE! Our gift to you just for trying our home subscription service.

BIG SAVINGS AND FREE HOME DELIVERY

Each month, you'll receive the four newest titles as soon as they are published. You'll probably receive them even before the bookstores do. What's more, you may preview these exciting novels free for 10 days. If you like them as much as we think you will, just pay the low preferred subscriber's price of just $3.75 each. *You'll save $3.00 each month off the publisher's price.* AND, your savings are even greater because there are never any shipping, handling or other hidden charges—FREE Home Delivery. Of course you can return any shipment within 10 days for full credit, no questions asked. There is no minimum number of books you must buy.

4 FREE BOOKS

FREE BOOK CERTIFICATE

4 FREE BOOKS

ZEBRA HOME SUBSCRIPTION SERVICE, INC.

YES! Please start my subscription to Zebra Historical Romances and send me my first 4 books absolutely FREE. I understand that each month I may preview four new Zebra Historical Romances free for 10 days. If I'm not satisfied with them, I may return the four books within 10 days and owe nothing. Otherwise, I will pay the low preferred subscriber's price of just $3.75 each; a total of $15.00, *a savings off the publisher's price of $3.00.* I may return any shipment and I may cancel this subscription at any time. There is no obligation to buy any ship-ment and there are no shipping, handling or other hidden charges. Regardless of what I decide, the four free books are mine to keep.

NAME

ADDRESS   APT

CITY   STATE   ZIP
(   )
TELEPHONE

SIGNATURE   (if under 18, parent or guardian must sign)

Terms, offer and prices subject to change without notice. Subscription subject to acceptance by Zebra Books. Zebra Books reserves the right to reject any order or cancel any subscription.

"Well . . . if you really think our presence could make a difference . . ."

"I'm sure of it."

Quickly Chandra gathered her thoughts. Naturally, she told herself, it didn't matter to her whether Julian won or lost, but there was no denying she'd be considerably more in the public eye as the wife of a rising young undersecretary. What's more, she was curious to see the Ware estates in Buckinghamshire.

"You've convinced me, Irene. I'll go."

"I *knew* you wouldn't fail Julian," said Irene, smiling in delight.

Chandra felt rather ashamed of herself.

Busily making plans, Irene said, "Miss Banks and Lily should go, too. We'll have a real display of family unity. And Tristan could be our escort. Surely his colonel will grant him a few days' leave."

In the event, Tristan's colonel was amenable. The following day a rather impressive cavalcade set out for the country. Julian's womenfolk rode in the berline, with Tris riding beside the postilions, and a fourgon heavily laden with luggage following behind. A third vehicle carried Ramesh and the abigails.

The journey across Middlesex and into Buckinghamshire took almost five hours, but Chandra didn't find it tedious. She had a natural curiosity about her surroundings, and it was pleasant to get away from the city into the green coolness of the countryside.

"Oh, how lovely," she breathed, as they began moving into an area dominated by a great range of chalk hills, heavily wooded on its crests with glorious beech trees.

"The Chiltern Hills," said Irene. "Ashley always feels he's nearly home when he glimpses them."

Passing prosperous-looking villages and rich two-hundred-acres fields separated by leafy hedgerows, they entered a narrow valley which gradually widened out beside a rushing little stream. A small village clustered beside the stream, dominated by an ancient church and a well-proportioned stone house surrounded by a wall. A road led from the village up a long sloping wooded ridge.

"That's Wolverton Abbey on the crest of the hill," said Irene. "And over there, near the church, is the dower house. It's vacant now, of course. We have no dowager countess! I've often thought it would make a fine country residence for you and Julian."

"Oh, Chandra, it looks like a lovely house," said Lily excitedly. "And you'd be so near Irene and Ashley."

Suddenly Chandra felt extremely guilty. No one except Frederica knew that her marriage was purely temporary, that she intended to leave England as soon as she'd solved the mystery of her father's murder. Lily had apparently come to terms with her new life in England; it would come as a shock to her when Chandra uprooted her. Julian, too, expected her to remain in England after their divorce. And Irene, dear Irene, who'd been so kind and loving. For the first time, it occurred to Chandra how grieved Irene would be to discover that the woman she'd befriended had been living a life of lies.

"Would you like to see the dower house now?" Irene inquired.

"Oh. No. Later, perhaps."

The cavalcade of carriages passed under the arches of a large gatehouse, attended by bowing caretakers, and swung up the steep driveway of an extensive park to the crown of the hill and the imposing hulk of a vast stone residence. Servants swept out of the great entrance doors to greet them.

"I'll tell you what," Tristan said to Lily when he'd helped her down from the carriage, "let's go for a jaunt about the countryside. It's only mid-afternoon. We've loads of time before dinner."

"I'd like that," said Lily with a dimpling smile. "You won't expect me to ride?"

"No, of course not. I know you don't like to ride." He gave her a teasing look. "Although, coming from a girl who once rode on elephants, it's hard to understand why you're afraid to get on a horse! No, there's a dog cart in the stables we could use. I learned to drive in it."

Lily's eyes sparkled. "Perhaps you could teach me to drive."

Dear Tristan, thought Chandra as she watched the laughing young couple. *He's been such a good friend to Lily. Without him, I don't think she could have adjusted to life in England.*

"Miss Banks? Do you care to go with me and Lily?"

"My old bones are tired enough after five hours in the carriage," said Frederica firmly. "I'm for a nap."

Chandra said, "Some other time, Tris. I must unpack."

"There's been some kind of habitation on this site since the late eleventh century," observed Irene, as they trailed into the house. "It was an abbey originally, of course. But then, early on, the abbot crossed swords with William Rufus, and the upshot was that the king granted these lands to the first baron, Adam Ware."

Chandra could well believe in the antiquity of the house, as she followed her abigail and several footmen with her luggage up steep, winding staircases and through labyrinthine corridors to her bedchamber. The house had obviously been added onto haphazardly for centuries. It would be extremely easy to lose oneself in those endless, secretive corridors.

Her bedchamber was very large, with massive, old-fashioned furniture. Her abigail began immediately to unpack her bags. The girl paused as she opened the doors of the heavy oaken wardrobe. "Ma'am, the master's clothes are in here," she began.

The door opened and Julian pushed into the room. He stopped, looking thunderstruck, on the threshold. "What are you doing here?"

"That'll be all, Betsy. You can finish later," Chandra told the abigail hastily. The girl hurried way.

"Well, what *are* you doing here, Chandra?"

"I've come to help with your campaign."

"The devil you did. I didn't ask for your help, I don't need your help, and I'd like you to leave as soon as possible."

"Irene seems to think you need help," observed

163

Chandra. "Ashley wrote to her that your campaign wasn't going well. She says you need the support of your whole family. So we all came down, Irene and I and Freddie and Lily and Tristan."

"This was Irene's idea?" Julian bit his lip. "All right," he said grudgingly. "I daresay it can't do any harm for the pair of you to act as my hostesses." He glanced at her luggage piled in the center of the room. "Are you aware that this is my bedchamber?"

"Yes. The servants who brought up my luggage must have assumed—"

"Must have assumed we were dewey-eyed newlyweds, anxious to share the joys of the marriage bed. A natural mistake, doubtless."

Chandra flushed. "I'll have my abigail ask the housekeeper for another room. I'll be out of your way in a few minutes." She headed for the door.

"I'd think twice about that if I were you," came Julian's amused voice from behind her.

She whirled around to stare at him. "What do you mean?"

He grinned, saying, "If you ask the housekeeper for a separate room, the news will be all over this corner of the county in hours that young Mr. and Mrs. Ware, married for—how long is it, five, six weeks?—are already estranged. The prattle boxes will speculate that I've been straying. No, Carlton House to a charley's shelter, that wouldn't shock the people around here. They've known me since I started in the petticoat line. No, they'll speculate that *you've* been straying, and I've cast you out of my bed. Or that you've cast me out, perhaps because I beat you. Or—Good God!" He struck a hand to his forehead in a theatrical gesture. "I hope they won't think that I can't—er—perform."

"You're enjoying yourself, aren't you?" snapped Chandra. "Well, it doesn't signify. Your constituents can think what they like. I haven't any intention of sleeping in this room with you."

The impish amusement faded from his face. "Pray

164

disabuse yourself of the notion that I have any desire for you to do so," he said coldly. "However, since you came down here without being asked, we're both obliged to abide by the consequences. Like it or not, we'll share this bedchamber. Now that I've committed myself to this campaign, I don't propose to lose it because of a naughty tale from the boudoir. The election is touch-and-go. In fact, I've been trailing my opponent from the beginning, and I'm still behind. The faintest hint of scandal could tip the scales. And you might reflect that a toothsome little morsel of gossip like this, if it wafts its way to London, won't improve your social career, either."

Chandra opened her mouth to object vociferously, and closed it again. She wanted attention, she craved attention, as the best means of achieving her goal, but her fragile reputation couldn't survive malicious laughter. At length she said, "If you'll promise not to—to—"

"Promise not to do what? This?" Suddenly Julian reached out a long arm and pulled her against him. He looked down at her with a mocking smile. Slowly the blue eyes darkened, the smile disappeared from those sensual lips, and his arms tightened around her until she could feel something sharp and hard pressing against the tender flesh of her side. His watch fob, she realized later when the encounter was over.

"No," she muttered, fighting a teacherous urge to relax against that hard body.

Instantly he released her. The mocking smile was back on his lips. "You have my promise, although it's quite superfluous. You don't tempt me, my dear. I won't come near you tonight—or any night."

Ashley was surprised and not entirely pleased to see his wife at Wolverton Abbey. "You'll tire yourself out, entertaining for the electors," he protested, when he walked into the drawing room before dinner to greet Irene.

"Nonsense, my love. I'll merely preside at the head of the dinner table. Chandra and Frederica and Lily will do

165

the really onerous work, like pouring the tea for the ladies!"

"You can count on us," Frederica assured Irene, her eyes twinkling. "That is, if Tristan can be persuaded to drop his plans to show Lily the entire county of Buckinghamshire."

A strong sense of humor wasn't among Ashley's virtues. He said curtly to Tristan, "You won't have time to go gallivanting about the countryside. You'll come canvassing with me and Julian."

Dinner in the cavernous dining room of Wolverton Abbey—Irene and Ashley, at opposite ends of the interminably long table, virtually had to shout to make themselves audible to each other—was an uncomfortable affair for Chandra. Julian wore his normal charming, considerate public face, but she kept thinking with increasing dread of the shared bedchamber upstairs. The thought of being in such close proximity to him throughout a long night raised goose pimples on her skin.

In the event, she needn't have worried. Julian lingered downstairs with Ashley and Tristan, discussing the campaign, after the ladies retired to bed. Toward midnight, wearing her most conservative dressing gown, buttoned high in the throat, she was nervously pacing up and down the bedchamber when Julian strode in. She turned her eyes involuntarily on the great tester bed.

He gave a short laugh. Motioning to the door opening off the bedchamber, he said, "Not to worry. I'll sleep in the dressing room. As I'm sure you observed, it contains a settee." He walked over to the bed, and before her affronted gaze quickly stripped it of several blankets and most of the pillows. "It's a warmish night. You won't need these," he said blandly. "In any case, I refuse to be a perfect gentleman. You'll have to sacrifice something. I need a few creature comforts. Good night, Chandra."

She was relieved to see him disappear into the dressing room, but she didn't sleep well. Through the closed door, she was acutely conscious of stirrings and rustlings as Julian settled in. Once, in the middle of the night, she heard a loud thump and an even louder string of curses. She'd noticed that the settee wasn't very long. Julian must have fallen out of it.

On the following morning, Chandra began the most singular week she'd experienced since her arrival in England. Night after night, she joined Irene in welcoming the more prominent families of the borough to dinner. Afternoon after afternoon, she and Irene, assisted by Freddie and Lily, poured numerous cups of tea for the ladies of the area. Between times, they rode in cavalcades along leafy country lanes, waving to prospective voters, or stood in front of the hustings on the Wolverton village green, listening with admiration while Julian, or occasionally Ashley, gave a rousing speech. Even Tristan was pressed into service. After his first speech he came down from the platform quaking with fright.

"You were wonderful, Tris," Lily assured him.

"Was I?" replied a dazed Tris. "I can't remember a word I said."

However, at the end of the week, with only two days remaining before polling day, Julian's camp was in disarray. Late one evening the family sat in the great drawing room after the last of their dinner guests had departed, and Julian remarked, "It's no good, you know. I'm still trailing. Carstairs"—the local man who had set up his campaign—"Carstairs says the votes aren't there."

"But how can that be?" Chandra protested. "The crowds have been so enthusiastic. I haven't heard one word in your disfavor from anyone."

"That's because you've been talking to my supporters, or at least to near supporters, or to people who might be *disposed* to be supporters. All things considered, I'm running about even with my opponent except for a block of votes in the hands of several important freeholders in the outlying districts. These men—two of them, especially—can virtually dictate how their neighbors and tenants will vote, either because of their influence in the community or through their control of land leases. They

167

support my opponent. I haven't been able to win them over."

"I see." After a thoughtful pause, Chandra asked Tristan an apparently inconsequential question. "Tris, didn't you tell me once about some duchesses who campaigned for a man named—what was it now?—oh, yes, a Mr. Fox."

"Lord, yes." Tristan chuckled. "That was the Duchess of Devonshire and her sister, Lady Duncannon, canvassing in person for Charles James Fox. Oh, what a stir that caused! The ladies stormed through Westminster, going from house to house and shop to shop. The opposition tried to howl them down for ungenteel and unladylike behavior, especially when it was learned that the duchess had kissed a butcher to obtain his vote! And once"—he began to laugh—"once a heckler offered her grace a halter to hang herself with, and she handed it back to him, saying she didn't wish to deprive him of a family relic."

The others laughed at Tristan's sally, but Chandra noticed Julian's eyes fixed on her in a speculative look. She glanced away from him, asking Irene about the next day's activities. Before the party separated for the night, she managed to get Tristan off by himself to ask him for the names and the directions of the recalcitrant freeholders.

"Why do you want to know?" Tristan demanded.

"Oh . . . just curious." She gave him a friendly poke. "You know how we females are."

She rose earlier than usual next morning. She was fully dressed, sitting at a chair by the window drinking her tea, when Julian, following the routine they'd fallen into, rapped on the dressing room door and emerged into the bedchamber, yawning and trailing bedclothes. His eyes narrowed as he glanced at her gypsy bonnet, fastened under her chin with violet ribbons that matched her sprigged muslin gown. "Are you off somewhere at this hour?" he asked.

"Oh, I thought I'd take an early morning drive, before

168

Irene puts me to work again. It's such a glorious day, with everything so fresh and green and blooming."

"I didn't realize you were so fond of nature," he commented, his tone faintly skeptical. Hearing a knock at the door, he moved off to admit his valet into the bedchamber. Chandra bit her lip. He was beginning to know her too well. She would have to be more careful in future to guard her tongue and even her thoughts.

By nine o'clock she was driving down the long sloping driveway of Wolverton Abbey in the Daylesford landau, with Ramesh sitting in imposing dignity on the box beside the coachman. Chandra unfolded her parasol against the bright June sunshine, and watched the lovely verdant Buckinghamshire scenery roll by. Some five miles from the Daylesford estate, the coachman turned into a narrow lane, edged with hedgerows, and drove through an arched gateway into a well-kept cobbled courtyard. A substantial, comfortable-looking house faced the gateway, and around to the rear, Chandra caught a glimpse of stables and other outbuildings.

A squarely built, middle-aged man in a serviceable coat and gaiters and a wide-brimmed hat appeared from the direction of the stables, talking to one of his laborers. He paused, his eyes passing slowly from Ramesh to Chandra and, finally, to the door of the landau with its gilded crest.

Chandra smiled at him. "Mr. Peddrick?"

"That's my name." The man sounded, not surly, exactly, but extremely reserved. "And ye, I take it, ma'am, are a member of the Ware family. Not her ladyship. I know her. Would ye be Mrs. Julian Ware?"

"I am. I've taken the liberty of coming to your house today, Mr. Peddrick, to ask you to give your vote to my husband."

The grizzled brows drew together over the freeholder's eyes. "Then ye've come for naught, Mrs. Ware. I'm supporting your husband's opponent, Mr. Redgrave."

"Yes, I'm aware of that. But I'd like you to reconsider which man would best represent you in Parliament. Unlike my husband, Mr. Redgrave has no experience of

169

political affairs. What's more, he has no knowledge of military affairs. Now, my husband was a soldier for many years. Shouldn't we make use of his experience, his expertise, in this great crisis in which England is fighting to the death with Napoleon?"

Patriotism was quite the wrong argument, Chandra realized in dismay. Mr. Peddrick's face had turned an alarming shade of purple.

"No, we should not make use of any such experience," he roared. "It's fire-eating military men like Julian who're sending this country straight to perdition, and I want no part of him! And I'll thank ye, ma'am, to get off my property. Ye'll do no good for your husband here."

"Ebenezer," called a warning voice. Chandra looked up to see a stout lady in a mobcap and apron standing in the doorway of the house. The lady came down the steps and walked over to the landau. "Good day, Mrs. Ware," she said, bobbing a curtsy. "I'm Marcy Peddrick." She turned a reproving gaze on her husband. "Ye're no' being very hospitable to Mrs. Ware, Ebenezer."

"No more did I ask her here," said Peddrick sullenly. He swung on his heel and stalked away.

Mrs. Peddrick looked aghast. "I'm so sorry. He doesn't really mean to be rude. It's just that . . . Mrs. Ware, will ye no' come in the house and have a glass o' my gooseberry wine?"

Chandra was well aware that Mrs. Peddrick didn't want her company any more than her husband did. However, the freeholder's wife, obviously a sensible soul, didn't think it was politic for her husband to insult a member of the county's leading family. The invitation to take refreshments was her way of making amends.

Over glasses of wine and little cakes in Mrs. Peddrick's painfully neat parlor, the two women made small talk for several moments. Then Chandra said abruptly, "Why is your husband so opposed to military men? Oh, I know there's a good deal of sentiment in the county against the government prosecution of the war—"

Mrs. Peddrick's eyes filled with tears. "Mrs. Ware, we

lost two grandsons in the retreat to Corunna. Just boys, they were. Sixteen and eighteen. The only grandsons we'll ever have. My husband fair adored them, never having gotten along, as ye might say, with our son. My daughter-in-law, she can't have any more bairns. My husband thinks English soldiers should never have been sent to fight the Portugees's war for them."

"Believe me, I can appreciate your loss," said Chandra earnestly. "I'm a soldier's daughter. My father fell fighting for his country." She mentally crossed her fingers. It wasn't exactly a lie, even though Major Geoffrey Meredith had died defending, not his country, but the East India Company and the Begum of Bhulamphur's jewelry.

"I'm that sorry," said Mrs. Peddrick, wiping her eyes with her apron. "Then I fancy ye'll understand my husband's feelings, too."

"Oh, I do. But I also agree with *my* husband, that we must fight Napoleon wherever we can, even if it means shedding the blood of English boys, rather than face far greater bloodshed later, when Napoleon will have conquered the entire world."

Good Lord, I've been listening to too many of Julian's speeches. I'm beginning to sound like him, Chandra thought. She took a lace-edged handkerchief from her reticule and delicately touched her eyes. "I miss Papa so much," she said bravely, "but I *know*, if he were still here, he'd be supporting Julian." She rose, holding out her hand. "Thank you for the wine. It was delicious. It's been a pleasure meeting you."

As she drove away from the Peddrick farm, Chandra felt depressed. So much for her attempt to canvas votes *à la* the Duchess of Devonshire. Mr. Peddrick had virtually thrown her off his property. His wife? Well, she'd listened, but she wasn't a voter. How much influence did she have with her husband?

Her next foray into electioneering was considerably more exciting. Approaching a farmhouse on a hill by a winding lane, the coachman drove the landau past a fenced field in which cattle were grazing. Suddenly shrill screams split the air, and Chandra gazed with horror as a small child came running frantically across the field toward them, with a snorting bull in close pursuit. Two men, one brandishing a pitchfork, were chasing after them, but it was obvious the bull would reach the child before the men did.

Without a moment's hesitation, Ramesh leaped down from the driver's seat and over the fence. He snatched up the child and jumped back over the fence, leaving a portion of his long flowing robe entwined around the horns of the enraged bull.

The men came running up. While one of them warded off the bull's lunges with the pitchfork, the other scrambled over the fence into the lane. He gasped, "Is my wee girl hurt?" He was an enormous man, with shoulders like a blacksmith. He looked fully capable of handling his angry bull without the use of a pitchfork.

Holding the trembling child close in his arms, Ramesh looked over the little girl's head to her father. "Your daughter is unhurt, sahib."

"Thank God! Give her to me, man."

Gravely Ramesh handed the child to her father, who cuddled her and scolded her lovingly for sneaking into the field. At length he looked up, his eyes widening, as he seemed to notice for the first time, in his agitation, Ramesh's unusual garb.

"Who in the fiend's name be ye?" he blurted.

Ramesh made a low salaam, impressive as always despite the large hole in his robe. "I, sahib, am Ramesh Lal, the servant of the Lady Ware."

"Lady Ware? There be no such—" The farmer looked at the crest on the door of the landau. "Ye're the wife of Julian Ware," he said, almost accusingly. "Lord Daylesford's brother. Feller who's standing for election from Wolverton. Wants to send all our English boys off to be slaughtered by them bloodthirsty Froggies."

Chandra smiled at the farmer. "Yes, I'm Mrs. Ware. And you must be Mr. Gaines. I came here to solicit your vote, sir, on behalf of my husband, but I see it's a very bad time for you. You've been worried about your daughter, and you'll want to bring her straight home to her mother. I do hope, though, that you'll give some serious thought to my husband's candidacy. I assure you he *doesn't* wish to send our brave English boys off to be slaughtered!"

The farmer gave her a long, considering look. "Begging your pardon, Mrs. Ware, 'tisn't what I've been hearing. Your husband's opponent, Mr. Redgrave, *he* says folk like Mr. Ware will drag us into a blood bath in that there Peninsula." He inclined his head toward Ramesh. "I thank ye, sir, for saving my little girl. Good day to ye, and to ye, ma'am." Clasping the child more closely to his chest, he turned to walk up the lane.

Considerably chastened, Chandra drove back to Wolverton Abbey. Why had she thought she could influence the freeholders when Julian hadn't been able to move them during the past three weeks of the campaign? Not wanting to feel any more foolish than she did already, she didn't mention her visits to anyone.

Polling day finally came. As an early dusk was falling, the polls were declared closed. Waiting for the final count, the party from Wolverton Abbey sat in the best parlor of the Wolverton Arms, opposite the village green and the hustings. At one point, Julian gazed around the family circle, raising a glass of wine in salute. "You all know I'm not going to win," he said with a wry smile. "But it wasn't from want of trying, or from want of help from all of you. Thank you, every one of you."

Chandra raised her glass of wine to her lips to answer the toast, conscious of a deep sense of regret. From her years of living with Asaf Khan, despite his many faults, she'd learned to appreciate gallantry in any form. For a moment she wished, for Julian's own sake, and not for any social benefit she might gain for herself, that he had won the election.

Carstairs, Julian's campaign manager, burst into the inn parlor. "Mr. Ware, Mr. Ware, you've done it! The final count is Ware, 251, Redgrave, 237. They're calling for you on the hustings. You must come speak to them!"

Tristan leapt from his chair, shouting with joy. Irene rushed to Julian, throwing her arms around him and kissing his cheek. Lily followed suit, and, somewhat more sedately, Frederica. A sudden, expectant silence descended on the room. Feeling every eye upon her, Chandra slowly walked up to Julian. "Congratulations," she said, placing her hands on his shoulders. She lifted her head and pressed her lips to his. He tensed, and then, in a fraction of a second, his mouth responded. Their lips clung, the pressure deepened, and Julian's arms went around her waist. Her breathing quickening, Chandra pulled away. She forced a laugh, saying, "My love, we're making a spectacle of ourselves! And besides, your constituents await you."

Julian and his party walked out of the inn to the village green, which was thronged with electors and their families. Someone had lighted a vast bonfire, and the children in the crowd were cavorting joyously around it. Making his way through his jubilant supporters, smiling and reaching out to shake their hands, Julian reached the platform. He climbed up on it, waited through a loud burst of cheering, and lifted his arms for silence. "My good friends, you've heard me speak too often and too long these past few weeks. I won't bore you with another speech. I'll simply say that I appreciate your support from the bottom of my heart, and I'll do my best to represent your interests in the House."

The crowd gave him another round of enthusiastic cheers, and then Julian left the platform to join his family. As he walked toward them, two men intercepted him. The flickering flames of the bonfire picked out their figures in the gathering dusk clearly enough for Chandra to recognize them. One man was solidly built with a brimmed hat set squarely on his head. The other was an enormous man with shoulders like an ox. They spoke briefly to Julian, shook his hand, and moved off. When Julian came up to the family group, Ashley said curiously, "That was old Ebenezer Peddrick, wasn't it, and Jack Gaines with him? What did they have to say?"

174

"It seems that both gentlemen switched their votes to me, and so did many of their friends and tenants. That's why I won the election."

"By Jove, what made them do that?" asked Tristan blankly.

Julian gave Chandra a long, inscrutable look, but said nothing to her. To Tristan he replied, "I daresay it was my eloquence—or yours, Tris. You were coming on to be a regular Demosthenes!"

Much later that evening, after a family dinner of celebration at the Abbey, Chandra dismissed her abigail and waited for Julian's knock on the dressing room door. When he entered, she motioned to a pile of pillows and neatly folded blankets. "All ready for you. You must be grateful that this is the last night you'll be sleeping on that settee."

"I find I can get used to anything, including a permanent crick in my back," he said dryly. Making no move to pick up the blankets and pillows, he cleared his throat, saying, "The freeholders, Peddrick and Gaines, informed me tonight about your visits to them. Ebenezer Peddrick said his wife persuaded him to support me, largely, I gather, because 'Mrs. Ware's father died fighting for his country.' Jack Gaines changed his vote because 'that peculiar-looking feller in the long dress and funny hat' saved his daughter from being gored to death by a bull."

Julian began to laugh. "Oh, I wish I could have seen Ramesh snatching the child from the horns of that bull!" He cocked his head at her, his eyes still dancing with mirth. "Of course, I wouldn't have put it past Ramesh to incite the bull to charge in the first place, just to give himself the opportunity to be a hero!"

Chandra grinned. "No, no, you wrong him. Ramesh would never put a child in danger. You may find it hard to believe, but he's very fond of children."

Julian wasn't paying attention to what she was saying. Instead, he was staring at her, as if he were looking at her for the first time. He said abruptly, "That's a beautiful

175

dressing gown you're wearing. The creamy yellow color suits you exactly. But then, all the clothes you wear now are beautiful. *You're* beautiful . . ." He broke off, flushing. "Well, I wanted you to know I appreciate what you did. Apparently I owe you my seat in Parliament."

Their eyes locked together, and Chandra had the sensation of a slow heat rising in her vitals. Suddenly she wanted to feel those strong slender fingers on her silk-clad shoulders and around her waist, and the warm clinging touch of those sensual lips on . . .

"No!" she exclaimed.

Julian looked surprised. "You're being too modest. I'm certain I'd have lost the election if you hadn't gone to see the freeholders."

"No, no, that isn't what I meant." Chandra was beginning to recover herself. She couldn't allow Julian to realize how much his nearness affected her. "I only meant to say that you've no need to feel grateful to me. I did what I did out of self-interest. I wanted to protect my business investment in you."

His face changed. Smiling derisively, he said, "But, of course, I knew that. However, I can't seem to escape the strictures of my old nanny. She pounded into me that I must always, always, thank people who do me a favor. Consider yourself thanked, whatever your reasons were." He picked up the pile of pillows and blankets. "Good night, Chandra."

Chapter Eleven

The door of Chandra's sitting room was open. She glimpsed Julian walking down the corridor from his rooms and called out to him.

Lounging against the door frame, he surveyed the mound of papers on her desk. "Are those invitations or bills?" He sounded faintly amused.

There'd been a subtle change in her husband since their return from Buckinghamshire and the Wolverton elections a week ago, Chandra realized, although she couldn't put a finger on it. He was still cool, still aloof, and no one overhearing their private conversations could have mistaken their relationship for other than what it was, an essentially impersonal one, except when they were squaring off with each other over some vexatious topic. But most of Julian's prickly resentment seemed to be gone. He was no longer openly hostile; instead he appeared wary, as if he were waiting for something, as yet unknown, to develop in their association.

Most probably, Chandra mused, Julian's softened attitude was due to the assistance she'd given him during the election campaign, and it might not last, but at least their daily routine had ceased to resemble a carnage-strewn battlefield. Perhaps he was simply too busy with his new duties as Undersecretary for War to concern himself with his marital situation.

"They're invitations," Chandra said in reply to Julian's

question, waving at the stack of papers on her desk. "All the bills go to Ramesh now."

"Oh? How is he adjusting to the new regime?"

"Well, it hasn't been very long, of course. He's still convinced his way of dealing with tradesmen is superior, I think, but he's becoming reconciled to the wrongheaded English temperment."

Julian laughed. "He's also earning very large sums of money." Pushing himself away from the door frame, he asked, "You wanted to see me about something?"

"Yes. I have four requests for the honor of our company on Thursday evening next, and I can't decide which to accept." She handed him the invitations. "Help me choose."

He studied them carefully. "Lady Jersey's party would probably be the most amusing, but it's Lombard Street to a China orange you'll meet more influential people at Lady Melbourne's house." He raised an eyebrow. "That *is* what you're asking me, is it not? You want to know which of these affairs will best advance your social ambitions?"

"Precisely." Chandra met his eyes in a challenging look. "That's my only criterion."

His lip curling slightly, Julian handed the invitations back. "Then, since simple enjoyment of social pleasures has nothing to do with the matter at hand, I'd advise you to accept Lady Melbourne's invitation. She can do more for you than Lady Jersey. You'll excuse me? I have an appointment with Lord Castlereagh this morning."

"Wait, Julian. You haven't forgotten about our ball tonight?"

"How could I?" He grimaced. "For the past four days this house has been in an uproar. Servants cleaning every available surface, tradesmen delivering enough supplies to feed half of London. Even my valet has been affected. He thinks I should have ordered a new coat. No, I haven't forgotten. I'll return in good time to play host."

Nodding, he left the room. Chandra continued to scribble her acceptances and regrets. Frederica wandered in from a shopping expedition. "They're already putting

178

up the marquee over the entrance and laying the carpet on the steps," she reported excitedly. "And the florists are here, and best of all, it looks like beautiful weather for your first big entertainment, Chandra."

Chandra felt faintly troubled. Freddie seemed to have blocked the realities of their situation out of her mind. She was enjoying the heady excitement of being a part of London's social whirl, and she sometimes gave the impression that she expected their life in London to continue indefinitely. It was weeks now since she'd mentioned any fears or qualms about Chandra's scheme to discover Geoffrey Meredith's killer, or the fact that their stay in England, and Chandra's marriage, were purely temporary.

Suppressing her uneasiness, Chandra smiled affectionately at Frederica. Motioning to the package in the ex-governess's hand, she asked, "And what have you been up to this morning? Something to help you primp for the ball tonight?"

"My dear, at my age primping wouldn't do a deal of good," Frederica replied tartly. "No, I've been to Hatchard's book store. I found a copy of Mrs. Edgeworth's novel, *Belinda.* I enjoyed her *Castle Rackrent* so much."

"Did Lily go with you?"

"No. She went with Tristan to Spitalfields market to buy a goldfinch. A singing bird, mind you, on the day of your great ball! You'd suppose she'd have more important things to do today." Frederica paused, then said suddenly, "I think it was merely a pretext to go off with Tristan. Chandra, I'm becoming concerned about Lily. She spends far too much time with Tris. Before we know it, she might fancy herself in love with him."

Frowning, Chandra said, "You're exaggerating, surely. They're just friends. When I see them together, they often remind me of a pair of young puppies playing together. Lily's only seventeen, after all!"

"Yes, and well you know that in India, and in England, too, many young girls are mothers at seventeen!"

"Nonsense, Freddie," said Chandra impatiently, but

not without a shade of guilt, too. Lulled into security by Lily's apparent happiness, she hadn't been paying a great deal of attention to her niece of late.

Chandra had been grateful to Tristan for befriending Lily, who had been welcomed into the Ware family's social circle, but without any great enthusiasm. Lily had made no close female friends, and she was rarely invited to intimate gatherings where she could meet unmarried girls of her own age. The affairs to which she was invited were all large, crowded, and impersonal. The color bar was very much there, in Chandra's opinion, but Tristan's cheerful friendliness had gone a long way to obscuring it for Lily.

"Nonsense," Chandra said again, more to reassure herself than Frederica. "Tristan wouldn't allow himself to fall in love. Much as he resents his mother's constant efforts to pair him off with an heiress, he knows very well he must marry well. And he knows, too, that Lady Eversleigh and the Ware family would violently oppose such a match with a girl of Lily's background."

"'Where your treasure is, there will your heart be also,'" said Miss Banks, the clergyman's daughter.

"Don't you quote the Bible at me, Freddie," said Chandra crossly. "Look, do you have a spare minute? Please go see if Ramesh is being too autocratic with all the temporary servants we had to hire for the ball. I fear he's already struck terror into some of their hearts."

"Oh-h-h," breathed the abigail, settling a toque of feather-light green Parisian gauze on Chandra's head and stepping back to view the effect. "Oh, ma'am, you look like a fairy princess!"

Chandra rose from the dressing table and walked over to the cheval glass to get a full-length view of herself. She did look like a fairy princess, she thought, or at least as lovely as one. She could hardly have failed to do so in this beautiful gown of gossamer white net over an emerald green satin petticoat with a flounce of exquisite lace at the hem, trimmed with tiny knots of green leaves and miniature yellow roses. The dress had scarcely any bodice, with the neckline cut so low and the waist so high that rather a large amount of creamy skin was exposed. Asaf Khan's elaborate diamond necklace complemented rather than overpowered the gown, and after all these weeks of Irene's careful tutelage, Chandra knew better than to pile on several additional strands of pearls and a number of gold chains.

With one last look in the mirror, Chandra picked up her embroidered reticule and left the bedchamber. As she emerged from her door, Julian was swinging down the corridor from his rooms. He stopped short at the sight of her. Her heart caught at the quick blue flame that ignited his eyes. He drew a deep breath. "Congratulations," he said quietly. "You look utterly magnificent. There's not a woman in London who can touch you tonight."

"Thank you." She glanced at his long, lean form in the superbly fitting black tailcoat and breeches and the white-on-white damask waistcoat and masterfully tied cravat. "You—you look complete to a shade yourself."

Smiling faintly, he extended his arm. "Then shall we go downstairs and be magnificent together?" he said gravely.

They walked down the staircase to the front hall, where Ramesh stood erect as a ramrod in his best brocade *izar*, confined at the waist with a brilliant red cummerbund. The turban wound around the tall conical cap was red also. He bowed low to his master and mistress. To Chandra he said, "Lady, will you inspect your house to ensure it is in perfect order to receive your guests?"

Chandra spoke in Hindi. "I don't need to inspect the house. The arrangements have been under your guiding hand, my good old friend, and I know all is in order."

The wonderful mustachios registered Ramesh's gratification. "I do but my feeble best, lady."

Pulling out his watch, Julian said, "It's time to go to the ballroom, Chandra. Our guests will soon start arriving."

An hour later, when she and Julian had left the receiving line and the dancing was in full swing, Chandra realized she had a triumph on her hands. Not a soul who mattered in London society was missing from the ranks of her guests. The government was well represented by several cabinet ministers, including Lord Castlereagh and the Prime Minister himself, Lord Portland. The influential patronesses of Almack's were there, and the leading hostesses of the ton. Beau Brummell came to show off his perfect tailoring and his wit. And, toward midnight, the supreme accolade: puffing for breath after the climb up the staircase from the foyer, the Prince of Wales, red-faced and obese, walked slowly into the ballroom.

His rather prominent eyes beaming with admiration, His Royal Highness raised Chandra's hand to his lips. To Julian he said with an affable smile that took the sting out of his words, "Can't imagine how an ordinary dull feller like you managed to catch such a beautiful wife."

"It was pure luck, sir, or perhaps it was clean living and the purity of my soul," Julian replied solemnly.

"What? Eh?" Momentarily the prince looked confused. Then he burst into a laugh, clapping a hand to Julian's shoulder. "You sly dog!"

"If you'll come with me, sir, I daresay you'd like a rubber or two of whist before supper."

Chandra's memories of the ball were a series of shifting, disconnected scenes. Basil Forrest arrived late, doubtless to avoid Julian in the receiving line, and kept strictly out of his host's way. His dark, spaniel-like eyes turned wistful when he realized Chandra's dance card was completely filled. However, he managed to sit with her for a few minutes when he fetched her a glass of ratafia. "I was pleased, but rather surprised, to receive an invitation to the ball, Chandra."

"But why? You're my friend, even if I don't see as much of you as I'd like."

"Well . . . you know." Basil jerked his head in Julian's direction. "He don't like me. Chandra, I thought you'd be interested in this: I met a feller the other day who knew your father in Bombay."

"Bombay?" For a moment Chandra was confused.

Geoffrey Meredith had, so far as she knew, never set foot in the Bombay presidency. His entire Indian service had been spent in Calcutta and Bhulamphur. Then her mind cleared. As long as she remained in England, she told herself, she must remember to think of Freddie's brother, Walter Banks, as her father. "Did your friend know my father well?" she asked.

"No, no, a mere casual acquaintance. He was surprised to hear that Captain Banks became so wealthy. Indigo plantations, wasn't it? Or so I told him."

Extricating herself from Basil with some difficulty, Chandra sat out the next dance with her sister-in-law.

"Lady Melbourne was telling me that you and Julian were the handsomest couple she'd ever met," said Irene with a teasing smile. "And according to the *on dit*, that's the opinion of an expert, at least so far as male beauty is concerned!"

Beneath the determinedly bright smile, Irene didn't look happy. There were dark circles under her eyes, marring the delicate porcelain skin.

"Aren't you feeling well, Irene? You shouldn't have felt obliged to come. It's only a ball, after all."

"Now you sound like Ashley." This time Irene's attempt at a smile was a total failure.

Taking her sister-in-law's hand, Chandra said, "What's wrong? Won't you let me help? You've done so much for me, I'd like to repay a little of my debt to you."

Irene shook her head, blinking against a film of tears in her eyes.

"Tell me, Irene."

"I—oh, it's Ashley." Irene kept her eyes lowered, and her soft voice was nearly inaudible. "There's something dreadfully wrong, and he won't talk to me about it. You know how he always tries to keep worries from me. But I know him so well, you see. I can tell when he's troubled. For the past few days, something has been tearing him apart. Chandra, I can't bear it. I love him so much. He's all I have, he's all that matters to me in the world."

Chandra felt a sudden pang, almost a physical pain, at

183

the throbbing note of adoration in Irene's voice. She knew Ashley returned his wife's love in full measure. What must it be like, to be loved so completely, and would she never experience it herself? She said slowly, "Irene, would you like me to speak to Julian?"

"Oh, no. Oh, please don't." Looking up, Irene drew a sharp breath. "There's Ashley, coming toward us. Talk about something else—tell me a joke—he mustn't realize I'm blue-deviled."

When Ashley came up, Chandra took a closer look at him. She'd noticed earlier in the evening that his limp was more pronounced than usual. Now she observed the deep lines in his face. The blue eyes, so like Julian's, were dark and lifeless.

He bent over Irene. "I think I should take you home, love. You look so tired." To Chandra he said, "You won't mind if we go, I'm sure." He spoke with his usual cold politeness.

Chandra thought, *If I stayed married to Julian for twenty years, Ashley would never totally accept me as a member of the family*. Aloud, she said, "Ashley is right, Irene. There's no reason for you to stay. I'll come see you tomorrow."

As she stood watching them walk slowly toward the entrance of the ballroom, Julian strolled up to her. "Is Irene ill?"

"No. A bit tired, that's all. Ashley's taking her home."

"Good. She always tries to do too much." Chandra heard the affection in his voice. Julian was very fond of his sister-in-law. He looked down at Chandra, an ironical smile wreathing his lips. "You realize, I presume, that with this ball tonight you've achieved your ambition? As a hostess of the ton, you're a *succès fou*. By tomorrow, the prattle boxes will be comparing you with Lady Jersey, or Countess Lieven." The irony in his smile grew more pronounced. "Actually, have you considered that I've become superfluous? You really don't need me any longer to sponsor you and introduce you."

He was baiting her, Chandra knew that, but it was more

than that. He was making it clear he'd like nothing better than to be free of her ahead of schedule. "Oh, but I do need you, Julian," she said coolly. "Imagine the scandal if we were to separate after only a few weeks of marriage."

But his attention had wandered. Mrs. Artemus Taney was bearing down on them. "Oh, God," he muttered, "I didn't know you'd invited that dreadful woman here tonight." He composed his face into a stony politeness as Mrs. Taney stepped up to them.

"Mr. and Mrs. Ware, I've been dying to give you my joyful news," gushed the wife of the East India Company director. "My dear husband has just acquired an estate in Buckinghamshire near Wolverton Abbey. Artemus tells me there are splendid coverts on the property. You must join us for the hunting in the autumn, Mr. Ware."

"Er—thank you, but I'm rarely in Buckinghamshire these days," Julian said lamely.

"Pray excuse me, Mrs. Taney, I must have a word with my aunt," said Chandra, taking the coward's way out and ignoring Julian's anguished glance. She knew she would hear from him later on the subject. She sighed. As long as there was any possibility that the Taneys and their East India Company friends could supply her with clues to her father's death, she must continue to invite them to her house. But oh, how Julian did hate to be toad-eaten!

Unfortunately, associating with the elder Taneys also meant associating with their obnoxious son, she reflected, spotting Alfred Taney off to the side of the room, talking to Lily and Tristan. Smitten by calf love for Lily, Alfred had continued to haunt the house, although Lily never responded to his overtures. As Chandra watched the trio, Lily suddenly walked away in the direction of the ballroom door. Her face was flaming. His hands clenched, Tristan made a slight abrupt movement toward Alfred, then followed Lily.

Oh, the devil, thought Chandra. What had the dreadful Alfred been saying to Lily? She glanced quickly around. A country dance was just forming. She didn't think many people had observed the brief confrontation between Lily and Alfred. Thank God for Tris. He'd soothe the girl's ruffled feelings. She turned, fixing a bright smile on her face, at the sound of a voice behind her.

"I believe this is our dance, Mrs. Ware?"

"Indeed it is, Lord Castlereagh."

As they walked to join the set, the Secretary for War murmured, "I've been hearing tales of your electioneering in Bucks. May I thank you on behalf of my department? Without your help, I'd be minus a most valuable undersecretary."

Chandra said saucily, "I assure you I mean no offense, sir, but some day I'd like to help Julian be Secretary for War himself!"

The expression softening the features of the notoriously frozen-faced Castlereagh might almost be described as a smile.

As Chandra was coming off the floor with his lordship after the dance, Tristan's mother hurried up to her. Muttering an apology to Castlereagh, Lady Eversleigh drew Chandra aside. "You must come with me, Chandra. It's urgent."

"Come with you where? Georgiana, I have guests. I can't leave—"

"Only to the morning room. But you must come, if you're to prevent all of us from landing in the basket. Disaster is staring us in the face!"

Chandra stared at Lady Eversleigh's agitated face. "What disaster?" she asked, bewildered. "You sound positively dicked in the nob, Georgiana."

"Please keep your voice down," hissed Lady Eversleigh. "Do you want everyone to hear us?" She put her hand on Chandra's arm. Her fingers felt like talons. "Well? Are you coming?"

Shrugging, Chandra allowed Georgiana to lead her away. In her present mood, Lady Eversleigh was quite capable of making a scene. They walked in silence down the staircase to the ground floor, past the drawing room and the open door of the library, where a number of guests, the Prince of Wales among them, sat playing cards. Lady

Eversleigh threw open the door of the morning room and pulled Chandra inside. "There they are," she exclaimed, pointing dramatically to Tristan and Lily. "Speak to them! Tell your sister she must not ruin my son's life. Tell Tristan he must remember what he owes to his family. Neither of them will listen to me!"

Tristan, red-faced and angry, and Lily, pale and trembling, stood together with clasped hands, staring defiantly but not speaking. With a sinking feeling that disaster might well be creeping up on her, Chandra said to Georgiana, "What's happened?"

"Well, a few minutes ago I chanced to look into this room—"

"Don't tell whiskers, Mama," said Tristan coldly. "The fact is, you followed Lily and me in here."

Her eyes shooting sparks, Lady Eversleigh snapped, "And if I did? I merely came to remind you how very indiscreet it was of you and Lily to go off for an intimate tête-à-tête in the midst of Chandra's ball."

"Indiscreet, my eye and Betty Martin," said Tristan hotly. "Alfred Taney made an improper advance to Lily. She was so distressed that she retreated to this room, and I came along after her to comfort her."

"And that was why I found the pair of you passionately embracing, was it?" retorted his mother. "Some comfort!"

Lily's pallor flamed into an embarrassed red. "You're twisting things, Lady Eversleigh, making it all sound so ugly. Tris and I haven't done anything wrong. We told you—"

Georgiana swung on Chandra. "They told me they'd fallen in love and planned to marry. Well? What do you have to say to that?"

"Is this true, Lily?" Chandra felt her fingernails digging into her palms as she clenched her hands by her side.

"Yes." Lily's words came in a rush. "It all happened so fast, Chandra, but Tris and I meant to tell you right away, you and Freddie."

Chandra said in a tight voice, "Lily, I think it would be best if you went to your bedchamber. If you were to return

187

to the ballroom, someone would be bound to notice how upset you are."

"But, Chandra—"

"Please do as I say."

Pressing her lips tightly together, Lily gave Tristan one last, long look and left the room.

"Tristan, I doubt that you're much interested in dancing at this point," said Chandra. "I daresay you'd prefer to leave the ball. Georgiana, perhaps you'd like to leave also."

Lady Eversleigh swelled with outrage. "Well! You're ejecting me as if I were some dunning tradesman? Your husband's only aunt? Without the courtesy of discussing with me what we're to do in this grave family emergency?"

"Mama." Tristan took his mother's arm. His face was pale and set. "Chandra is right. We're none of us in a state to discuss this"—his mouth twisted—"this *emergency*. Come. I'll take you home."

Chandra went back to the ballroom. Somehow she got through the rest of the dancing and the elaborate supper and the farewells to her guests without betraying her worries about Lily. Except possibly to Julian.

Standing with Chandra at the door of the ballroom as the last of their guests went down the stairs, Julian remarked, looking at her with curious eyes. "You don't seem to be relishing your triumph. Why not, I wonder?" He flashed her another of his ironic smiles. "I don't remember much Latin from my misspent days at Eton, but one phrase leaps to mind: *'Veni, vidi, vici.'*"

Chandra's badly frayed nerves snapped. "I'm no Julius Caesar, and I haven't conquered anybody," she said crossly. "And I'm in no mood for your little jokes. I *am* tired, and I'm going to bed. Good night, Julian."

She went up the stairs, aware that Julian's surprised gaze was boring into the back of her head. Reaching the door of her bedchamber, she hesitated, then continued down the corridor to Lily's room. With only a peremptory knock, she pushed open the door and walked in. Lily sat on the edge of her bed, mopping her eyes with a damp handkerchief. Frederica sat beside her, her arm around Lily's shoulder.

Frederica rose and walked over to Chandra, saying in a low voice, "I was afraid something like this might happen. You wouldn't believe me this morning, when I warned you Tris and Lily might be falling in love."

"Well, the damage had already been done, it seems," said Chandra wryly. She walked over to the bed. "Lily, dear, I know you've very unhappy—"

Wiping away a fresh flood of tears, Lily quavered, "Lady Eversleigh said the most dreadful things. She said if Tris married me he'd be cast out of society. His friends would all abandon him. He'd be forced to sell out of his regiment. Chandra, none of those things are true, are they?"

Chandra hesitated, picking her words carefully. "Georgiana was coming it too strong, perhaps, but . . . Lily, it's true you can't marry Tristan. I'm sure you know why."

Swallowing painfully, Lily said, "Lady Eversleigh said it was because I'm only half English." The hot blood flooded her face. She looked away, whispering, "Except she didn't put it like that. She said—she said I had mongrel blood."

"Oh, what a cruel thing to say," cried Frederica. "Georgiana Eversleigh is a monster."

"She's not a very nice woman," Chandra agreed. "She doesn't care a fig for anybody's feelings save her own. But she's right about this, Lily. Society would regard Tristan's marriage to you as a disgrace because you're a half-caste."

"But, Chandra, why? I know my father was an Indian, but my birth has never made any difference to you, or to Freddie. Nor to Grandpapa Meredith. I remember how kind and loving he always was. And it doesn't matter a whit to Tris, either, that I have mixed blood."

"It matters to London society. They wouldn't accept you as Tristan's wife. Be sensible. Think about our voyage from India. Remember how many of the ladies snubbed you? Think about your life here. Haven't you noticed how

189

careful all the fond mamas are to keep their daughters from your contaminating company?"

Wincing, Lily said fiercely, "A plague on society. Tris and I will be happy just with each other. The only thing is . . . Tris is worried that he won't have enough money to support me. But you'll help, won't you, Chandra? Asaf Khan left you that huge fortune—"

"No, I will not. I won't lift a finger to help you marry Tris. In fact, I forbid you to marry him. It would be a tragedy for both of you."

Lily clenched her small fists and glared at Chandra. "Then we'll get married without your help! You can't stop us!"

"We'll see about that. If necessary, I'll send you out of England with Freddie, to a place where Tristan can't find you, until you come to your senses."

Wailing loudly, Lily threw herself on the bed in a storm of tears. An unfamiliar expression of hostility appeared on Frederica's face. She said, more angrily than she'd ever spoken to Chandra, "You're as bad as Georgiana. What possessed you to speak so cruelly to the child? You may be able to dictate to Lily, but don't think you can tell me what to do." She sat down on the bed, patting Lily's shoulder, murmuring broken phrases of comfort.

Throwing up her hands, Chandra left the room. In the corridor she collided with Julian. He put out a hand to prevent her from falling. "What's the matter?" he asked.

She shook her head. "Nothing."

"Don't pitch that gammon to me. You're in the megrims. And I heard somebody crying out." He glanced at the closed door of Lily's bedchamber. "Is it Lily?"

"No. Yes." She made a quick resolve. "Julian, I must talk to you." Taking his hand, she pulled him along the hallway to her room and closed the door. Her abigail, waiting to put her to bed, stood up, gazing uncertainly at Julian. "Come back in half an hour," Chandra told her.

After the maid had left, Julian glanced around the room and remarked, with a grin, "What do you suppose the ton would say if they knew this was only the second time I've set foot in my lady wife's bedchamber?" At Chandra's hostile look, he shrugged. Sitting down, he spread his arms over the back of his chair and settled himself comfortably. "What's this about Lily?"

Chandra paced the floor nervously. "She's fallen in love with Tristan, and he with her, that's what. They're talking of getting married. I can't make Lily see reason. I want you to talk to Tristan."

"No."

She stared at him in disbelief. "Why not?"

"Because I'm not Tris's guardian. He's of age. I won't interfere in his life."

"You can't mean you approve of this match!"

"No, I don't. Lily's a lovely girl. I like her very much. But—"

"But she's not good enough to marry your cousin. Isn't that what you were about to say?"

Julian bit his lip. "No. It isn't that Lily isn't good enough," he floundered. "Oh, the devil, you know as well as I do that a man in Tris's walk of life must choose a suitable partner, a girl of good breeding who matches him in family background."

"Unless such a man needs money badly—to keep himself out of debtors' prison, for example—in which case he can lower his standards," Chandra exclaimed in a sudden flash of anger.

Julian's face turned to stone.

"I'm sorry," she said after a moment. "That wasn't very helpful. I agree with you that a match between Tris and Lily would be very ill-advised, because of her background. I think she, at least, might be totally ostracized. I know quite well she's been tolerated by London society only because she's the great Julian Ware's sister-in-law and a connection of the Earl of Daylesford. I'm convinced your Aunt Georgiana will never accept Lily as Tristan's wife, nor will your brother Ashley. Under those circumstances, do you suppose anyone else will receive them?"

"Probably not."

"Then do something!"

"There's nothing I can do. I've no authority over Tris. He must live his own life."

"Julian, please reconsider," Chandra pleaded. "Tristan idolizes you. I know he'd listen to your advice." Memories of her sister Phoebe's tragedy flooded into Chandra's mind. Speaking in a low voice, almost as if she were talking to herself, she muttered, "Lily simply doesn't realize what bitter unhappiness she faces in a mixed marriage. The hostile, hateful glances. The constant snubs. The vile gossip behind her back. The worries about her children's future . . ."

Chandra fell silent. She stood staring into space, remembering those nights in her childhood when she'd lain awake, listening to Phoebe's muffled sobbing in the next room, and how often she'd wondered why the officers' wives in Bhulamphur never invited Phoebe to their quarters.

Julian's voice broke into her reverie. "You seem to know a great deal about Anglo-Eurasian marriages," he said curiously. "Was that how it was with your father's second wife? And is that why you're so afraid for Lily?"

For several seconds Chandra stared uncomprehendingly at Julian, before she realized how close she'd come to revealing the true circumstances of her background. He knew nothing of the Meredith family and her sister Phoebe's love affair that had resulted in Lily's illegitimate birth, and he must continue to remain in ignorance. He must continue to believe that Chandra's "father" was a Captain Banks, who had married as his second wife a woman of color.

"Yes," Chandra said after a moment. "That's why I'm afraid for Lily. My—my stepmother was a very unhappy woman. She was never really accepted by my father's English friends." She looked hopefully at Julian. "Now that you know, will you speak to Tristan?"

He shook his head. "A gentleman doesn't tell another gentleman, even his own cousin, how to conduct his life. If Tris asks my opinion, I'll give it to him. But I won't thrust it on him."

Chandra glared at him as he sat, calm and unmoved, in her favorite chair beside the fire. She burst out, "Oh, you smug Englishmen, with your persnickety notions of honor! Well, *I* won't stand still and do nothing. I'll prevent this marriage if I have to shut Lily up in a nunnery to do it!"

Julian rose from his chair and walked to the door, where he turned to say coolly, "You have the instincts of an autocrat, Chandra. Someday you'll discover you can't always have your own way."

Chapter Twelve

On the following morning, as Chandra's abigail was putting the final touches to her hair, Frederica came to the bedchamber. Chandra nodded a dismissal to her abigail.

The ex-governess looked as though she'd spent a sleepless night. She said abruptly. "I was rude to you last night. I'm sorry."

"It's all right. You were upset. So was I."

"Yes. Chandra, you and I have talked so often about Lily's future. We've agreed she'd have a better chance of making a good marriage in some place without a color bar. Heaven knows, I wouldn't have wanted Lily to fall in love with Tristan, but now that it's happened . . ." Frederica spread her hands helplessly. "Is the marriage really such a hopeless idea? Shouldn't we at least think about accepting it? The child is so unhappy."

"Better a little unhappiness now than a great deal of unhappiness later," said Chandra sharply. "Have you forgotten how much Phoebe suffered? Lily's very young. After we leave England, she'll gradually forget about Tris."

"Oh." Frederica looked a little startled. "I don't think Lily's thought very much recently about leaving England."

It hasn't occurred to you, Freddie, either, Chandra thought.

Frederica said, with a hint of nervousness, "Tristan is

downstairs in the morning room. He wants to talk to you."

Chandra didn't have the faintest doubt about the topic Tristan wanted to discuss. She gave the governess a hard look. So Tristan had first sought out Freddie as an ally, and obviously she'd encouraged him. Shrugging, Chandra said, "All right. I'll see him. I daresay it's best to make my position crystal clear from the very beginning."

Frederica's face fell. "Chandra, you won't be too severe? Perhaps I should go with you."

"No, I'd rather see him alone."

Tristan rose when Chandra entered the morning room. He looked more serious and, yes, older, than she had ever observed him. "Good morning, Chandra. I believe you know why I'm here. I want your permission to marry Lily."

Sitting down, Chandra said calmly, "I can't give it." She reiterated the arguments she'd used with Julian the night before.

Tristan heard her out. "I don't care what people will think," he said mulishly.

"Your mother?"

"I'll take care of Mama," he snapped.

"Well, then, what about your colonel? Or, rather, his wife? I understand she's the daughter of an earl. Very proud. A high stickler. Do you think she'd welcome Lily into the regiment?"

Tristan's expression changed.

"And how about Irene?"

"Irene?" Tristan was outraged. "Irene is the sweetest, kindest—"

"Do you think she could hold out against Ashley, if he decided not to receive Lily into the family? You know, better than I, how much he prides himself on the Ware family lineage." Chandra rose. "I must go, Tris. I promised Irene I'd visit her this morning. Think about what I've said. You wouldn't want Lily's marriage to you to be a source of unhappiness to her, rather than joy."

Half an hour later, a footman ushered Chandra up the

195

stairs to the second floor of Daylesford House. Irene was resting on a chaise longue in her sitting room, her legs covered with a fleecy Angora shawl. She was very pale, and the dark circles that had marred her fair complexion the evening before were still visible under her eyes.

"Oh, Irene, you don't look well," said Chandra guiltily. "You shouldn't have come to the ball. It was too much for you."

"Not a bit of it. I'm just a little tired," Irene replied with an attempt at cheerfulness. Almost at once her mouth drooped. "I don't think Ashley slept at all last night," she murmured, half to herself. "Oh, if I only knew what was troubling him, I might be able to help." She gave her shoulders a shake. "Perhaps it's simply that his leg is paining him more than usual," she said, though it was obvious she didn't believe what she was saying, and gracefully turned their conversation to other subjects.

Chandra left Irene after a short visit, feeling depressed that she couldn't offer more comfort to her sister-in-law. As she came down the stairs, she slowed her steps in surprise. Ashley was waiting for her at the foot of the staircase.

"Chandra, will you please come into the library? I'd like to speak to you."

In the library, Chandra settled into a chair and gazed curiously at Ashley, who seemed too restless to sit down. He paced up and down, his left leg dragging noticeably. The deep lines in his haggard face made him look a generation older than Julian, although the brothers were only three years apart in age.

"Chandra, I need your help," Ashley began abruptly, forcing out the words as if they hurt his throat to say them. Which was probably true, thought Chandra. Ashley had never bothered to hide from her how much he resented Julian's forced marriage to a woman who was far beneath the Ware family socially. How it must gall Ashley now to be obliged to ask that woman for a favor.

Pausing in his restless pacing, Ashley faced Chandra, his hands clenched at his sides. "I must have twenty-five thousand pounds immediately," he blurted. "I can't tell you when I'll be able to pay the money back." A faint color came into his pale cheeks, and he looked down at the floor. "Probably never," he muttered.

"That's a very large sum," Chandra observed after a moment.

Ashley glanced up quickly. "Too large even for you? Julian seems to think you're as rich as Croesus," he sneered. He cut himself short, biting his lip. "Forgive me, please. I—I'm not myself today."

Chandra didn't allow herself to display any sign of anger. "I *am* very rich, Ashley. And I'm willing to help you, but twenty-five-thousand pounds is an exceedingly great amount, even for me. If this is a gambling loss, a debt of honor, as the Pinks of the ton put it, I fear I can't advance you the money. I don't believe in debts of honor."

"Oh, God, if only it *were* a debt of honor . . ." Ashley swung away, going to the window where he stared blindly out at the plane trees in Berkeley Square. After an interval, he turned around, his face ravaged. "I'm being black-mailed. For a number of years I've patronized an establishment run by a woman named Caroline Onslow. She's now retiring. It's been suggested to her that she publish her memoirs. For a substantial sum, she's willing to omit my name from these memoirs. She's asking for twenty-five thousand pounds."

Chandra said, "This 'establishment,' I take it, is a brothel?"

Ashley's mouth twisted. "Caroline Onslow preferred to call it a 'palace of pleasure.' She was used to boast about her exclusivity. She served only the top ranks of society, the aristocracy, the gentry, rich cits if they had enough money. For them, she provided the most accomplished ladybirds, a luxuriously appointed house, and excellent food."

Giving him a direct look, Chandra asked, "Why are you so disturbed, Ashley? I understand it's not uncommon for gentlemen to go to these places. Doubtless you'd be humiliated to have your name mentioned in this book, but you'd be one of many. I collect your reputation might be a trifle tarnished, perhaps, but not ruined."

"You don't understand," said Ashley in a strangled voice. "I can't allow Irene to be hurt."

Chandra hesitated. "I don't mean to pry, but surely Irene wouldn't be too shocked to learn you'd patronized a brothel? From something Julian once told me, you and she haven't been . . ." Her voice trailed away in embarrassment.

"You're trying to say that Irene and I haven't been living together as man and wife for some years now, because of her delicate health. That's correct. The doctors say a pregnancy could be fatal." Ashley's voice was so brittle that Chandra knew he was clinging to his self-control by the slenderest of threads. "And, yes, I daresay she may suspect I've been seeking physical release elsewhere. If she does suspect, I believe she's forgiven me for it."

"Well, then . . . ?"

Ashley's false calm broke, and his anguish was out in the open. "God, Chandra, you still don't understand. I haven't been sleeping with Caroline Onslow's prime lightskirts. I couldn't bear to touch them. Irene's face kept getting in the way. So I turned to little girls, eight, ten years old. I've been making love to children."

Chandra gasped. The sick disgust she was feeling must have been apparent on her face.

"Go on, say it," exclaimed Ashley bitterly. "You can't hate me any more than I hate myself. But you see, don't you, why I can't permit Caroline Onslow to put my name in her damned memoirs? It would kill Irene."

"Yes," said Chandra, thinking of Irene's fragile health and her near idolization of Ashley. "I think it might."

"I'd gladly kill myself if I thought it would do any good," Ashley went on dully. "Caroline couldn't blackmail me if I were dead. I told her as much. She laughed at me. Whether I was alive or dead, it made no difference. She said she'd get the money from my brother and his rich wife. She said the Ware family would pay anything to keep such a juicy scandal out of print."

198

Desperation cracked Ashley's voice. "Chandra, will you help me? Five days ago, Caroline Onslow sent me an ultimatum: produce the twenty-five thousand pounds by Friday—that's tomorrow—or she'd write to Julian. Please don't allow that to happen. Finding out about this filth would destroy every shred of love and respect Julian has for me. And it would be so useless. There's no reason why he should know about this. He doesn't have any money. It's you who must make the decision to pay or not to pay Caroline Onslow."

It took Chandra mere seconds to make up her mind. She'd come to love Irene, and she couldn't allow her sister-in-law's happiness and her health to be destroyed. And, despite Julian's arrogance, his undisguised eagerness to be rid of her, she had no wish to inflict unnecessary pain on him, either. She knew how much he loved his brother. Also, Chandra reminded herself, it would certainly damage her budding social reputation if Ashley's shameful secret were exposed.

"Very well, Ashley. I'll give you the money, subject to two conditions."

The hope died on his face. "What are they?"

Trying to keep the distaste out of her voice, Chandra said, "For Irene's sake, I want your promise that you'll never lay a finger on a child again."

Ashley turned a pasty white. "I promise."

"Good. In addition, you must allow me to take charge of the arrangements to pay this woman."

"You mean you'll go to see Caroline? No! I won't have it! I haven't sunk so low that I'd let you contaminate yourself by having anything to do with that harridan."

"I'm sorry, Ashley. I must insist."

"But why—?" Ashley made a bitter gesture of complete surrender. "All right. I can't stop you."

"Where does this woman live?"

"Henrietta Place."

Chandra lifted an eyebrow. "A very good address."

Ashley smiled mirthlessly. "Nothing but the best for our Caroline and her toplofty clientele."

Rising, Chandra said, "I'll take care of this right away. You can put it out of your mind."

As she walked to the door, Ashley said, "Wait, Chandra. I haven't thanked you."

Chandra paused. Her clear gaze skewered him. "I don't want your thanks. I'm not doing this for you."

"Yes. I know. It's for Irene." Ashley paused. "Chandra, you won't tell Julian?"

"No. Goodbye, Ashley."

Leaving Daylesford House, Chandra ordered the coachman to take her to Harley's Bank in Lombard Street. On the long drive into the City along Oxford Street, her thoughts wandered. She should be wallowing in enjoyable memories of her triumph at the ball last night, she reflected ruefully. Instead, the ball seemed to have receded into the past. It didn't seem important, now, after everything that had happened since. Lily's love affair with Tristan. The revelation of Ashley's shameful hidden life.

In Lombard Street, Simon's clerk greeted the bank's most important customer with a beaming smile and showed her into his employer's inner office immediately, without bothering to check with Simon. "Mr. Harley's free, Mrs. Ware, and I know he'll want to see you."

His face lighting up, Simon came from behind his desk to grasp Chandra's hand. "It's been so long since I've seen you," he said wistfully. He looked with frank admiration at her pelisse of pale apricot-colored sarcenet and the Leghorn bonnet tied with matching ribbons. "You look so beautiful."

Sitting down opposite the desk, Chandra said, her eyes twinkling, "Thank you. I'm only beginning to realize what a perfect guy I must have looked when you first met me." She added reproachfully, "It's not my fault we haven't seen each other recently. Why didn't you come to my ball last night?"

He shook his head, smiling faintly. Returning to his chair behind his desk, he said, "It was kind of you to send me an invitation, but you shouldn't have done it. Ours is a business, not a social, relationship."

"Simon! We're friends!"

He shook his head again. "I'm your man of business. I don't belong among your aristocratic friends." He looked at her keenly. "It's been a while since we talked. I don't wish to pry, but . . . Are you satisfied with your arranged marriage? Has it accomplished what you thought it would?"

"Oh, yes. I'm well on my way to becoming the most prominent hostess in London! Would you believe it, the Prince of Wales was a guest at my ball. Our future king!" Chandra cleared her throat. "Simon, I need twenty-five thousand pounds. Immediately. Well, by tomorrow morning at the latest, but I'd prefer to have the money this afternoon."

The young banker's steady gray eyes gleamed with a sudden anger. "I was afraid of this," he snapped. "Ware had a bad night at the tables, did he? It was only a matter of time before he started playing ducks and drakes with your fortune. The man's been a gambler for years. You don't have to allow him a shilling, you know. That trust I drew up protects your assets absolutely."

"Simon, for heaven's sake, the twenty-five thousand pounds isn't for Julian. It's—" Chandra cut herself short. "The money's not for Julian," she repeated.

Simon said abruptly, "Chandra, are you being blackmailed?"

Chandra gasped. "No. Certainly not." Her voice took on an irritated edge. "And not to be rude, but I must tell you I think you *are* prying into my affairs. Now, when can I have the money?"

Simon gulped. "Not until I find out what you intend to do with it."

"You've gone too far, Simon. It's my money, and I can do what I like with it. Either you produce that twenty-five thousand pounds by tomorrow morning, or I transfer my account to another bank."

Pale, but resolute, Simon said, "That's your prerogative. I think you *are* being blackmailed, however, and as long as I'm your banker I won't advance you the money to victimize yourself. What you don't realize is, if you pay what these people demand, they'll keep coming back until they've bled you dry."

Chandra's anger faded. She said, smiling, "Simon, we like each other too much to be cutting up stiff like this. I know you're trying to help, but I assure you, on my word of honor, I don't need help." A note of steel sounded in her voice. "Much as I value your friendship, however, I can't allow you to dictate to me. I meant what I said: either your provide the money, *my own money*, or I find another banker."

After a long pause, Simon's shoulders slumped in defeat. "Yes. All right. I'll bring the money to you in a few hours." He hesitated, turning a pleading gaze on Chandra. "Promise me you'll be careful. You could be in danger."

"Simon, don't worry. I'll be in no danger at all."

True to his word, Simon arrived in Grosvenor Square slightly more than two hours later. A footman showed him into the morning room, where Chandra was waiting, dressed for the street and pacing impatiently up and down the room.

"Thank you for being so quick," Chandra said, reaching for the bank draft in Simon's hand.

He put the hand holding the bank draft behind his back. "I won't let you go alone to wherever it is you're going. I'm coming with you."

"Simon, you ninnyhammer," began Chandra in exasperation. She paused. She needed the twenty-five thousand pounds by tomorrow at the latest. There wasn't time to transfer funds to another bank. "What about a compromise? You can go with me, but you'll remain in the carriage while I transact my business. No, wait," she added at the automatic protest she saw forming on his lips. "If I don't return to the carriage, say, in half an hour, you can come charging in after me. That's my final offer."

"I accept," said Simon reluctantly.

"Done. I'll ring for my carriage."

In the foyer, a few minutes later, Chandra and Simon encountered Julian as the footman admitted him into the house. He looked at them with a faint air of surprise. "Off somewhere, are you? Dare I guess, Harley, that you're taking my wife to investigate some profitable new business scheme that will increase her already vast fortune?"

Chandra heard the tinge of mockery in Julian's voice, mingled with condescension. She'd long suspected he felt nettled by the realization that Simon not only knew all the details of their forced marriage, but had also been instrumental in arranging it. Simon apparently heard the note of mockery, too. He colored, although he kept his voice composed as he replied, "Come now, Mr. Ware. You must know I can't divulge my client's financial affairs to an outsider."

The barb struck home. A momentary glint of anger showed in Julian's eyes. Quickly recovering himself, he said smoothly, "I stand rebuked. Your professional discretion is admirable." He bowed. "Good day, Harley. Chandra, do enjoy your excursion."

As he and Chandra emerged from the door of the house, Simon muttered, "That husband of yours obviously agrees with me that I don't belong in your social circle, wouldn't you say?" He paused, taking a long look at Chandra's carriage drawn up in front of the door. Ramesh stood in solitary dignity on the rear platform.

Chandra chuckled. "Now you see why I don't need you as a bodyguard." It was some weeks since Ramesh had been providing a sideshow for the public by accompanying her on her outings about town. For one thing, he'd apparently become convinced the streets of London were safe. For another, Chandra suspected Ramesh was fully occupied in his role as tyrant-in-chief to her household.

Simon looked more closely at Ramesh. "Is that a sword in the fellow's sash?"

"Indeed, yes. That's a *talwar*. You know, a kind of scimitar. Ramesh is very proficient in its use."

"Splendid," said Simon hollowly. He remained silent during the short drive from Grosvenor Square up New Bond Street to Henrietta Place, where the carriage stopped in front of Number 17. Simon handed Chandra down when the door opened and stood looking up at the large and stately house. "You're sure you don't wish me to go in with you?"

"Very sure." Chandra waved to Simon and walked up the steps of the house, followed by Ramesh. A manservant who opened the door fell back, his eyes widening, at the sight of Ramesh's imposing form in the towering blue turban.

"Mrs. Onslow, please," said Chandra.

"Yes, ma'am. Er—who shall I say—?" Clearly the man was little accustomed to female callers who were obviously ladies of quality. Chandra handed him her card. He bowed, leading the way to a large drawing room, where he left them.

Chandra gazed around the room, which was furnished in the latest Egyptian style. Actually, it resembled her own drawing room, which she had now learned to see with Irene's discriminating eyes. If she were planning to stay permanently in England, Chandra reflected, she would get rid of her Nile boat settee and her crocodile sofa and the pyramids and obelisks that littered her formal rooms. She would furnish her house to look more like Daylesford House. She wrinkled her nose. The drawing room was permeated by a cloying, almost overpowering perfume, or, rather, a mixture of scents competing with each other.

A tall, plump woman entered the room. Caroline Onslow was not in her first youth, though she was heavily painted to disguise her age. She was wearing a silk gown that Chandra, with her newly discovered fashion sense, pronounced vulgar and unbecoming.

The woman hesitated. "Mrs. Ware? I expected to see— Well, no matter." A smug, gloating smile appeared on her face. "You're very prompt. I like that. We can do business." Her gaze shifted to Ramesh, and the smile faded into a look of astonishment.

204

Obviously Mrs. Onslow had expected to see Ashley. Or possibly Julian. But no, she'd only *threatened* to contact Julian. She hadn't yet done so. Chandra said, "Yes, I'm Mrs. Julian Ware. I collect you know my reason for coming here."

"Indeed. Will you sit down? Would you like some refreshment?"

"No, thank you. And I prefer to stand." Chandra opened her reticule and took out the bank draft. "Mrs. Onslow, this is a draft for twenty-five thousand pounds. I believe that's the amount of the blackmail you're demanding from Lord Daylesford to keep his name out of your forthcoming memoirs."

Under the thick coat of paint Caroline Onslow's face reddened at the cool contempt in Chandra's voice. "Blackmail? Coming it too strong, Mrs. Ware. Memoirs are supposed to be truthful, and I shouldn't wish to cheat the public. Actually, it's my tender heart that impels me to offer Lord Daylesford an opportunity to keep his affairs private."

"Pray spare me the hypocrisy," retorted Chandra. She put the bank draft into Mrs. Onslow's eager hand. "This is yours with the understanding that you'll omit all mention of my brother-in-law from your filthy memoirs."

"I swear it. You and your lordship will hear no more from me."

Chandra smiled unpleasantly. "There's no need to perjure yourself. If you print one word about the Earl of Daylesford in your memoirs or in any other publication, you won't live to enjoy your profits." She turned to Ramesh, saying, "Show the lady your *talwar*."

As Ramesh approached her, slowly sliding the long glittering curved sword from its sheath, Mrs. Onslow shrank back with a gasp of fear.

"Give the lady a closer look, Ramesh. Yes, that's right," Chandra said calmly, as Ramesh advanced the scimitar to a point six inches from the woman's bulging eyes. "Now, then, Mrs. Onslow, listen to me very carefully. If you put my brother-in-law into your book, my servant Ramesh will carve your heart from your body and feed it to the vultures. Or perhaps you don't have vultures in England? Well, you must have some kind of carrion-eater. Your heart won't go to waste!"

The brothel keeper's face had turned ghastly pale. She tottered to a chair, trying to speak, but only a frightened squeak escaped from her mouth.

"Sheathe your *talwar*, Ramesh," said Chandra. "I think Mrs. Onslow and I understand each other. Do we not, ma'am?"

The woman found her voice. "Yes. Oh, yes." She looked up at Ramesh and shuddered. "Please take him away. I think I'm going to be ill."

Simon was waiting on the pavement in front of the carriage when Chandra and Ramesh came down the steps of Number 17, Henrietta Place. His face was a study in mixed emotions. Relief at seeing her safe and sound warred with feelings of bourgeois prudery. "My God, Chandra," he blurted, "I've heard of this place. It's a— a—"

"It's supposedly a superior brothel, catering to the aristocracy and gentry," said Chandra. "However, I can't imagine why it's so well-patronized. I'm glad to see the last of it. It has the most frightful odor. It smells like a—" She blinked in self-discovery. "I daresay it smells exactly like a brothel. I wonder why brothel keepers think that men find such odors alluring?"

Simon turned red.

When Chandra entered the foyer of the house in Grosvenor Square an hour later, a footman gave her a message. "Mr. Ware's compliments, ma'am, and he would like to see you in the library at your convenience."

"Yes? You wanted to see me, Julian?" said Chandra as she entered the library a moment later, stripping off her gloves.

Julian was sitting behind the desk, frowning at a piece of paper in his hands. "Yes. Sit down," he said curtly.

Raising an eyebrow at the brusque command, Chandra said nothing, but sat down.

"Where've you been?" Julian barked.

Chandra eyed him coldly. "I'm not answerable to you for my whereabouts. For your information, however, I was out. On an errand."

"By any chance, were you making arrangements to pay a little blackmail to Caroline Onslow?" Observing Chandra's start of surprise, Julian said grimly, "I thought so. I remembered your excursion this afternoon with your banker friend."

"How—?"

"Mrs. Onslow wrote to me, of course." Julian motioned toward the piece of paper in his hand. "The lady doesn't realize I have no access to your moneybags. She tells me she'll be obliged to mention some discreditable facts about my brother in her memoirs unless I'm prepared to pay up."

"She gave Ashley until tomorrow," Chandra blurted. She cut herself short, remembering the Onslow woman's greeting: "Mrs. Ware? I expected to see—Well, no matter. You're very prompt." Of course. Chandra had been mystified at the time. Now she understood. Suspecting that Ashley would be unable to raise the money, and unwilling to suffer any delay in getting her hands on it, Mrs. Onslow had greedily made good on her threat to contact Julian even before Ashley's grace period had expired. She'd expected to see Julian at her house, not his wife, of course. She didn't know that Chandra controlled the purse strings.

Julian stood up, tearing the brothel keeper's letter into shreds. The blue eyes were brilliant with anger. "I'm putting an end to this skullduggery right now. My brother should never have come to you about his problems. I forbid you to pay this woman a ha'penny. I intend to inform Mrs. Onslow she can publish and be damned!"

A puzzled frown creased Chandra's forehead. "But Julian, the scandal—"

"Oh, I know what you're going to say," he interrupted

207

her impatiently. "Ashley came to you because of Irene. He's afraid the shock of finding out about his conduct in such a public way would be too much for her, but that's patent nonsense. She's by no means a terminal case, and what's more, she's a sensible woman. Her feelings will be hurt to learn her husband's been patronizing a brothel, but she'll realize the scandal will be a nine days' wonder and will soon be forgotten. I'm sure she'd agree that we— you—shouldn't give in to a blackmailer. If we pay what Mrs. Onslow demands, she'll be back next month, or next year, with another demand."

Chandra felt a hollow sensation in the pit of her stomach. It was obvious Julian didn't realize the enormity of Ashley's offense. He must have assumed from Caroline Onslow's letter that his brother had merely been one of the lady's many regular customers. Chandra understood why Julian didn't want to pay blackmail. He would have reasoned that, although it would grieve the adoring Irene to see her husband's transgression in print, Ashley had been no more guilty than most men. It would sicken Julian to learn his brother was a molester of children. She'd promised Ashley not to tell him. In any case, she'd already paid Caroline Onslow. Julian was arguing against a *fait accompli*.

Lord, what a shocking coil I've gotten myself into this time, she thought.

"So if Harley has already withdrawn money from your account to pay the Onslow woman, Chandra, you can tell him to redeposit it."

Drawing a deep breath, Chandra said, "It's too late. I've already paid her. I've just come from Henrietta Place."

Julian's face turned to granite. "How much did you pay her?"

"I—that's my affair."

"I asked you a question. How much?"

Under that burning blue stare, Chandra found herself telling the truth. "Twenty-five thousand pounds."

He stared at her, stupefied. His hands clenched into fists. "That's a good five times what she could expect to

208

collect from anyone else. You've made the lady's fortune for life. She'll be back, you know."

"No, she won't. That's why I insisted on paying her myself. I took Ramesh with me, and threatened to turn him loose on her if she so much as breathed Ashley's name in public. And in any case, Julian, it's my money. I can do what I like with it."

"Money!" he exploded. "You think money can do everything, solve everything, don't you? You used your fortune to force me into this infamous marriage. You paid for my reelection campaign, not out of any personal feeling, but to put another feather in your social cap. Now, without the courtesy of consulting me, you've paid an exorbitant sum to my brother's blackmailer. And don't try to gammon me by saying you did it for Irene. You were afraid your precious social reputation would be tarnished if the world knew your brother-in-law patronized a brothel!"

"Are you finished?"

Julian glared at her. "My God, if only I *were* finished with you! You promised to release me in a year. That leaves me with roughly nine months to go. Nine months of living in the same house with a venal selfish woman, who cares for nothing except money and what it can do for her!"

Chapter Thirteen

"Will you wear the pearl earrings today, ma'am?"

"What?" Lost in her thoughts, Chandra blinked at her abigail's reflection in the mirror of the dressing table. "Oh. Yes. The pearl earrings will do very well, Betsy."

"You're not feeling ill, ma'am?"

"No, not ill at all. Just woolgathering," said Chandra ruefully. "Thank you. That will be all."

It was more than woolgathering, Chandra reflected, when the abigail had gone. She was in domestic difficulty. It was the third day after her set-to with Julian over the blackmail payment she'd made to the brothel keeper, and she was beginning to feel like a pariah in her own home. Two out of three of her family members were out of charity with her.

Not that she and Julian were openly feuding. That same day, after their quarrel over Caroline Onslow, he'd actually apologized to her for his outburst. "I said too much. I'm sorry," he'd said stiffly. "If we're to live together for the next nine months, the least we can do is to be civil to each other."

It wasn't an olive branch. It was merely a very tenuous offer of truce. As an ex-military man, Julian was saying, in effect, that the war wasn't over, but for the present, it would be more comfortable for both of them not to be dodging constant bullets. He'd been rigidly formal to her ever since, even on the occasions when they'd appeared together in public.

But at least they *were* speaking. Lily wasn't talking to her at all. Since the morning after the ball, when Tristan had failed to persuade Chandra to consent to his marriage to Lily, the girl had barricaded herself in her bedchamber, refusing to allow Chandra to enter.

Chandra's lips tightened. It was sad and ridiculous, after the dangers and anxieties they'd endured together during their captivity in Asaf Khan's camp, for her and Lily to be so estranged. She got up from the dressing table and made for the door with a purposeful stride. Walking down the corridor to Lily's room, she tapped on the door. "Lily, may I come in?"

No answer. Chandra tried again. "I know you're angry with me, but can't we at least talk?" Still no answer. Out of patience, Chandra tried the door handle, which turned under her hand, and marched into the room.

Lily jumped up from a chair by the window. Her delicate features looked pinched, and the great dark eyes were swollen from crying. "This is the outside of enough," she exclaimed bitterly. "In addition to everything, now you're depriving me of my privacy."

Keeping her voice low and soothing, Chandra said, "I just want to put things straight between us, Lily." Looking at her niece's woebegone expression, which suddenly reminded her of the younger Lily, caught up in some childhood tragedy and coming to her not much older aunt or to Freddie for comfort, Chandra unconsciously murmured Lily's Indian name. "Nalini, darling—"

"Don't call me that!"

"But Lily, Asaf Khan, and everyone in the encampment, called you that for ten years. It's your name, or at least one of them."

"It's an Indian name. I'm not Indian. I'm English! And I'm going to remain English. I'll be Tris's English wife!"

"No. That's impossible. Haven't you listened to a word I've been saying? I'm very fond of Tris, and under different circumstances, I'd love to acquire him as a nephew, even though he'd think, of course, that he was becoming my brother-in-law! But I can't let you risk a terrible unhappiness." Chandra hesitated. "Freddie and I haven't spoken very much to you about your mother . . ."

The swift, angry color flooded into Lily's pale cheeks. She marched to the door and threw it open. "I won't listen to any more of this. You always think you know best. You manipulate people like pieces on a chessboard, to try to get them to do what you want them to do. Well, I'll not let you manipulate *me*. I'm going to live my own life as I choose, and that includes marrying Tris. Please go now."

Shrugging, Chandra walked out of the room. The door slammed behind her. Frederica was standing in the corridor. Chandra said to the ex-governess, "I suppose you heard that."

Frederica nodded. She looked subdued. In fact, since the ball, she'd largely avoided Chandra's company. Chandra knew she was spending most of her time with Lily.

"Lily doesn't want to talk to me, but I know she talks to you," said Chandra. "You've been sympathizing with her, haven't you? Well, I sympathize with her, too, you know. However, I'm a realist. So, I've always thought, are you. Why can't you see that, by encouraging Lily's feelings for Tristan, you're only pushing her down the road to tragedy?"

"Chandra, more than once you've accused Lily of not listening to you. *You* never listen to anybody. She just told you that you always think you know best. Perhaps you do, most of the time, but you're not infallible. In any case, you can't go on trying to manage Lily's affairs for her. If she chooses to make mistakes that will ruin her life, that's her right."

It was one of the very few times since Chandra had grown up that Frederica had spoken to her so sharply. Nettled, Chandra retorted, "I can keep her from making this mistake, Freddie, and I propose to do so."

Throwing up her hands, Frederica, without saying a word, opened Lily's door and disappeared inside.

Sighing, Chandra went down to breakfast. Julian rose from the table as she entered the dining room. He said,

"Good morning," bowed slightly and left the room. *La, Mr. Ware, let us be civil at all costs*, she thought resentfully. She failed to eat her usual hearty breakfast, and had to force herself to keep her engagement with Basil Forrest to go riding.

Mercifully, she soon found the hussar captain's company to be more soothing than otherwise. At least Basil's flirtatious remarks and frequent inanities kept her from brooding over her troubles with Julian and Lily. At one point, however, Basil turned serious. "You'll scarcely credit this, Chandra: the other day I very nearly got myself leg-shackled."

"Really? You're thinking of getting married? Famous!"

He gazed at her reproachfully. "I've sometimes thought you had a heart of stone. Now I'm sure of it."

"Basil! What a thing to say."

"Well, how could you think I'd marry someone else, when I'm so much in love with you? I know, I know," he added, as she opened her mouth to protest. "You're a married woman, far out of my reach. Though how happy you can be, married to a hell-kite like Julian Ware . . . But that's by the by. I was on the verge of popping the question the other day. Very nice gal. Bit of money. Decent family background. But I couldn't do it. Felt like desecrating a shrine, you know? Because I still love you."

Torn between amusement and pity, Chandra could think of nothing to say, except, "Pleae don't wear the willow for me. I'm not worth it."

"Let me be the judge of that." Basil grabbed for her hand to press it to his lips. The sudden movement caused his horse to rear.

He's not a very good horseman, thought Chandra, stifling an urge to laugh. *I wonder how he gets by in the Hussars?"*

When she returned from her ride, feeling somewhat more cheerful, she found she had a visitor. Tristan's mother was waiting for her in the drawing room. Georgiana's costume and coiffure were meticulous, as usual, but her forehead was scored by a deep frown. "My dear Chandra, what a shocking coil!"

"Is something wrong?" asked Chandra, pretending to an ignorance she didn't feel. There was but one topic that could engage Lady Eversleigh's interest and emotions, and that was the welfare of her adored only child.

Georgiana tossed her a glance of angry impatience. "Really, my dear. What could I be referring to except Tristan and Lily? My son informed me last night he intends to marry your sister." She fixed Chandra with a challenging stare. "I must tell you I am unalterably opposed to such a match. Mind, I *like* Lily very much. She's a dear girl. But her—her ancestry prevents her from being a suitable wife for Tristan. My son's lineage on the Ware side goes back centuries to a Norman barony, and the Lorings, too, are a very ancient family."

"You needn't explain," Chandra interrupted her. Much as she agreed with Georgiana about the unsuitability of the match between Lily and Tristan, it was still distasteful to hear Lily described as unworthy. "I'm opposed to the marriage, too. It could only bring unhappiness to both of them."

"Oh. Precisely." Georgiana seemed quite taken aback. Obviously she hadn't expected such prompt agreement. "Well, then, what are we to do about the situation?"

"Nothing."

"Nothing?"

"Nothing except to stand firm. Acting as Lily's guardian, I've refused my consent to the match." Chandra mentally crossed her fingers. Lily didn't have a guardian. Her mother had died in the massacre at Bhulamphur without having made any legal arrangements for her. Chandra went on, "Without my consent, Lily and Tristan can't get married. Lily is under age. I consulted a solicitor yesterday. According to Hardwick's Marriage Act of 1753, the marriage of a person under the age of twenty-one is illegal without the consent of a parent or guardian."

"Oh, capital." Lady Eversleigh's face was radiant with relief. Then another thought struck her. "You'll not let Lily and Tristan argue you into changing your mind?"

she asked anxiously.

"No. Don't worry, Georgiana. Tristan and Lily are not going to get married."

The following day, shortly after noon, Chandra remembered her reassuring pledge to Lady Eversleigh with the taste of sawdust in her mouth. After a late breakfast and a long session with Ramesh over the household accounts, she was dressing to attend an exhibition at Somerset House with Irene, when Lily's abigail came to her bedchamber. The woman was holding a folded slip of paper in her hand. She looked flustered. "Mrs. Ware, this 'ere note is fer ye. It's from Miss Lily."

Taking the slip of paper, Chandra didn't unfold it immediately. She looked curiously at the abigail, who, it was obvious from her guilty expression, had already read the note. "What's the matter?" Chandra said quietly.

"Miss Lily, she's gone, ma'am." The abigail's voice took on an excited squeak. "Last night, she said 'as 'ow she wanted ter sleep late this morning, so I didn't bring up 'er tea as usual. But a bit ago, when she 'adn't rung fer me, I went to 'er bedchamber, wondering, y'know, if she'd taken sick or something, an' she weren't there. The room, it was ev'ry which way. Miss Lily's clothes scattered all over. A portmanteau missing from the wardrobe. An' that note. I brought it straight ter ye."

Chandra unfolded the note and read its brief contents. She crushed the bit of paper into a ball, and then smoothed it out and tore it into tiny pieces. Calmly she said to the abigail, "Go back to Miss Lily's room and tidy it. Then find Miss Banks, and ask her to come here. After that, go about your usual duties. You're not to answer any questions about Miss Lily's absence, is that understood?"

"Oh, yes, ma'am." The abigail scuttled out of the room.

Chandra sat down by the window, oblivious of the glorious July sunshine pouring into the bedchamber. She stared unseeingly down into the large, circular, railed garden in the center of Grosvenor Square. What was she to do? Lily had eloped. "Tris and I have gone off to get married," her terse little note had announced.

Chandra slapped a fist into her other hand. Why hadn't the possibility of elopement occurred to her? Yesterday the solicitor she'd consulted had specifically informed her that under Scottish law, parental consent for the marriage of minors was unnecessary. But, of course, she knew why the thought of elopement hadn't entered her head. She'd simply assumed that Tristan was far too proper to subject Lily to a havey-cavey runaway ceremony in Gretna Green, or one of the other Scottish marriage mills, a ceremony around which gossip and scandal might linger for years to come.

Well, apparently she'd been wrong about Tris and his notions of propriety. She looked up at a knock on the door. "Yes?"

Lily's abigail peered into the room. "Ma'am, Miss Banks ain't in the 'ouse. The footman, 'e says she ordered the carriage this morning ter go out shopping."

"Very well. That will be all."

So. She'd have to do without Freddie's help, unless the ex-governess returned very shortly from another of her interminable shopping expeditions. Time and speed were all important. For, without conscious thought, Chandra had decided what she must do.

She rang the bell for her own abigail. When the girl arrived, Chandra gave her a series of terse instructions. "Tell Mr. Ware's valet I wish to see him. Send word to the stables that I want the traveling chaise immediately. Then pack a small portmanteau with several changes of clothing. I'm going on a short journey. You won't be accompanying me."

Chandra sat down to write a brief note to Frederica, informing her of Lily's elopement and what Chandra intended to do about it. Julian's valet arrived even before she finished the note. He was seldom far away from Julian's bedchamber, where he spent hours lovingly attending his master's wardrobe. "You wished to see me, ma'am?"

"Yes. Do you know where I can find Mr. Ware?"

The valet shook his head. "Not precisely, I fear. This

216

morning he went to his offices in Downing Street, as he usually does." The valet glanced at the clock. "He might be at White's now, or he'll no doubt be arriving there shortly. Would you wish me to send him a message?"

"That won't be necessary. Please pack a portmanteau or valise with whatever clothing and other necessities Mr. Ware may need for a stay of several days, and bring it to this room."

"Mr. Ware is going out of town? He didn't tell me."

"He doesn't know about it yet," Chandra replied coolly. "Do as I say, please, and do it as soon as possible. By the way, Mr. Ware will not require your services on this trip."

The valet's mouth dropped open. "I won't be going with him? But who will brush his coats, see to the blacking of his boots?"

"I'm sure Mr. Ware will manage to struggle along without you for a few days," Chandra said dryly.

Half an hour later, dressed in a walking dress and a plain pelisse and bonnet, Chandra climbed into the traveling chaise drawn up before her door. The few pieces of luggage she was taking with her were piled on the roof. "White's Club, St. James's Street," she directed the groom who was putting up the steps. The groom was one of two stablehands who would be acting as postilions until the first posting stop to change horses, at which point the grooms would return to Grosvenor Square with Chandra's team. The groom blinked at Chandra's order, scratched his head, hesitated. "Yes, ma'am," he said finally, and closed the door of the carriage.

Not long afterwards, when the chaise stopped in front of a graciously proportioned building at 37-38, St. James's Street, the same groom opened the door of the vehicle. "Ye'll be wanting me ter take a message ter some'un in the club, ma'am? Mayhap ter the master?"

"No. Let down the steps, please."

"Ye're never going inside, ma'am?"

"I am."

"But—"

Chandra descended from the chaise and sailed past the

staring and speechless groom and up the steps of White's. She walked into the foyer, where the hall porter, in powdered wig and black breeches, swooped down on her with a horrified cluck. "Ma'am, ma'am. Ladies aren't allowed on these premises."

Chandra fixed him with a quelling stare. "Is Mr. Julian Ware here this afternoon?"

"Yes, ma'am, but—"

"Tell him his wife wishes to speak with him."

"Really, ma'am, I can't allow—"

"Give Mr. Ware my message now," said Chandra firmly. "Tell him it's a matter of life or death." When the porter still hesitated, shifting from one foot to another in an agony of indecision, she added, "I don't intend to move an inch from here until I've seen Mr. Ware. And if you lay one finger on me to put me out, I assure you, you'll be sorry."

With a shrug of defeat, the porter turned away. As Chandra stood in the foyer, impatiently tapping her foot, a number of the club servants wandered in and out, gazing at her surreptitiously with awestruck eyes. Several gentlemen, members of the club, paused momentarily to stare at her in stunned silence as they entered or left the premises.

In a few moments, Julian came striding down the corridor. His face was a frozen mask, though his voice was composed as he said, "Chandra. The porter said there was an emergency. Will you come into the library? There'll be more privacy there." He took her arm, his fingers biting into her flesh as they walked up the stairs to the library. There, closing the door behind them, Julian exploded into fiery anger.

"Damnation, Chandra, you've finally gone too far. You've made me look like an absolute gudgeon by invading my club, dragging me out of a whist game in front of a roomful of my friends and acquaintances. Have you taken leave of your senses? Or are you out to ruin both of us?"

"Julian, I need your—"

Too incensed to listen to her, Julian cut her off. "Don't

you realize you've probably damaged your standing—and mine!—beyond repair, by coming here? No lady of quality who values her reputation will dare even to set foot in St. James's Street in the afternoon, let alone enter a gentleman's club! What possessed you to do such a thing? The porter said something about life and death. If there's a crisis of some kind that warrants my attention, couldn't you have sent one of your servants to the club with a message?"

"No. That would have taken too much time. Julian, you must come with me immediately. I have a chaise waiting out in front, and I had your valet pack a bag for you."

"You *what?*" Julian's blue eyes darkened with rage, and a muscle twitched in his forehead.

"Lily has eloped with Tristan. We must go after them. They can't have gone too far today. Lily's delicate, she'd need to rest. I don't know exactly when they left. It was probably quite early this morning. If we hurry, we might catch up to them by late this evening, or sometime tomorrow." Chandra studied her husband's furious face, saying impatiently, "We're wasting valuable time. Come *on*, Julian."

"No," said Julian flatly.

"You can't mean that! This is Lily's entire future. It's Tristan's future. We can't let them ruin their lives with this disgraceful runaway marriage."

"I told you once I had no authority to interfere in Tris's affairs, remember? That's still my position. And now, if there's nothing further, I'd like to get back to my whist game. I was within a hand of winning another rubber when you interrupted me."

The cold indifference in Julian's tone lashed Chandra into a rage. "You go back to your whist game, and by tomorrow morning at the latest, you'll be dealing your cards in a Newgate prison cell! Don't forget, I still hold your promissory note."

"Up to your old threats?" Julian exclaimed contemptuously. "I never before met a woman with less of a sense of honor. Hasn't it ever occurred to you that it might be unfair and dishonorable to keep battering me with that promissory note, once I'd given in to your original demands? I've kept my end of the bargain. You should keep yours, by returning the damned note to me at the end of this confounded year of marriage."

"I warn you, I'm desperate—"

Julian glared at her. "For an intelligent woman, you can be positively bird-witted. I've already pointed out to you that you can't afford to use my promissory note against me every time you want to force me into another of your sapskulled schemes. Toss me into debtors' prison, and you throw away everything you've gained by marrying me. The scandal would ruin you."

Chandra's shoulders slumped. Her anger dissolved into sheer misery. "I know, I know, but better my ruin than Lily's," she said in a low, desolate voice. "That's what this marriage will do, ruin any chance she has for happiness." She drew a long, steadying breath. "You're right. It *is* dishonorable to keep threatening you with the promissory note. Besides, I can't waste time now making the arrangements to put you back in Newgate," she added with a note of bitter derision. "With every minute that passes, I'm falling further behind Lily and Tristan." She turned to leave the room.

"Chandra, wait. You're not going off by yourself? Is Ramesh with you? It's three hundred miles from London to Gretna Green."

Pausing with her hand on the door handle, Chandra threw him a backward glance. "No, I didn't bring Ramesh. I thought you'd be coming with me, naturally. Goodbye, Julian. Good luck with your whist game."

"Oh, the devil." Julian sounded goaded. "I'll go with you. If you hadn't driven me into such a rage with your infernal intrusion into the club . . ." He clamped his lips shut, biting off any other revealing words. After a moment he said, "Mind, that's all I'll do, go with you. I still believe I've no right to interfere in Tris's affairs. However, I agree with you about the elopement. It could be an endless source of grief and scandal. I'll point that out to Tris. If he then chooses to ignore my advice, so be it. He can go his way. Understood?"

"Yes. Oh, yes." Chandra said in relief. She'd lived long enough in England to know that ladies didn't travel alone, without a male escort or even an abigail. She'd counted on Julian's company. His easy air of authority, his familiarity with traveling by post chaise, would speed up the chase and provide, if need be, the muscle necessary to force the truants back to London. Because, although Julian might have decided he wouldn't coerce Tristan into giving up his plans to elope, she had no such scruples. If only she could catch up with Lily, she'd make very sure her niece returned to Grosvenor Square with her, unmarried. She smiled gratefully at Julian. "Thank you."

He gave her a curt nod. "I'll just fetch my hat and coat."

The postilions drove the chaise at a brisk pace out of Mayfair and up the New Road, past the brick kilns and dairy farms of Islington, then along the Great North Road, through Highgate and across the lonely stretches of Finchley Common to Barnet in Hertfordshire.

Chandra sat tensely, watching the neat houses and small factories and later the farms and fields flash by. "Oh, I hope we can go fast enough to catch them," she murmured, her earlier confidence beginning to evaporate. She stole a look at Julian. He leaned against the squabs on his side of the carriage, his face turned to the light breeze blowing in through the open window of the chaise. The lines of annoyance were still etched on his features, and he was maintaining an aloof silence. There was no doubt he'd accompanied her very much against his will. A random thought crossed her mind: she and Julian had been living in the same house for weeks now, and they were still strangers. Would they ever know each other better?

"Do you think we can, Julian?"

He aroused himself. "Can what?"

"Catch up with Lily and Tristan. They have a long head start. Five hours or more, I'd guess."

He shrugged. "We'll know more after I start questioning the hostlers and innkeepers at the posting stops. It will doubtless mean driving through the night," he warned. "Even so, Tris may have the same idea." He moved restlessly. "We'd make more speed if I were driving my curricle. God, how I hate to be driven."

At Barnet, their first posting stop, amid the bustle of hostlers changing horses and inn servants dashing out to offer refreshment, Julian left the chaise to make his inquiries. He climbed back into the carriage shaking his head. "No one remembers them," he reported. "You'd think with Lily's distinctive appearance—" He darted a quick look at Chandra. "No offense, but she *is* very dark-complexioned. But perhaps she's veiled. That would account for it. I must remember to ask about that in Welwyn."

"They may have left London at the height of the morning traffic. Perhaps the hostlers were too busy to notice one young couple in a posting chaise."

"Perhaps."

But at Welwyn, fourteen miles from Barnet, Julian's inquiries at the White Horse Inn were no more productive. Nor did he obtain any information at Baldock, twelve miles farther along the Great North Road. It was now nine o'clock, and Julian suggested a quick meal in the coffee room of the inn.

Chandra merely nibbled at a piece of bread and drank some coffee. "I can't understand why we don't find some sign of them," she fretted.

Julian chewed ruminatively on a bit of beef and washed it down with several swallows of wine. "We may be on the wrong track entirely," he said suddenly. "Did Lily's note say specifically she and Tris were going to Gretna Green by post chaise?"

Putting down her cup, Chandra stared at Julian. "No. She didn't mention Gretna Green, or post chaises, either. She simply wrote that she and Tristan had gone off to be married and not to worry about them. I assumed, naturally, they were going to Gretna Green."

"It's the closest Scottish marriage mill, but there *are* others. Lamberton, for example, and Coldstream, near Berwick. Only a little farther from London."

"What—Julian! If they're not going to Gretna Green, are we on the wrong road?"

He shook his head. "Not necessarily. You more or less follow the same route as far as Ferrybridge. That's . . . oh, a hundred and forty miles from here. Thirteen or fourteen hours of driving. What concerns me isn't so much the destination. Tris isn't very plump in the pocket, you know. Perhaps he couldn't afford to pay the post charges for a journey of six hundred miles or more. Did Lily have any money that you know of?"

"A few pounds only. She charged everything she bought to my account."

"It's possible they went by mail coach to save money. Did you see Lily last night?"

"No, but I heard her talking to Freddie in her bedchamber."

"Then she and Tris couldn't have traveled by the mail. Those coaches all leave at night from the Post Office. Tris probably booked seats on an ordinary stagecoach. That would explain why we haven't found a trace of them."

"What do you mean?"

"Stagecoaches don't stop at posting houses, which is where we've been changing horses. From now on, I'll start making additional inquiries at all the inns where the stagecoaches stop. The problem is—"

"The problem is that inn servants and hostlers probably don't pay as much attention to coach passengers as they do to private travelers, who pay more, and from whom they can expect tips. Lily and Tristan might easily go unnoticed."

"Yes. Tris may have had that in mind." Julian rose. "Shall we go? It's a long road to Ferrybridge."

The rest of the night and the succeeding day became an interminable blur to Chandra. The unfamiliar towns and villages flew by. Stilton, Stamford, Grantham, Newark, Barnaby Moor, Doncaster. The counties merged into one

223

another. Huntingtonshire, Lincolnshire, Nottingham-shire, Yorkshire. At each stop Julian made inquiries in the posting inns and the coaching establishments. There was no news of Lily and Tris.

As the night and then the morning wore on, Chandra dozed briefly between stops, rousing to wakefulness whenever the wheels of the carriage sank into an unusually deep pothole. Apparently Julian dozed also. She caught an occasional glimpse of him with his chin on his chest. In the afternoon a cold, interminable downpour of rain slowed their progress. In Ferrybridge at six o'clock in the evening, after a time-consuming and fruitless search through all the inns of the town for some trace of the fugitives, Julian called a halt. At that point, they were a little over half the distance to the border. Julian ordered the postilions to put up for the night at the King's Arms, on the main street of Ferrybridge. When Chandra protested, he said grimly. "You're dropping from fatigue. I'm in no better case. We need a good meal and some rest in a proper bed. We'll start after them again early tomorrow morning."

"But—"

"No arguments, Chandra."

She stumbled getting out of the chaise in the courtyard of the King's Arms, and would have fallen except for Julian's steadying hand. She realized he was right. They needed rest before they could go on. She comforted herself with the thought that perhaps Lily and Tris had been forced to stop, too. Lily had never had a great deal of stamina.

While Julian arranged for accommodations with the landlord, a servant showed Chandra into a private parlor, where a table had been set for dining in front of the fireplace. A modest fire burned in the grate, for which Chandra was grateful. After the rains this afternoon the weather had turned frigid for July. The air felt very cold and damp. She took off her bonnet and spencer and sat down at the table.

When Julian came to the parlor, he carried with him an

opened bottle of claret and a pair of glasses. Pouring each of them a drink, he said, as he settled himself opposite her at the table, "The landlord tells me he has a haunch of beef and some fine fat ducks all ready to serve. They'll be here shortly. A good thing, too. I'm famished."

He looked very tired, as tired as she felt, Chandra thought. She hadn't been to bed for almost a day and a half. Neither had he. He needed a shave. The faint dark shadow on his chin and cheeks didn't detract from his good looks. It merely made him resemble a handsome and rather raffish brigand.

Taking a few sips of her wine, Chandra reverted to the subject foremost on her mind. "What will we do tomorrow, Julian?" she asked with a worried frown. "You didn't get news of Lily and Tris today at any of the inns in town here. And you've told me the road to Gretna Green diverges from the route to Coldstream, the other marriage mill, at Ferrybridge. So which road will we take in the morning?"

"The road to Carlisle, probably. Gretna Green is the more likely place for Tris and Lily to choose to be married. It's a little closer to London."

"But if they've gone to Coldstream . . ."

Julian shrugged. "Then we'll have chosen the wrong road." He lifted his voice to call out, "Come." Several servants entered the room carrying covered dishes from which steam was escaping. Soon the table was covered with an array of appetizing food. Julian tackled the roast beef, the ducks, and the venison with gusto. After a few moments, noting that Chandra hadn't touched her food, he reached across the table to place his hand on hers. "You must eat to keep your strength up. The chances are good, you know, that we'll be hot on Lily's heels tomorrow."

Chandra could hear a note of real concern in his voice. Tears prickled the back of her eyelids, and she blinked them back. Managing a smile, she said, "The venison smells delicious. I believe I'll have some." In fact, she realized, she was very hungry. She ate heartily, had several glasses of claret, and was mildly surprised to find that she and Julian were having a relaxed, perfectly ordinary conversation about anything and everything except their truant relatives. Julian kept away from the subject of the elopement, and Chandra followed his lead.

At one point she said, "I haven't been keeping up with the newspapers, I fear. Is the war in the Peninsula going well?"

"I'm optimistic. Wellesley's army began crossing into Spain two days ago. Sir Arthur will fight a major battle soon, I think. The French commander, Marshal Victor, is at Talavera, only seventy miles from Madrid, and in position to join forces with Marshal Jourdan. Wellesley must go after the French, before Victor can link up with another army under Soult. Yes, I believe there'll be a decisive battle in a matter of days or weeks."

"You were an officer in the—what was it? Oh, yes, the dragoons. Do you ever wish you could join Sir Arthur's army in the Peninsula?"

His eyes lighted up, and he said eagerly, "If I could only serve in one campaign . . ." He shook his head, smiling ruefully. "It's not for me. I sold out of my regiment at Ashley's request to ensure I wouldn't die in battle before I fathered an heir to the title, and so far, of course, I have no heir—" He broke off, flushing. "And, considering my marital circumstances, no possibility of an heir in the immediate future," he muttered. The fragile air bubble of unaccustomed friendliness between them disintegrated.

He quickly changed the subject and, soon afterwards, suggested they go to bed. Which caused an immediate renewal of hostilities, when Chandra realized that she and Julian were about to occupy the same quarters for the night.

Chandra stared at him in surprise when, after unlocking the door of a room for her and standing aside to allow her to enter, he followed her inside. Her eyes narrowed when she observed two portmanteaux in the center of the room. One of them was Julian's.

"The servants must have misunderstood the landlord's instructions," she said. "They've assumed we're sharing a bedchamber like any respectable married couple. You *did* order two rooms?"

"No," he replied coolly.

Chandra's eyes shot sparks. "Why not? Are you telling me the inn is full up?"

"I have no idea. I didn't order separate bedchambers because I've stayed in this establishment previously, the landlord knows me, and he congratulated me on my marriage. Did you wish me to intimate we're already so estranged after a few weeks of marital bliss that we're unwilling to sleep in the same room?"

Chandra bit her lip. "No." She thought for a moment. "We could go to another inn and pass ourselves off as brother and sister."

"You must take me for a ninnyhammer," Julian retorted. "I haven't the faintest intention of rousing the postilions and dashing about the town to find another inn. If I don't get some sleep soon, I'll collapse. So will you." He walked over to the wardrobe, stripped off his coat and waistcoat and hung them up. He turned back to her in his shirtsleeves and sat down in an armchair, where he began tugging off his Hessians.

"I—am—not sleeping in that bed with you," Chandra enunciated in the careful accents of controlled rage.

"Oh, damn it to hell," Julian said wearily. "Haven't I made it clear by this time that I harbor no libertine aspirations toward you? I'll sleep in this chair, or on the floor, it doesn't matter. The moment I close my eyes, I'll be deep in the arms of Morpheus." Tossing a boot on the floor, he followed it with the other, and then leaned back in the chair, stretching out his long body, and closed his eyes. In a few moments, his breathing deepened and slowed.

With a sigh of exasperation, Chandra gave up the unequal battle. Acutely conscious of her tired muscles, she looked longingly at the bed. She slipped out of her shoes and put her bonnet and brief spencer into the wardrobe. Then she paused. If she could disrobe, she would certainly rest more comfortably, and her frock would remain unwrinkled. Luckily, she didn't require the services of an abigail to undress. She was wearing a chemise-robe of thin jaconet muslin which buttoned down the front, and her short buckram corset also tied at the front.

She glanced uncertainly from Julian's somnolent form to the bed. Was he really sound asleep? Well, no matter, she thought crossly. If he was feigning sleep, he was welcome to play Peeping Tom, because she was *not* going to lie down in that tightly laced corset, which she despised and only wore because her abigail seemed to think it was immoral for a lady to leave off her stays. With a quick, apprehensive look at Julian, who didn't move a muscle, she stripped off her frock and corset. Clad only in her knee-length cotton drawers and a petticoat with an attached bodice, she shivered in the chill of the room, the aftermath of the heavy rains of the afternoon, and dived into bed. The warmth of the coverlets felt very welcome. She must have fallen asleep immediately.

She was cold. Her coverlets had slipped off during the night, Chandra thought drowsily, reaching out to pull the blankets back over her. The coverlets didn't move. She tugged again, meeting resistance, and then, at the sound of a muttered curse, she rolled over to stare disbelievingly at the form lying beside her. At the same moment, Julian stirred in his untidy cocoon of blankets, and without opening his eyes, put out a long arm and draped it across her body. Still seemingly asleep, he pulled her close and snuggled his head into the hollow of her throat. The movement disarranged the blankets, bringing their bodies into close contact, and Julian relaxed against her with an inarticulate murmur of pleasure.

Chandra pushed energetically against his shoulder, trying to dislodge him. "Julian, wake up!"

He lifted his chin, opening his eyes with a look of startled surprise that seemed entirely genuine. "Good God," he muttered. "I remember now. I woke up during the night petrified with cold, so I slipped under the covers.

I didn't think you'd mind."

Their faces were very close together. She could see clearly the tiny black hairs on his cheeks and upper lip. She had an odd sensation that she was drowning in the intense blue of his eyes. They stared at each other in a breathless silence in which Chandra imagined he must be able to hear the wild pounding of her heart. Slowly he bent his head, pressing warm, seeking lips against hers in a kiss that was totally unlike the savage, hurting kiss he'd forced on her on their wedding night. His mouth grew more urgent, and he shifted his position until he was holding her against him with both arms in a hard embrace. She was falling into a mindless abyss of sheer sensual delight when she became aware of the unfamiliar, enticing, swelling pressure against her thighs and recoiled in a rush of blind panic. Wrenching her lips from his mouth, she struggled to release herself. "Julian, you can't . . . You *promised*," she panted.

Instantly his arms relaxed. He moved away from her to the far side of the bed, looking at her with dazed eyes. "I'm sorry. I was half-asleep. I must have thought . . ."

Chandra sat up, drawing a deep breath. "You thought I was one of your ladybirds, I daresay," she said in a hard voice. "You had no right to get into my bed."

Julian's lips tightened. "If I'd perished of cold, I'd have been of no use to you in this mad chase to the border, did you think of that?" he retorted. He rose, padding to the bell rope in his stockinged feet. "I'll order some tea and some hot water. I need a shave."

"And I need to get dressed. Turn your back, please."

By the time the servant's knock sounded, Chandra had hastily tied her corset and buttoned on her chemise-robe. Julian opened the door to find himself confronting, not the expected inn servant, but a tall and impressive figure in an enormous blue turban and a flowing, full-sleeved *anga*.

"What the devil?" said Julian rudely. "What are *you* doing here?"

Ramesh touched the floor in a graceful salaam.

229

Straightening, he said, with the faint overtones of hostility he always exhibited toward Julian, "I come with a message for my lady from the mem-sahib Banks."

"*Ramesh?*" Chandra raced to the door. She stared at the tall figure incredulously. "Freddie sent you after me? Is something wrong?"

"I cannot say, lady. Here is the message."

Ramesh handed Chandra a sealed note. As she was tearing it open, Julian asked Ramesh curiously, "How did you find us? And how did you travel?"

A faint prideful quiver of the mustachios. "The mem-sahib Banks, she instructed me to hire a post chaise and inquire for you and my lady at every posting station until I reached the border of some place called Scotland."

"Good God," said Julian in a hollow voice. "Did—I daresay you attracted considerable attention. People in this part of the world have never seen—er—a representative of your race."

"Everyone gawked at me, yes," replied Ramesh coldly. "Infidels have no manners. I ignored their rude stares."

"Julian," Chandra exclaimed. She'd turned very pale. "Lily and Tristan didn't elope to Gretna Green. Freddie says they were married in London yesterday by special licence."

"That's impossible. Lily's a minor. No bishop would have granted a special licence without the consent of her parent or guardian. You never signed any such consent, did you?"

"No," said Chandra grimly. "But I think I know who did."

Chapter Fourteen

Chandra and Julian arrived back in London at noon of the following day, after another wearying nonstop journey of over thirty hours. Ramesh had made his own way back to the city.

During the return drive from Ferrybridge in the chaise, Chandra sat in silence much of the time, brooding about Lily's marriage and what she could do about it. Julian wrapped himself in silence, too, more oppressive and uncomfortable than the silence that had enveloped him on the journey north. At that time Julian had also remained aloof, coldly annoyed because Chandra had embarrassed him by invading the sacred male precincts of White's, and still nursing a resentment against her for paying Caroline Onslow's blackmail demands without consulting him.

This silence was different. It was not so much a silence as the unspoken clamoring of thoughts and emotions straining to break through the barrier of chilly hostility that separated them. In the intervals when she wasn't worrying about Lily and Tristan, Chandra couldn't prevent the memories of Julian's kiss and the pressure of his lean, hard body against her soft flesh from invading her mind.

Several times, when she glanced at him out of the corner of her eye, she caught him looking at her, his mouth tensed, the hand on his knee clenched into a fist. Was he remembering, too? And was he feeling unutterably relieved, as she was, that they hadn't broken the terms of their business bargain by crossing over into the dangerous territory of sexual relations? She'd always sensed, from the time of their first stormy encounter on the Woolwich road, that, despite their differences, a very strong physical attraction existed between them. Now she realized how wise, and how fortunate, she'd been in avoiding all occasions of intimacy with him. Until now.

When the chaise rolled to a stop in Grosvenor Square, Chandra left Julian to settle with the postilions and marched up the steps and into the foyer of the house. She cut off the footman's respectful salutation, saying curtly. "Tell Miss Banks I wish to see her immediately in my sitting room."

Chandra was dealing with her abigail, who was distressed with the condition of her mistress's rumpled dress and spencer, and especially with the disheveled contents of the portmanteau a footman had just brought up to the room, when Frederica made a tardy appearance. Chandra suspected, from the ex-governess's faint expression of guilt, that she'd deliberately delayed her arrival.

Motioning to the abigail to leave, Chandra faced Frederica. "Well, Freddie?"

"Obviously Ramesh caught up with you. I'm so glad. One of the servants told me it takes three days to get to the Scottish border. You might have been on the road almost a week. I do hope you're not too tired," Frederica said, twisting her fingers together nervously. "When I came home and found your note saying you and Julian were going to Gretna Green after Lily and Tris, I didn't know what to do at first. Then I thought of sending Ramesh off in a hired chaise. Where did he find you?"

Chandra cut her off ruthlessly. "Stop dithering, Freddie. I want to know about that special license. How did Tristan lay hands on it? No bishop will grant a special license to a minor without the sworn consent of a parent or guardian. *I* never gave my consent to Lily's marriage."

A sudden color appeared in Frederica's cheeks. "No, you didn't. *I* did."

"I thought as much," said Chandra grimly. "May I point out that you're neither a parent nor a guardian?"

"Nor are you. Lily has neither. I gave my consent as Lily's aunt. That's who you've been saying I am, since we arrived in England. I took advantage of it," retorted Frederica. She appeared to be rapidly regaining her usual poise.

"Freddie, how could you stab me in the back like this?" Chandra burst out. "You know I've had only one thought, to save Lily from unhappiness."

"That was my thought, too," snapped Frederica. Her voice softened. "Of course, on the face of it, this marriage is unwise. I'd hoped the attraction between Lily and Tris wouldn't become so serious. But it did. I think Lily and Tris really love each other. I tried to persuade Lily to give Tris up, just as you did, but nothing either of us has said has made them change their minds. So, finally, I decided to help them, when Lily confided to me that she and Tris were planning to go to Gretna Green. She told me she'd offered to go live with Tris as his mistress. Naturally, he refused her, suggesting instead that they elope to Scotland. I thought, and still think, that a marriage by special licence, with a member of the family in attendance, was preferable to elopement. I hoped you'd feel the same."

"Well, I don't," exclaimed Chandra, her eyes blazing. "I could have handled the situation if you hadn't interfered. Without your faked consent, Tris could never have obtained that special licence. If he and Lily had eloped to Scotland, I'd have caught up with them before they could go through a ceremony. But no, you had to go and play sentimental mother hen. I hope you're satisfied. You've ruined Lily's life!"

Frederica faltered, "Even if you're right, and I don't think you are, it's too late. What's done is done."

"Don't be so sure of that. Under the law, that marriage is illegal. It could be annulled."

"You wouldn't do that. You *couldn't* do that."
Frederica looked appalled. "Chandra, Lily and Tris are so
happy. Wait till you see them. Of course, they're not in
London now. They've gone to the country to stay with
Tris's brother."

"I don't know that I want to see them," said Chandra in
a hard voice. "Oh, don't worry about an annulment," she
added bitterly. "That marriage is illegal, but I can't prove
it without plunging Lily into even more public disgrace,
and without exposing all the lies I've had to tell about our
family. I'll have to accept it, put as much grace as possible
upon it, at least in public. But I'll never forgive you for
this, Freddie. You've betrayed my confidence. I can never
trust you again."

"In that case, perhaps, you'll want me to leave your
household," replied Frederica stiffly. "I realize I have no
claim on you whatsoever."

"Spare me a Cheltenham tragedy. No matter what
you've done, you're still a member of my family, and
always will be. I don't want to talk anymore. Would you
please go?"

Even as Frederica left the room, looking stricken and
suddenly much older, Chandra felt a twinge of remorse. In
all their years together—and Freddie had joined the
Meredith household several years before Lily was born—
governess and pupil had never before had a violent
quarrel. Chandra knew her anger had prevented her from
being entirely fair. Whatever Freddie had done, it had been
done with the best of misguided intentions. Which,
however, hadn't prevented a disaster.

Chandra felt desolated. The close little family circle of
three, who had sustained each other during the years of
captivity in Asaf Khan's camp, had fallen apart. She
thought of Lily. What more could she have done to make
the girl see reason? Love! Chandra clenched her fists. What
an overrated, flimsy emotion upon which to base the
whole of your life. "Love" had destroyed her sister
Phoebe's happiness. Now it was about to destroy the

234

happiness of Phoebe's daughter, and there was nothing Chandra could do about it. All too soon, the gossip and the slights would begin to erode Lily's romantic delight in her marriage.

Chandra sighed. She knew she couldn't sustain her bitterness and her resentment. Eventually, she would have to make her peace with Frederica, and with Lily, too. As she'd told Freddie, the two of them were her family, and always would be. But she didn't want to deal with her problems now. She was so weary after the bone-jarring drive from Ferrybridge. She desperately wanted to lie down in her comfortable bed and drown all her problems in oblivion.

A knock sounded at the door. A footman presented her with a folded note on a salver. "Tell her ladyship I'll be with her as soon as I can," she told the footman.

She closed the door, shrugging resignedly as she began to strip off her travel-worn garments. She'd have to face Lady Eversleigh sometime. Better to do it now and get it over with.

When Chandra entered the drawing room a little later, Georgiana was sitting tensely upright on the crocodile settee. "Chandra! What are we to do about this tragedy?" she exclaimed, in dramatic accents worthy of the reigning queen of the theater, Sarah Siddons.

"If you're speaking about Lily's marriage to Tristan—"

"What else? I've been calling here every day for three days, since I found Tristan's note announcing he and your sister were getting married. Where have you been? Yes, and Julian, too?"

"Chasing off to Scotland to prevent Tristan's and Lily's elopement to Gretna Green," said Chandra dryly.

Lady Eversleigh looked at her blankly. "But they were married by special licence."

"Yes, so I've discovered."

"Well, but how did that happen? You told me yourself, not above a sennight ago, that you, as Lily's guardian, would never consent to the match. So how did

235

Tristan get that licence?"

Chandra replied reluctantly, "My aunt swore she was Lily's guardian and gave her consent."

"What?" Lady Eversleigh's thin, elegant form swelled with outrage. "But then this so-called marriage is illegal. We can—"

"We can do nothing," Chandra interrupted her. "We'd simply create a bigger scandal. Lily could never hold up her head again after both a runaway marriage *and* an annulment."

"I don't care about Lily," snapped Georgiana. A bright red spot of color burned on either cheek. "It's different for men. In a short while after an annulment, no one would hold such a—such an *indiscretion*—against Tristan. He'd still be in a position to make an eligible match."

"There will be no annulment."

Georgiana lost control of herself. "Oh, I knew from the very beginning you'd mean trouble for our family," she exclaimed, her voice rising hysterically. "Julian should never have married you. All your money couldn't make up for your lack of background, your vulgarity. Do you realize the embarrassment we used to feel at your outlandish clothes, until darling Irene took you in hand? But now you've gone too far. I won't allow you to sacrifice my son to that mongrel sister of yours. Tristan's lineage on both sides of his family has gone unsmirched for centuries. He must make a good marriage, too, to carry on the line. I demand you start annulment proceedings immediately."

Shaking with rage, Chandra cried, "And I won't allow *you* to call Lily a mongrel! The marriage stands!"

Georgiana jumped up from her chair. "We'll see about that," she screamed. "I'll go to the Lord Chancellor. I'll go to the Archbishop of Canterbury. I'll raise such an outcry that you and your sister will be forced out of society."

"What's the meaning of this bobbery? I could hear your voices from the staircase," said Julian from the doorway of the drawing room. He'd shaved and changed his clothes, Chandra noted. Once more he looked the picture of lounging elegance. He stared down his nose at Lady Eversleigh. "What's this about forcing Chandra out of society, Aunt Georgiana?"

"Your wife won't lift a finger to free Tristan from this dreadful marriage," Lady Eversleigh replied in a shaking voice. "Tristan obtained that special licence under false pretenses. The marriage can be annulled. Julian, make Chandra see reason. You must agree we can't have our family line contaminated by such a mésalliance. It's bad enough that *you* married beneath you, but to bring a half-caste into the family will disgrace us forever!"

Julian froze Lady Eversleigh with a glance of cold fury. "I must ask you to leave, Aunt Georgiana. I don't allow anyone to speak of my wife or my sister-in-law in such terms in my presence. And let me warn you: you'll catch cold if you persist in your attempts to destroy Tristan's marriage. You'll lose your son. You'll lose me, for whatever that's worth. You'll no longer be welcome in this house."

Georgiana's bosom swelled. "We'll see what Ashley has to say to this. *He's* the head of our family."

"Ashley's a bigger snob than you are, but family loyalty counts for a great deal with him, too. I'll warrant he'll close ranks wtih me over this. Goodbye, Aunt Georgiana."

Lady Eversleigh looked disbelievingly at Julian's grim face. Then, her face a mask of shock, she left the drawing room.

Chandra turned to Julian. "Thank you for supporting me and Lily."

"There's no need to thank me. I—"

"You didn't do it for us," finished Chandra. "I know. You did it for your male ego, and your family honor, and heaven knows what else. But thank you, anyway."

His mouth tightened. He hesitated, visibly forcing back a reply. After a moment, he bowed stiffly, saying, "I'm off to Downing Street to see if I'm still a member of the government. I've neglected my duties shamefully for the past few days, while I've been roaming the highways. I'll

237

return in time to escort you to the Mannerings' ball. That is, if you still care to go? In view of Lily's situation, I mean."

"Why not?" Chandra gave him a cool, direct look. "Isn't the ball one of the most important events of the Season? I collect we should appear in public as though nothing were amiss."

His lips curled in an ironic smile. "Forgive me. I was in danger of forgetting your priorities. Social glory above all things, regardless of domestic upheavals, what? Until tonight, then."

Smarting from the flick of contempt in his voice, Chandra drooped as she watched Julian leave. Already weary because of the long journey from Ferrybridge, worried about Lily's future, she also felt emotionally exhausted after her confrontations with Frederica and Tristan's mother and now this exchange with Julian. When a footman arrived shortly afterward with a card on a tray, she was tempted to turn the caller away until she read the name on the card. "Bring Mr. Harley here," she said.

The young banker's steady gray eyes and diffident smile were a welcome sight to Chandra's battered sensibilities. "Oh, Simon, I'm so glad to see you!"

Simon appeared startled but pleased. "I'm very happy to see you, Chandra." His smile faded. "You don't look well. Have you been ill?"

"I'm only a little tired. Do sit down." She chuckled, quite unconvincingly. "I daresay you have business papers for me to sign? You never come to see me unless it's on business!"

Simon took a seat beside her on the crocodile settee and looked at her keenly. "You're more than tired. Something's wrong. It's not the Onslow woman again, is it? She's not demanding further blackmail?"

"Oh, no. It's not Caroline Onslow who's concerning me. She'll never bother me again. She's too afraid of Ramesh and the vultures." Chandra burst into a genuine laugh at Simon's mystified expression. Sobering, she added, "I *have* suffered a little setback. Doubtless the news will be all over London soon. I might as well tell you. My sister Lily has secretly married my husband's cousin, Tristan Loring."

"Yes, I know of Mr. Loring. He's a military man, isn't he? His brother is Baron Eversleigh?" Simon hesitated. "May I guess? Mr. Ware and his family aren't best pleased with the marriage because of Miss Lily's—er—mixed blood."

Chandra nodded. "Nor am I, Simon. I can't see any happiness ahead for her. As you once told me, the London ton is a very closed society. I don't think Lily and Tristan will be accepted."

"I'm sorry to say so, but I fear you're correct." Simon cleared his throat. "You're upset. Perhaps I should go. My news can wait."

"What news?" Chandra glanced at his empty hands, noticing for the first time that he hadn't brought with him his usual portfolio. "You didn't come on business," she said slowly.

"No. Not exactly. Do you remember asking me, some time ago, to be on the watch for the names of individuals, connected either with the East India Company or the Indian army, who had returned to England with a fortune approximately ten years ago? Are you still interested in such information?"

"Yes." Chandra began to tremble.

Heavily, almost reluctantly, Simon said, "Recently I came across the name of a man who returned from India at about that time. This man went out to the Calcutta Presidency a poor man; he came back immensely wealthy. He was the younger son of a prominent family, who, through the family influence, had been appointed a collector in the Board of Revenue. I looked into the salaries of collectors. They're paid a base salary of fifteen hundred rupees a year. In addition, they receive one percent of the revenue they collect. In the larger revenue districts that amounts to approximately 27,500 rupees. In the past, collectors augmented their salaries by engaging in private trade. They're now forbidden to do so. So, as I reckon it, this man made a top salary of, at the very most, three thousand pounds a year. His stay in India lasted under two years, and yet he returned a nabob. Where did his fortune come from?" Simon cleared his throat. "Is this the kind of information you were looking for?"

Chandra said urgently, "What's his name, Simon?"

He told her.

She put her hands to her face, and the tears began to stream from her eyes in an emotional release. Simon's dry words had rung true. She might have reached the end of her long search.

Since her arrival in England, she'd made many contacts, mainly through Basil Forrest and the Taneys, with individuals formerly connected with the East India Company. A few of these people had engaged her suspicions briefly, but none had seemed to fit the composite mental picture she'd formed of the man who'd planned the massacre in Bhulamphur. None of them had aroused in her an instinctive feeling that she'd met her father's murderer.

But this man Simon had described, he was different. All the pieces seemed to fit. She had good reason to believe that this man, out of all the great and fashionable and wealthy people she'd met since her marriage to Julian, was the conscienceless villain who had ordered the massacre at Bhulamphur. She was justified in everything she'd done since she'd arrived in England from India. Now she could expose her father's murderer.

Her tears continued to fall. The shattering news she'd just received, hard on the heels of the tensions and quarrels and disappointments of the past few days, had broken down her defenses completely. She cried like a child, as she'd never cried during those lonely, frightening years she'd spent in Asaf Khan's encampment.

Simon said tensely, "Chandra, darling! What have I said? How can I help you?" He wrapped his arms around her in a close embrace. Still crying, Chandra relaxed gratefully into the comfort of his shoulder. At last she stirred, sitting upright and attempting to wipe the tears from her cheeks with her fingers. "Here," said Simon, handing her a handkerchief. "Better now?"

She nodded, attempting a watery smile. "Bless you, Simon."

With an inarticulate groan, Simon grabbed her by both shoulders. "I can't bear to see you so unhappy. It's Ware, isn't it? That man's never brought you anything but grief! I should never have consented to help you enter into this accursed marriage. Oh, Chandra, I love you so much. I know I'm not good enough for you, but at least if you'd married me—" Before Chandra, petrified with shock, could stop him, he swooped to kiss her clumsily, impulsively.

"You haven't forgotten our engagement to drive this afternoon, I trust?" From behind them, Basil Forrest's voice rose in a shrill shriek. "Chandra!"

Simon lifted his head with a start, his face turning scarlet. A moment later, Forrest's angry hands tore him away from Chandra and jerked him to his feet. "Keep your hands to yourself, you filthy cit," Basil snarled, cocking his fist.

Evading Forrest's inexpert punch, Simon pushed him so hard that the hussar captain staggered and fell, hitting his head against a table with lion's paw feet. Disregarding him, Simon said in a low voice, "Please forgive me for embarrassing you like this."

"It's all right, Simon." She hesitated. "I'm sorry."

"No need to be. I've always known . . . ." He shrugged. "Goodbye, Chandra." He walked toward the doorway.

Shaking his head dazedly, Forrest scrambled to his feet and would have lunged after Simon, if Chandra hadn't caught his arm. She said peremptorily, "Basil. Stop this."

"But the fellow forced his attentions on you," Forrest protested, glaring after Simon as he vanished into the corridor.

"You're mistaken," Chandra said, releasing the hussar's

241

arm. "Simon did not force his attentions on me. He's my good friend."

Forrest stared at her. "Good friend? How good a friend?" A scowl twisted his face. "Are you telling me you've taken him as your lover?"

"Oh, don't be a cloth-head. Of course Simon isn't my lover."

"Then why were you crying? Don't deny it. Your face is all tearstained."

Chandra sighed. "Perhaps I am a little sad today, but it's nothing to do with Simon. It's something purely private. Basil, would you please go? I'm really not up to visitors today. I'm sorry about our drive. I'd quite forgotten it."

Throwing his arms around her, Forrest exclaimed, "My darling girl, I can't leave you when you're unhappy. Please, please let me comfort you. Let me show you how much I love you. You know I'd give my very life for you!"

"Basil, let me go this instant."

"I can't let you go. You inflame me, Chandra. For months I've longed to hold you like this." Forrest bent his head, seeking her mouth, and as his faintly wet lips brushed her cheek, Chandra shuddered. Struggling to free herself, she twisted her head back and forth, trying to avoid his kisses. Finally she broke his hold by shoving strongly at his chest with both hands.

She raced to the bellpull. "If you don't leave, I'll call Ramesh. You know him. He could break your neck with the fingers of one hand."

Forrest took a step toward her. "You wouldn't let him do that," he said with a coaxing smile.

The accumulated strains of the day caught up with Chandra. Something snapped in her mind. She heard herself saying, "Oh, wouldn't I? I'd enjoy seeing Ramesh do it. Basil, I want you to go, and I don't want you to come back. I can't put up with your foolishness any more. You've bored me to tears for long enough."

He recoiled as if she'd struck him with a whip. His face was a pasty white. "Is that what you really think of me?

What you've always thought of me? You've smiled at me, and allowed me to ride with you, dance with you, escort you all over London, and all the time I've *bored* you?" Reading the truth in her set, telltale expression, he burst out, his voice trembling with angry hurt, "Do all men bore you? Or is it just me? You didn't look bored when I caught that Harley fellow pawing you. I think he *is* your lover!"

"That's enough, Basil. Just go."

Forrest opened his mouth and closed it again. Then, his shoulders slumping, he turned and walked out of the room.

Biting her lip, Chandra watched him go. Had she made a mistake, letting Basil Forrest know what she really thought of him? Would he now start spreading gossip about her? Could she really afford to change any of the relationships in the intricate web she'd been weaving since she came to England? Perhaps she should have been patient, keeping to the status quo, preserving all the contacts she'd made to date, until it was time to make her final move.

Tristan Loring looked into the card room at White's, locating his cousin at his customary table in the far corner, the usual pile of winnings at his elbow. Tristan walked over to Julian's table. Waiting until the hand had been played, he leaned over his cousin's shoulder. "Julian, could I talk to you?"

Julian glanced up with an expression of faint surprise from the cards he was shuffling. He lifted an eyebrow, saying, "Back from your wedding trip so soon? Give me a few minutes while I finish this rubber, Tris. I'll see you in the coffee room."

Half an hour later, when Julian dropped into a chair opposite his young cousin in the coffee room, he lifted a finger to a waiter and ordered a bottle of claret. From the faint slur in his voice, it was obvious he'd been drinking for some time. He said with a mocking smile, "Well, Tris, you led us a merry chase, by God! Chandra assumed, of course, that you and Lily had eloped to Gretna Green, so off we hared along the Great North Road, hoping to catch you before you reached Scotland. We got all the way to Ferrybridge, before Ramesh reached us with Miss Banks's message that you and Lily had been married by special licence."

Flushing, Tristan said belligerently, "I hope you don't expect me to apologize for causing you an inconvenience! You had no right to interfere if I *had* chosen to go to Gretna Green."

"Lily is a minor, and she *was* living under my protection, recall." Julian's voice was soft, but there was an edge to it.

Tristan flushed even more deeply. "Julian, I had to marry Lily out of hand. We knew Chandra would never consent to the marriage, and Lily was afraid Chandra would send her away, out of England, perhaps back to India. We might never have seen each other again!"

The waiter arrived with the bottle of claret. Waiting until the man had left, Julian poured himself and Tristan some wine. Lifting his glass, Julian said, "I've no wish to quarrel with you, Tris. What's done is done. I wish you happy."

Tristan's tense features relaxed a little. He gulped down half a glass of wine. "Thanks, Julian. I'd hoped the rest of the family would feel the same way." He finished his wine and reached for the bottle, saying with a catch in his voice, "Lily and I went to see Mama this morning, as soon as we returned from Eversleigh Manor. She wouldn't receive us."

Julian nodded. "Aunt Georgiana always wanted you to marry an heiress."

"Lily could be an heiress ten times over, and she'd still be outside the pale as far as Mama is concerned," said Tristan bitterly. "And all because Lily's blood isn't pure English. What does it matter?"

"It could matter to a great many people, and not just to your mother."

"I know." Tristan swallowed hard. Suddenly he looked very young and vulnerable. He said slowly, "I thought Chandra was exaggerating when she claimed society wouldn't accept Lily as my wife. But if Mama's reaction this morning is any indication of how others will feel . . . What if my colonel's wife should cut Lily, too, for example? I tell you, if marrying me were to give Lily a moment of unhappiness, I'd never forgive myself. Julian, that's why I've come to you. If you and Chandra and Ashley and Irene give our marriage your approval, the rest of our acquaintances would likely come around. Is Chandra very angry with us?"

"I fear she is."

"But you can talk her around, can't you?"

Julian made a quick, involuntary movement. He poured himself more wine and emptied the contents of his glass. "When did anyone, let alone her own husband, ever talk Chandra into anything?" he said savagely. He beckoned to the waiter and ordered another bottle of claret.

"You and Chandra have quarreled?" faltered Tristan. "Over me and Lily?"

"Yes, we've quarreled, but not over you and Lily. We needn't go beyond ourselves to find something to quarrel about, I assure you. We're like a pair of hounds, constantly at each other's throats."

The waiter brought the second bottle of claret and uncorked it. Julian poured wine into his glass and motioned to Tristan with the bottle. "A little more for you?"

"No, thank you." Tristan looked uneasily at his cousin, who sat with his eyes cast down on the table, sipping his claret morosely. "Julian, I didn't know you and Chandra were—were having difficulties. You always seemed like the perfect couple. I'm sorry."

Julian lifted his head. "What?" His eyes cleared, and he shot Tristan a twisted grin. "Good God, what fustian have I been spouting? I must watch myself. I've been dipping too deep of late. No, Tris, Chandra and I are not having difficulties. We had a little quarrel, over nothing im-

245

portant." He rose, saying, "Which reminds me, we'll have another little quarrel if I don't get home. I promised to take Chandra to a ball tonight." He clapped his hand on Tristan's shoulder. "Chandra is more hurt and anxious than angry with you and Lily. I think she'll come around. Be patient. And I'll speak to Ashley and Irene."

His eyes shining, Tristan clasped his cousin's hand. "Thanks, Julian. I could always count on you."

"Including dragging you out of every scrape known to man," Julian complained, as they left the coffee room together. "I don't think you've ever been properly thankful, you young villain." They retrieved their hats and walked out of the club. On the entrance steps Julian collided with a tall figure in a wasp-waisted coat of the latest cut.

"Here, you, why don't you look where you're going?" asked Basil Forrest truculently. A strong odor of Blue Ruin wafted from his willowy form. He peered at Julian out of unfocused eyes. "Oh, it's you, Ware."

Nodding curtly, Julian edged himself to the right and prepared to step down and around the hussar captain, who moved with him and stood like a swaying tree, blocking Julian's exit.

"Will you please remove yourself, Forrest, or must I make you?" Julian said coldly.

"I'd like to see you make me do anything, damn you. Why do you always treat me as if I were some kind of noxious insect? You look straight through me as if I were invisible. You're doing it now, confound you!"

Julian's lip curled. "Let me make myself clear, once and for all. I choose my friends and acquaintances, and they don't include Captain Sharps. My wife may choose to receive you, but I won't spend a minute in your company. Are you going to move?"

Forrest stood his ground, hugging his arms to his narrow chest and glaring malevolently at Julian. "Move? Why should I move for the likes of you? Who are *you* to give me orders? A seedy politician who's not clever enough to grasp the fact that his wife is making him the laughingstock of London! A cuckold who doesn't realize his beautiful wife is planting horns on his head with her banker friend!"

Julian shot out his fist and knocked Forrest down. He stepped around the hussar captain, went down the steps, and walked toward a waiting hackney cab.

"Julian," called Tristan warningly.

His hands clenched, Julian whirled to face Forrest. But the captain was not disposed for any more fisticuffs. He ripped off an elegant yellow glove and whipped it across Julian's face. "Name your second, Ware."

Chapter Fifteen

Chandra put down her book impatiently, when she realized she'd read at least ten pages without remembering a single detail of Evelina's escape from the foppish Sir Clement Willoughby's infamous attempt to abduct her after the opera. Looking disdainfully at the book, Chandra wondered why Miss Fanny Burney was one of Freddie's favorite authors. *Evelina* was a very dull book.

But, to give the famous lady novelist her due, the dullness of *Evelina* wasn't responsible for Chandra's woolgathering this morning. She'd picked up the book in the first place in an attempt to distract her mind from the many problems demanding her attention on this lovely July day, when she should have been out driving, or riding in the park, or shopping with Lily.

Lily. Her niece's hasty, misguided elopement was the least of Chandra's worries, though it still pressed heavily on her spirits. However, the marriage was a *fait accompli*. She could do nothing about it for the moment, at least. Overshadowing Lily's predicament in Chandra's mind was the shocking news she'd learned from Simon yesterday: the identity, or what she believed to be the identity, of Geoffrey Meredith's murderer. Now that the time had come to start putting in motion her plans to expose and punish her father's killer, she felt far less confident of her chances for success. Reality had set in.

Achieving her goal would be far more difficult and dangerous than she'd imagined during her days in Asaf Khan's encampment.

Her mind turned to Julian. He'd acted so strangely last night. For one thing, he'd been half-sprung when he returned to Grosvenor Square to escort her to the Mannerings' ball, and he continued to imbibe during the evening. But the liquor didn't entirely account for his curious mood, a mixture of excitement, hostility, and something else. The excitement she couldn't account for. The hostility toward herself was self-explanatory; their relations had always been adversarial, and never more so than now, after her invasion of White's Club and their mad dash for the Scottish border to prevent Lily's elopement. The "something else" . . .

Chandra's cheeks burned, as she remembered how Julian had acted last night, during and after the Mannerings' ball. The "something else" had been unmistakable. It was sensual attraction, in evidence whenever they were in close contact during the evening. When he helped her into the carriage, his hand had tightened on hers. When he reached out to adjust the shawl that had slipped off her shoulders, his fingers lingered on her bare flesh. When she took his arm to walk up the staircase to the Mannerings' ballroom, she could feel the tensing of his muscle beneath the fine broadcloth sleeve. And at the end of the evening, when he walked with her to the door of her bedchamber, he'd paused, swinging around to face her. His blue eyes were brilliant with a dancing hot flame. He put out his hand, brushing his fingers gently across her cheek, down her throat, into the filmy lace of her brief bodice. The touch of those knowing, caressing fingers sent a tremor through Chandra's body.

"Don't!" she exclaimed, edging back against the door.

He'd laughed then, dropping his hand. "Are you quite sure you mean that?"

"Very sure. You're foxed, Julian."

He'd laughed again. "Not too foxed to know what I

want. Or what you want." He slipped an arm loosely around her waist. "You know there's something between us, Chandra. You can't deny it."

He spoke lightly, almost with a tinge of amusement. He wasn't pressing her, but even the light physical contact between them was causing her heart to flutter wildly. She couldn't, she mustn't, give in to an insidious desire to relax into his embrace. From the very beginning, she'd known it would be fatal to allow any kind of a personal relationship to develop between them. Pushing his arm away, she said breathlessly, "There's nothing between us except a few meaningless words spoken over us by a preacher."

His reaction was immediate. His face changed. The dancing blue flame died out of his eyes. "And business," he replied coolly. "Don't forget business. You got my name and my position. I got a reprieve from debtors' prison. Value received on both sides, I'd say. Thank you for reminding me. Goodbye, Chandra."

This morning, recalling the scene, she moved her shoulders restlessly. She hadn't been able to sleep last night, for remembering every detail of the encounter with Julian outside her chamber door after they'd returned from the ball. Why couldn't she stop thinking about it? Julian had been half-seas over. He'd have pressed his attentions on any female within reach. It didn't mean anything, not to him, and most certainly not to her. But why had he said goodbye, instead of good night?"

She lifted her head, as the sound of urgent voices and scuffling noises outside in the corridor broke into her thoughts. At the same time, Frederica slipped into the room without knocking. Her face was pale. "Chandra, it's Julian. Tristan's just brought him home. He's hurt."

Chandra raced for the door. In the hallway, she could see Julian lurching toward his bedchamber, supported by Tristan on one side, and on the other by a stranger. His coat and waistcoat had been stripped off, and his white shirt was streaked with blood. A rough bandage was tied around his upper left arm and shoulder.

Darting out to confront the three men, Chandra exclaimed, "In God's name, Julian, what's happened?" His appearance appalled her. His face was ghastly pale and drawn with pain.

"It's nothing," he muttered thickly. "A scratch."

Tristan said in a low voice, "Julian's been shot, Chandra. Tell you about it later. The doctor's got to get the bullet out."

"Shot? My God! What can I do?"

The stranger glared at her. "Absolutely nothing, ma'am, except to get out of our way. You're interfering in my treatment of my patient. I want him in bed as soon as possible."

Standing tensely in the corridor with Frederica, dodging bustling servants who were bringing hot water, fresh linens, and restorative drinks to Julian's bedchamber, it seemed to Chandra that hours had elapsed before Tristan emerged from Julian's room. He hurried to Chandra, putting his arm around her. "Come sit down in your sitting room and we'll talk. You, too, Freddie."

Chandra was surprised to find her hands trembling in Tristan's strong grasp, as they sat together on a settee in her little sitting room. I'm reacting like any dutiful wife to news of her husband's injury, she thought in some confusion. She heard herself saying in a voice sharp with anxiety, "Now tell me what happened, Tris. Is Julian badly hurt?"

"No, no. Oh, granted, it's more than a flesh wound. He took a bullet in his left shoulder. But it's a clean wound. The bullet didn't touch the bone. He didn't lose much blood. The surgeon got the bullet out in a trice. Says he doesn't expect any complications, but Julian will be feeling pretty weak for a few hours. The doctor's keeping him in bed."

"Well, I should think so!" exclaimed Frederica.

Chandra sank back against the cushions in relief. "Who shot him? Why?"

Instead of answering, Tristan stared at her in embarrassment.

"Well, Tris?" Chandra gaped at him. "Don't tell me it was you?"

"Me! In heaven's name, why would I shoot Julian? No, it was that fellow, Basil Forrest. The hussar captain who's always hanging about after you." Tristan shook his head, saying reproachfully, "Never could see why you tolerated him. He's a Bad Man. Responsible for the suicide of one of Julian's great friends, did you know that?"

Chandra stared at Tristan in stupefaction. "Basil shot Julian? How—? Why—?"

"It was a duel, of course. Forrest forced a quarrel on Julian last night in front of White's. They met this morning at Westbourne Green, near Paddington. I was acting as Julian's second, and he told me beforehand he intended to delope, and he did. He fired straight into the air. He thinks duels are stupid, y'know. Says a duel proves only one thing, that one fellow can shoot straighter than t'other." Tristan shook his head. "Julian also told me he thought Forrest would shoot to kill. Forrest did. But he's a bad shot, fortunately." Tristan's face turned an angry red. "By God, if that slimy hussar had killed Julian, I'd have seen him in the dock for murder. And if the jury had refused to convict, I'd have shot Forrest out of hand myself."

"And he'd have deserved it, too," declared Frederica indignantly.

But Chandra felt something like a cold fist squeezing her heart. Now she understood why Julian had said goodbye, and not good night. He'd thought there was a good chance he wouldn't survive the duel. Her lips stiff, she asked, "Why did Basil challenge Julian to a duel?"

Tristan turned an even deeper red. Avoiding her gaze, he mumbled, "Well, Forrest and Julian have never hit it off. Julian always cuts the fellow dead, and Forrest resents it. And they were both castaway last night, Forrest especially.

He was sodden with Blue Ruin. Can't even drink like a gentleman."

Tristan was too open-natured to be a good liar. Chandra said curtly, "Out with it, Tris. There's more to this quarrel than dislike."

"Oh, the devil, I *knew* we couldn't keep it from you. You've always been as shrewd as you could hold together. Very well, Chandra, if you must have it, Basil informed Julian you were planting horns on his head with your banker friend, Simon Harley, and Julian milled the fellow down. Naturally. Forrest demanded satisfaction. Well, I suppose you could say he *was* the injured party."

"The injured party," repeated Chandra hollowly. Of course. In a fit of anger and anxiety yesterday, she'd told Basil what she really thought of him, and ordered him out of her life. So then he'd set out to drink himself into oblivion, and it had been sheer bad luck that he'd encountered Julian on the steps of White's. Julian had delivered another of his set-downs, Basil had retaliated verbally, and what followed was inevitable. In his stiff-necked masculine pride, Julian would neither refuse the challenge nor shoot to defend himself. He could easily have died. It was all her fault.

Tristan's voice broke into her thoughts. ". . . So I don't think there'll be any gossip."

Chandra looked at him blankly. "What?"

He said with a patient air, "I don't think you need worry about gossip. Before we left Westbourne Green this morning, I got hold of Forrest and put the fear of the devil into him. If ever I heard one slanderous word about you and Harley, I told Forrest, I'd thrash him down the length of St. James's Street, and then, if he demanded satisfaction, I'd damned well give it to him. Only, I'm a crack shot, and *I* wouldn't delope!"

"That's good. Thank you, Tris." Chandra's words were perfunctory. Somehow, gossip seemed a minor evil compared to the enormity of Julian's brush with death.

Tristan cleared his throat. "Chandra . . ." The words

came in a rush. "I know you must be very angry with me and Lily. She's afraid you'll never forgive us. But I told her I was sure you'd never cast her off. You love her too much for that."

Chandra looked at Tristan's tense young face and sighed. "Of course, I love her. She's my nie—my sister. And it's not a question of forgiveness. All I ever wanted was Lily's happiness."

"And you think she won't have it with me. Chandra, I promise you I'll do everything in my power to make you change your mind about that. Lily's happiness will come before everything else in my life, until the end of time. Won't you help me? Won't you receive Lily and publicly approve our marriage? Where you lead, others will follow, I'm sure of that. And Lily will be overjoyed to know she's no longer estranged from you."

Chandra strongly doubted that her approval, or lack of it, would have any effect on the attitude of society toward Lily's marriage, but she saw little point in reminding Tristan of that. Suddenly she laughed, saying, "Tristan, you wretch, if you thought to turn me up sweet, you were perfectly right!" She leaned over to brush her lips against his cheek. "Tell Lily to come see me. No, wait. Where are you and Lily staying? With your mother?"

"No. Mama has washed her hands of us. We've taken rooms at Fenton's Hotel, until we can find lodgings."

"Indeed you're not. You're staying with me and Julian."

Out of the corner of her eye, Chandra saw Frederica's face flood with relief. Tristan jumped up from the settee, smiling with joy. "Bless you, Chandra. I can't wait to tell Lily the wonderful news. And don't worry about old Julian. He'll be fine."

After Tristan had left, Frederica said, "You'll never be sorry you've reconciled with Lily."

Chandra smiled at the ex-governess. "Oh, you. You must have known I couldn't stay angry with her. Mind, I still think I was right. I doubt very much that the ton will accept this marriage."

"You always think you're right," retorted Frederica, with a return of her old asperity.

Chandra laughed. "Freddie, I'm sorry I spoke so sharply to you yesterday."

Frederica patted Chandra's arm without speaking. After a moment, she said, "Shall I tell the housekeeper to have Lily's old rooms prepared for her and Tris?"

"Yes, thank you, Freddie."

Frederica went to the door. As she opened it, a footman, his hand poised to knock, stepped back from it. "Yes, what is it?" Chandra asked.

"Lord and Lady Daylesford ter see ye, ma'am." The footman's face wore a curiously wooden expression. No doubt the servants already knew all about the duel, thought Chandra resignedly.

"Tell his lordship and her ladyship I'll be right down."

As Chandra entered the drawing room a few minutes later, Irene was sitting quietly on a sofa and Ashley was pacing nervously up and down the vast room, his limp more pronounced than usual. When he limped badly, it was always a sign of inner perturbation. He stopped abruptly when he saw her. She realized with a slight shock that she hadn't seen him since the day, over a week ago now, when he'd begged her for the money to pay Caroline Onslow's blackmailing demands. While Chandra hadn't wanted or expected his gratitude, the open hostility in his voice was unexpected as he said, "What's this about Julian fighting a duel with the likes of Basil Forrest?"

Chandra said in surprise, "How did you find out about it? The duel took place only hours ago."

"My friend Jack Jermaine came around this morning to tell us about it. It was all over White's last night."

"Chandra, is Julian hurt?" asked Irene anxiously. "All we know is that there was a duel. We came the moment we heard."

"He was wounded, but not seriously. He was shot in the shoulder. The surgeon's already removed the bullet, and he told Tristan—Tris was Julian's second—the surgeon told Tristan he doesn't expect any complications."

"Thank God," murmured Irene. "What good news, Ashley."

"Yes." Ashley stared at Chandra. "How did Julian come to fight Forrest? Julian despises the fellow. Says he's a Greek, and worse."

Chandra hesitated. "Perhaps you'd better ask Julian," she said at last.

Frowning, Ashley gazed at her for a long moment. His voice rasped as he said, "You know the reason for the duel, don't you? Why are you being so evasive?"

Curbing her irritation, Chandra replied, "If you don't mind, Ashley, I'd prefer not to discuss my husband's private affairs."

"Oh, come, it's rather late to be playing the dutiful wife, isn't it? Damnation, Julian's my brother. I demand to know why he allowed a scruffy court card like Basil Forrest to call him out." Ashley's gaze sharpened. "Lombard Street to a China orange, *you'll* turn out to be at the bottom of it all. You've meant nothing but disaster for Julian since the first day he met you!"

"Ashley!" exclaimed Irene in horror. "How can you speak to Chandra like that?"

His expression altered, but before he could reply, Chandra's own temper got the better of her. She said coldly, "If you must know, my dear brother-in-law, Basil Forrest accused me of cuckolding Julian with my old friend, Simon Harley, and Julian knocked Basil down."

"Oh, Chandra, how dreadful for you," breathed Irene in an anguished whisper.

"Well? Is it true?" sneered Ashley.

In an icy tone Chandra had never before heard her use to her husband, Irene said, "Ashley, that was unpardonable. Apologize to Chandra immediately."

Ashley colored, gulped, turned pale again. His voice sounded strangled as he said, "I beg your pardon, Chandra."

256

She inclined her head.

"Excuse me. I'm going up to see how Julian goes on," Ashley muttered. When he'd gone, Irene slumped back against the upholstery, looking alarmingly pale. Chandra hurried to her side.

"Darling Irene, you're ill." Chandra rummaged in Irene's reticule for a vinaigrette bottle and waved it slowly beneath her sister-in-law's nose. Slowly Irene began to recover her color.

"Thank you, Chandra. I'm fine now, truly." Irene caught Chandra's hand in a surprisingly strong grip for one so frail. "My dearest, Ashley didn't mean what he said to you. It's just that he's so concerned about Julian. His fears for Julian's safety simply ran away with him, and he struck out at the first person he could find to blame for his brother's condition. You understand, don't you?"

"Yes, of course. Don't worry about it, Irene," Chandra said soothingly. She thought it quite likely that Irene's defense of Ashley was at least partly justified. The two brothers were very close, and Ashley had arrived at the house in Grosvenor Square not knowing whether Julian was dead or alive. It *was* natural for him to vent his feelings by lashing out at the first available victim.

But Chandra also suspected another, and very human, reason for Ashley's antagonism toward her. She'd saved him from a public exposure that he'd feared might affect his wife's health and sanity. Although his first instinct probably had been to feel grateful, his next reaction might well have been anger. Anger that he'd been forced to reveal to Chandra his dreadful secret, anger that he was now under a debt to a woman he disliked and despised, a debt he could never repay.

Still clinging to Chandra's hand, Irene murmured, "Ashley's been under a strain for so long. Something is still weighing on his spirits, and, try as I may, I can't persuade him to talk about it. He just denies there's anything wrong."

Chandra squeezed Irene's hand in silent sympathy.

There was little she could say. She surmised that Ashley was not only feeling a heavy goad of guilt, but he might also have acquired such a taste for unnatural practices that he was continually fighting against the temptation.

"Well, of course he'll solve the problem, if it *is* a problem," said Irene with a determined cheerfulness. "Ashley is so strong." Withdrawing her hand from Chandra's, Irene sat upright, saying, "I was planning to come see you today, even before we heard about Julian. Georgiana visited me yesterday. Would you believe it, she wanted my promise that Ashley and I would bar the doors of Daylesford House to Lily and Tris! She had the bacon-brained notion that if we refused to receive Lily, Tris would start divorce proceedings! At least, I *think* that's what she meant."

"And what did you say?" asked Chandra, smiling at Irene's indignant expression.

"Why, I told Georgiana I'd as lief bar *her* from my door! Lily is family now, doubly so, as Julian's sister-in-law and Tris's wife."

Irene looked up as Ashley returned to the drawing room, appearing more composed than when he'd left. "I talked briefly with the doctor, who was just leaving," he reported. "He told me Julian was in no danger whatever, unless he developed a fever, which the surgeon didn't anticipate. The doctor's given Julian a dose of laudanum, which should make him sleep for some time."

Irene gave him one of her warm, sweet smiles, in which there was no hint of the strain she'd displayed to Chandra. "You must feel so relieved, my dear."

"Yes." He said hesitantly to Chandra, "I'd like to say again I'm sorry for what I said to you."

Controlling the aversion she couldn't help feeling toward him, Chandra said, "There's no necessity for that. It's a trying time for all of us." She was rewarded by Irene's quick smile of relief.

After Ashley and Irene had gone, Chandra sat ir-resolutely for several minutes in the drawing room, before she started up the stairs and down the corridor of the second floor toward Julian's bedchamber. She tapped lightly on the door, and Julian's valet, Bates, answered immediately.

"I'd like to see my husband," Chandra said in a low voice.

The valet bowed and stood aside to allow her to enter. She walked over to the big, old-fashioned tester bed, another of the pieces of furniture belonging to the former owner that she'd thriftily decided not to replace when she refurbished the house. She stood beside the bed, looking down at Julian's still figure.

His face was waxy pale, almost deathlike. Even though he was deep in drug-induced sleep, she could see the lines of pain creased into his features. He looked so defenseless, shorn of his usual poise and arrogance, and with his closed eyelids, with their fan of absurdedly long black lashes, hiding the electric vitality of his blue eyes.

"Should he be so pale?" she whispered to the valet.

"Mr. Ware *was* shot, ma'am. And it's not a pleasant experience to have a bullet extracted, let me tell you. It stands to reason Mr. Ware wouldn't look quite the thing. But we must hope for the best. The doctor says Mr. Ware will be all right, barring a fever."

"I suppose," murmured Chandra doubtfully. "You'll call me, if—if anything happens?"

"Assuredly, ma'am."

Chandra went to her own bedchamber to take up an uncomfortable vigil. She was worried about Julian. The ominous mention of a possible fever had brought back terrible memories of an incident in Asaf Khan's encampment. One of the Pindari chief's lieutenants, his leg wounded in a plundering raid, had developed a high fever which resulted in successive agonizing piece-by-piece amputations of the limb, and, finally, death.

Chandra made no attempt to evade her feelings of guilt. She was responsible for Julian's injury, and she'd be responsible for his death, if it occurred. If she hadn't come to England to pursue her vendetta against her father's murderer, he would never have met her. If she hadn't forced him into a marriage he despised, he would never have been drawn into her affairs, and he wouldn't now be lying wounded in his bed. Because, however much Basil Forrest had resented Julian's cutting set-downs in the past, it was the hussar captain's infatuation with Chandra that had caused him to issue his challenge to Julian yesterday.

Compelled by a sudden impulse, Chandra walked over to the massive wardrobe and reached back into a corner of the top shelf to remove an object wrapped in a shawl. She placed the object on a small table, unfolded the shawl, and opened the carved wooden box that contained the diamond and emerald parure of the Begum of Bhulamphur. The myriad diamonds flashed with a scintillating blaze in the rays of the brilliant July sun streaming through the windows, and the huge emerald pendant in the necklace burned with an intense green fire.

Chandra hadn't looked at the jewels since her arrival in Woolwich, so many weeks ago, when she'd shown the parure to Frederica and revealed her plans to use it to trap her father's killer. She hadn't wanted to look at the jewels. She hadn't wanted to be reminded that the glittering things, so beautiful and yet so evil, had caused so many deaths. Papa was dead, and her sister Phoebe, and the Begum and her servants, and so many Sepoys from her father's regiment. All because an unknown, greedy man had schemed to possess the Begum's jewels and her gold, whatever the cost in human life.

Chandra closed the box with a snap, wrapped it in the shawl, and put it back in the wardrobe. Difficult as it had been to gaze on the jewels and bring back the dreadful memories of the massacre in Bhulamphur, she mused, perhaps she'd needed to see them, to be reminded of her reason for coming to England. Because the mysterious villain who'd caused her and her family so much suffering was no longer unknown. Provisionally, at least, she could now pinpoint a name and a face. She mustn't allow anybody or anything to get in the way of her purpose.

Throughout the rest of the day, Chandra went back several times to Julian's rooms to check his condition. For many hours she could see no difference in him. His valet continued to sit watchfully at his bedside, observing him as he lay pale and unmoving, sunk deep in the oblivion of laudanum. Toward late afternoon, however, as she approached Julian's door, she heard a voice raised in anger and the sound of breaking crockery. She hurried into the room and came to an abrupt stop to avoid colliding with the valet, who stood in the middle of the floor, mournfully surveying the smashed remains of a china bowl, from the shards of which a thin gray liquid was seeping into the carpet.

"And if you come near me one more time with that poisonous stuff, Bates, you can consider yourself dismissed," Julian snapped. He was sitting up in bed, one hand clamped to his injured shoulder, and his face was faintly flushed.

"Yes, sir. The doctor did say, sir, that you were to have the gruel." Gazing at Julian's implacable expression, the valet sighed in resignation and bent to collect the pieces of broken china.

Julian flinched when Chandra walked over to the bed and placed her hand on his forehead. "What's that for?" he growled.

"You're a little flushed. I thought you might have a fever," she said in relief. His skin wasn't hot. The flush, she surmised, was the product of annoyance, not fever.

"Are you in much pain?" she asked.

"I don't feel the urge to stand up to several rounds with some Pet of the Fancy, if that's what you mean."

Finished with clearing the carpet of the debris of broken china, the valet went to the table on the other side of the bed and picked up a glass containing what appeared to be port wine. "The doctor also left this for you, sir."

Julian took the glass and raised it to his lips. Without a word he handed it back to the valet. "There's laudanum in

261

that wine. I can smell it."

"Yes, sir. The doctor did say the wine would disguise the taste."

"I don't want it. Take it away."

"But, sir, you'll need it for the pain."

"Take—it—away. I don't propose to be drugged senseless a second time. And bring me something to eat. Half a chicken, for instance, or a few rashers of bacon. And a bottle of claret."

"Sir, the doctor said you were to have only light foods. Gruel, or perhaps broth. Toast and tea."

At the look of growing wrath on Julian's face, Chandra intervened. "You really shouldn't eat too heavily right away, Julian. We had some wonderful beef soup for lunch. Perhaps you could have some of that now, and a bit of toast and a cup of tea. Then, later, for supper, you might have something more hearty."

For a moment, Chandra thought he would remain adamant. Then, grudgingly, he said to the valet, "Very well, Bates, I'll have some of that soup and toast. But I warn you, that's the last pap I'll eat today."

"Yes, sir, I'll bring the soup right away, sir."

After Bates left, Chandra looked closely at Julian, who was in obvious discomfort, having difficulty holding himself upright. "If you're going to continue sitting up, let me arrange some pillows behind your back," she suggested. Slipping her arms around his sound shoulder, she gently inserted pillows behind him, trying not to notice the smooth flesh and the rippling muscles of his naked chest and back. She pulled the coverlets up around him and moved back from the bed, saying, "Is that better?"

"Yes. Thank you." He added gruffly, "There's no need for you to fuss, though. It's a mere flesh wound."

"Don't you try to bubble me," Chandra retorted. "There's a hole in your shoulder."

He attempted to shrug, and grimaced with pain.

Chandra said suddenly, "Julian, I'm so sorry you're hurt. I know it was my fault."

His eyebrows drew together, and the blue eyes turned chilly. "What do you mean? As I remember it, Basil Forrest pulled the trigger of the pistol that shot me."

"Yes, but he was really angry with me. We'd quarreled that afternoon, when he found me with Simon—" She broke off, biting her lip. Julian was staring at her with an unreadable expression. "Of course, you'd probably have taken up Basil's challenge whether you believed the filth he was spouting or not," she went on hastily. "I've heard about the peculiar English male code of honor. But I assure you there wasn't a word of truth in anything Basil may have told you about me and Simon."

"I know that." His tone was perfectly matter-of-fact.

"Oh." Now it was her turn to stare.

"I've seen you with Simon Harley," Julian said coolly. "If you two are lovers, it must be the most tepid romance that ever set a maiden's cheek ablush! And besides, I know you, Chandra. While we're legally tied to each other, I don't think you'd make me the sport of gossips by planting horns on my head."

"No, of course, I wouldn't do that." Chandra's mind was whirling with confusion. Was Julian aware of the compliment he'd just paid her? After all these weeks of bitterness and estrangement and misunderstandings, he'd told her, in effect, that she had a rock-bottom core of integrity that had won his respect. Or had he? Misgiving struck. Perhaps she's simply read too much into what he'd said. But then, what had he meant?

The valet returned at that moment with a kitchen maid carrying a tray, and Chandra beat her retreat, saying hastily, "I'll look in later, Julian."

She wanted to examine her jumbled thoughts, but she had no opportunity to do so. As she stepped into the corridor, she met a file of maidservants and footmen who were heavily laden with an assortment of valises and portmanteaux. In reply to her query, one of the footmen said, "Oh, yes, indeed, ma'am. Miss Lily an' her new husband, they're come ter stay. Miss Lily, she says they'll

263

wait fer ye in the morning room."

As Chandra entered the morning room shortly afterward, Lily rushed up to her with an ecstatic embrace. "Oh, Chandra, darling, I can't thank you enough for having us here. It's so good to be back!"

"Nalini." The pet Indian name came out naturally. All of Chandra's lingering anger melted away. Returning Lily's embrace, she exclaimed, "I'm so glad to see you."

Flashing a pleased grin at both of them, Tristan inquired, "How's Julian? Resting comfortably? Famous! I knew he'd have no problems." He bestowed a hasty hug on Chandra, saying, "I'll leave you two to a cozy chat. I must go. I have a review this afternoon. The Prince of Wales is coming." He brushed Lily's cheek in a brief kiss and left.

Chandra gave Lily a close look. In repose, the girl's dark, piquant face seemed subtly older, and there was a shadow behind the great brown eyes. Lily was no longer a kittenish little girl.

"Chandra, I'm so sorry we caused you such grief. We never meant to. It was just that Tris and I loved each other so much, and we wanted to be together."

"I know. Don't put yourself into a taking. I really do understand. Lily, are you happy?"

For a moment, the dark eyes lighted up. "Oh, yes. Tris is so wonderful." The glow faded quickly. "But—"

"But?"

Lily hesitated. Then, "Perhaps I should have listened to you, for Tris's sake, not my own. *I* wouldn't change anything," came her words in a rush. "We were so sure, you see, that, once we were actually married, everything would be all right."

"What's happened, Lily?"

"Well, Lady Eversleigh won't receive us. How can she act so to her only child, Chandra? But there, I daresay I shouldn't be too surprised. She's never liked me. Today, though . . . Tris suggested I call on his colonel's wife. Mrs. Lovejoy's servants told me she wasn't receiving, though

264

the carriages were lined up in front of her house, and I could hear a clamor of voices from the drawing room. I hated to tell Tris. He was counting so much on Colonel and Mrs. Lovejoy's friendship."

"Don't think about it. The lady may change her mind later." Chandra tried to inject optimism into her voice, but she didn't feel much hope.

Neither, apparently, did Lily. "Well, we'll see, won't we?" she murmured, sounding unconvinced. She brightened a little a moment later, when Frederica swept into the room with outstretched arms. Watching the pair with a catch in her heart, Chandra reflected wistfully that, even in the darkest, most terrifying days of their captivity in Asaf Khan's encampment, Lily had at least been able to count on unqualified love and approval from herself and Freddie.

Early that evening, dressed for dinner, Chandra left her bedchamber and walked down the corridor to Julian's room. When the valet opened the door, she stepped inside and paused in surprise. Julian was sitting in an armchair in front of a table that was set for dining. His black curls were neatly brushed, he'd been shaved, and he was wearing a dressing gown, with the empty left sleeve tucked into the loosely tied sash.

"Julian! Should you be out of bed? What did the surgeon say when he called this afternoon?"

"Told me to stay flat on my back until his next visit," Julian said with a grin. "But I am *not* about to eat my first decent meal today in that blasted bed."

The valet, Bates, removing the covers from several dishes on an adjacent serving table, murmured, "Perhaps you'd care to share Mr. Ware's dinner, ma'am?"

"Oh, I'm not sure . . ."

"No problem at all, ma'am. I'll ring for more plates and silver."

Several minutes later, facing each other across a well-laden table, Chandra and Julian exchanged glances of blank surprise.

"How did this happen?" said Chandra, with a rather weak attempt at a laugh.

"You know what I think?" said Julian suddenly. "I think Bates is thoroughly sick of being incarcerated with me all day, and he's decided to turn over his nursemaid duties to you for a while."

Chandra's laugh this time was genuine. "Oh. Well, in that case, I'd better make myself useful." She placed some roast beef, a piece of ham, some stewed carp and some asparagus on Julian's plate, cut the meat into bite-sized bits, and poured him a glass of claret.

It was a meal Chandra never forgot. A number of disparate factors—an excellent claret, a hint of illicit intimacy, Julian's partial helplessness from his injury, Chandra's relief at seeing him on the road to recovery—combined to break down the barriers of constraint that normally inhibited them when they were together. Before Chandra quite realized what was happening, they were speaking more naturally to each other than they ever had before, exchanging views, telling jokes, slipping easily into a bantering give-and-take.

At one point, Julian regaled Chandra with tales of Parliament and the War Office. She laughed until she cried as he described how the Duke of York's love letters to his greedy mistress, Mrs. Clarke, had been read aloud in the House of Commons. "And they weren't even very good love letters."

Chandra told Julian about the effect Ramesh's exotic appearance had had upon the startled inhabitants of Woolwich when she and Frederica and Lily had first landed in England. "The children followed poor Ramesh around until you'd think he was the Pied Piper of Hamelin."

"Ramesh has been in your employ for a long time, I take it," said Julian idly.

"Oh. Yes. Many years. He was my hus—he's an old

family servant." Chandra tensed as she realized how close she'd been to talking about Asaf Khan.

"You never speak much about your life in India," Julian went on. "Where was it you lived? Bombay? Or was it Calcutta? It seems to me I've heard your aunt mention Calcutta."

"We lived for a time in Bombay," said Chandra with a dry mouth. She rose, saying, "I think I should go. This is Lily's first night back, you know. You look tired, too."

As he braced his weight on his good arm and pulled himself up from the armchair, Julian gave an involuntary grunt of pain. He swayed, catching at the chair.

"You should go back to bed immediately. You've overtired yourself." Chandra put her arm around his waist.

"I'm all right," he replied impatiently, but he allowed her to walk with him to the bed. He stood waiting while she pulled back the coverlets and fluffed the pillows.

"You'll rest more comfortably if you take off your dressing gown," said Chandra rather nervously as their eyes locked together. Without looking down, he fumbled one-handed with the sash on his robe, and Chandra put out her hand automatically to untie the sash and slip the dressing gown from his injured shoulder. Almost before she'd registered the fact that he was wearing only his thin cotton underdrawers, the silk robe fell to the floor in a slithering heap and Julian reached out his right arm to pull her to him.

His mouth descended on hers, hard, hungry, demanding. She made one feeble, ineffectual effort to pull away, and then, as waves of fiery longing surged through her, she relaxed against him, feeling an unfamiliar urgent throbbing in her pelvis. Moving his head from side to side, he forced her lips apart and thrust his tongue into her mouth, exploring the delights within, caressing her tongue with his, until she was trembling with desire.

When he finally lifted his head to look down at her, his breathing was rough and uneven, and his blue eyes were blazing with passion. "Chandra, I want you, I need you," he muttered thickly, and with one fluid motion he sank down on the bed, drawing her with him, cradling her with his good right arm.

"Julian, please . . . we shouldn't . . ."

"Why shouldn't we? You're my wife." His searching lips traced feathery kisses on her eyelids, her cheeks, her throat, and came back to her mouth in a scorching kiss. His hand lingeringly caressed her breast and then slowly slipped inside the satin of her brief bodice. She gasped with a fiery pleasure that was almost pain, and at the same moment she realized he was using his left hand. "Julian! Your shoulder!"

"The hell with my shoulder," he murmured, and pulled her closer to him, until she could feel the swelling in his groin. Shaking with the enticing danger of the contact, she twined her arm around his neck and pressed against him. With a little groan, he buried his face in her hair, whispering, "You smell like flowers. I'd know your scent anywhere. It intoxicates me. *You* intoxicate me." The whisper deepened in her ear. "Chandra, I have to know. Are you a virgin? I don't want to hurt you."

Virgin. In a flash of memory, she could see Asaf Khan's burly form sitting on the edge of her divan, she could feel the gross touch of his trailing fingers and hear his muttered, "My beautiful virgin, more exquisite than the blessed *houris* of Paradise, why did you come to me when it was too late?"

"No! I can't—" She pushed desperately at Julian's chest to release herself, and scrambled to her feet beside the bed. Her breath coming in great irregular gasps, she stared down at him. He lay back against the pillows, his eyes wide and dazed, his right hand clutching his wounded shoulder. The white bandaging was splotched with crimson.

"Oh, God, Julian, your wound's broken open." After a frantic glance around her, Chandra grabbed a linen napkin from the supper table and leaned over Julian, pressing the napkin to his shoulder. She recoiled when he grasped her arm with a surprising strength and shoved her away from him.

"Don't touch me."

"But Julian, you must let me help you—"

"I don't want your help, I don't want you near me, ever again. This is the last time I'll let you make a fool of me with your tempting, beautiful body. There's something evil in you, Chandra, something perverse, that drives you to lure a man to the point of sexual frenzy, before you tear yourself away like a virtuous but slightly tarnished virgin."

Feeling a knifelike pain in her heart as she saw the spreading stain on his bandaged shoulder, Chandra said pleadingly, "Please, Julian, no matter what you think of me, let me help you."

Julian's voice was weaker now, almost inaudible. "Call Bates. He's probably lurking somewhere out in the hall. I'd rather bleed to death than have you touch me."

Chapter Sixteen

Her hand raised to knock, Chandra stood hesitating before the door of Julian's bedchamber. A chambermaid, broom and dustpan in hand, came down the hall toward her, staring curiously. "Good morning, ma'am."

"Good morning." Chandra waited until the maidservant had walked on, and then, exasperated by her cowardice, she rapped purposefully on the door. "How is Mr. Ware feeling this morning?" she asked the valet, Bates, when he answered her knock.

"Come in, Chandra," Julian called from inside the room.

She drew a breath of sheer relief when she saw him sitting in front of a serving table, raising a cup to his lips. He was wearing his dressing gown, with the left side of it draped loosely over his injured shoulder.

"Oh, I'm so glad," she exclaimed. "You're none the worse for—" She broke off, feeling the hot color rush to her cheeks. "Has the doctor seen you today?"

He put down his cup and poured more tea with a steady hand. "Yes. Bates insisted on calling him in last night, also."

"Your shoulder? It didn't continue bleeding?"

"No, I'm in prime twig, or soon will be. But thank you for your concern." The blue eyes, chilly and emotionless, stared straight through her. "Don't let me keep you," he added politely.

A moment later, Chandra was standing outside the door again, blinking her eyes against a rush of stinging tears. So this was how it was going to be for the duration of her marriage to Julian. He'd made his position very clear. Henceforth they would live as strangers, cold, remote, without a vestige of warmth or companionship. Or passion, she thought, clenching her hands.

There *had* been passion between them last night. She couldn't deny it. She couldn' blame Julian, either, for becoming so furious with her. It must have seemed to him that she'd deliberately led him on, responding to his kisses and his embraces only to refuse and humiliate him so cruelly in the end.

Her face flamed. She'd been so close to surrender. Last night she'd wanted Julian as much as he wanted her. But thank God, her ugly memories of Asaf Khan's last futile, fumbling efforts to renew his male vitality had intervened to prevent that surrender. Very soon, now, she would expose and punish Papa's murderer, and then she would leave England, trailing a shambles of scandal behind her as her real identity and the magnitude of her lies and deceptions became known. How much easier it would be for both her and Julian to cut their ties, if they hadn't succumbed to the fiery passion that had hovered over their relationship since the first day they'd met.

"Good heavens, Chandra, why are you standing there like a pillar of salt?"

Chandra turned to greet Frederica, reflecting with a wry amusement that the vicar's daughter could never rid herself of Biblical allusions. "Just thinking, Freddie."

Frederica said in alarm, "Julian hasn't taken a turn for the worse? You look so grave."

Chandra took a deep breath. "No, not at all. He's mending apace. Bates can't keep him in bed. Julian insisted on getting up to eat his breakfast."

"Oh, that's wonderful news." Frederica didn't seem to notice any constraint on Chandra's part. "Shall we go down to breakfast? I'm famished. Lily, of course, is keeping to her bed. How that girl hates to get up in the morning!"

Chandra ate a large plate of bacon and kidneys and buttered toast, washed down with several cups of tea, without really tasting a mouthful, and without arousing Frederica's anxieties about her state of mind. Freddie was immersed in a blissful euphoria about Chandra's reconciliation with Lily. Her antennae, usually so sensitive, hadn't picked up on Chandra's mood.

After breakfast, Chandra sent for Ramesh.

The Pathan saluted her with his customary sweeping salaam when he entered the morning room. "My lady wishes to confer with me?" he asked in Hindi. "I trust your servant has given you no cause for dissatisfaction?"

"No, of course not, Ramesh. You are ever my true and faithful henchman," Chandra replied, in the flowery phrases that came to her so naturally when she was speaking Hindi. "I have summoned you on an affair of the utmost importance."

She paused, as a footman appeared at the door. "Captain Forrest wishes to see you, ma'am," said the footman.

Chandra's flesh crawled. "Tell the captain I'm not at home," she began, and paused. "No. Ask him to come here." To Ramesh she said, "I will confer with you later."

"Your merest wish is your humble servant's command." The Pathan's face was impassive, but Chandra wasn't deceived. She'd seen the quick glow of interest in his dark eyes at the mention of her "important affair."

When Basil Forret entered the morning room, Chandra was shocked at his appearance. The hussar captain had neglected his usually meticulous toilet; his cravat was badly tied, his coat was wrinkled, and his Hessians lacked a mirrorlike gloss. His eyes were bloodshot, his hands were shaking, and his skin had the pasty appearance of one who had been so castaway that he'd just shot the cat.

He fastened the bloodshot eyes on Chandra. "I feared you wouldn't see me," he mumbled.

"I was tempted not to," said Chandra coldly. She could hardly bear to look at him. She had to resist an overwhelming urge to summon Ramesh to toss Basil out.

272

But no, until her mission here in England had been accomplished, she couldn't break any of the intertwining strands in the web she'd woven to trap Geoffrey Meredith's killer.

Forrest continued in hopeful tones, "Ware wasn't badly hurt, I hear. A clean shoulder wound, I believe."

"No, he's recovering. No thanks to you."

"Chandra, I swear I never meant to harm Ware. Lord help me, I've never before fought a duel! But I was drunk, and when he looked down his nose at me at White's, in that toplofty way of his, well, something snapped."

"Is that why you informed Julian I was cuckolding him with Simon Harley?"

Basil's flush concealed the pastiness of his skin. "It—it slipped out before I could stop myself. I didn't really mean it. Chandra, I've come here to beg your pardon. I'll gladly apologize to Ware, too, if you wish. Just don't close the door on our friendship. Without that, I don't see how I can go on. I love you so much—" He took a quick step toward her, recoiling at the sudden flash of green fire from her eyes.

"Don't ever mention the word love to me again, Basil."

"No—no. But you *will* forgive me? You'll let me see you?"

Chandra saw her way out and took it. "Yes, I forgive you, but as for seeing me . . . Basil, you must understand how awkward it would be for me to meet you in my husband's presence. Perhaps you shouldn't call on me for a little."

"Oh. But later, when Ware's fully recovered? We might go riding, at least?"

"Yes, later." Much later, Chandra silently resolved.

No sooner had she succeeded in getting rid of Basil Forrest, stammering and inarticulate in his joy, when a servant brought word of other visitors. With an inward groan, she said, "Ask Mr. and Mrs. Taney and Mr. Alfred Taney to come to the morning room."

Mrs. Taney's beady little eyes were avid with curiosity as she took a chair opposite Chandra, saying, "Captain

273

Forrest was just leaving as we came in the door."

"Yes?" Chandra shot the woman a cool glance that said plainly, "No trespassing."

Mrs. Taney swallowed. "We came to inquire about Mr. Ware's health. We've been so concerned about him, haven't we, Artemus, Alfred?"

"Hmph," muttered Artemus Taney. He was a dour, unprepossessing man who rarely opened his mouth. Chandra would have had trouble recognizing him outside his wife's company. She'd often wondered how such a man had managed to acquire power and vast wealth in the East India Company.

"Hmph," echoed the dreadful Alfred, whose complexion appeared spottier than ever.

"Thank you," replied Chandra graciously to Mrs. Taney, "but, indeed, there's no need for your concern. My husband is enjoying a speedy recovery from his—his indisposition."

"How splendid. We've also heard of an exciting event in your family. We'd like to wish Miss Lily happy." She cast significant glances at her husband and son.

"Hmph," said Mr. Taney again.

"Like to wish Miss Lily happy," muttered Alfred morosely. Chandra wondered how soon he would fancy himself violently in love with another girl, now that Lily was out of his reach.

"And last, but not too much the least, one hopes," Mrs. Taney continued, "we've come to invite you and Mr. Ware to a house party at our new estate in Buckinghamshire in September, when we'll have finished the last of the renovations on the property."

Chandra beamed. "I'm delighted to accept for myself. I'm sure Julian will be pleased, too." I'll never have to lay eyes on the Taneys' Buckinghamshire estate, she thought gratefully; by September I'll be long gone from England. I won't have to cultivate these obnoxious social climbers and their equally obnoxious friends any longer. Aloud, she said, "I'm planning a gala evening soon. You'll be receiving an invitation. I hope you can come."

When at last a footman had ushered out a gratified Mrs. Taney, her silent husband, and her oafish son, Chandra breathed a brief prayer of gratitude, and sent for Ramesh. He planted himself in front of her with his great arms folded across his chest, declining, as he usually did, to sit in her presence.

Speaking in Hindi, which always seemed to feel more natural between them despite Ramesh's excellent command of English, Chandra said, "My good friend, I wish to give a great entertainment, one that will surpass any social event that has ever been presented in London. You will be in charge of the arrangements."

Inclining his head gravely, Ramesh said, "As you command, lady. When will this event take place? Soon, I trust. It is now the second week of July. I am told that this Season they speak of will be over at the end of the month, and then all the fashionable people will leave London."

Chandra nodded. "Yes, we'll be cutting it pretty fine, but I don't anticipate any problem. Shall we say two weeks from now? That will be the very end of the Season. I daresay you'll need that much time to prepare the Pantheon for the festivities."

"The Pantheon? I do not know the place, lady. Will you not be entertaining in your own house?"

"No, it isn't big enough," said Chandra calmly. "I plan to invite over a thousand people."

Ramesh's dark eyes widened. "A thousand people. This will indeed be a very great event."

Chandra smiled at him. "As I told you, the most splendid social occasion in the history of London. I want you to provide magnificent food, music, and entertainment in the Indian style. Something that will remain memorable in the minds of my guests after I am gone."

Ramesh shot her a piercing glance. He lowered his voice, saying, "So, lady, have you decided at last that it is time to leave the land of the infidels?"

Ignoring the sudden constriction in her throat, Chandra said, "You read my mind, Ramesh. Yes, after this great party, my farewell gala to all the people I've met here in

London, I will be leaving England."

"Allah be praised. Will the lady Nalini and the mem-sahib Banks accompany us?"

"Oh, yes." Chandra sounded much more positive than she felt. She knew in her heart it would be difficult to persuade Lily to leave Tristan, even after Geoffrey Meredith's killer was exposed and the repercussions of the scandal further endangered the fragile foundations of her marriage. As for Frederica, the ex-governess might feel it her duty to stay behind to support Lily.

"And the sahib Ware?" continued Ramesh.

"Mr. Ware will not be going with us. He will stay in England."

"Ah." The sound was a soft growl of satisfaction. After a moment, Ramesh inquired, "This Pantheon, can you give me some information about the place, so that I may serve you more capably?"

"The Pantheon, Ramesh, has been called the most beautiful building in Europe. It has an enormous central rotunda, with numerous smaller rooms, vestibules, card rooms, supper rooms, and the like. It was a very fashionable place when it was first built. Then, some years ago, there was a disastrous fire. Since it was reopened, it's been used primarily for exhibitions and occasional public masquerades. I think it will be a most suitable location for my gala. Now, then, several months ago, I asked my banker, Mr. Harley, to look into the matter of renting the Pantheon at some future date. The owner of the building, a Mr. Crispus Clagett, was most amenable. You may contact him at the Apollo Gardens on Westminster Bridge Road. And Ramesh, you need spare no expense."

The dark eyes gleamed, and the expressive mustachios quivered. With a sweeping salaam, Ramesh said, "I shall expend every effort within my power, lady, to make your farewell gala worthy of the widow of the great Asaf Khan."

The next few days were among the busiest in Chandra's life, as she applied herself to sending out invitations to, at a final count, eleven hundred and forty people. The guest list contained the names of every person in London who

276

had any pretensions to being a member of the ton, including all the hostesses of Almack's and representatives of the foreign diplomatic corps. The list also included the names of all the military and East India Company contacts that Chandra had made through Basil Forrest and Mr. and Mrs. Taney.

More than once, as Chandra scribbled the words of the invitation over and over again, she longed for the services of a social secretary, only to remind herself, with a curious ache in her heart, that very soon now she'd be living in a place where she'd have no need for a social secretary. In the meantime, she made do with the help of Lily and Frederica, and, occasionally, that of an unwilling Tristan, until the drudgery of addressing the invitations was completed.

Reaction to the proposed entertainment at the Pantheon was predictably varied. Lily and Tristan were bemused, but excited. Tristan said to Chandra with a grin, "The ton will talk of nothing else for months—no, *years* to come. You'll be the most famous hostess in London, and after it's observed that Lily and I are very much in your good graces, some of your triumph is bound to rub off on us!"

Irene was initially aghast at the news. "Rent the Pantheon for a private party?" she faltered. "Dearest Chandra, you wouldn't wish to be thought the least bit ostentatious, I'm sure." Chandra could sense the un-uttered word, vulgar, lurking in the back of Irene's mind.

However, after Chandra explained that she needed more room than the house afforded in order to invest her party with a Northern Indian motif, complete with papier-mâché elephants and tigers, for lack of the real thing, and how she would be grieved to omit the presence of any of the kind people she'd met in London to date, Irene became reconciled to the idea of the Pantheon. "Oh, I daresay the idea is a trifle out of the way, Chandra, but doubtless people will simply think of you as a refreshing original," she'd said indulgently. She also undertook to convert Ashley. "For, although I know some people think dear

Ashley is stiff and toplofty," she told Chandra, "I assure you he's no such thing."

Frederica was harder to persuade. "Could I speak to your privately?" she'd said quietly, after Chandra had announced at the breakfast table that the Pantheon would be the site of a lavish event to be attended by over a thousand guests.

When they were alone together in the morning room, Frederica went straight to the attack. "You've discovered, or you *think* you've discovered, who ordered the massacre at Bhulamphur," she said accusingly.

"Yes, I think I have."

"And you're giving this event so you can act as a stalking horse to lure this man into betraying himself."

"Yes, Freddie. As I told you I intended to do, the day we landed in Woolwich from India."

"Chandra, are you positive about this man's identity?"

"Reasonably so. I won't know, beyond all doubting, until I've forced him into the open."

"Then you have no real proof, nothing you could take to the authorities."

"No. If I had proof, of course, it wouldn't be necessary to host an elaborate festivity at the Pantheon in order to trap the man."

Frederica said in a shaking voice, "Chandra, I beg of you, don't go on with this dangerous scheme. If you've actually found Major Meredith's murderer, he could turn on you and kill you, before you have the opportunity to expose him."

"I suppose that could happen." Chandra shrugged. "It's a chance I must take."

"Listen to me. I know your father wouldn't want you to avenge him if it meant endangering your own safety. Can't you let Major Meredith rest in peace, and get on with your own life?"

"You want me simply to forget how Papa died, and the Begum and her servants, and the Sepoys in Papa's regiment?"

"Better to forget than to risk your whole future, your

278

marriage, your very life, on some mad scheme of revenge!"

Stung, Chandra said curtly, "I don't have a marriage. You know that better than anyone. Whatever else I'm risking by pursuing Papa's murderer, I'm not risking a happy married life." Her expression softened, and she put her arm around Frederica. "There's nothing you can say to make me give up my plans, you know. But I really need your help. Won't you give it to me?"

"Can I do anything else?" muttered Frederica in a low voice. She left the room, looking strained and unhappy.

Julian's reaction to the party was one of pure indifference.

As she was working in her sitting room one morning, several days after she'd begun her preparations for the gala at the Pantheon, she spotted Julian walking past her door, and called, "Could I talk to you, please?" He paused, hesitating noticeably for several seconds, and then stood in the doorway, gazing at her with a look of polite inquiry.

She hadn't seen him for several days. He'd made it quite clear at their last meeting, on the morning following the shattering scene in his bedchamber, that he preferred not to speak to her. However, she'd gathered from Lily and Tristan and Frederica, who paid him daily visits, that he was rapidly throwing off the effects of his wound. This morning, dressed for the street, he looked much his usual self, except that he was still pale. She could only guess at the discomfort he must have endured while he was forcing his injured shoulder into his tightly fitting coat.

"Good morning," she said. "I'm happy to see you looking so well."

"Thank you." The tone was flat, the blue eyes chilly. He might have been replying to the greeting of someone who was the barest of acquaintances.

"Julian, have you heard anything of my plan to hire the Pantheon for a gala evening?"

"Tristan mentioned something about it."

"You don't object?"

Shrugging, he said, "Would it make any difference if I did object?"

"Well, I'd rather you approved, naturally, since you'll be acting as my host. That is, I hope you will."

He cut her off. "Shall we abandon the pretence that my wishes have any influence on the conduct of affairs in this house? You'll do exactly as you choose, as you've always done. And yes, I'll act as your host. Our bargain still stands."

"Julian—" At his look of blank disinterest, Chandra abandoned her impulse to mend fences, to attempt to return in some degree to the wary truce under which they'd been living before the duel and its aftermath. "Thank you," she said quietly.

From his vantage point in a balcony on the second-floor loggia, Julian looked down into the huge rotunda of the Pantheon, which someone had informed him was modeled on the Church of Saint Sophia in Constantinople. He could well believe it, at least so far as size was concerned. Despite its size, the great room didn't appear crowded, though it seemed to him that virtually everyone he'd ever met, and many that he hadn't, were assembled on the floor below. More than eleven hundred people were there, so Tristan had informed him. He stiffened. He'd spotted Basil Forrest among the crowd, and the dreadful Taneys. Had Chandra invited every riff and raff in town?

At the moment, the guests were watching with absorbed interest a troupe of *nautch* girls performing their graceful, swaying dance on the stage. Preceding the dancers' performance, there had been a concert of Indian music, as well as entertainment of a more popular nature provided by such artists as snake charmers and practitioners of the famous Indian rope trick.

Splendid as the rotunda was in its own right, with its *giallo antico* pillars, beautiful stucco work, and the magnificent paintings in the dome, Chandra and Ramesh had added their own embellishments. Enormous gilded papier-mâché elephants stood on either side of the stage, equipped with lavishly decorated *howdahs,* or riding seats. A pair of realistic tigers, also of papier-mâché, grimaced snarlingly at guests as they entered. At intervals around the room, servants in Indian dress slowly pulled the cords of huge *punkahs,* or swinging fans, their frames covered with iridescent silks and dripping with heavy gold fringe.

Julian remarked to Frederica, "The Indian decor is quite impressive."

"A great deal of bother over nothing," she said shortly. He looked at her in surprise. It wasn't like Frederica to be ungracious.

Tristan leaned over to say, "Are those dancers genuine, Freddie? Lily says you've seen *nautch* girls perform many times in India."

Frederica sniffed. "They look perfectly genuine to me, though I can't imagine where Ramesh found them. There can't be many *nautch* girls in London." Again her tone was short, as if at bottom she disapproved of the entire idea of the gala.

"There probably aren't *any nautch* girls in London," said Lily, giggling. "I wouldn't put it past Ramesh to round up *amahs* and other Indian servants working in the city and teach them the steps himself!"

Ashley, with Irene on his arm, joined the others on the balcony, where Chandra's family members had established themselves from the beginning of the evening in an informal group, to greet the guests.

"We've just come from the supper rooms," announced Irene in awed tones. "There are two of them, you know. One of them has every delicacy known to man, including a stuffed peacock, and the most gorgeous collection of hothouse blooms I've ever seen. But the other supper room, the one with the Indian dishes! In the first place, in the center of the table, there's a fountain flowing with wine. It was delicious, but a kind I never tasted before."

"Shiraz, probably," said Lily knowledgeably. "Asaf— we were used to drinking it in India. It's a very fine wine. Imported from Persia." Her eyes sparkled. "Irene, did you say the food in one supper room is exclusively Indian?"

"Yes, but don't ask me to describe it," said Irene with a little laugh, "except for an enormous turkey, which I'm told is essential to every Indian dinner."

"Did you see something that looked like a boiled chicken with almonds and raisins?" asked Lily. "My very favorite dish! I haven't had any since we sailed from Bombay! Or *palau*, perhaps, cabobs of beef and mutton, roasted with herbs and garlic?"

"My love, there's a greedy glow in your eyes," exclaimed Tristan with a grin. "Restrain yourself. You shall have all the dumpoked fowl, or whatever that chicken dish you like so much is called, but only after you've given me several dances."

Under cover of Tristan's raillery, Ashley said in a low voice, "Julian, I don't like to think about the cost of this evening. Thousands and thousands of pounds, and for what? A mere vulgar display. Elephants and tigers and those peculiar hanging fans! You should have put your foot down."

Before Julian could reply, Irene nudged her husband, saying warmly, "I think it's a wonderful party. Something decidedly out of the ordinary. I'm enjoying myself immensely. But, Julian, where's our hostess? You said Chandra would be arriving later, but how much later? The gala's been in full swing for over an hour now. She's not ill, is she?"

Julian shook his head. In public, during the past two weeks, he'd done his best to behave as normally as possible toward Chandra. Not to anyone, not even to Irene or his brother, had he given any indication that Chandra had delivered such a body blow to his pride that he could hardly bear to be in the same room with her, for fear of what he might do if he came in the slightest physical contact with her. Or of what her faintest touch might do to him, he thought savagely.

"No, Chandra isn't ill," he replied to Irene with an effort. "I think she simply wants to make a grand entrance, after all the guests are present."

Irene's soft blue eyes twinkled. "I've heard rumors of

the most beautiful gown that ever graced a ballroom."

Smiling, Julian let the remark pass, but he was sure Chandra wasn't making a delayed entrance merely to show off an extravagant ball gown. His thoughts drifted. Dressed for the gala, he'd knocked at Chandra's door earlier in the evening, telling her abigail he would wait for his wife downstairs. Chandra had called to him, "Please come in, Julian."

Entering the room, he'd found Chandra sitting at her dressing table, wearing a dressing gown. Her face was pale, her manner preoccupied, and her fingers were tearing nervously at a bit of ribbon. "You're not ready," he'd said in surprise. "Aren't you well, Chandra?"

"I'm very well," she'd exclaimed impatiently, almost angrily.

"You don't look—"

"I'm very well," she repeated. "But I don't wish to leave yet for the gala. I'd like you and the others to go on ahead of me. I'll be there shortly."

He'd bowed, saying, "As you wish," and had gone downstairs to join Tristan and Lily and Frederica. But during the drive to the Pantheon, and while he was greeting and mingling with the guests, he'd wondered what was in Chandra's mind. In all the months he'd known her, he'd never seen her so grim and tense, so turned inward on herself, not even on their wild dash to the Scottish border, when she'd been so concerned about Lily's future. Perhaps he was being fanciful, but he had the impression that Chandra was facing some great crisis, one in which she was poised on the knife edge of disaster.

The clanging sticks and the jangling bracelets of the *nautch* girls became silent, as they sank to the floor in a final bow and rustled off the stage in a flutter of varicolored skirts. Taking their place was an orchestra of conventional musicians who began tuning their instruments for the start of the ball proper. But drowning out the toots, hoots, and scraping of strings of the musicians came the high clear call of a trumpet. The loud murmuring of the huge crowd gradually died away, and eyes began turning, like the growing surge of an ocean wave, toward the door of the ballroom.

Julian watched bemusedly as a clear path opened between the ranks of guests to allow the passage of an elaborately carved litter with an arched canopy and silken curtains and strings of tinkling golden bells, borne on the massive shoulders of four turbaned bearers. The curtains were drawn, concealing the identity of the occupant. The palanquin swayed slowly across the floor toward the stage and stopped in front of it. At that moment, Ramesh, dressed in a tall red turban and *kurta* and *izar* of brilliant red brocade, appeared on the stage. He pulled open the curtains on the side of the palanquin facing him, and put out his hand to assist the occupant to get out.

"God!" muttered Julian at his first glimpse of Chandra. He had never seen her look so beautiful, or so different, or so remote from anything he'd ever known of her. She was wearing a loose coat of cloth of gold, richly embroidered with seed pearls and tiny winking diamonds, over voluminous pantaloons of emerald satin. A diaphanous veil of golden tissue failed to conceal her auburn hair, worn as Julian had first seen it in Woolwich, pulled to the crown of her head in a topknot, from which a heavy braid hung down her back. She must have saved the thick rope of hair that she'd sacrificed to the hairdresser at Irene's behest all those months ago, Julian thought. Then he wondered why so unimportant a detail had occurred to him, as his eyes fastened on the unfamiliar, magnificently ornate parure of diamonds and emeralds Chandra was wearing.

Diamonds and flawless emeralds flashed from the chandelier-type earrings, from the tiara fastening her veil, from the heavy bracelets on her arms, and the intricate strands of the necklace, with its enormous emerald pendant, virtually covered Chandra's breast. For a moment Julian was reminded of her appearance as he'd first seen her, draped with an overwhelmingly vulgar display of gems. She didn't look vulgar tonight. The flamboyant jewels enhanced but didn't overpower her richly colorful costume and her natural beauty. His pulses stirred. She was an exotic, enchanting, Eastern fairy tale princess come gloriously and mysteriously to life.

The single high penetrating note of the trumpet sounded again, silencing the babble of comment, admiring or speculative, that had risen from the crowd when Chandra emerged from the palanquin. She stepped forward to the front of the stage, raising her arms, the gems of her bracelets scintillating in the brilliant glow of the chandeliers.

"My friends," she began, projecting her voice over the crowd, "I bid you welcome to my gala. I wanted, of course, with my dear husband's concurrence . . ." She paused, lifting her eyes to Julian in the balcony; he bowed gravely, suppressing an urge to wring her neck for her hypocrisy. She continued, "I wanted to give you all an evening of great enjoyment as a thank you, at this, the end of my first Season in London, for the warm welcome you've extended to a stranger in your midst. I came to England not knowing a soul. Now I feel I have a myriad of friends. As you will have observed from my costume and my elephants and tigers—I'm so sorry they aren't the real thing!—I thought it only fitting, in planning this entertainment, to combine the flavor of my home in northern Indian with the civilized beauty of this great English building. And now I hope you will have great pleasure in the remainder of your evening here."

With an enchanting smile, a graceful curtsy, she left the stage, and the orchestra struck up. From his position on the balcony, Julian watched her making her slow way along the side of the ballroom, pausing every few seconds to greet her guests.

Beside him, Irene said, wide-eyed, "I've never seen anyone look as exquisitely beautiful as Chandra does tonight. Those emeralds! The pendant must be the size of a small hen's egg! Why have I never seen them before? I can easily imagine a queen wearing them, or an empress."

"They did belong to an empress long ago," said Frederica in an odd, choked voice. "Later they became the property of the wife of a ruler in northern India. Some years ago, a villain hired a bandit chief to steal them. Since this villain wished to keep his identity secret, his only contact with the bandit was through the medium of notes signed with a secret symbol. The bandit betrayed the villain and kept the jewels for himself. The bandit didn't fear retribution because he had learned the identity of the villain, and had retained as a hold over him the notes signed with the secret symbol.''

"What a fascinating story," exclaimed Irene, her eyes keen with interest. "But how, then, did the jewels come into Chandra's possession?"

"But that's what makes the story even more fascinating, Irene," chimed in Lily. "Our papa—Freddie's brother, you know—saved the bandit chief's life, and in gratitude the man gave the emeralds to Papa."

Irene looked entranced. "It's like a fairy story! But I still don't understand why Chandra's never worn them."

"I wish she hadn't worn them," Frederica burst out. "They're evil, evil—"

Julian glanced at her sharply. No doubt about it, the ex-governess was under some great strain. Now that he thought about it, Lily wasn't herself, either. There'd been an air of suppressed excitement about the girl during the whole evening. Tristan seemed to be infected, too, though to a lesser degree. Julian's mouth hardened. Was something going on among Chandra's family members that he didn't know about, something, very probably, he wasn't meant to know?

Frederica drew a deep breath and tried to smile. "Excuse me for talking such fustian. I collect you'll think I'm a superstitious old lady." The cloud descended again on her face. "Somehow, though," she said slowly, almost as if she was speaking to herself, "I can't help feeling that objects with such a bloody history must bring bad luck with them."

Tristan said quickly, "That's quite enough about emeralds when something important like dancing is in progress. Come along, Freddie, Lily. I insist you both dance with me, one at a time, of course."

Julian had a distinct impression that Tristan had hurried Frederica away, not only to give her time to compose herself, but to prevent her from saying any more about the emeralds. What was it about those glittering baubles that was troubling her? Were the emeralds also connected to Chandra's mood of grim preoccupation earlier this evening in her bedchamber? Frowning, Julian headed downstairs to the ballroom to ask his wife some leading questions. But, as happened so often when he escorted Chandra to a social event, he caught only glimpses of her. She danced every dance with someone else. He had no opportunity to speak to her until the evening was over.

"That will be all, Bates."

"Yes, sir." The valet eyed Julian as he tied the sash of his dressing gown with quick, impatient fingers. "Your shoulder's as good as new, I'm glad to see," Bates said approvingly. "You have the full use of your arm again. Good night, sir."

After the valet's departure, Julian walked down the corridor and rapped at Chandra's door. Her abigail opened the door and stood aside to allow him to enter. "I wish to speak to your mistress in private for a few minutes," he told the girl. He closed the door and stood with his back against it.

Chandra was sitting at her dressing table. She had discarded her Indian finery and was wearing a silk robe. The heavy false braid had been discarded and her dark auburn hair was loose around her shoulders. She looked tense and tired, in sharp contrast to her air of smiling triumph at the gala. Gazing at his set face, she said, "It's very late, Julian. Whatever it is you wish to say, can't it wait until tomorrow?"

"I won't keep you long. I simply want a brief explanation for the charade you mounted this evening."

"Charade?"

"Yes, charade. Do you take me for a gull? You didn't

give this lavish entertainment, complete with elephants and tigers and snake charmers and the Lord knows what, merely to thank more than a thousand people for being friendly to you. You don't even like most of them. Why, you actually invited Basil Forrest and the Taney family to the gala, for God's sake, and by this time, I know what you think of *them!* No, you wanted all those people there for quite another reason, and I want to know what it was. I think it had something to do with those damned emeralds."

Her expression changed. "Oh, the emeralds. You considered them overly ostentatious, I daresay. That's why I haven't worn them previously."

"Coming it too strong, Chandra. You wore those emeralds deliberately. You wanted people to talk about them. You set Tristan and Lily and Frederica to spreading the tale of the bandit chief who stole the empress's emeralds, and by the end of the evening, everyone in the ballroom knew all the details."

"That's ridiculous."

"Is it? People were repeating the story in almost exactly the same terms. Very odd, when you reflect how much idle gossip changes from mouth to mouth. And I kept hearing the same phrases over and over again. 'Miss Banks told me . . .' 'Lieutenant Loring swore the story is true . . .' 'Mrs. Loring assured me . . .' No, Chandra, you instructed your family to spread the tale, all right. That was why Freddie was so nervous tonight, and why Lily was excited nearly to the verge of hysteria."

Chandra's attempt at a derisive smile was ghastly. "You're letting your imagination run away with you."

"No, I don't think so." Julian studied her beneath drawn brows. "You're not going to tell me about it? Very well. I'll find out for myself."

Chapter Seventeen

Chandra glanced out the window of the carriage at the distant range of heavily wooded hills and felt a sense of relief. She was approaching the Chiltern Hills in Buckinghamshire. Her long journey of five hours from London was nearing its end. In another hour or so she'd be arriving at the principal seat of the Ware family, Wolverton Abbey.

She turned again to the newspaper she'd brought with her, partly in order to while away the tedium of the journey, but mostly to divert her thoughts from the danger she might be facing in a matter of hours. She'd read and reread this copy of *The Morning Chronicle* so many times, she reflected, that she should have been able to repeat every word from memory. However, the only item she'd really noticed had to do with a battle in the Peninsula. Sir Arthur Wellesley had just won a great battle in Spain, at a place called Talavera, and the French forces were in full retreat toward Madrid. It was a battle Julian had been convinced was coming, she remembered. He'd spoken of it at dinner, that night they'd spent on the road during their abortive pursuit of Lily and Tristan to the Scottish border.

Julian. Putting down the newspaper, she thought back to the scene in her bedchamber last night after the gala. He was beginning to know her too well. Without any real facts to go on, he'd sensed that the gala had merely been an elaborate stage production, designed to mask a far more serious design beneath it, and he was determined to get to the bottom of the mystery. She smiled a little grimly. Doubtless he could do it, once he put his mind to it. Julian was a resourceful man. But time was against him. Fortunately for her, not enough hours remained for him to ferret out her secret and disrupt her plans.

She wondered what his reaction would be when he received the note she'd left for him this morning. It was an exact copy of the notes she'd written to Frederica and Lily and to Irene. It had stated briefly that she was exhausted from her efforts in organizing her gala at the Pantheon, and had retired to the dower house at Wolverton Abbey for a few days to rest in solitude. She wanted no visitors. She'd instructed her servants to give the same message to anyone who called at the house in Grosvenor Square in her absence. Within a few hours, it should be widely known in London that Mrs. Julian Ware had retired to the country. Alone.

Chandra shivered, though the midsummer breeze blowing in through the opened window of the carriage was almost too warm for comfort. Soon, if her calculations had been correct, her father's killer would be stalking her into Buckinghamshire. She shivered again, as she suddenly remembered stories she'd heard about tiger hunts in Hindustan. The hunters would first tether a live domestic animal, a goat or a lamb, in a clearing, then wait in platforms among the trees to shoot the tiger when he arrived to seize his helpless prey.

The man who'd ordered that massacre in Bhulamphur was like a tiger, ruthless and cunning and single-minded. In order to lure him out of hiding, she'd deliberately made herself his prey. She had no choice, because, although she believed she knew the identity of her tiger, she had no proof. No proof at all, as a matter of fact, except in the mind of the murderer. Her one bit of concrete evidence, the note written to Asaf Khan, giving instructions for the massacre and signed with the symbol of interlocking circles, was literally useless, unless she could force its author to acknowledge it.

From her standpoint, the note had always been the weakest link in her chain of revenge. Her task had been to persuade the murderer, once she'd succeeded in finding him, that the note could hang him. And so the gala at the Pantheon last night had had a twofold purpose.

On the one hand, by wearing the emeralds, she'd revealed her identity. The emeralds would have meaning only for the "tiger." No one, except the tiger and Asaf Khan, knew the Begum of Bhulamphur had been secretly carrying the jewels in her effects at the time of the massacre. To the world in general, the emeralds had simply vanished. No one except the tiger knew that Asaf Khan had retained them as his share of the loot. And therefore, if Chandra was wearing the emeralds, she had some connection with Asaf Khan. The tiger might even suspect that she was the child, Diana Meredith, grown up. The bodies of Diana and Lily and Frederica Banks would not have been found among the corpses at the site of the massacre, of course, but the authorities might have, and probably did, assume the three had wandered off to die in the jungle. Now the murderer might realize that Asaf Khan had simply abducted Major Meredith's remaining family members.

On the other hand, by enlisting Lily and Tristan and Frederica to spread a garbled history of the emeralds at the gala, Chandra had hoped to convince the tiger, not only that she had a piece of paper in some unknown's handwriting and signed with someone's strange device, but that *she might know who had written it.* The story circulating at the gala had stated quite plainly that the bandit chief had learned the identity of his accomplice. If the tiger believed the story, he'd be compelled to act. He couldn't be certain that Asaf Khan had revealed his accomplice's identity to Chandra, but he could take no chances. He must corner Chandra, force her to give him the note, and then kill her. And that was why she was going alone to Wolverton Abbey, to give him an easy opportunity to corner her.

In this confrontation, she hoped to trick the tiger into confessing his original crime, and then to hand him over to the authorities. In any event, his attempt to kill her, whether or not it succeeded, would send him to the gallows, because she'd have with her a witness. Ramesh.

Deep in her thoughts, she hadn't noticed that the carriage had turned off the main road into a narrow valley. She'd traveled this familiar road beside the rushing little river many times before, during her visit to Wolverton Abbey to help Julian in his election campaign. It seemed so long ago. In minutes the valley widened out, and the carriage entered the hamlet of Wolverton, clustered on the banks of the stream. The sound of wheels on the village street attracted the attention of the children playing on the green, and brought their parents to the windows and doorways of their houses to stare at the Daylesford crest on the doors of the vehicle.

The carriage rolled past the ancient church and stopped in front of closed doors in a high wall surrounding a pleasant stone house. In a moment, Ramesh jumped down from his perch beside the coachman and pushed open the gates. The coachman guided the carriage into a large forecourt. Ramesh made his stately way up the steps to the door of the house and knocked. After an interval of several minutes, a neatly dressed middle-aged woman answered the door and stared at Ramesh in some confusion. Her gaze shifted to the carriage with its crested door, and her confusion vanished. She hurried down the steps and across the courtyard. Peering in the window of the carriage, she exclaimed, "Mrs. Ware! I had no idea ye was coming."

The woman was a stranger to Chandra, who said, in some surprise, "You know me?"

"Oh, indeed, ma'am. Many's the time I seen ye with Mr. Julian in the village. When he was here earlier this summer, y'know, for the election."

A simple explanation, Chandra thought. During her brief stay in Wolverton, she hadn't associated with any of the villagers enough to know them by sight, but, of course, they would all recognize the Earl of Daylesford's sister-in-law.

"The Earl and Countess and Mr. Julian, be they coming down to Wolverton, too?" asked the woman.

"No. I came by myself. And since I'm alone, I'd prefer to stay in the dower house, if that's possible, rather than rattle around in that vast pile up the hill like a very small pea in a very large pod."

"Well, now," the woman began doubtfully, "no 'un's lived here since his lordship's mother died. A few 'ears back, that was."

"Are you the housekeeper?"

"After a fashion, ye might say. My name's Annie Pope. I lives in the village, but I comes in several days a week to keep it tidy, like, and the fires lit in bad weather, against the damp."

"Well, Annie, do you think you could take care of me for a few days? I've merely come here to rest a bit, so I won't require elaborate meals, and I certainly won't be entertaining. And, of course, since I've brought my manservant with me, you needn't stay here at night. I expect you have a family in the village."

"Yes, ma'am." The woman's face cleared. "In that case I'll do my best for ye, o' course. I'll have the holland covers off the furniture in a trice, and then I'll make ye up a comfortable bed. But meanwhile, I expect ye'd like a good strong cup o' tea, and p'raps some o' the nuncheon I was about to have. Please to step inside, Mrs. Ware."

The housekeeper walked to the front of the carriage to speak to the driver. "The coach house is outside the wall in a separate building," she told him. "Ye'll find sleeping rooms above it. The gardener sleeps there, too."

Chandra listened intently to the woman's remarks about the coach house. Later, after a cup of tea and some scones and some cold meat, which she insisted on taking, to the housekeeper's discomfiture, in the cozy, scrubbed kitchen, she asked Annie to take her on a tour of the house.

While it was still daylight, Chandra wanted to see every detail of the house and its surroundings. She needed to know the layout of the rooms, the position of the doors, the possible entrances into the walled enclosure from the coach house or the kitchen garden, in order to plan her defenses.

It was a charming, gracious house, built on a much smaller scale than the mansion in Grosvenor Square. It had obviously not been refurnished in many years, but Chandra found she liked the graceful, old-fashioned furniture and the faded, jewel-toned rugs. Annie Pope, becoming more comfortable with Chandra by the minute, chattered away as she walked through the rooms, telling stories about Julian's grandmother and mother, who had both occupied the house at different times, when each had become the Dowager Countess of Daylesford.

When Chandra had finished her tour of the premises, it was still only mid-afternoon. Too restless to stay indoors, she wandered into the pleasure garden behind the house. The garden was small and unpretentious, much like the house itself, with narrow walks among informal flower plantings, a few shade trees, and a modest foundtain, apparently fed by the boisterous little brook flowing down the hill behind the house.

Chandra settled onto a bench set beneath one of the trees, gradually surrendering to the peace of the place. In some indefinable way, the lovely little garden reminded her of the luxuriant harem gardens in Asaf Khan's encampment. Probably, she decided, it was the soothing sound of the water flowing from the little fountain that had stirred her memories.

The idea of using the dower house for the final act of her drama had sprung from an idle remark Irene had made during the election campaign. Irene had said, "The dower house would make a perfect country retreat for you and Julian."

Already, after these few minutes of exposure to it, Chandra had realized she could easily come to love this gem of a house in its quiet, verdant corner of the English countryside. For a fleeting moment, she allowed herself to imagine what it would be like to share the dower house with Julian. Then reality set in, leaving a desolate little ache in her heart. In a few hours or days, she'd be leaving Julian and England behind her. She'd come so far in time and space from the days of her captivity in Hindustan, she reflected. Now she was at the end of another cycle in her life, facing an uncertain future.

Or *was* she at the end of her stay in England? Suddenly misgiving assailed her. She sat up, straight and tense, on the edge of the bench. What if she was wrong? During these past few weeks, she'd been so sure she'd found her tiger. Simon's description of the man had fit in every detail. But suppose those details of the man and his history amounted only to a vast coincidence? Suppose the eleven-hundred-and-forty people who'd thronged the Pantheon for her gala hadn't included her tiger among their number? An appalling thought struck. Was it conceivable she hadn't yet met her father's killer? The man might already be dead. Or still in India. Or . . .

Chandra stood up abruptly. The sunny peace of the garden had faded. She had to face the possibility that her vigil at the dower house might end in failure. She might be forced to return to London to begin her search for Papa's killer all over again. She might never find him. Freddie had always thought her quest was hopeless. Then, as Chandra walked slowly out of the garden, she felt a chilling sensation of certainty. She might not have pierced her tiger's true identity, but, whoever he was, she knew beyond doubt, he would soon be prowling about the dower house, seeking to devour his prey.

As she entered the front hall of the house, she encountered Annie Pope, breathless and red-faced. The woman exclaimed, "Oh, ma'am, not to be forward, like, but it's not seemly for that servant of yours, the one wearing that tall blue thing on his head, to be pawing about among your undergarments in your portmanteau, and so I told him! And then he said—he said—ma'am, I can't repeat it."

Chandra lifted her eyes to observe Ramesh slowly descending the stairs. He came to a stop in the hallway, stolidly planting his feet and crossing his arms as he bent on the housekeeper a long, intimidating stare that made the woman quail and step back.

"It's quite all right, Annie," said Chandra soothingly. "I didn't bring my abigail with me—silly girl, she's afraid of the country!—so Ramesh was merely unpacking my belongings. He's a very old family servant, who's accustomed to turning his hand to almost any household chore."

"Yes, ma'am," said a subdued Annie.

Ramesh continued to stare at her, and Annie went off down the hallway with a curious sideways motion, as if she was unwilling to expose her unprotected back to his unfriendly gaze.

Chandra murmured in Hindi, "You frightened the poor wretch, Ramesh."

"The woman does not know her place, like so many females among the infidels," replied Ramesh loftily. "I showed it to her."

The look of amusement in Chandra's eyes was replaced by an angry spark. She snapped, "This is no time for games. Play the petty tyrant to my servants as much as you like, *after* we leave here. Until then, keep in mind we came here for a purpose."

The impassive dark face registered no emotion, but Ramesh bowed in a graceful salaam, murmuring, "Your servant is gravely at fault. My lady's honor and her safety are at stake, and I must let nothing interfere with my duty."

Chandra bowed her head. "So be it." After a moment she said, "You have familiarized yourself with the house?"

"Yes, lady, and with the gardens and the outbuildings and the outlying areas. Praise be to Allah, you have chosen this place well. The tiger will have little cover in which to stalk his victim."

Chandra looked at Ramesh curiously. So he, too, was thinking of their secret adversary as the tiger. At times she'd been convinced Ramesh could read her mind, but in this instance the explanation for their parallel line of thought was probably not mind-reading, but their common knowledge of big game hunting in Hindustan.

The afternoon wore on. Chandra tried to keep herself occupied. She read a little, took a short walk into the village, sat for a while in the garden, ate the simple supper Annie Pope prepared before she left for her home and family in Wolverton. At ten-thirty, when the long northern twilight had completely turned to darkness, Chandra went up to her bedchamber. After half an hour she put out her lamp and walked to a window, drawing the curtains back and looking down at the pleasure garden and the outbuildings beyond the rear wall of the house. A moment later, the door of the bedchamber opened, and Ramesh slipped silently into the room.

It was about a week after the full of the moon, and the half moon was rising to cast a pale light across the landscape. From her position at the window, however, Chandra could see nothing moving. She didn't expect to see anything. She and Ramesh had agreed it was highly unlikely the tiger would strike that first night. She'd told no one of her plans to leave London to go to the dower house, and, by the time the tiger learned of her whereabouts, it would be too late for him to make his plans and put them into operation that day. Nevertheless, Chandra had decided to leave nothing to chance. She and Ramesh would follow the same procedure tonight that they would employ tomorrow night and any subsequent night.

Taking off her slippers, she slipped into bed, still fully dressed, and pulled up the coverlets. In her right hand she held the wickedly sharp poniard with which she'd defended herself from the bandits on the Woolwich road. The curtains of the tester bed shadowed her head and upper torso, but the room and its furnishings were dimly visible in the light of the rising moon. She could make out Ramesh's tall form, clad in a loose dark garment, in the corner of the room nearest the door, but only because she knew he was there. Anyone entering the room would be unlikely to notice him.

The hours dragged by. Midnight. Two in the morning. The moon began to set. Not a sound had disturbed the silence except the soft soughing of the wind in the shade trees of the garden, and the occasional hoot of an owl. Weary as she was in both body and spirit from the strain of the past few days, Chandra didn't feel sleepy. She lay rigidly awake, intently listening for a sound that never came. Then, at daybreak, she gradually drifted into an uneasy sleep. She woke at noon, unrefreshed and heavy-eyed, when Annie Pope came into the bedchamber with a tray.

"I was worried about ye, ma'am," said the housekeeper. "I was afeared ye might be sick, sleeping so late. That man in the blue hat, he said as how ye wasn't to be disturbed, but what does a man know about females, I ask you?" The housekeeper's voice swelled with virtue. "I *knew* ma'am, that ye'd like some tea and bit of toast, even if ye had the headache or some such thing."

"Thank you, Annie." Chandra's somber mood lightened with a flicker of amusement. The housekeeper obviously considered that she'd gotten some of her own back with Ramesh.

The rest of the day passed uneventfully. As she had yesterday, Chandra took a short walk and later spent some time in the garden. The vicar of the village church came to call, respectful to his patron's sister-in-law, but plainly curious about her solitary visit. After supper, Chandra sat for a time in the drawing room, working rather aimless stitches in a piece of embroidery. Then, shortly after ten, she went upstairs to her bedchamber, walked back and forth across the room occasionally so that a passerby could see her shadowy movements against the draperies, and

298

finally put out her lamp. As before, she drew the curtains and got into bed fully dressed, with the poniard in her hand. Soon Ramesh glided silently into the room and took up his station.

Chandra waited tensely, scarcely moving a muscle. She knew in her bones that the tiger would strike tonight. His nerves must be stretched as tightly as hers. He could no more bear the strain of a postponement than she could. Yes, he would come tonight, and he would come as silently as possible, concealing the noise of his passage by leaving his transport on the far side of the village: a horse, most likely, or a curricle and pair driven without a groom. After all, the tiger would want no witnesses of his own to his night's work.

Chandra and Ramesh had discussed the best ways of affording the tiger an easy entrance into the house. The gates in the wall were no problem. They were merely secured by latches. The locks on the front and back doors were simple ones, but the tiger might fear he'd make too much noise if he tried to force them. The downstairs windows presented a much better opportunity. A few snips of a glasscutter would allow him to obtain entry, but Chandra had made it even easier. It was a very warm night, and earlier, when she'd sat with her embroidery in the drawing room, she'd opened the windows and had neglected to close one of them securely. Surely the tiger would be bound to try the windows? Her flesh crept. Perhaps, even at that early hour, he'd been lurking nearby. Perhaps he'd actually observed her failure to latch the window.

The silent minutes crept by. The half moon rose and and slanted its pale rays into the room. Chandra began to feel cramped, and she cautiously changed her position. More waiting, until she wanted to scream from the tension. In the corner, Ramesh stood like a statue, his dark skin and dark clothing making his presence barely perceptible.

It was well after midnight, though Chandra couldn't

know the exact time, when she heard the sound of wheels some distance away, from the direction of the village. She started. The road from the village went past the dower house, shortly to disintegrate into a rough track leading only to several isolated farmsteads in the hills. Surely no self-respecting, hard-working farmer would be abroad at this hour. But just as surely, unless he was a very stupid man, the tiger wouldn't neglect the most elementary precautions to conceal the sound of his presence. Chandra didn't think she was dealing with a stupid man.

The carriage, if that was what it was, came slowly along the road from the village, and then, as Chandra lay without moving, petrified with shock, she heard the vehicle turn into the drive leading to the coach house. The tiger was either very stupid or very self-confident.

She could sense Ramesh's tense readiness, though he made neither sound nor movement. In a minute or two she heard a faint creaking noise from the gate nearest the coach house. A moment later someone tried the front door, without success. Then a moment of silence, followed shortly by the sound of soft footfalls on the uncarpeted stairs. The tiger had found the open window of the drawing room, and he was so sure of himself that he hadn't bothered to remove his boots.

Steeling herself to lie motionless, hardly daring to breathe, Chandra waited, as the creeping sounds seemed to become frozen in time. The tiger came up the stairs and padded along the hallway. He paused several times. Why, Chandra wondered? He must know, if he'd been skulking outside, which room she was occupying.

The footfalls approached her bedchamber. The door opened, and a tall figure entered the room. Simultaneously, Ramesh's shadowy form moved, lightning-swift, and pounced on the intruder from behind, encircling the man's throat with an iron arm.

"Damn it to hell, is that you, Ramesh? Take your hands away, before you break my neck!" The identity of the choked voice was unmistakable.

"Julian!" gasped Chandra. It didn't occur to her until much later that she never for a split second believed that Julian was her tiger. "Let him go, Ramesh."

"But, lady—"

"Release Mr. Ware." Chandra threw back the coverlets and stood up, her poniard glittering in her hand in the moonlight as she stepped away from the concealing shroud of the bed curtains.

With Ramesh hovering closely behind him, Julian advanced into the room. His clothes were disheveled, and he was rubbing his throat. Even in the dim light, she could see he was furiously angry. "Good God," he growled, looking at the poniard, "have you taken to sleeping with that thing? And by all that's holy, what's Ramesh doing in your bedchamber in the middle of the night?"

The abrupt break in the tension left Chandra feeling weak. Her voice shook as she asked, "What are you doing here, Julian?"

"More to the point, what are *you* doing here?" he retorted.

"I—I told you in my note. I was exhausted after the gala. I needed rest and privacy. I also told you I didn't want visitors."

"Doing it rather too brown, my girl. You've never been exhausted in your life. You've got more energy than one of those elephants Lily is always talking about. No, the more I got to thinking about what you'd said in your note, the more I realized you had some scheme in mind. A scheme that was probably connected to that infernal gala and those emeralds. So late this afternoon, right in the middle of a debate in the House, I decided to come up here to find out what was what." He cast an irritated glance at the hovering presence behind him. "Confound it, Ramesh, I won't have you breathing down my neck. Move off. And can't we have some light? Must we go on talking in almost total darkness?"

Chandra was thinking more clearly now, and suddenly the enormity of her husband's presence here at the dower

301

house struck her like a blow. "Julian, please do as I say and leave here immediately," she said urgently. "I'll explain later, but you must go now."

"I've no intention of leaving until I find out what's going on here, so if you want to get rid of me, start talking."

"Silence," hissed Ramesh, who had taken up a position at the side of the window. "Someone just entered the garden from the rear gate," he whispered, continuing to peer downward.

"In God's name, Chandra what *is* this?" Julian muttered angrily.

Chandra clapped her hand across his lips. She breathed in his ear, "I beg of you, don't say anything, don't make a noise. In a minute or two, someone will come into this room and try to kill me. Ramesh is prepared for him. Please, Julian, this is a matter of my life or my death. Promise me you won't interfere."

Julian stiffened, and made an instinctive move to push her away from him. Then, after several long, agonizing moments, he nodded. Shaken with relief, Chandra removed her hand from his mouth. "Thank you," she whispered. "Please stand in the corner by the door." After an indecisive fraction of a second, he moved to obey. Ramesh was already in position opposite him. Chandra slipped into the bed and drew up the coverlets.

For what seemed an eternity, but which couldn't have been more than several minutes, Chandra waited for the tiger to pounce. She sensed rather than heard his slow silent progress through the darkened rooms below and up the stairs. Then he seemed to pause. What was taking him so long? She heard the faintest sound of a latch being gently pulled back on the door of one of the bedchambers nearer the stairwell. He was checking to see where she was. So he hadn't been lurking outside the house earlier in the evening. Otherwise he'd surely have known which bedchamber she was sleeping in. She suppressed a horrified gasp. If the tiger *had* been keeping surveillance on her

302

earlier tonight, he'd have seen or heard Julian drive up in his curricle.

Chandra held her breath. The latch of her bedchamber door gave an infinitesimal squeak. The door opened gently, and a shadowy presence drifted across the threshold, stopping to glance toward the bed and take his bearings. He was dressed all in black, with what appeared to be a black hood covering his entire head and face.

Ramesh struck again with the speed of a panther, but this time he didn't have the easy, swift success he'd had with Julian earlier. Perhaps Ramesh had been able to subdue Julian so quickly because the latter had come into the room unsuspecting. On the contrary, the tiger's senses were alerted for danger, and he fought savagely for several minutes to free himself from Ramesh's grasp. But finally the Pathan's giant strength prevailed. He wrapped his long arms around the tiger in a vicelike grip that held him completely immobile.

Chandra slipped out of bed, picked up a small bottle filled with asbestos and acid from her night table, and with trembling fingers inserted a wooden splint into the bottle. The sulphur-tipped splint ignited, and she quickly lit the lamp. In its light, the occupants of the room resembled the figures in a still life tableau: the motionless Ramesh and his rigid prisoner, Julian standing, momentarily petrified with shock, in his corner, and Chandra herself, with her hand stretched out to the lamp.

Chandra disrupted the tableau. Taking a long, steadying breath, she stepped up to the tiger and snatched the hood from his head.

"My God! Ashley!" Julian rushed from his corner to stare disbelievingly at the haggard face of his brother. His voice tight with fury, he barked to Ramesh, "Let him go." Ramesh looked inquiringly at Chandra, who hesitated for a brief moment and then slowly nodded. Ashley swayed, then caught his balance. His eyes glittered in his pallid face, and his mouth was working, but he said nothing. He seemed to be in some kind of a stupor. His eyes fixed unwaveringly on Ashley, Ramesh remained close beside him.

Julian turned on Chandra. "What's the meaning of this? You said someone was coming to kill you. You can't mean Ashley—"

Chandra held her hands tightly clenched together to prevent them from shaking. Keeping her eyes fixed on Ashley, she began speaking in a low, emotionless voice. "Eleven years ago, in northern India, an official of the East India Company—or an officer in the Indian army, I didn't know which at the time—conspired with a Pindari bandit named Asaf Khan to ambush a caravan and rob the Begum of Bhulamphur of her jewels and gold. During the ambush a great many people died, including my father, Major Geoffrey Meredity, my sister, Phoebe, and the Begum herself. My governess and my niece, Lily"—out of the corner of her eye Chandra saw Julian's start of surprise—"and I were carried off to captivity. Some years later I became the child bride of Asaf Khan. Before he died, he gave me the emerald parure I wore on the night of the gala at the Pantheon, and he told me the story of the massacre."

Shifting her gaze to Julian, Chandra said levelly, "I came to England last January determined to find my father's murderer. I had no idea who he was. However, I'd inferred that he came from a prominent family, had seved with the East India Company, and had returned to England some ten years ago with a large fortune. I had one clue: a message in the murderer's handwriting, signed with a peculiar symbol. Soon I realized I could never find the murderer on my own. I must have access to the top ranks of London society. So I married you for your position, Julian. I also cultivated more modestly placed people like Basil Forrest and the Taneys for their Company contacts, and I asked my friend Simon Harley to be on the watch for people who'd returned from India with mysteriously large fortunes."

Julian's face had been steadily growing grimmer. He

interrupted her now, glancing from her to Ashley, who still appeared to be in a curious trancelike state. Chandra wondered if Ashley could actually hear what she was saying. Julian said to her roughly, "What's this got to do with my brother? Yes, he served briefly in India, and yes, he came back with a modest fortune. But so did many others."

With a pang of pity, Chandra realized that Julian was refusing to allow himself to draw the obvious conclusion: that Ashley's very presence in this room connected him with Chandra's story.

Still addressing herself to Julian, Chandra went on, "I didn't have the faintest initial suspicion of Ashley. Why should I? No one told me he'd served with the East India Company. It was most unlikely on the face of it, for the heir to a great title to accept a minor position with the East India Company. You see, no one had told me, either, that you and Ashley had an older brother, who died soon after Ashley returned from India, making him the heir. Simon Harley learned that Ashley had served a scant two years with the Company, returning suddenly with a very large fortune. Not the modest sum he apparently reported to you and the rest of your family, Julian. Rather, an immense sum in gold, a fortune, presumably, that soon disappeared into the hands of gaming hell proprietors. So Ashley became my prime suspect, but I still wasn't sure of his guilt. You were right about the gala at the Pantheon. Its sole purpose was to show off the Begum's emeralds and to circulate the story of the incriminating note with its betraying symbol. Then I came down here to the dower house to see if the killer would take the bait. As you see, he did."

Julian recoiled, as if Chandra had struck him a blow. In a last-ditch effort to deny the ugly truth, he said desperately, "God, Ashley, don't stand there like a graven image. Say something. For whatever reason you came here tonight, it can't have anything to do with theft and murder. You must have some explanation for being here.

Chandra must have the wrong information."

Ashley didn't stir. Only his eyes, deeply, intensely blue, and so like Julian's, seemed sentient, moving from his brother to Chandra.

"There's no mistake, Julian," said Chandra quietly. "I have proof. Ramesh?" She held out her hand to the Pathan, who, after a long, piercing look at her, reached into a pocket in his voluminous garment and produced a slip of paper, grimy and much creased. She handed the paper to Julian. "That's the note my father's murderer sent to Asaf Khan, setting up the massacre. Is that Ashley's handwriting?"

As Julian scanned the letter, he muttered on a note of rising hope, "No, of course, it's not Ashley's writing. Oh, it's a bit like—"

"He probably tried to disguise it," Chandra cut in quickly, but she felt a faint qualm of doubt.

Julian wasn't listening. He was staring at the signature, a series of intricately interlocking circles. "Oh, my God," he murmured brokenly. "It's our secret symbol, Ashley, the one we used to sign all our letters when we were boys." Anguish ravaging his face, he turned on his brother, waving the letter. "This will send you to the gallows. Nothing can save you. Why did you do it? No matter how much you needed money, how could you kill for it?"

In a sudden manic burst of energy, Ashley sprang toward Julian, clawing for the letter. "Give it to me," he screeched. "Without it, that bitch-wife of yours can't prove anything!"

Though he was caught momentarily off balance by surprise, Ramesh lunged at Ashley. A moment later, the Pathan stumbled backward, clutching at his arm, his fingers already stained with blood from the wound inflicted by the knife that had unexpectedly appeared in Ashley's hand.

Ashley was now out of control. Knife raised, he slashed at Chandra, screaming, "You're next, whore! Do you think I'd let you put me in the dock, ruin my darling

Irene's life, stain the Ware name for all time?"

Julian leaped at his brother, grasping for the hand holding the deadly knife. Ashley desperately resisted. For several minutes, Chandra could only stand helplessly by, watching the two men as they struggled in fierce, panting silence for the control of the knife. Then, with a strangled groan of agony, Ashley dropped to the floor. Julian stood like a statue, his eyes wide with shock, as he stared at the reddened blade of the weapon in his hand.

Still clutching his wounded arm, Ramesh sank unsteadily to his knees beside Ashley. The Pathan put out his hand, groping inside Ashley's clothing. After a long, terrible moment, Ramesh looked up at Julian. "Sahib, your brother is dead."

Chapter Eighteen

The library of Daylesford House was so quiet that the ticking of the clock on the mantel was clearly audible, almost intrusive. Glancing at the clock, Irene broke the silence, saying in a low voice, "They must be at the cemetery by now. Soon they'll be lowering Ashley into his grave, throwing the sods of earth on his coffin—" Her voice broke, and Chandra leaned from her chair to clasp her sister-in-law's hand.

Irene had maintained a stoic composure until now, though Chandra thought she looked so frail in her widow's cap and dress of deepest black that a strong breeze could have blown her away.

"I wish I'd been able to go to the church and the cemetery," Irene whispered, "to say goodbye."

"I wish so, too, darling," Chandra murmured, "but ladies don't go to funerals, you know."

Irene bowed her head. "Yes. I know."

"Well, I, for one, think it a very good thing. We females are the weaker sex. We can't bear as much as men," declared Georgiana. Tristan's mother, to Chandra's relief, had made up the family quarrel, at least to the extent of attending Irene on the day of the funeral. However, the Dowager Lady Eversleigh still studiously refrained from speaking to Lily.

How I hate black, thought Chandra. How does it help the dead to swathe oneself in musty crape? She glanced at the other women in the room. Georgiana was chic, as always, in her mourning clothes, but unrelieved black made Lily look swarthy and more foreign than ever. The somber clothing did nothing for Frederica's appearance, or that of the young Lady Eversleigh, the wife of Tristan's elder half brother.

A footman entered the library with a tea tray, which Irene waved away.

"Dearest Irene, you must have something. A cup of tea, at least, and one of those little sandwiches," urged Georgiana. "You must keep up your strength, as Ashley would wish you to do." The dowager wiped an easy tear from her eye. "Dearest Ashley," she murmured. "It was so like him to give his life for another." Her cool glance swept over Chandra, saying as plainly as words that Ashley's sacrifice had been misguided.

Chandra looked away. She didn't care a fig for Georgiana's opinion, or for those of the world at large. It was for Irene's sake, and Julian's, that she'd allowed her father's killer to go to his grave a hero.

Her thoughts drifted back reluctantly to that terrible night at the dower house . . .

Looking down at Ashley's still figure, Julian said in a torn voice, "I killed my own brother."

"It was an accident, Julian," Chandra said quickly, hardly able to bear the raw grief in his face.

She wasn't sure he'd heard her.

"Perhaps it's better this way," Julian muttered. "At least I won't have to see him on the gallows." He raised his clenched hands. "But oh, God, what will it do to Irene to learn that her husband was a thief and a murderer? And that I killed him to prevent him from killing my wife? How can I tell her?"

Chandra made her decision without conscious thought. She heard her voice saying, "Irene need never know. We'll say Ashley's death was an accident."

Still sounding dazed, Julian asked, "What do you mean? How could we make people believe Ashley's death was an accident?"

"With a well-crafted lie. On an impulse—we *are* newlyweds, after all!—you decided to join me here in Wolverton, and you asked Ashley to go along with you for the company. However, you left London so late—which is perfectly true—that you didn't arrive at the dower house until the middle of the night. Just as you got here, you heard me screaming, so you entered the house through the drawing room window, dashed up the stairs to my bedchamber, and found me being attacked by an intruder, or several intruders, we can decide that later. A villain had already wounded poor Ramesh. So then, when one of the intruders came after me with a knife, Ashley threw himself in front of me and took a fatal blow. You were unable to pursue the attackers, because you and I had our hands full, tending to the wounded. Unfortunately, we couldn't save Ashley."

. . . And that was how Ashley became a hero, Chandra reflected, as she poured milk into a cup of tea and urged it on Irene. No one had questioned the story of how Ashley died. If the authorities had made even a cursory investigation, they might have discovered that Julian and Ashley had left London separately. But they hadn't investigated. Ramesh, of course, would have cheerfully allowed himself to be flayed alive before he'd contradict his mistress's account of the tragedy.

Chandra looked up at the sound of footsteps in the corridor. Julian entered the library, followed by the other menfolk in the family, Tristan and his elder brother, the present Lord Eversleigh. Julian, his face pale and haggard, walked over to Irene, sank down on his knees beside her chair, and gathered her into his arms. He murmured, "Dearest Irene, Ashley is at peace."

Chandra walked up the steps of the house in Grosvenor Square, feeling a vast sense of relief that the long, somber day of Ashley's funeral was coming to an end. She was relieved, too, to get away from the sorrow-laden atmosphere of Daylesford House, at least for a little while.

For this evening, Tristan and Lily and Frederica had volunteered to stay on with Irene. Julian had accompanied Chandra home.

As they entered the foyer, the footman murmured, "Good afternoon, my lord, my lady."

It wasn't, of course, the first time in the past four days that Chandra had been addressed as "my lady," but she was still not accustomed to it. On Ashley's death, Julian had become Earl of Daylesford, and she, in an ironical twist of fate, was now a countess.

As Chandra started up the stairs, Julian said, "I know you must be tired, but could I have a word with you? In the library, perhaps?"

"Yes, of course."

In the library, Julian closed the door behind them and turned to face Chandra. Ashley's death had left its mark on him, she thought. He looked worn and saddened, and the blue eyes had lost their electric spark. He must be racked with guilt for the killing of his brother, however justified his actions had been. Probably the guilt would never leave him entirely.

Julian said abruptly, "I just wanted to thank you properly for allowing my family to bury Ashley with honor. I don't think Irene could have survived the shock of knowing what he'd done. She's always put him on a pedestal."

"There's no need to thank me. I love Irene, too."

"Ashley wasn't all bad, you know." Julian's voice had an undercurrent of pleading. Chandra was suddenly glad she'd never told him about Ashley's shameful sexual deviance with little girls.

"Now that you've given me the details of Ashley's scheme to rob the Begum, I've been doing a lot of remembering," Julian went on. "I believe Irene was unwittingly the cause of his decision to turn criminal. He'd adored her from the moment they met, you know, when both of them were still in their teens. But Irene's father wouldn't hear of a match between his daughter and a penniless younger son, who was a near cripple, besides.

So Ashley went out to India, hoping to make his fortune, and, soon after he arrived, he received a frantic letter from Irene, telling him her father was pressuring her to marry someone else. He must have become desperate then. He had to have money immediately, if he was to have a chance to marry Irene. It doesn't excuse what he did, of course."

"No, but it makes it easier to understand," replied Chandra quietly. It felt so odd, she thought, for her and Julian to be talking together in this way, like two people with a normal interest and concern for the other, after all those months of embattled relationship. She hesitated. "I might as well tell you now. I plan to leave England as soon as I can put my affairs in order. You'll have your freedom earlier than you'd planned."

"You're going away?" he said blankly. "But our agreement was for a year. At the end of that time, you said, you'd be established as a London hostess on your own . . . Oh." A twisted smile appeared on his lips. "I was forgetting. You never wanted social success for its own sake, did you?"

"No. I needed, or I thought I needed, my position as Mrs. Ware to meet prominent people, so I could discover Papa's murderer." She shrugged. "Well, I've done that, for what it's worth, so—"

"So now there's no reason for you to stay in England," he finished. "I understand. Would you mind telling me where you intend to go?"

"I'm not sure," Chandra said slowly. "The only place I can really call home is India. Originally I'd planned to settle in one of the Portuguese or French enclaves in the south of India, where the color bar isn't important, for Lily's sake. But now, with her marriage to Tristan . . ." She shrugged again. "Perhaps I'll go to Calcutta. I lived there when I was a child. People there might welcome a wealthy woman, even one who was divorced."

An oddly started expression crossed Julian's face at her casual reference to their coming divorce. After a moment he said, "Will your aunt—? There, I'm forgetting again.

312

Miss Banks isn't your aunt, and Lily isn't your sister. Will Miss Banks be accompanying you?"

"I don't know. I hope so, but I haven't asked her. Freddie is English-born, you know. She may prefer to stay in England with Lily. Of course, she's free to do whatever she wishes. I'll see she doesn't worry about money."

Julian gave her an intent look. "If Miss Banks and Lily stay, and you go, it might be very lonely for you. As I understand it, you three have been together for many years."

"Yes, Freddie came to us before Lily was born. They're all the family I have and, of course, I'll miss them. But naturally, they have every right to lead their own lives," said Chandra, trying to sound matter-of-fact as a sudden hard lump formed in her throat. She paused, her forehead furrowed in a thoughtful frown. "So much has happened recently, so fast," she murmured. "I've been forgetting a plan I had. Julian, could I ask you to help me?"

He answered promptly. "Of course. What do you want me to do?"

"Well, as you know, I've never believed Lily will be accepted fully in Tristan's world. His colonel's wife has already snubbed her. Georgiana still refuses to accept her. So, some time ago, I thought of a possible solution. What if Tristan were to obtain a commission in the East India Company army? I think he and Lily would encounter much less prejudice in Bengal or Bombay. Would it be possible to obtain such a commission, do you think? Could you use your influence with the government? It *is* the government, isn't it, that ultimately controls the East India Company?"

"Yes, the Board of Control has governed 'John' Company since 1784, and the president of the board is a member of the cabinet."

"Do you know him?"

Julian smiled. "As well, I daresay, as any lowly undersecretary can know a high and mighty member of the cabinet! I'll be happy to look into a commission for

313

Tristan. I don't think it will be difficult to arrange."

Chandra's eyes shone. "Then we could all be together in India. Thank you, Julian."

"Come in," Chandra called. She was standing by the window, looking idly down at the garden in the middle of the square. The trees were still fresh and green, the flowers were still blooming, but the sun wasn't as warm, and summer was undeniably drawing to a close. August had merged into September, and tonight was her last night at the house in Grosvenor Square. Soon she must dress for dinner.

She turned away from the window as Frederica entered the bedchamber. The governess glanced at the pile of luggage ranged against the wall near the door, saying, "You're all packed, I see."

"Yes, except for what I'll need tonight. Are you finished with your packing, Freddie?"

"Almost." Frederica's voice sounded flat.

Chandra gave the ex-governess a searching look. "Freddie, are you sure you really want to go with me? You can change your mind, even at the last minute, and stay in England if you like."

Frederica shook her head. "No, my dear. Oh, for a little while, I was tempted to stay here. I'd discovered how much I missed England and English ways. But I don't have any family or old friends here any more. I'm sure I'd be very lonely. No, I want to be with you and Lily. You're the only family I have. And now that Tristan has his commission, and he and Lily are going with us, we'll all be together again."

"Then why don't you sound happier about it?"

"I'm worried about *your* happiness, Chandra," Frederica said simply. "I don't believe you really want to leave England."

Chandra made a quick, involuntary movement. "Stuff and nonsense! Why would I want to stay here?"

"To be with your husband. Where you belong."

314

Chandra felt the hot color flooding her cheeks. "Don't talk fustian. Julian doesn't want me, and I don't want him. You know perfectly well ours was a marriage of convenience."

"It may have started out like that, but it's more than that now," Frederica retorted. Before she could say anymore, a knock sounded at the door.

Grateful for the interruption, Chandra went to the door and opened it. A footman was standing in the hallway. Chandra turned back to Frederica with a note in her hand. "Simon Harley is here. I'll see you at dinner, Freddie."

Simon rose from his chair as Chandra entered the drawing room, her hands outstretched. "Simon, I'm so glad to see you."

"It's your last day in London. I wanted to say goodbye," said Simon, grasping her hands.

He'd been such a rock of comfort to her, this quiet man with the kindly gray eyes, thought Chandra with a catch in her throat. He'd always been there in the background when she needed him, but he'd never been intrusive. During the past few weeks, she'd been happy to see a great deal of him as he continued his kindly care of her, making a final check of her investments, arranging for the transfer of her funds to India, conferring with her on the termination of the lease on the house in Grosvenor Square, and the disposition of the furniture and the horses and carriages. Simon had even looked into sailing schedules to India, and had booked passages for Chandra's party to Calcutta.

"Thank you for all you've done for me, Simon. You've been a wonderful friend. I'll miss you."

"And I you. Do you think you'll ever return to England?" asked Simon wistfully.

Chandra shook her head. "I doubt it. Of course, I'd like to see you and my sister-in-law, Lady Daylesford, again one day, but otherwise . . . I have nobody in England to come back to."

"Mr. Ware? I mean, Lord Daylesford?"

Averting her face, Chandra said, "Julian and I are going

our separate ways. As soon as we're divorced, there'll be no further contact between us."

"Chandra, when that happens, will you consider coming to me?"

She leaned over to kiss him gently on the cheek. "Simon, I'm sorry."

"I know. You don't love me, not the way I love you." He put his arm around her and hugged her briefly. "Goodbye, Chandra. I wish you a safe voyage and a long and happy life. It's been the greatest pleasure of my life to have known you."

Tears were stinging the back of her eyes as Chandra went upstairs to dress for dinner after Simon left. More likely than not, she and Simon would never meet again.

She took pains with her appearance for her final dinner in Grosvenor Square. She put on a gown of gossamer, tissue-thin silk in a pale green shade that brought out the color of her eyes. When her abigial suggested she wear the Begum's emeralds, however, she pushed them away with a shudder. The beautiful, evil things had caused enough grief. She should get rid of them. Sell them and use the proceeds for charity. Perhaps it would be possible to establish schools for the half-caste children of Bengal. That would give some meaning to poor Phoebe's wasted life.

Chandra had planned the dinner in the vast dining room with its Egyptian wallpaper and lion-legged furniture, as a farewell meal for the family. It was generally known that Chandra was planning a trip to India, but only the members of the family knew the move was permanent. As it happened, the dinner wasn't very festive, except for the enjoyment Tristan and Lily took in it. They were in high spirits, excited about the prospect of a new life in India. Irene, ethereal in her widow's weeds, and Frederica were subdued.

Julian was reserved and quiet, almost indifferent. It struck Chandra that, though they'd lived in such close proximity these last weeks, they hadn't really interacted on a personal level. Possibly they'd both been too preoccupied. Julian had been busy with the details of settling Ashley's estate and helping Irene to cope with her widowhood. Chandra had been winding down her affairs in England. They hadn't spoken of divorce or speculated on the future.

Tristan and Julian took only token sips of their port at the end of the meal, and immediately joined the ladies in the drawing room for coffee. Then it was time for Irene to go. She clung to Chandra, whispering, "I'll miss you so much. I wish you and Julian had been able to work out your problems."

"It wasn't in the cards, dearest," Chandra murmured. "Goodbye, Irene."

A little later, the abigail helped Chandra into her dressing gown, tidied the dressing table, and asked, "Will there be anything else, my lady?"

"No. I'll see you in the morning."

The abigail lingered. "I jist wanted ter thank ye, my lady, fer finding me the position in the other Lady Daylesford's house."

"That's all right. However, I'm sorry to lose you, Betsy." The girl had flatly refused to go to India. Chandra suspected that Ramesh had filled her head with tales of poisonous cobras and rampaging bull elephants. In Calcutta, Ramesh intended to preside over a household of docile native servants.

After the abigail left, Chandra walked to her sitting room and sat down at her desk. She dipped a pen in the inkwell and put it down again, without touching it to paper. Hesitating a moment, she opened a drawer in the desk and took out a slip of paper, which she unfolded and read several times. Then, taking a deep breath, she left the room, still holding the piece of paper, and walked down the corridor to Julian's chamber.

"Come in," he called in answer to her knock. She found him standing at the fireplace, staring down into the small fire, one arm hooked over the mantel, the other hand holding a glass of wine. He wore only his shirt and black evening breeches. He looked up with a faint air of surprise

317

as Chandra approached him.

"I was going to write to you, leaving you a letter with this enclosure," Chandra said, handing him the paper. "Then I thought better of it. We should talk."

Julian took a quick look at the promissory note that had trapped him into his marriage with Chandra. "Thank you," he said, laying it carelessly down on the mantelpiece. "You needn't have bothered. I had no fears you'd use it against me again."

"No, I've done enough damage with it, haven't I?" Chandra bit her lip. "Julian, I visited a solicitor yesterday about our divorce. I had no idea the process was so complicated. Did you know?"

He gave her a level look. "I knew."

"The solicitor said that before the case could even go before the House of Lords, you would have to obtain a decree in a church court, granting a divorce *a mensa et thoro*. I believe that's equivalent to a judicial separation. Next, you'd have to institute, and win, an action in common law, resulting in recovery of damages against my—my paramour. Only then could the case go forward to the House of Lords."

He straightened his tall form and put down his wine glass. "I have no intention of branding you an adulteress in open court," he said curtly.

"Oh." Chandra couldn't quite conceal her sensation of relief. "Well, then, the solicitor suggested our best solution would be to apply to have the marriage declared null and void from the beginning."

"On what grounds? Because the marriage was never consummated? That wasn't because we were physically unable to have relations, just that we never chose to sleep with each other."

Chandra winced at the sting of bitterness in his voice. "The solicitor said you might be able to plead absence of consent, meaning, in this case, fraud as to the nature of the contract. We deliberately entered into the marriage without the intention of consummating it."

"I see. Yes, it's worth trying. I'll look into it."

"Don't worry if you can't get an annulment," Chandra said quickly. "I promise I won't fight a divorce granted on the grounds of my adultery. I'll come back from India, if need be."

"I've already said I won't sue you for adultery."

"But Julian—" She stared at him in rising distress. "What will you do, then? You *must* obtain a divorce, so you can marry and have children. You're the last of your line."

His mouth tightening, he looked back at her, and said nothing.

"I've ruined your life, haven't I?" Chandra burst out. "I forced you into this marriage, and now you can't get out it, not unless you perjure yourself, and you've refused to do that." She hit her clenched fist into an open palm in helpless anger. "If there was only something I could do to make up for this . . ."

He came away from the mantel with a lunge and placed his hands on her shoulders. "There is something you can do. You can stay here with me."

She looked up into his eyes, burning now with a fierce blue flame. "But, Julian," she faltered, "you never wanted this marriage."

"I want you, Chandra. God, how I want you," he said huskily, as his hands slid off her shoulders and his arms locked around her. "Don't leave me," he muttered against her lips, and then, as the pressure of his mouth deepened and grew more urgent, Chandra surrendered to the waves of fiery desire surging through her. She wound her arms around his neck, responding to the eager seeking of his lips, exulting in the feel of his hard body against her soft flesh.

He lifted her in his arms and carried her to the bed. As he threw himself down beside her, gathering her into a crushing embrace, he murmured, "I love you, Chandra. Stay with me, let me teach you to love me back."

"It's too late for that. I love you now. I've loved you for a long time . . ." And then she couldn't say any more, because he'd stopped her mouth with his hungry kisses.

* * *

Chandra awoke with a start, looking with dazed eyes at the powerful bare arm wrapped around her. In a moment, memory returned. She gently stroked the handsome, lean-planed face pressing against her shoulder, and ran her fingers through the dark springing curls. The blue eyes opened, and the sensual lips curved in a smile. "I want to wake up just like this every morning for the rest of my life," Julian said contentedly.

Someone knocked on the door of the bedchamber. Chandra realized that an earlier knock had awakened her.

"Go away," Julian called.

"Sahib, I must talk to you."

Julian exclaimed in disgust, "Oh, for God's sake." He slid out of bed, reaching for his dressing gown.

"Julian—"

But Julian was already opening the door. "Well?" he said to Ramesh.

"Sahib, my lady is not in her bedchamber . . ." Ramesh looked past Julian into the room, and froze. He said to Chandra, in a voice of outrage, "Lady, it is time, and past time, to depart. The carriages await."

"My wife isn't going anywhere," said Julian coolly. "She's staying with me. You can remain with us, Ramesh, in your present capacity, or you can return to India. The choice is up to you."

For a long, hard-breathing moment, Ramesh struggled to make up his mind. Then he bent in a graceful salaam. "I am your humble servant, sahib," he told Julian, as he passed forever under the yoke of the infidel.